THE EARL'S BLUESTOCKING BRIDE

JAYNE RIVERS

Copyright © 2024 by Jayne Rivers

All rights reserved.

No part of this book may be reproduced in any form or by any electronic or mechanical means, including information storage and retrieval systems, without written permission from the author, except for the use of brief quotations in a book review.

This book is a work of fiction. All people, places, events and organizations within it are fictional or are used fictitiously. Any resemblance to real people, places, events and organizations is entirely coincidental.

Editing by Hot Tree Editing.

Proofreading by Proof It Write.

Oops detection by Anne Victory Editing.

Cover design by EDH Professionals.

*To the people who read and loved
The Duke's Inconvenient Bride,
and convinced me to turn
it into a series.*

CHAPTER 1

*London,
October 1820*

Andrew Drake, the Earl of Longley, had outdone himself this time. He sat on his bed, admiring the necklace displayed in a box on his lap, the glittering facets of the rubies reflecting the candlelight back at him.

It was exquisite. The workmanship—faultless. The gems—flawless. The design—bold without being gaudy.

Florence would be delighted, and when his mistress was pleased, she rewarded him in all sorts of creative and delicious ways.

He traced his fingers around the edge of the largest ruby, set in silver and surrounded by smaller but no less perfect specimens, imagining how it would look around her pale, elegant neck. Perhaps she would allow him to strip her of everything but the necklace and—

A knock at the door interrupted his musings. He scowled. His servants knew better than to interrupt him during the nights he spent with Florence. Especially when he was supposed to be leaving soon, and she'd pout and sulk if he was late.

"What is it?" he demanded.

"A Mr. Harold Fisher is in the drawing room, my lord," the butler, Boden, called through the bedroom door. "He wishes to speak with you."

Andrew frowned. The name was familiar, but he couldn't quite recall where from. He carefully set the necklace down, then paced to the door and opened it. Boden, a gray-haired man of indeterminate age, straightened his shoulders, instinctively standing taller while simultaneously dipping his chin.

"Apologies, my lord. He would not be deterred," he said.

Andrew waved his hand dismissively. "Never mind that. You're just doing your job. Did Mr. Fisher tell you what his business is?"

"No, my lord. But he gave me his card. Would you care to see it?"

"Yes, please, Boden."

Boden extracted a plain white calling card from his front pocket and offered it to Andrew, who accepted the card and read the details printed neatly in the center.

Harold Fisher, Esq.

Smith & Fisher Co.

"Ah. He is Albert Smith's business partner. Unusual for him to call on me." With a sigh, he pocketed the card. "Please inform Mr. Fisher that I will be with him soon."

Boden bowed. "Very good, my lord."

Andrew rolled his eyes as the butler turned away. No matter how many times he told Boden he didn't have to refer to him as "my lord" every single time he spoke, there was no stopping the man. It wasn't sufficient to show his respect once or twice in a conversation—he must do so incessantly.

Curious what had brought his man of business's partner to Drake House, Andrew strode back to the bed, where he folded silk around the necklace, placed it in its box, and closed the lid. He checked his attire in a full-length mirror beside the wardrobe and straightened his cravat. That done, he headed downstairs.

Boden had left Mr. Fisher in the blue drawing room. As Andrew approached, he spotted the small, neatly turned-out man standing stiffly in front of an empty writing desk, his hands folded over his lower abdomen.

"Good evening," Andrew said as he entered. He offered Mr. Fisher his hand, and they shook briskly. "I understand you wish to speak with me."

Mr. Fisher's small brown eyes darted left and right. "I'm not sure that 'wish' is the correct term, my lord. It's more that I must speak with you regarding an urgent matter."

Andrew's eyebrows drew together as he studied the other man. Sweat was beaded at Mr. Fisher's hairline, and he was quite pale.

"Do you feel well?" he asked. "Would you like me to call for tea?"

Mr. Fisher shifted from one foot to the other, and a droplet of sweat trickled down the side of his face. Really, this was most unusual. The fire wasn't lit, and the air in the drawing room was verging on cold.

"No, thank you." Mr. Fisher adjusted the collar of his shirt, subtly tugging it out as if he were having difficulty breathing.

Andrew took a step back. "I say, man. Are you ill?"

"My only illness is of the heart and soul," Mr. Fisher said mournfully.

Andrew glanced at the large grandfather clock ticking away the seconds in the corner. "I'm afraid I can't dally long. I have an appointment to keep."

Mr. Fisher's throat bobbled. "This may take precedence, my lord."

Andrew gestured impatiently. "Tell me."

How bad could it be? Perhaps Mr. Smith was ill, and his business partner had come to advise the earl that some of his holdings would need to be managed by someone else. Surely the man couldn't have died. He was relatively young, and he was perfectly healthy the last time Andrew had seen him.

"I'm sorry to tell you that Albert Smith is gone." Mr. Fisher pressed his palms together in supplication.

Andrew tilted his head to the side. "Gone where? For how long?"

"Erm… indefinitely, I suppose."

Andrew rubbed his temples. "Please speak plainly."

Mr. Fisher squeaked. "Mr. Smith disappeared several days ago, and no one has seen him since."

Andrew's breath caught. "Has anyone checked his home? He could have taken ill or been in an accident."

Mr. Fisher shifted his weight again. "That's the first thing I did when he failed to show up at the office for the second day in a row without sending word as to why. My assistant reported back that his house had been emptied of personal belongings. I verified this myself."

"Did he move houses?" Because Andrew couldn't think of any other explanation.

"Not within London." Mr. Fisher inhaled deeply and visibly braced himself. "Upon further investigation, we discovered that Mr. Smith seems to have boarded a ship bound for Spain. He is fleeing the country."

Andrew shook his head. That made no sense. "Why would he need to flee? Was he in debt?"

If possible, Mr. Fisher paled even more. "I asked myself those same questions. Apparently, my business partner has not been handling his client's affairs as successfully as he portrayed."

A sinking feeling settled in Andrew's gut. Somehow, he knew that whatever Mr. Fisher was about to say, it wouldn't be good.

"Go on," he prompted.

Mr. Fisher wrung his hands. "It seems Albert invested heavily in a company that was attempting to build a smaller scale steam locomotive to be used for personal transportation. Unfortunately, the company has gone bankrupt and all the money he invested on behalf of our clients has been lost."

The sinking sensation worsened. "I recall him mentioning that invention. He said it sounded promising. I believe some of my fortune was invested."

Mr. Fisher wet his lips. "Yes, my lord. A substantial amount. More, I believe, than what you agreed to. He has been forging approvals for investments he considered worthy—presumably assuming that if they paid back well, no one would question him. But that isn't all."

"Dear God. What else? And how much more did he invest beyond what we discussed?" Had he lost enough money to feel the pinch? While his family had never been as wealthy as that of his close friend, the Duke of Ashford, was, they were rich enough that they'd never had to worry about their finances.

"A lot more." His shoulders slumped, and he stared down at his hands. "And what was not lost, Mr. Smith appears to have taken."

Andrew stared at him. "I beg your pardon?"

Mr. Fisher raised his chin. "I regret to inform you that the Drake fortune is almost completely gone. What was not lost to bad investment, Mr. Smith stole to fund his travel abroad. I can only assume that he intends to stay on the Continent for a long time and enjoy a lavish lifestyle."

Andrew's mouth fell open, but he snapped it shut again. His mind was whirring frantically, and he felt sick to his stomach. "How did this happen?"

Mr. Fisher backed up a step. "As I said, Mr. Smith was forging client approvals. He had a copy of your seal made and mimicked your signature. In this way, he entered into deals without your knowledge, invested more than he should have, shifted money to his own accounts, and sold off two of your unentailed properties."

"He sold two of my properties," Andrew sputtered. "That's impossible!"

The backs of Mr. Fisher's legs hit the desk. "I assure you, it's not. When the investments started going downhill, he tried to fix the problem by selling Rosewill Cottage and the dower house that was formerly attached to the Longley Manor estate."

Andrew's heart thudded rapidly. This was unbelievable. It couldn't be real.

Ten minutes ago, he'd been admiring the finest jewels money could buy, and now he was being told he was almost broke. Not only that, but his former man of business had sold off the homes he'd set aside for his mother and sister in the event he passed away unexpectedly and left them without protection.

"Are you perfectly serious?" he asked quietly.

Mr. Fisher ducked his head. "I fear so, my lord. You have my utmost apologies. I had no idea what Albert was doing until it was already too late. I understand, of course, if you wish to employ another firm to manage your estate, and I can only pray that you do not see fit to punish me for my partner's actions."

Pinching the bridge of his nose, Andrew drew in a deep breath and tried to calm himself. This was all happening so quickly. He needed time to think.

"I have employed an investigator to track down Mr. Smith," Mr. Fisher continued. "There is a chance that some of your fortune can be reclaimed. However, until we have returned him to England, we cannot be sure exactly how much is in his possession."

"Indeed, he must be found," Andrew muttered. "How much money, exactly, do we have left?"

Mr. Fisher bit his lip. "I could not tell you from memory, but we have the records at our office if you wish to review them. Unfortunately, you are not the only one of Albert's former clients I have had to visit today, although you are most assuredly the one who has suffered the greatest losses."

Andrew trudged to a chaise positioned against the wall and dropped onto it, wishing it were just a little softer. "I appreciate you bringing me this news, even if it is unwanted. I'll be in touch." Once he'd time to fully comprehend the magnitude of what had happened. "Please see yourself out."

Mr. Fisher bowed deeply. "My most sincere apologies. I assure you, we are doing all that we can to track my erstwhile business partner and to protect what you have left."

He bustled out before Andrew could reply, perhaps sensing that he may not like whatever he had to say.

"My lord?"

Andrew glanced up. Boden stood in the doorway, his posture impeccable, his expression giving no indication of whether he'd overheard their conversation.

"Please summon the dowager countess, and have Mrs. Baker bring us tea and biscuits."

Boden nodded and swept out, leaving Andrew alone in the silence. He dropped his face into his hands. He was torn between a desperate desire to know exactly how bad the situation was and the urge to bury his head in the sand for as long as possible.

Unfortunately, being the earl meant he couldn't afford to remain in the dark. His mother and sister were relying on him to provide for them, as were the dozens of servants employed by the Drake family across their holdings.

He couldn't let them down.

He gazed blankly at the wall, listening closely for footsteps in the corridor. The patterned wallpaper, in shades of navy and pale blue, swam before his eyes. The ornate gold trim, so carefully crafted, blurred into indistinguishable squiggles and masses.

"Andrew? What on earth is wrong?"

Pulling himself together, he looked toward the doorway, where the dowager countess, Lady Drake, stood with a furrowed brow and a curious slant to her mouth.

"I'm afraid I've just received bad news," he said, hearing himself as if from a distance.

Lady Drake moved farther into the room, her skirts—a similar shade to the wall—swishing around her ankles. "Has there been a death?"

"No." Although, in a way, this felt similar. He couldn't believe he'd been careless enough to lose everything. He wasn't the only one who would pay the price for this. His mother had trusted him to care for her. How could he do that if he had very little to his name?

"Then what?" She gave a little laugh. "You're worrying me."

He patted the chaise beside him. "Sit, Mother."

She sat, her head held high despite the gray-streaked auburn hair piled atop it. Her hazel eyes gleamed, but the corners of her mouth were tight. "What is it?"

He took her hand, wishing with everything he had that he could wake up and discover this had all been an awful dream. He waited a few seconds before deciding that simply wasn't going to happen.

"Mr. Smith, my man of business, fraudulently invested our money in a company that has gone bankrupt."

"Oh no!" Her hand flew to her mouth.

Andrew gestured for her to wait. "That which he has not lost, he has, apparently absconded with—including the proceeds of the sale of both Rosewill Cottage and the dower house."

She lowered her hand, obviously confused. "I didn't know we had sold them."

His nostrils flared, but he reined in his temper. "Nor did I."

"Oh." She gazed blindly around, not taking anything in. "Oh."

She stood and paced the length of the room, her skirt fluttering around her slender frame as she muttered under her breath, a frantic edge to her usually composed demeanor.

"Mr. Smith's business partner is attempting to have him apprehended and returned to London. Hopefully, we may reclaim some of our lost fortune from him. However, I do not think we can rely on that."

If Mr. Smith had known things were going downhill, it seemed likely he'd have taken steps to ensure he was able to disappear once he left the city. He must know that the only way he would get away with defrauding one of the most prominent members of society was by becoming a ghost.

Lady Drake paused in her pacing. "How dire is the situation?"

He rested his forearms on his thighs. "We will know tomorrow. But from the sounds of it, we can't expect much."

"It isn't right." She grabbed fistfuls of her skirt and clenched and unclenched her hands. "He can't get away with this."

"Hopefully, he doesn't." Andrew rose to his feet, his legs trembling beneath him. "In the meantime, we need to decide what to do if we don't get any of our money back."

The sensible thing would be to start releasing members of staff from their contracts, but most of their servants had worked for the Drakes for years, if not decades. He didn't want to be responsible for causing them any hardship—especially not because of his own laziness.

Perhaps if he'd paid more attention and been more actively engaged with their investments and finances, this wouldn't have happened. He'd been too blasé, believing them safe because of all the generations of wealthy Drakes who'd come before them.

"Is that a possibility?" the dowager asked, one of her hands subconsciously smoothing over her simple chignon. "That we will not see anything he has taken?"

Andrew pressed his lips together and struggled not to show how scared he was. "We must prepare for the worst."

"Very well." She nodded to herself and tapped her index finger against her pointed chin. "Lord, it is difficult to think during such stressful times. I suppose, if we need to replenish the coffers, that the fastest and most obvious way to gain access to money is through marriage."

He gasped. "Surely you aren't suggesting that we marry off Kate? She's far too young."

Lady Drake tsked. "Of course not." She gave him a pointed look. "Even if Kate were of an age to marry, she would require a dowry, which it seems we do not have. You, however, do not require a dowry, and I know for a fact that there are many girls from wealthy families who would happily become the next Countess of Longley."

Dear God.

She wanted him to marry?

He knew he would have to do so at some point, if only to secure an heir for the next generation. He had nothing against the idea of taking a wife, but he always believed that when he did so, it would be because a particular lady had caught his interest, rather than as a sacrifice on the altar of matrimony to restore his family's fortune.

He strode out of the room, down the corridor, and pushed open his office door. Without looking around, he went straight to the cabinet, pulled out a bottle of his favorite brandy, and poured a healthy portion into a glass. He tossed it back, wincing as the alcohol burned down his throat, then poured himself another.

Hell, if he were broke, this bottle may be the last one he

would be able to enjoy until they'd solved their financial dilemma.

He sipped the brandy this time, then, after a brief hesitation, poured a sherry for his mother and carried both glasses back to the drawing room. He passed hers over. She accepted it without comment and drained the glass almost as quickly as he had.

"There must be another way," he said, his chest tight with panic.

"We can think on it," the dowager said, eyeing her empty glass with disapproval. "But I believe marrying an heiress with a substantial dowry is the most straightforward way to obtain more money. I know you don't wish to marry for such crass reasons, but you can't rule it out yet. Just consider it. Perhaps one of the heiresses will appeal to you."

He huffed. "That would be convenient."

However, it seemed unlikely. Even if he found an heiress he was attracted to, how could he justify marrying her under false pretenses?

"Marriages of convenience are not uncommon among the ton," his mother murmured, as if privy to his thoughts.

"Usually, both parties are aware of what they are participating in when that occurs," he replied. "I, for one, would rather the ton not know of our changed fortune. Do you feel differently?"

Lady Drake scrunched her nose, and after a long hesitation, she shook her head. "No."

The clock ticked over the hour, and Andrew jolted, recalling his scheduled rendezvous with Florence.

Damn it, he wouldn't be able to continue to keep his mistress in the fashion to which she was accustomed. Depending on the state of the ledgers when he reviewed them tomorrow, there was a possibility he could still afford to provide for her, but it would require a significant reduction in her circumstances.

Florence wouldn't tolerate that. She'd lived lavishly for most of her life—first as the bastard daughter of a marquess and a widowed viscountess, and later, after their deaths, as one of the most sought-after companions for gentlemen of the ton.

She wouldn't respond well to being offered less. It would be better to free her to seek other protection. He ought to give her the necklace as a parting gift, but considering he didn't know his family's financial standing and the necklace was worth a small fortune, he simply couldn't justify doing so.

Perhaps he could sell the necklace. The jeweler he'd bought it from may be willing to buy it back, or else he could pawn it—although if he liquidated it that way, he was certain he'd receive far less than what it was worth.

"All right." He set his glass on a table. "Tomorrow, I will confirm how grave the damage to our financial position is. If we need money immediately, there are a few high-value items we can sell. Longer term, I will consider the possibility of marriage while we wait to hear whether Mr. Smith is apprehended and, if so, how much—if any—of our stolen money we can expect to be returned."

The dowager nodded. "I will compile a list of potential brides with large dowries."

He shot her a look. "No schoolroom chits."

She scoffed. "As if I would match you with a child. Have faith in me, Andrew."

He tried to smile but couldn't quite manage it. "I always do." He wiped his moist palms on his trousers. Time to face down a very unhappy Florence. "There is something I must do. I'll be home later."

She tapped her cheek, and he dutifully kissed it.

"We will get through this," she murmured.

God, he hoped so.

He left the drawing room and called for one of his more

discreet carriages. It met him out the front of the house, its simple black panels and white doors giving away nothing of who the carriage belonged to. Perfect for a clandestine meeting.

A footman opened the door, and Andrew climbed inside. He gazed through the window as the carriage began to bump across the cobblestone driving circle and back out onto the street.

The evening was completely dark except for the slight illumination cast by oil lamps. The lamps were fewer and farther between as they neared the edge of Mayfair and pulled onto a side street.

Florence resided on the second floor of a tidy house on a quiet residential street generally occupied by those on the fringes of the ton. His driver stopped outside, and Andrew waited until the footman opened the door before stepping down.

"Please wait here," he told the driver. "I won't be long."

The man's expression gave nothing away. "Yes, my lord."

Andrew unlocked the front door—he had a key because he paid Florence's rent—and took the stairs to the second floor. He knocked on the muddy green door and waited. It took a good minute to hear movement inside.

The door opened, and Florence's stunning face appeared in the gap, her high cheekbones emphasized by the play of shadows across her skin. Her full lips formed a pout, and her dark blue eyes narrowed.

"You're late," she said tartly. "I'm not sure that I should let you in."

He winced. "I have a good reason."

She arched an eyebrow in a way that clearly said she doubted his explanation would be sufficient. "Do tell."

He worried his lower lip between his teeth. "May I come in?"

She cocked her head. "That depends on whether I find your excuse to be reasonable."

All right. He supposed he was doing this right then and there.

"Unfortunately, I received the news today that my man of business defrauded me and ran off with my remaining fortune, bound for Spain." He spoke quietly so as not to be overheard by nosy neighbors. "As you'll understand, we must tighten our purse strings."

She opened the door wider and crossed her arms. "Do not tell me that you intend to abandon me."

His stomach dropped. "It's not like that. I can pay for your lodgings for another month. That gives you plenty of time to seek an alternative arrangement. I know you have many admirers."

She rolled her eyes. "I do not care about other admirers. I want you, my lord." She swayed closer, wrapping her arms around his neck, and the floral scent of her perfume washed over him. "I'm not finished with you yet. I have confidence we can come to an agreement."

Reluctantly, he disentangled himself from her. "I'm afraid not." His mother and sister must come first. "There is a possibility I will have to marry."

"You intend to become a fortune hunter?" She sounded horrified.

"If I must." From her obvious distaste, he assumed that would be the end of the matter, but she pressed closer to him again.

"You'll be back." Her fingers trailed down the side of his face. "I don't mind if you spend some naive debutante's dowry on me. In fact, nothing would thrill me more."

CHAPTER 2

Light streamed through the tree branches ahead, and Joceline's heart lifted. She battled through the brush, fueled by the desperate hunger gnawing at her insides.

As she drew closer, she saw buildings and heard the hum of voices.

Lord have mercy. It was civilization.

After three weeks of being stranded in the wilderness of a foreign country, she was finally safe.

Miss Amelia Hart placed her quill in its holder, excitement thrumming through her. The latest installment of her adventures of Miss Joceline Davies was complete.

Butterflies swooped in her gut as she lifted the quill back out of its holder and scrawled "The End" beneath the final sentence.

There. That was so much more satisfying.

She rose from her chair behind the heavy wooden desk in her parents' yellow drawing room and stretched her arms above her head, working the kinks out of her back.

She wandered to the large windows that looked out onto the square, rolling her wrists back and forth as she did so. She'd been stooped over the desk, writing frantically, for far longer than she'd intended to. She got that way when she neared the end of a story. Thoughts of it consumed her until she jotted the final words.

Amelia gazed out the window, watching a pair of women stroll through the garden in the center of the square with a maid trailing behind them. The last rays of the sun streamed through the glass, warming her skin, and she smiled.

What adventure would she send Joceline on next?

Perhaps she could travel to the Continent and discover the remnants of a lost civilization or journey to the Americas and explore the new world. Maybe Joceline would remain closer to home and uncover a hidden structure in the wilds of Cornwall or the expanses of Cumbria.

There were so many possibilities.

Amelia turned away from the window and crossed the room to the bookshelf against the internal wall. Most of the household's books were stored in their library, but her father kept their most impressive tomes on display in the drawing room so that guests may admire them, and Amelia had discreetly added a couple of her favorites over the years.

She withdrew a leatherbound illustrated world atlas and carried it to the desk, then shifted her pile of handwritten paper aside to make room, taking care to ensure it remained in order.

Flipping through the stunning images and elaborately drawn maps inside the atlas, she considered where she might send her heroine, pausing each time a picture caught her eye. The Amazon jungle sounded thrilling. Or perhaps one of the desolate, snow-covered countries to the north.

The door flew open, and Amelia's mother, Mrs. Hart, marched into the room, her dark eyebrows knitted together.

"You look frightful." She shook her head, and her pretty features pinched. "It's a disgrace. Your hands are covered with ink, and what on earth have you done with your hair? You look common."

Amelia's heart fell, and her good mood slipped away. Her mother often had that effect on her.

"I'm in the privacy of my own home, Mother. It doesn't matter if I am slightly unkempt." In all honesty, Amelia was not in a particularly worse state than usual. Yes, perhaps she'd dressed her own hair in a loose coil, and maybe it was coming down around her shoulders, but what did it matter if no one could see her?

Mrs. Hart harrumphed, her full lips twisting with displeasure. "You won't marry into the aristocracy with that attitude. You need polish. Sophistication. Go and clean yourself up this instant."

Amelia glanced at the window, hiding her expression from her mother. She did not wish to marry into the aristocracy at all. That was Mrs. Hart's ambition. She'd married beneath herself and regretted it ever since, but now her husband was rich enough to buy their way into an even more exclusive level of society than Mrs. Hart's parents had belonged to, if only Amelia would cooperate.

"Are we going somewhere?" Amelia asked. The trouble with her mother's plan was that Amelia had no desire to join the ton. She'd enjoyed growing up outside of high society. She'd been allowed to roam across the countryside as a child, and her father had encouraged her schooling and interest in literature.

She'd been happy. At least until her mother had decided that Amelia should become a duchess or a marchioness. She would no doubt settle for her becoming a countess or viscountess, but anything less than that was simply unacceptable.

Mrs. Hart stopped and folded her palms over her skirt. "No, but once you are married, you must maintain your appearance at a certain standard. I don't trust you to recall something so important later, so it is best we train you into it now."

"I'm not finished, though," Amelia protested.

Mrs. Hart cast a cursory glance at the atlas. "Nothing is more important than preparing to become an aristocratic wife—especially not your silly scribbling. Do as I say."

With a sigh, Amelia stood and left the atlas where it was. She didn't dare pack it away or even close it. That would invite further attention from her mother, who might decide to have a maid toss the book into the fire so it would not steal any more of Amelia's focus.

She did, however, gather her papers and carry them out of the room with her. She kept her work in a locked drawer in the writing desk in her bedchamber. She feared if Mrs. Hart had access, she might take it into her head to destroy all of Amelia's hard work.

She'd spent years honing her craft and learning how to tell stories in a way that interested people. Not to mention the time she'd dedicated to creating her fictional alter ego, Miss Joceline Davies.

Joceline was everything Amelia wished she could be. Adventurous. Outgoing. And, above all, independent.

How Amelia longed to have a distant relative bequeath a fortune upon her, as had happened with Joceline. Then she wouldn't be required to play the games of the ton or engage in the social posturing which she'd never fully understood.

Alas, no matter how rich her father might be, Amelia had no money of her own. Ergo, she must abide by her parents' rules, and for now, that meant seeking an aristocratic husband.

She took the stairs to the second floor and turned into the west wing, where the family's private chambers were located. She entered her bedroom, set the papers on her writing desk, and rang for her maid, then thumbed through the pages as she waited.

Mary breezed into the room and bobbed a curtsy. "How can I help, miss?"

"Can you please arrange for hot water and soap to be delivered to my chamber?" Amelia asked, gesturing at her ink-streaked hands. "I'm under orders to get clean."

Mary's lips pinched together. "I'll make sure it's your special soap."

"Thank you, Mary."

The maid left, and Amelia considered how lucky she was to have Mary, who didn't bat an eyelid at any of Amelia's eccentricities and sometimes actively encouraged them.

She returned with two footmen carrying a pail of hot water between them and guided them on its placement. Amelia placed a cushion on the floor and knelt on it, holding out her arms so that Mary could scrub them.

The block of soap was slightly scratchy as she ran it over Amelia's skin, and it smelled of peppermint. She had never asked what was actually in it, but she knew it cleaned ink better than anything else she'd tried. There was a reason her mother didn't realize exactly how much time she devoted to her "silly scribbling."

When her hands and forearms were blemish free, Mary patted them dry with a towel.

"Would you like to change for dinner now?" she asked.

Amelia glanced out the window. The sun had dropped beneath the horizon, and the gray of dusk had descended. "I suppose I'd better. The pale blue dress, please."

While it wasn't an evening gown, the blue dress suited Amelia's coloring, which would please her mother. Any small ways in which she could win Mrs. Hart's approval were best taken advantage of, since there were many more significant ways in which she'd never have it.

Mary removed the dress from the closet and laid it on the bed. Amelia turned her back to Mary, and the maid quickly undid her laces so the dress dropped to the floor and pooled around her feet. She stepped out of it, clad in only petticoat, chemise, and stays, and ducked to assist Mary in sliding the blue dress over her head.

Mary buttoned the back of the dress with deft movements. "There you are, miss. Would you like anything done with your hair?"

Amelia sighed. "Yes, please." She pulled out the padded bench from the foot of her bed and perched on it, presenting Mary with her back.

She gazed at the blue embroidery on her gold bedspread as she waited for Mary to return with a hairbrush and supplies. It was a good thing she liked blue, considering the fact that Mrs. Hart had seen fit to surround her with the color for her whole life. Growing up, most of her outfits had been blue, and her bedchambers had also been decorated in the same hue.

Amelia tended to think it was because her vivid blue eyes were both the only part of her appearance that could be solely attributed to her mother and the most noteworthy part of her.

With the exception of her eyes, she was rather plain. Dark hair, pale skin, an average build that was neither slender enough to make her appear fragile nor curvaceous enough to attract men's attention. She was neither beautiful nor ugly. Perfectly designed to be part of the background.

Mary removed the ties from Amelia's hair and brushed its length. Amelia closed her eyes, enjoying the sensation. It was lovely to have someone brush one's hair. As a young girl, she'd often wished for a sister so they could take turns dressing each other's hair, but the Harts had not been blessed with a second child.

As Mary brushed her hair back from her face and began to pin it into place, Amelia spoke.

"I completed Miss Davies's most recent adventure today. Would you like me to read it to you after dinner?"

"Oh, yes, please. That would be wonderful."

Amelia smiled. For all she knew, Mary only humored her because it was her job, but Amelia preferred to think that she genuinely enjoyed the stories.

"The other maids will be eager to hear what trouble Miss Davies gets herself into next," Mary added. "I always let them know what she's up to, although I'm sure my storytelling isn't nearly as good as yours."

She slid a pin into place near Amelia's hairline. Amelia winced as it caught the skin.

"Sorry," Mary murmured.

"Don't worry about it," Amelia said. "And I have no doubt you're a superior performer to me. My flair is for the written word, not the spoken."

Mary hummed thoughtfully. "I believe you could be good at anything you set your mind to."

Amelia laughed. "How very diplomatic of you."

They fell silent while Mary finished winding Amelia's hair into a tidy arrangement on the back of her head, with a loose curl positioned on each side of her face. By the time she stepped away and placed the brush and remaining hairpins on a cabinet, it was almost dark outside. No doubt dinner would be served soon.

Amelia thanked the maid, locked her papers in her writing desk, and wandered downstairs. The dining hall was well lit with dozens of candles positioned down the center of the table and attached to the walls.

She rolled her eyes internally at the wastefulness of the extravagance. There was no reason for them to eat every meal in the formal dining hall, but her mother insisted it was "most proper."

Amelia claimed the seat to the left of the table's head. Her mother and father swept into the room arm in arm a moment later. Her father held out the chair at the right of the table's head for her mother and waited for her to lower herself down before sitting at the head himself.

"Good evening, Mia," Mr. Hart said, smiling warmly. He was a slightly portly gentleman with dove-gray eyes and a thick gray mustache.

"Walter," Mrs. Hart chastened. "Remember what we discussed."

"Ah." He nodded. "Rightly so. My apologies, Amelia. I forget that you're not my little girl anymore."

"I'll always be your Mia," Amelia replied, ignoring her mother's sigh of exasperation. There was no reason for family to stand on formality—especially not in private.

"Please refrain from saying such things in front of potential suitors," Mrs. Hart said as footmen carried in platters laden with food.

"I will hold my tongue in front of potential suitors," Amelia replied dutifully.

She doubted there would be any. At least, not unless they were fortune hunters. This was her second season, and to say the first had been a dismal failure would be an understatement. The only men who'd looked at her twice were those in want of her father's dime.

Other gentlemen seemed to be put off by either her family's position—very much outside the ton's inner circle—her somewhat plain looks, or her mother's obvious aspirations as a social climber. If none of those things scared them away, then the fact that she was incapable of polite small talk seemed to do the trick.

"I have been researching," Mrs. Hart declared.

Both Amelia and her father cringed. Nothing good ever came of Mrs. Hart's research.

"There is one duke, a marquess, and two earls seeking wives this season."

Mr. Hart reached for the mutton and cut off a portion. Following his cue, Amelia served herself potatoes, peas, beans, and mutton. Whatever came next would surely be best endured with a full belly.

"Would you like to know which ones?" Mrs. Hart asked, a disapproving groove between her eyebrows that said she'd expected more interest.

"Of course, dear." Mr. Hart's knife chinked against the china as he sliced through a piece of mutton. "I'm curious how you ascertained that these particular men are seeking a wife."

"They accepted invitations to the Wembley ball on Saturday."

"I... see." He clearly didn't.

"Obviously, bringing a duke into the family would be the most impressive coup." Mrs. Hart selected dainty portions of each dish for herself. She was of the belief that women ought not to eat much more than birds did, and her slim, girlish figure was evidence of that. "However, the Duke of Wight may be past the age of being able to produce an heir."

Amelia's jaw dropped. "The Duke of Wight must be at least seventy!"

Mrs. Hart nodded. "Ergo, marrying him would leave you unencumbered much sooner. But, as I said, if any of his three previous wives haven't been able to bear him an heir, we must assume the problem lies with him and that you would have no more success."

"Three previous wives?" Amelia was astounded. If he weren't a duke, this man would surely be a cautionary tale. Three wives could not have died of natural causes.

"The first wife died of consumption, the second in a carriage accident, and, rumor has it, the third jumped from a cliff because she was so heartbroken at not being able to provide an heir," Mrs. Hart explained.

Or the cunning old duke had them all killed.

Amelia didn't voice the suspicion. Her mother would consider it yet more proof that all her reading and scribbling had rendered her fanciful.

"How unfortunate for him," Mr. Hart muttered.

Amelia forced herself to eat her mutton before it went cold. Chewing it was hard work, and she had a sour taste in her mouth.

She didn't want to marry an aristocrat. Or, she supposed, not more than she wished to marry any other man. But she especially didn't want to marry someone who might throw her off a cliff should she fail to get pregnant.

"Indeed." Mrs. Hart sipped from a glass of water. "The Marquess of Overton may be a better choice. He is rich, titled, and younger."

Stuffing a chunk of potato into her mouth, Amelia managed not to respond. The chances of the Marquess of Overton being interested in her were slim to none.

"And?" she prompted, because they may as well get this conversation over with.

Mrs. Hart smiled, pleased with her cooperation. "The Earl of Winn and the Earl of Longley."

Amelia looked down at her meal to hide her grimace. The Earl of Winn was a lecher and a drunk. "I don't believe I'm acquainted with the Earl of Longley."

"No, you wouldn't be." Mrs. Hart sounded smug about having information that her daughter was not privy to. "He attended only one—maybe two—balls last year, with his childhood friend, the Duke of Ashford."

"Ah." Amelia poured water from a jug into her glass. "The one who was jilted and then married his former fiancée's twin sister."

"Exactly." Mrs. Hart's cobalt eyes were practically glittering. "We all know that men tend to settle down in groups. Ashford did so last year, and I'm certain that Longley intends to do the same this season. Perhaps you will be the one to win him."

"Perhaps." Amelia swallowed, her throat tight. She didn't believe she had any hope of landing a decent aristocratic gentleman. She just had to pray that her mother would be satisfied with a peer's younger sibling or, if she was lucky, a baron.

All Amelia personally wanted was someone kind who would allow her to pursue her own interests. If they were an intellectual themselves, that would be desirable, but beggars couldn't be choosers. In this case, despite their wealth, they were very much beggars as far as the ton was concerned.

They finished their meal, and then she and her mother retired to their chambers while Mr. Hart vanished into his office. Amelia retrieved her writing papers from her desk, locked the drawer behind her, and took the stairs back down to knock on her father's door.

"Enter," he called.

She turned the handle and stepped inside, leaving the door ajar, her papers clutched in one hand. "Hello again, Father."

"My dear." His eyes creased at the corners. "What brings you here?"

"I completed a written project today, and I would be interested to hear your thoughts—if you have time to read it."

He beckoned her forward. "Let's see, then."

Amelia closed the distance between them and offered him the papers, but just before he could take them, her mother rushed past her and knocked them out of her hands. Amelia gasped as the papers fell to the floor, completely out of order. She dropped to her knees and scrambled to gather them up.

"Enough!" Mrs. Hart cried. "No more of your scribblings. You will never secure a betrothal with anyone of the peerage if you persist with these bluestocking tendencies."

Amelia snatched up the last sheet of paper and shakily rose to her feet, holding them tightly to her chest so her mother could not touch them again.

"If I were to be published," she began quietly.

"You would bring shame to the Hart name," Mrs. Hart snapped. "I tell you, no one wants a bluestocking wife."

Tears prickling in her eyes, Amelia looked to her father for support. Surely he would intervene. After all, during her formative years, he'd allowed her to sit with him while he worked. He'd explained business concepts to her and gifted her the books that had expanded her mind. He would defend her now.

But no. There was a quiet apology in his eyes, and yet he said nothing. Perhaps she should have expected that. However much he cared for her, he always allowed his wife to make the decisions about her life.

He gave a small shrug. "I am sorry, Amelia. Your mother knows best in these things. You should listen to her."

CHAPTER 3

"Thanks for agreeing to meet with me. I must say, I'm surprised to see you away from your wife," Andrew said to the Duke of Ashford as they met outside the entrance to the Regent, the gentleman's club of which they were both members.

Vaughan grimaced as the doorman held the door for both of them. "I'd rather not be in London so soon after Lilian's birth, but I had an urgent business matter that needed attending to. I'll return to the country as soon as possible."

They shucked their coats and passed them to an attendant.

"A private room?" their host asked, bowing deeply.

Andrew glanced at Ashford. For the conversation he had in mind, privacy would probably be best. "Yes, please."

The host led them through the foyer and down a corridor. He turned into the third room on the left, which contained only two well-padded leather chairs and a small drinks table.

"Brandy?" he asked.

"Yes," Ashford said. "Thank you."

The host nodded. "A server will be with you momentarily." He bowed again and backed out of the room.

Andrew dropped onto the chair farthest from the door, ensuring he'd be able to see anyone passing by. He did not wish for gossip of his changed circumstances to spread.

"How is the lovely Emma?" he asked, gesturing for his friend to join him. "Is she recovering well after the birth?"

"She is incredible." The corners of Ashford's mouth twitched up. On anyone else, it could hardly be considered a smile, but for him, this was practically beaming. "She is wonderful with Lilian, and she's already up and about the house. She's taken a couple of walks outside, but I've asked her not to do so while I'm gone so I don't have to worry."

Longley grinned. "You're smitten. And this from the man who didn't want to wed."

"Marriage agrees with me," Ashford said simply.

A server entered, carrying a tray on which stood a decanter of brandy and two glasses. He placed a glass in front of each of them and filled them, then retreated to the corner to await further instruction.

Andrew raised his glass and inhaled the sharp scent of brandy along with the underlying hint of cigar smoke that permeated the Regent. He sipped and then set the glass down. He steeled himself. If anyone could understand his situation—at least in part—it was Ashford.

"I hope marriage will agree with me too," he said, watching the duke for a reaction.

Ashford frowned. "I distinctly recall you saying last season that you did not intend to wed for quite some time."

"Yes, well, circumstances have changed."

Ashford picked up his brandy and cradled it between his palms. "How so?"

Andrew glanced at the server, who was gazing at the wall, obviously listening but doing his best not to appear as though he were. "Excuse me," he said.

The server looked over.

"You are dismissed. Please close the door behind you."

His face creased with disappointment, but he sketched a quick bow and glided out.

"This is confidential," Longley murmured to an intrigued Ashford. "The only other people who know are my mother and the company that manages my affairs. I've lost almost our entire fortune."

Ashford's eyebrows flew up. "I beg your pardon? How can that be?"

Andrew grimaced. "We are not near to the poorhouse, but unless I take drastic action, we will have to release the majority of those employed by the Longley estate and begin selling off our higher-value items."

He briefly explained the situation with Mr. Smith and his mismanaged and misappropriated funds.

"I've been over the records. I've combed through every detail. Unless Mr. Smith is apprehended upon arrival in Spain, with my money still in his possession, we're in trouble. Even if we get back what's left of our fortune, we'll have to substantially change the way we manage the estate."

Ashford rolled the glass between his palms. "Hence the need to marry. You're seeking an heiress, I assume?"

"I am," Andrew confirmed. "Mother has provided me with a list of suitable options."

She'd been rather quick to do so, as a matter of fact. It made him wonder how closely she'd been monitoring the marriage mart over recent years. Perhaps she'd hoped he might take an interest and she'd wanted to be ready if he did. Of course, he doubted she'd ever have expected that to happen under such dire circumstances.

Ashford emptied his glass in one gulp and plunked it on the table, then held out his hand. "Do you have the list on you?"

Andrew extracted the folded paper from his front pocket

and passed it over. Ashford carefully unfolded the paper, then smoothed it out on the table. His eyes skimmed down the names. There were six in total.

"I believe they're ordered according to the size of their dowry." He hated how crass that was, but unfortunately, it was necessary.

"I met one of these girls last year." Ashford didn't look up. "Lady Esther Bowling. If I recall correctly, she had a penchant for elaborate feather hairpieces."

Andrew smirked. "Yes, I remember meeting her too. She made quite an impression."

"Do you know any of the others?" Ashford asked.

"Miss Caroline Wentham is very pretty." Although she reminded Andrew of a bird of prey. There was always a hungry gleam in her eye that made him feel hunted.

Ashford tapped the paper. "What about the chit at the top of the list? Miss Hart."

Andrew shrugged. "Never met the girl. Her father is in mining. Rich as Midas, and in search of a titled husband for his darling daughter."

"Does the origin of his money bother you?" Ashford asked.

"Not particularly." Andrew tended to think men ought to be applauded for becoming successful enough to rise above their station of birth. However, not many members of the ton agreed with him, and he imagined the Harts' social invitations were few and far between. The more snobbish of their number wouldn't want to sully themselves with such an acquaintance.

"Lady Elizabeth Holden." Ashford drummed his fingers against the wood. "Why is that name familiar?"

"She married young to an extremely rich elderly gentleman who left her most of his fortune. Now, she seeks a husband her own age."

Andrew didn't fancy his chances with Lady Elizabeth. She

could afford to be selective, and something told him that she may not find favor in a nearly destitute earl, even if he was passably handsome.

Lady Esther and Miss Wentham were not societal outcasts, nor were they on the shelf. They also had options—although he gave himself better odds with them than with Lady Elizabeth. Miss Hart, on the other hand, was not in a position to cast aside potential suitors.

"The other two?" Ashford asked. "Miss Cahill and Miss Carruthers?"

Andrew shook his head. "I have not made the acquaintance of either. I have it on good authority that Miss Cahill is something of a shrew and that this is intended to be her final season. If she does not find a husband, her parents are retiring her to the country."

He felt for the girl. Considering he had a younger sister of his own, he knew how difficult life could be for women who could not—or chose not to—marry. Their futures were almost always dictated by their male relations. It was only right for family to care for their own, but all too often there didn't seem to be much "care" involved.

"Miss Carruthers is the youngest of the six. This is her first season. Her father is a cousin to the Earl of Wembley, and both he and her elder brother are independently wealthy. They have large holdings in Cumbria." He hadn't heard anything of her temperament, as no one he knew had met the chit.

"On the basis of what you've shared, do you have a preference?" Ashford asked.

Andrew shrugged. "I need to meet them. As usual, I have been inundated with invitations to balls. Unfortunately, I have had to accept far more of them than I usually would. If I want to meet these women without simply turning up on their doorsteps, then I must put in appearances."

Ashford winced. "I'm sorry that I can't be here to attend

them with you. It would be only right of me to stand by your side the way you did for me when I decided to take a wife."

Andrew waved his hand dismissively. "Don't dwell on it, my friend. I was in London and had nothing else to do with my time. You, however, have a duchess and a baby waiting for you in Norfolk. Such domesticity may be foreign to me, but I recognize its importance to you."

Ashford cocked his head. "Why is it that you've always delayed choosing a bride? You like to be around people—unlike myself—and women seem to find you charming. Why the resistance?"

Andrew paused to drink more brandy. Really, he ought to have asked the server to leave the bottle. "I'm not resistant to marriage. However, I've had no reason to rush until recently, and I don't want to be trapped with a woman I do not care for. I always thought the right woman would simply appear one day."

Ashford chuckled. "It doesn't work like that."

"Doesn't it? Did or didn't the Earl of Carlisle turn up in your office and propose a marriage between you and Emma? It sounds to me like that opportunity landed in your lap."

He scoffed. "Only because I put in the effort with Violet first, and I made up for not trying with Emma at the beginning—or at least, I did as much as I could. You know I'll never take her for granted."

Andrew softened. "I know. The entire ton knows how much you dote on that woman."

He'd once feared that Emma and Ashford would be a terrible match, given that they wanted such different things, but the sweet, reserved Emma had proven to be exactly what the surly duke needed.

"Perhaps marriage will surprise you," Ashford said.

"It's certainly turned you into a romantic."

A little smile twisted Ashford's lips, and he didn't seem at all bothered by the assessment. "Maybe so. But I think we've reached our limit of deep conversation for today. Would you like to join a card game?"

"I'd better not. I have no money to lose." He wasn't about to compound his poor luck by gambling away what little he had left.

Ashford shrugged. "Play with my money."

Andrew's heart squeezed. "No, but thank you, my friend. I appreciate the offer. Why don't you tell me more about your daughter?"

"Lilian is such a sweet baby. Good-natured. She looks so much like her mother." Ashford gazed somewhere over Andrew's shoulder, his smile turning dopey. "She's so small. The first time I heard her, I was afraid I might accidentally hurt her."

"But you didn't," Andrew reminded him.

"No, I didn't."

Ashford continued to wax poetic about his daughter for several minutes. Listening to him was easy. Andrew was glad to see his friend so happy. He was also pleased that Ashford hadn't been upset when Emma had given birth to a daughter. Considering he'd married her purely to obtain an heir, it had been a possibility he'd be displeased.

But no, he adored his little girl, and he and Emma would simply try again for an heir when she was well enough.

As Ashford trailed off, a thought struck Andrew.

"I say." He straightened in his seat. "You have a successful estate. I need a new man of business. Do you have any recommendations?"

Ashford hummed in thought. "My estate is managed differently than yours. I have an estate manager for Ashford Hall—you remember Cal, from school—and another who manages our smaller holdings. My estate managers do not involve themselves in my investments or business dealings unrelated to the properties."

"Hmm." Perhaps Andrew ought to consider arranging

something similar, although he now only had two property holdings, thanks to Mr. Smith: Longley Estate in Suffolk and Longley House in London. But he could hire an estate manager to be based in Suffolk and another person to oversee his finances.

"You want my opinion?" Ashford asked.

Andrew rolled his eyes. "I did ask, didn't I?"

Ashford looked irritated. "You ought not to rush into making any decisions while the loss and betrayal are still fresh. You're emotional, and any decisions you make now will be influenced by that. You'd be better off to wait for a week or two and then choose a plan of action based on what's rational."

Andrew tipped his head in acknowledgement. "Good point. I'll keep that in mind."

They talked for a while longer; then Andrew summoned a carriage to take him home, and Ashford headed to a business meeting.

As Andrew watched buildings pass through his window, it occurred to him that this was the time of day at which he'd usually be going to visit Florence. His gut twisted. Now, there was no willing woman waiting for him. He'd lost her, and all because he'd been foolish enough to put his trust in the wrong person.

The carriage turned off the street and passed through the stone gateway of Longley House. They stopped in front of the main door, and Andrew waited for the carriage to open, then stepped down. After a quick thank-you to his driver, he trudged up the stairs. His footman knocked, and Boden opened the door, welcoming Andrew inside and locking it behind him.

The downstairs area was dimly lit. He grabbed a candle and used it to light his path as he climbed the stairs and turned left toward his bedchamber. As he entered, he came to an abrupt stop at the sight of his sister, Kate, sitting on his bed.

He set the candle on the cabinet. "To what do I owe the honor of this ambush?"

She sat forward, her pale auburn hair spilling over her shoulders, her expression uncharacteristically serious. "Is it true that we are broke?"

Oh dear.

Heart heavy, he perched on the edge of the gray-blue bed cover and angled himself toward her. He couldn't hide this from her. That would be a disservice to her. Their financial situation would affect her as much as anyone else.

"We are not broke, no. We will not starve. However, we have lost nearly our entire fortune." Guilt swept through him. He should have protected her better.

He had let her down.

She took this in, biting her lower lip, her pointed chin—so like their mother's—quivering as she gathered herself. "What does this mean for us? Will I still be able to come out next season?"

"We will ensure it happens," he assured her, reaching for her hand. It sat limply in his. She did nothing to return the gesture.

"If I do not come out, how will I find a husband?" She met his gaze, her eyes—the gray of their departed father's rather than the hazel of his and his mother's—gleaming with tears. "Will I have to marry someone we already know? Or will I become a spinster and fade away in a cottage in the middle of nowhere?"

He winced internally, thinking of the country cottage he had, in fact, purchased for her in case she needed it, but which was no longer available to her.

"Don't cry," he murmured, at a loss as to what to do with her. He liked to make women laugh and smile, but he didn't know what to do with them when they were upset. "Whatever happens, I'll make certain that you are not miserable. If you want a season next year, then you will have it."

He didn't know how yet. She would require an array of dresses, jewelry, and a dowry. But he couldn't bear to see her unhappy, so he would find a way to ensure that she got her season.

He pulled her into an embrace. "Don't worry yourself, Katie. Mother and I will take care of it. Do you trust us?"

She nodded and swiped at her shining gray eyes, ready to spill over with tears at any moment. "Yes."

"Then believe me when I say that everything will be all right. Now, shall we get you to bed?"

He stood and helped her off his bed. She'd left a lantern on his cabinet, and she carried it as they walked the short distance along the corridor from his room to hers. He waited until she was tucked beneath her pastel pink bedclothes before closing the door quietly behind himself.

He rested his forehead against the door and closed his eyes, his bravado gone now that she wasn't around to see. He'd made a lot of promises to her. How could he possibly keep them?

With a groan, he straightened and strode on leaden legs back to his bedchamber. He helped himself to the bottle of whiskey hidden in the lower drawer of his nightstand, unscrewed the lid, and swigged it, enjoying the burn down his throat.

Soon, there would be no more bootlegged whiskey either. He returned the bottle to its hiding place and flopped onto the bed.

There was nothing else for it. He would simply have to find a wife with a hefty dowry.

Tomorrow, the hunt was on.

CHAPTER 4

Mary held up a sage-green dress, and Mrs. Hart clucked her tongue disapprovingly.

"Not that one," she said. "Put it back. Bring out the white one with the pale pink embellishments."

"White doesn't suit my complexion," Amelia complained. If she was to be forced to endure her mother parading her around like a prize filly for auction, she'd at least like to look as good as possible while it happened. "What about the blue?"

But Mrs. Hart shook her head. "No, the white showcases your purity. It's a more appropriate choice."

Good Lord. Knowing that the white was supposed to symbolize her untouched status somehow made her even more uncomfortable than she'd be simply wearing an unflattering color.

Mary flashed her a sympathetic look and hung the sage-green dress back in the wardrobe, then sorted through the options until she found the white dress Mrs. Hart had referenced. As she withdrew it, Amelia grimaced. Must dresses really be so… ruffled? She much preferred the simpler styles.

Mrs. Hart waved her forward. "Go on. Let's see it on you."

Amelia swallowed a sigh and stepped into the dress,

waiting while Mary pulled it up and cinched it at the back. The fit was slightly tight, but she suspected that was by design. Her mother wished she'd eat less, and what better way to achieve that than by purchasing dresses she couldn't breathe in properly unless she slimmed.

"Do a turn," Mrs. Hart ordered. "Hmm. Yes. That's perfect for the first ball of the season."

While Mary laced the back, Mrs. Hart studied the array of jewelry she'd laid out on the bed.

"The good thing about white is that you can wear any color of jewelry with it," she mused. "We can't settle for just anything, however. We must choose something that properly displays our wealth."

"I am certain most members of the ton are aware of the size of our fortune," Amelia said dryly. It was, after all, the only reason they were permitted among them. Well that, and the fact that her father's mines had made several key members of the aristocracy a lot of money.

"Then let's remind them." Mrs. Hart held up a necklace of rubies and diamonds, each one small but perfectly formed. "This will do, I think. The red of the rubies will go well with the pink embellishments on your dress, and diamonds…. Well, do I really need to remark on those?"

"I will put it on her after her hair is done," Mary said.

Amelia didn't argue. It was a nice necklace and far less gaudy than some of the ones her mother could have chosen. Personally, Amelia preferred not to wear jewelry at all, but until she was in control of her own destiny, she would comply. It wasn't as if she disliked jewels. She just found it uncomfortable to attract attention to herself, and jewelry was designed for that purpose.

Mary dropped her hands from the back of the dress and stepped away. Amelia tried to draw in a deep breath but couldn't quite manage to.

"Sit in front of the mirror, please, miss," Mary said.

"Of course." She lowered herself into the chair Mary had placed in front of the mirror, being careful not to burst the seams of the definitely-too-tight gown.

Mary removed the ribbon holding Amelia's hair and briskly brushed the length down her back.

"Make sure to use the jeweled pins," Mrs. Hart urged.

"Yes, ma'am."

As Mary began to arrange Amelia's hair into an elaborate knot on the back of her head, Mrs. Hart hovered over Amelia's shoulder so that they could make eye contact in the mirror.

"Do you recall which gentlemen we intend to impress?" Mrs. Hart asked.

"Yes." Amelia was careful not to move her head. "The Duke of Wight, the Marquess of Overton, and the Earls of Winn and Longley."

"Good girl."

Amelia was tempted to bark.

Mrs. Hart watched her with an unwavering gaze. "Remind me how we intend to capture their attention."

Amelia parroted her mother's earlier instructions. "By being demure, curtsying beautifully, and accepting every invitation to dance."

"Don't forget, there will be no mention of your fanciful scribblings. Nor should you mention any books you may have read."

Amelia frowned. "What if they refer to the book first? They may ask me if I have read a particular work."

Mrs. Hart laughed. "My dear, I can assure you that no gentleman will ask you about your reading habits." She shuddered distastefully as she voiced the phrase as if it were dirty and would sully her by association.

Amelia supposed that since she had made it through her first season without any discussion of books, it would be no sacrifice to promise to do so again. Her mother had a point, after all. Gentlemen didn't seem to admire ladies for their wit or their ability to read Latin or French.

"I will not mention fiction of any form," she agreed.

"Thank you." Mrs. Hart touched her shoulder lightly. "It is for the best. We will not secure a title if you do not try. You're a smart girl. You can make it happen if you wish to."

Amelia pressed her lips together. That might be one of the nicer things her mother had said to her. Not that Mrs. Hart was intentionally cruel. She was just self-centered and had a shallow view of the world.

Mrs. Hart excused herself to get prepared for the ball, and once she was gone, it didn't take long for Mary to pin Amelia's hair into place, frame her face artfully with curls, and arrange the necklace around the base of her throat.

"Good luck," she murmured as Amelia swept out of her bedchamber.

"Thank you," she called back.

Her father was waiting patiently near the bottom of the stairs. He turned toward her as she approached.

"Are you ready for a night of dancing?" he asked, looking her up and down.

"I suppose so." She actually liked dancing—not that she was the most graceful at it.

"I think—" He broke off as Mrs. Hart appeared like a vision at the top of the stairs. She was clad in blue, because of course she would never be seen dead in an unflattering color. Not that many colors looked ill on her mother, truth be told. "My dear, you look ravishing."

Mrs. Hart preened, fussing with her dark hair, which spilled over her shoulders like liquid silk.

Amelia pretended not to notice the way her father practically melted into a puddle at her mother's feet. No matter how much he may care for Amelia, that affection would never hold a candle to his complete adoration of his wife.

"Do you like it?" Mrs. Hart reached the ground floor and

gave a small twirl, her skirts rising high enough to reveal matching blue satin slippers.

Mr. Hart smiled and ran his hand over his balding head, clearly besotted. "You know I love to see you in blue."

Amelia sighed. She supposed her parents' relationship was sweet, in a way. Her father would happily worship her mother, and nothing made her mother happier than being worshiped. It may seem unbalanced, but they were harmonious, in a way. It was just unfortunate that she did not slot so easily into their dynamic.

"The carriage awaits," she murmured, afraid they might forget without her prompting.

Mr. Hart cleared his throat. "Of course."

He took her mother's arm and guided her out through the massive front doors to the carriage. The horses stood placidly, their sleek brown coats gleaming in the last of the evening light.

Amelia shivered and wished she had thought to don a pelisse prior to leaving her room. While the weather was fine, there was a chill in the air. They entered and settled in the carriage. Amelia sat with her back to the front and gazed out the window as the horses pulled them out onto the street.

They navigated through Mayfair until they joined a row of carriages queued outside an intimidatingly large house with Roman-style columns affixed to the facade and a domed turret on each side of the building.

The carriage carried them around a neatly maintained lawn to a cobbled bay beside the entrance. A footman opened the door, and Mrs. Hart nudged Amelia forward. She accepted the footman's assistance and stepped to the side while her parents disembarked,

The slight scent of cigar smoke lingered in the air. Perhaps some of the gentlemen had already sought refuge outside the ballroom.

She would too, if she were able.

Somewhere inside, a skilled pianist was playing Mozart. Mr. Hart linked one of his arms with Amelia's and the other with his wife's, and together they made their way up a short staircase and through the open doors. A footman gestured for them to cross the foyer and enter the ballroom on the other side.

The room was long and rectangular, with a wooden floor, white walls, and gold trim. The ceiling arched high above, and dozens of members of the ton were dressed in their finest and mingling throughout the room.

"Mr. Hart." The Earl of Wembley, their host, greeted her father with a tilt of his head. He turned to her mother. "Mrs. Hart. You are stunning, as always. And Miss Hart. A pleasure to see you here."

Mr. Hart shook the earl's hand. "Thank you for the invitation, Wembley."

"Of course, my good man. It's an honor to hold the first ball of the season. Please, come in and enjoy yourself."

Amelia curtsied to the earl and countess, who stood silently beside him, and moved farther into the ballroom, making way for the next guests to be greeted.

Mr. Hart surveyed those assembled. "I see an acquaintance of mine. I will keep him company while you ladies go about your business."

As he hustled away, Amelia narrowed her eyes at him.

Traitor.

He disliked these events as much as she did, preferring to keep to the fringes and make chitchat about mining and investments, leaving only to dance with his wife.

"Oh look," Mrs. Hart exclaimed. "It's Lady Bowling. If I recall correctly, she has a daughter your age. Come."

Amelia allowed herself to be escorted to join Lady Bowling and her companion, a pale young woman with an elaborate peacock-feather headdress twined into her hair, which was somewhere between ginger and blond.

"Lady Bowling," Mrs. Hart called, a little too loudly. "Such a pleasure to see you."

Lady Bowling flashed a fake smile. "Yes, a pleasure, Mrs. Hart." She glanced at Amelia. "Miss Hart."

Amelia curtsied. "Lovely to see you again, Lady Bowling."

Lady Bowling gestured at the younger woman. "You may have met Lady Esther last year."

Amelia curtsied to her too. "Lady Esther."

If her mother had drilled one thing into her, it was manners.

Lady Esther dipped her head in return. "Miss Hart."

"It looks like tonight will be a crush," Mrs. Hart said cheerfully. "Plenty of eligible gentlemen for our daughters to meet."

Lady Bowling looked around as if seeking escape. "Indeed."

Mrs. Hart's face lit up. "I say, I do believe that is the Marquess of Overton. Lady Bowling, would you do us the honor of an introduction?"

Amelia cast her eyes downward so as not to give away her shock at her mother's audacity. She was impressed, in a way. Her mother knew what she wanted and didn't intend to let any obstacles prevent her from achieving her goal. It was just a shame that her desires and Amelia's did not fully align.

"Of course." Lady Bowling curled her upper lip as if she'd smelled something foul. She led them through the crowd and to the side of the ballroom, where a handsome figure of a man with dark hair and an aristocratic nose was surveying the throng.

Amelia glanced at Lady Esther and found the other woman looking back. Lady Esther grimaced and moved her neck from side to side. Perhaps the headdress was heavy. Amelia wondered if it was Lady Bowling's choice to display her daughter in such a way, just as Mrs. Hart had been the one to select her unflattering and frilly gown.

"My lord." Lady Bowling swept into a dramatic curtsy as they reached the marquess.

The Harts and Lady Esther rushed to follow suit.

Lady Bowling rose. "You look very well tonight. Do you recall my daughter, Lady Esther?"

The marquess nodded and tipped his head toward Lady Esther. "You are as eye-catching as ever, Lady Esther."

Lady Esther giggled but didn't seem able to summon a verbal response.

Lady Bowling waved at Mrs. Hart and Amelia. "Have you met Mrs. Hart and Miss Hart?"

"I have not." The marquess gave a shallow bow. He caught Amelia's eyes as he rose. "Charmed."

Amelia's lips twitched. She did not think he was charmed at all. He had a slightly hunted expression that made her think of a fox that knew the hounds were on its tail. Of course, she kept that observation to herself.

"It's a pleasure to meet you," she said, offering him a small smile.

"A very great pleasure," Mrs. Hart added enthusiastically. "Do you intend to dance tonight, my lord?"

"Er, yes." The marquess shifted from one foot to the other. "I would be honored if Lady Esther and Miss Hart would each grace me with a dance. Provided that their cards aren't already full…." He sounded so hopeful that Amelia almost laughed.

Lady Esther rapidly proffered her card, giggling again. The marquess jotted his name beside one of her dances and then did the same for Amelia.

"You must excuse me now," he said, staring somewhere behind them. "I see… someone I must speak with."

Neither mother seemed concerned as he beat a hasty

retreat. They had accomplished their goal of securing dances for their daughters.

"Is that Lord Downing?" Mrs. Hart asked, subtly jerking her chin toward a man farther along the wall.

"I believe it is," Lady Bowling confirmed. "Shall we?"

Amelia didn't escape the clutches of her mother and Lady Bowling until her first dance with the aforementioned Lord Downing. She attempted to make small talk, but it was clear within the first thirty seconds of their dance that she bored him terribly.

Her next dance was with the Marquess of Overton, who at the very least seemed more inclined to carry on a conversation with her, even if it centered around how dreadful the weather had been.

Unfortunately, any joy she might feel as a result of this small win was overshadowed by the pain in her feet. The marquess was an atrocious dancer. However, he had been relatively pleasant to her, so she liked him more than Lord Downing.

On the side of the room, her mother kept widening her eyes and nodding meaningfully. Amelia wasn't quite sure what she was trying to convey, but there was little she could do to prolong their interaction considering her next dance was promised to the Earl of Winn.

Indeed, Overton quickly melted into the crowd and the earl materialized before her. He was a short man with graying hair, and his hand was clammy as it wrapped around hers. They began to dance a quadrille.

Winn's feet were quicker than Overton's, and he didn't step on her at all. However, he swayed in such a way that led her to believe he might be soused, and his eyes barely left the exposed skin of her throat and upper chest. At first, she thought he might be admiring the necklace, as her mother had intended, but she rapidly realized his thoughts were elsewhere.

Dreadful man.

As soon as the dance ended, she hurried toward the powder room without looking back. She paced the room, glancing at herself in the mirror each time she passed it. She winced. Her eyes were wide and agitated, and a faint flush had spread across her cheeks.

The door opened, and a short, curvaceous redhead strode inside. She came up short upon spotting Amelia.

"Do you need me to help you escape through the window?" she asked completely seriously.

Amelia laughed at the absurdity of the offer. "Much as I would like that, no. It's just…." She huffed. "Does the insincerity of this whole thing not grow tiresome?"

Her companion nodded. "No one says what they mean, and everyone is so polite and stiff. It's ridiculous. Yet this is the world we find ourselves a part of, and we must navigate it as best we can."

Amelia checked her hand for a ring and, seeing none, asked, "How many seasons have you had?"

The redhead sighed. "This will be my sixth."

Amelia prayed she did not have to endure another four seasons. She wasn't sure she would remain sane. She would almost certainly accept the suit of a halfway decent man before then if only to escape the unpleasantness of forced civility.

The redhead smirked. "Don't feel too sorry for me. It has been my choice not to wed. I intended to once, when I was much younger, but he, apparently, did not want me back."

Amelia's heart lurched. How awful to know who one wanted and be denied. "I am sorry."

The woman shrugged. "There is nothing for it. I am Helena, and you?"

"Amelia." She did not offer a last name, since Helena hadn't done so.

Helena closed the distance between them and patted her

shoulder. "Well, at least you no longer look as if you are considering fleeing. You should probably return before your mother sends out a search party, fearing that you are being debauched in some shadowy corner."

Amelia gaped at her. She could scarcely believe Helena had used the word "debauched" in polite company. Then she quietly laughed at herself. She shouldn't be so easily shocked. She had written plenty of scandalous things herself, although they were less of a debaucherous nature and were instead more in the vein of women doing things that society dictated they ought not to.

"I've shocked you." Helena appeared pleased by this.

"No. Well, yes, but only in a good way. You're right. I should return."

"Good luck," Helena called as Amelia strode out, her skirts brushing against her calves with each step.

She decided she liked Helena. She was exactly the sort of person who would have adventures like Joceline did. Not at all like Amelia herself.

"Amelia!"

She winced at the hiss from Mrs. Hart, who'd apparently been waiting beside the powder room door.

"You missed a dance," Mrs. Hart growled. "Fortunately for you, I was able to persuade the Duke of Wight to accept the next dance instead."

Amelia's heart sank, but she allowed herself to be drawn back into the crush. Her mother handed her over to the duke, who was waiting on the edge of the dance floor. They had met briefly earlier, and Amelia had been relieved that he'd been distracted by a friend at the time. She'd thought she'd had a lucky escape, but it would seem not.

"Miss Hart." The duke raised her hands to his lips and kissed the back, leaving a wet patch behind.

Amelia wished she could wipe it on her dress, but there was no way to do so without him noticing.

She curtsied. "Your Grace."

His gaze skimmed down her body, and she couldn't help but feel as if he were gauging her ability to bear children. For once, she thanked the heavens that she did not have particularly wide hips. The duke likely wanted someone more of Helena's proportions if his priority was to secure an heir.

But as he led her onto the dance floor for a waltz, of all things, it didn't feel as though he'd dismissed her potential to be the next Duchess of Wight. His hand on her waist dipped lower than necessary, and she stiffened.

"Were you in Town last season?" she asked to make polite conversation.

"I was in mourning," he said, "but I am finally ready to move on."

Ah, yes.

His late wife.

One of three late wives.

Amelia had no desire to become the fourth. At what point would the man admit that he might be the problem?

"How old are you?" he asked.

"Twenty-one, Your Grace." She'd had her first season slightly later than most debutantes because her mother wanted to ensure she could integrate as successfully as possible, having come from such a different background.

"Very good." His hand wandered lower again.

Amelia trod on his foot. "Oh, I'm sorry. I was distracted."

His hand returned to its former, slightly too low, position, and he bared his teeth in an approximation of a smile. "I expect you had less formal dance training than most chits."

She pretended not to understand the barb. He was trying to remind her of her place, which was lesser than the aristocracy.

They didn't speak for the remainder of the dance. As soon as possible, Amelia disentangled herself from him. She hurried to the drinks table, claimed a glass of lemonade, and forced herself not to gulp down the tart liquid in the unlady-like way she wanted to.

She looked around and couldn't see her mother. In need of a brief respite, she ducked behind an arrangement of shrubbery intended as decoration. There was a tickle in her nose, and she rubbed the side of it, thinking longingly of the chair in the corner of her bedchamber. She would so much rather be curled up there with a book.

"I say," a cultured male voice inquired from a few feet away. "Pray tell, who are you hiding from behind the shrubbery?"

CHAPTER 5

ANDREW STUDIED THE STRANGE WOMAN, INTRIGUED. She stared back at him with wide eyes the color of the sky on a clear summer's day. He'd been looking for her ever since speaking with her mother, but securing an invitation to meet Miss Hart had proven much simpler than actually locating the chit.

He'd never expected to find her behind the shrubbery.

"S-sir." She straightened and smoothed her free hand down the front of her dress. Something fascinating flashed through her eyes. "I was not hiding. I was merely… rearranging the greenery."

He chuckled, enchanted by the little liar. "There are servants for that."

Surely, she was used to having servants around. A man as rich as her father must have dozens of them.

Miss Hart raised her pert, slightly pointed nose. "I enjoy horticulture."

"You do?" he asked, amused.

"Yes." She sounded very uncertain. "It is a hobby of mine."

Entertained as he was by her falsehoods, he needed to know what she was doing over here.

He took two steps toward her, ensuring that no one would be able to overhear their conversation. "Did someone upset you?"

She sighed and squeezed those bright eyes shut, only for them to flutter open a moment later. "This"—she gestured at their surroundings—"is quite a change of pace for me. I simply needed a moment alone to gather my thoughts."

Guilt flashed through him. While he'd never been one to get overwhelmed by social events, Ashford was, so he was familiar with how debilitating it could be. She'd sought out a few seconds of peace, and he'd intruded like a clumsy oaf.

"My apologies for the interruption. If you need a while longer, I can stand guard and ensure no one approaches." It was the best peace offering he could think of, especially considering that he didn't wish to alienate Miss Hart.

It was refreshing to speak with a woman who wasn't either simpering at everything he said or too intimidated to respond.

She cocked her head. "I appreciate the offer, but I do believe it would be most improper. After all, we haven't even been introduced."

"Ah, but I have met your mother, and I am certain I have her blessing to introduce myself to you." Mrs. Hart had been practically gleeful when he'd asked her about her daughter. "I'm the Earl of Longley."

To his surprise, she cringed. "I see."

She didn't say anything more, and he wasn't sure why his identity caused her distress.

"Would you like to dance?" he asked, to break the silence. "Assuming this dance is not promised to someone else."

She laughed. "I am quite sure it is, but I'm avoiding taking part."

He grinned, relieved she was conversing with him again. "Well, what about the next one, then?"

"I suppose so." She held out her hand for him to look at her card.

He hid his amusement as he did so. He wasn't accustomed to young women being quite so unimpressed by him. He read the list of names on her card, his eyebrow rising. Mrs. Hart hadn't wasted any time in thrusting her daughter at every available titled man in the room, and a few second sons as well.

The next dance already had a name scrawled beside it, but he crossed it out and added his own. Her lips parted, and a breath gusted between them.

He put a finger to his lips. "Our secret. Trust me, you don't want to dance with Lord Brunner."

He half expected her to protest, but instead, her mouth curved into a sly smile.

"In that case, I appreciate your assistance."

The music ended, and he offered her his hand. "If we intend to dance, we must, unfortunately, leave the cover of your beloved shrubbery."

She stifled a laugh. "You are absurd, my lord."

He winked. "Better that than boring."

He guided her into position. She moved with the effortless grace of someone who had been dancing for years. No doubt her mother harbored long-held aspirations of marriage into the aristocracy and had been preparing her daughter for such. Although the fact that he'd found Miss Hart behind the shrubbery told him she was cut from a different cloth than her mother.

She swept past him, the soft fabric of their gloves brushing as they moved through the steps of the dance. He wondered how her bare skin would feel against his.

It was odd, but for some reason she fascinated him. She wasn't a great beauty by the ton's standards. Slim without being waifish. Dark hair rather than the blond that was currently in favor. Slightly taller than was usual for a woman.

Yet her eccentricities charmed him.

As she drew near, her remarkable eyes met his. Those were certainly noteworthy. As was the faint scent of peppermint that lingered on her skin.

"I appreciate you not treading on my feet," she said, humor gleaming in her eyes.

"I aim to please." The song rose to a crescendo. It would soon end, and a mild sense of panic rose within him at the thought of losing her company. "Tell me about yourself."

He spun her, and as she returned, her eyebrows were furrowed.

"What would you like to know?" she asked.

"Anything you care to share." They swayed past each other again, and he breathed in her minty aroma.

She considered this. "Very well. I enjoy learning about other places and civilizations."

He shook his head, his grin widening. "Of course you do."

A woman like Miss Hart would not be interested in ribbons or watercolors. She was of a different bent.

Her eyes narrowed. "What is that supposed to mean?"

"Only that you seem the type of person to be intrigued by the world around you."

"Oh." She clearly didn't know what to make of that.

The song ended, and he bowed to her and took her hand. "Allow me to escort you back to your mother... unless you'd prefer to return to hiding behind the shrubbery?"

"I was not—" She broke off, huffing in indignation. She rather reminded him of a cat with its fur puffed up. He knew better than to verbalize that though.

Finding Mrs. Hart proved simple. She was hovering just beyond the dancers, her expression conflicted.

"You were supposed to dance with Lord Brunner," she murmured, taking Miss Hart's arm.

"Forgive me," Andrew said, compelled to prevent Mrs. Hart from chiding her daughter. "I was so eager to dance that I ignored her obligation, even when she informed me of it."

"Oh. Well." Mrs. Hart seemed torn between continuing to reprimand Miss Hart and expressing her delight at his attention. "Next time, you will simply have to get in sooner to claim her first dance."

He inclined his head. "Indeed." He turned to Miss Hart. "May I call on you tomorrow?"

She stared at him, clearly baffled by his interest.

"Yes, my lord," Mrs. Hart rushed to say, her eyes narrowed at her daughter meaningfully. "We would love to welcome you. We'll be receiving callers tomorrow morning from 11:00 a.m."

He nodded. "I shall be there with bells on. Please excuse me, ladies."

With that, he bowed, pivoted, and strode away. Miss Hart was unlike any woman he'd ever met. He had a feeling he could grow to enjoy her company very much.

He made his way to the refreshments room and poured himself a glass of champagne. He dodged the Earl of Winn, who was swaying drunkenly toward him, and withdrew the list from his pocket. He'd made contact with four of the women tonight. Only two remained: Miss Carruthers and Miss Wentham.

He'd already crossed off one name. Miss Cahill, the first of the potential wives he'd encountered tonight, had been as shrewish as her reputation proclaimed. She'd made snide comments about the decor, other people's attire, and his own dancing skills.

Andrew knew he couldn't afford to be too selective, but he did not want an unkind wife. Thus, she was not an option.

Lady Esther Bowling had been reasonably pleasant, as he'd expected. Not much for chitchat, but she'd seemed good-natured. Lady Holden had been every bit as slippery as he'd anticipated. She was charming and beautiful, but aloof in a way that he expected meant she would not succumb easily to any man's charm.

He finished his champagne and went in search of Miss Wentham. He'd been unable to approach her so far because she had been constantly on the dance floor. However, he had secured her mother's word that she'd be available for this next dance.

Sure enough, Mrs. Wentham was standing next to the dance floor with her daughter beside her. Andrew had met Miss Wentham before but had not spent long in her acquaintance. She was a pretty blond girl with delicate features and a slightly hooked nose.

He circled around an arrangement of flowers, catching a faint floral scent, and stopped in front of them, sketching a quick bow. "Miss Wentham. Your mother advised me that you are available for the next dance. Is that so?"

"I am, my lord."

She offered him her hand, and he drew her onto the dance floor, where the dancing had temporarily ceased. They stood opposite each other, waiting as other couples joined them.

"I am surprised to see you here. I understand that you usually prefer social events of a different caliber."

Andrew wasn't sure whether to grimace or smirk. It seemed his reputation as somewhat of a rake preceded him. That was unfortunate in that it may prejudice some mamas against him, but it also rendered him intriguing to curious misses—such as Miss Wentham, if he were reading her correctly.

"I'm in search of a wife this season." He'd decided it was best not to play coy. He didn't want to risk putting anyone off by allowing them to be uncertain of his motives.

A violin began to play.

Her eyebrows rose. "Are you, indeed?"

Other instruments joined in, and the dancers started to move. As they circled around, Andrew spotted Miss Hart on the arm of Lord Brunner. Her mother must have pushed her to make up for the time she'd spent with him.

She looked most uncomfortable. Even from a distance, he could tell she didn't like Brunner being near her. She kept their touches as brief as possible, and her eyes were fixed somewhere over his shoulder. He couldn't help recalling how enjoyable their dance had been and feeling a flash of satisfaction that she so obviously preferred his company.

Miss Wentham followed his gaze as her feet moved effortlessly. She laughed, but rather than the sweet giggles of Lady Esther or the wry amusement of Miss Hart, hers was sharp enough to cut.

"What a joke that the Harts believe they can foist themselves onto polite society simply because they have money." She shook her head, her upper lip curled in a sneer. "No matter how nicely they dress or how well they polish their manners, they'll always have dirty roots."

Well. Apparently, Miss Wentham had no trouble vocalizing her opinion, and she was quite a snob. Andrew mentally crossed her off the list too. It was a shame. She was attractive, and her family was well respected, but he could not possibly tie himself to someone so judgmental.

"Don't you agree?" she asked as they separated and rejoined.

"No," he said shortly.

He'd never been one of the aristocrats who looked down their nose at people who made something of themselves from humble beginnings. They certainly had more to be proud of than he did. He'd inherited all he had, and he hadn't even been responsible enough to hold on to it.

The dance ended, and he escorted Miss Wentham back to her mother.

"Thank you for the lovely dance." He kept his tone polite. It did no good to be abrupt with anyone.

"I hope we'll see more of you soon." Mrs. Wentham sounded optimistic, but her daughter seemed less so. Perhaps she realized she'd erred in expressing her snobbery so openly to him.

He excused himself, internally debating whether to seek out Miss Carruthers or help himself to another champagne first, and perhaps a piece of cake. The idea of a sweet treat and more alcohol appealed, but he decided it was best to get the last of his conversations with prospective wives out of the way.

He wandered the gathering. Unfortunately, he did not know what either Miss Carruthers or her parents looked like. However, his mother had informed him that they were cousins to the Earl of Wembley, so when he spotted Lady Wembley, he hoped she would be able to aid him.

He silently thanked his lucky stars that the Wembleys' daughter had married last season. If not, he might find himself fending off Lady Wembley's attempts at matchmaking with her own daughter.

Normally, he wouldn't mind that, but from his understanding, the Carruthers were much wealthier than the Wembleys, and at the moment, unfortunate—and somewhat crass—though it may be, much depended on his ability to marry a fortune.

"Lady Wembley." He took her hand and bowed. "Might I trouble you for an introduction to your lovely niece?"

The corner of Lady Wembley's mouth hitched up. "It's true, then? The illustrious Earl of Longley intends to settle down?"

He straightened. "In this, the gossip is correct."

A dimple formed in one of her cheeks. "You are fortunate that I no longer have an unmarried daughter, Longley, or I might take offense at your interest in Miss Carruthers. As it happens, I am in a good mood, and she is a sweet girl. I shall be happy to make the introduction."

"Thank you, my lady. I can't imagine that you ever experience unpleasant moods. You are the height of graciousness."

She laughed. "And you, my lord, are a dreadful flirt. Come. Last I saw her, Miss Carruthers was near the lemonade."

She led him to the lemonade table tucked away in the corner of the ballroom. Hovering nearby was a relatively unremarkable girl with dark hair and a nice smile.

He assessed her quickly. Her dress was a pale shade of green that suited her well, and while she was not in anyone's company, she didn't seem to be attempting to disappear into the wallpaper.

She was, however, quite young. The youngest of the ladies he'd met tonight. His mother had promised him no schoolroom chits, but Miss Carruthers was surely not long past that age.

"Miss Carruthers," Lady Wembley called.

The girl turned toward them and, seeing Longley, swept a neat curtsy. "Aunt."

Lady Wembley drew up in front of her and gestured at Andrew. "This is the Earl of Longley. He wished to make your acquaintance."

"Lovely to meet you, my lord." Her voice was soft and cultured.

"The pleasure is all mine. I don't suppose your dance card is empty for the next dance?"

"It is." She held out her wrist and offered it to him.

He added his name, and they made polite small talk until the dance began.

When the dance was over, he returned her to the wall near the lemonade and parted with a few final words. He made his farewells and headed out of the building, taking the stairs down to where the carriages waited with a pep in his step.

Perhaps the evening had been exhausting, but he was in a good place to start planning. While both Miss Carruthers and Lady Esther remained valid options, neither had intrigued him as much as the woman he'd found hiding behind the shrubbery.

Miss Hart had been alternately awkward and witty. He suspected the awkwardness was a facade and that the witty, amusing woman was who she really was. Her, he wanted to know better. It didn't hurt that her mother had made it obvious just how desperate she was to make a good match.

His carriage pulled up. He got in and called out to the driver that he was ready to depart. They trundled through the gate and onto the road. It was truly dark now and slightly chilly. Andrew drew his jacket tightly around himself and dipped his chin down to conserve warmth.

The drive home passed far more quickly than the ride in the other direction had taken because traffic was far sparser. When they stopped outside Longley House, he thanked the driver and glanced up. Light shone through his bedroom window and also the one farther along, where Kate slept. His mother's room was dark.

Boden let him in and locked the door. Andrew bid him good night and climbed the stairs to his bedchamber. His eyes were heavy, but his mind was racing too much to be able to sleep soon, so he stopped by the library, found the book he'd been reading, and took it with him.

He opened his bedchamber and came up short, startled. "Kate."

His sister looked up from the sketch pad resting on her knee. From the doorway, he could tell she'd been shading in the portrait of a person, but he couldn't tell who. She closed the book and set it aside.

"Andrew. Mother said you wouldn't mind if I waited for you here."

"Of course not." He entered the room and closed the door. "Is everything all right?"

She spun the pencil between her fingers. There were dark smudges along their length and on her palms. Hopefully she hadn't smeared any of it on his bedding. "Did you meet anyone nice tonight?"

Ah. So she wanted to know how their prospects were looking.

"I did, actually."

She smiled ever so slightly, relief evident in the expression. "Is she a diamond of the first water?"

He sat on the edge of the bed and bent to remove his boots. "Actually, no."

"No?"

He didn't say anything more, knowing it would drive her crazy.

"Tell me," she whined. "Please, Andrew. I want to know."

He slipped off one boot and started on the other. "She's a merchant's daughter, and I get the impression she's rather unconventional."

"A merchant's daughter?" She sounded intrigued. "How is she unconventional?"

Smiling to himself, he removed the second boot, turned to face her, and recounted his first meeting with Miss Hart.

"I want to meet her," Kate declared when he'd finished speaking.

He chuckled. "Let's not get ahead of ourselves. There's every possibility that Miss Hart was not nearly as taken with me as I was with her."

Kate scoffed. "Of course she was. All my friends say how handsome you are. I am certain she noticed too."

"Yes," he mused. "Perhaps. But there is much more to attraction than appearances. She strikes me as the type of woman who will have a firm idea of what she wants, and I'm not certain I fit the bill."

She frowned. "When will you see her next?"

"Tomorrow."

"Good. We can plan out what you're going to say to her together."

Andrew glanced toward the window. Was he really willing to take advice from his baby sister?

He sighed. "What do you have in mind?"

CHAPTER 6

Amelia's hand flew across the paper as she jotted down ideas about what adventures might await Joceline next.

"Amelia!"

She froze, her hand an inch from the paper. Then, hearing her mother outside her bedchamber, she rushed to hide the paper beneath her pillow. She'd taken to working on her stories in private, since Mrs. Hart somehow always knew when she did so in the library, and she preferred not to deal with any more lectures than necessary.

Mrs. Hart breezed into the room and eyed Amelia with disapproval. "Stop lying about in bed. You ought to be preparing to receive callers."

Amelia checked the clock and winced. "I'm sorry. Time got away from me."

Mrs. Hart scowled. "Make sure it doesn't happen again. Our guests will be here soon, and you must look your best."

"Of course, Mother. I'll call for Mary now." She was just relieved her mother hadn't seen the papers and that she'd avoided a scolding. Mrs. Hart's temper was a fragile thing when it came to Amelia failing to live up to her expectations.

"No need. I will summon Mary," Mrs. Hart said. "You

must freshen yourself up. There's a pot of water in the corridor. Once you've done that, we can choose your dress."

Amelia's face fell. She'd hoped that she'd be able to select her own attire today, but since her mother was here, then she would simply have to accept whatever she thought was best.

"Yes, Mother."

Mrs. Hart left to find Mary, for which Amelia was grateful because it allowed her to dart into the corridor, retrieve the pot of warm water, and scrub her ink-stained hands with peppermint soap before anyone else could see them. She splashed her face and checked in the mirror to ensure there were no ink smudges on her cheeks or chin.

Mrs. Hart and Mary arrived seconds after she locked the desk drawer with her notes tucked safely inside.

"Good morning, miss," Mary said, dropping her chin respectfully.

"Hello, Mary," Amelia greeted in return.

There was nothing more she could say with Mrs. Hart present, so as much as she might like to ask what the other maids thought of her ideas for Joceline, some of which she'd shared with Mary last night, she would have to wait.

Never mind. Amelia could be patient.

Mrs. Hart removed a dress from the wardrobe, and Amelia exhaled a breath of relief. It was a simple frock of pale blue that would actually flatter her complexion and potentially even look rather nice.

"This one," Mrs. Hart declared.

Mary took it from her, laid it on the bed, and helped Amelia remove her nightgown. She folded the nightgown on the padded seat at the end of the bed and then positioned the dress for Amelia to step into.

Mary lifted the dress up over Amelia's hips, and they both ignored her mother's tutting about their difficult size—as if it were Amelia's fault they were not either willow slim or of the impressive proportions labeled as "childbearing."

She simply was as she had always been.

Average.

The worst possible outcome, as far as Mrs. Hart was concerned. At least if she were one extreme or the other, people would notice her.

"I think the pearl necklace today," Mrs. Hart mused.

Amelia almost chuckled. God forbid anyone forget for a single second just how wealthy the Harts were.

She held still while Mary buttoned the back of her dress, and her mother fetched the aforementioned necklace from a drawer and held it up in front of Amelia.

"Yes. That will pair nicely with the dress." She placed it atop the cabinet beneath the mirror. "I do wish you'd been more mindful not to waste the morning like a layabout. As it is, we don't have the time to dress your hair properly."

Amelia was quietly pleased that they would not be able to do anything too extravagant. It was an awful nuisance trying to comb out her hair after an event for which her mother insisted on an elaborate style. Her scalp always stung something fierce, and the tangles brought tears to her eyes.

"I am sure that Mary is more than capable of coming up with something appropriate in the time we have," she said, flashing the maid a smile.

Mary glanced at Mrs. Hart and, finding her waiting, nodded. "Yes, ma'am. I think, considering the hour, we would be best to leave her hair loose and perhaps swept over her shoulder. We can set a few curls around her face."

Mrs. Hart sighed and waved her hand dismissively. "Fine. But next time, I expect you to be prepared earlier."

She stalked out—no doubt to double-check her own appearance—and Amelia sat while Mary fixed her hair.

When her mother returned to escort her downstairs, she drew in a deep breath and braced herself for a morning of either painful chitchat or uncomfortable silence, depending on whether or not they received any callers.

She didn't have high hopes.

Last season, they'd prepared for callers many times, only to receive absolutely none or, at best, someone her mother considered subpar and in whom Amelia had no interest anyway.

Just because Mrs. Hart had decided to take a more aggressive approach this season by thrusting her in front of potential suitors didn't necessarily mean they would be more successful.

They took the stairs and passed by her father's office on the way to the drawing room they used to greet visitors. She peeked inside. Mr. Hart was bent over a ledger, a furrow of concentration between his eyebrows. She wished she could join him like she used to as a girl rather than going through this farce.

Alas, she was now a marriageable miss, not a child. She could not afford to flout propriety as she used to. No one cared if a merchant's daughter was eccentric, but the same could not be said of a woman of the ton. She must adapt or continue to be treated as less than their equal simply because of her birth.

Mrs. Hart summoned the housekeeper as they entered the drawing room.

"Please ensure we are prepared for callers," she ordered. "We will require tea, scones, and clotted cream."

Mrs. White nodded dutifully. "Yes, ma'am."

Mrs. Hart ushered Amelia over to one of the two chaises facing each other on the right side of the room. The regal blue-and-silver pattern of the fabric matched that of the wallpaper. Once again, her mother's love of blue had prevailed in this space.

"Sit," Mrs. Hart urged, looking around in search of any last-minute imperfection to tidy away.

Amelia personally thought her mother had done a wonderful job of making this room as grand as any possessed by the aristocracy, with paintings by well-known artists on the walls, a pianoforte in the corner, and a chessboard arranged atop a small table in front of the window.

Apparently satisfied, Mrs. Hart sat beside Amelia.

"Who do you think we can expect to call?" She sounded as excited as Amelia had ever heard her. "The Duke of Wight seemed quite taken with you. As did both the Earls of Winn and Longley. Could you imagine what a coup it would be if they all came to see us?"

"Quite a coup, indeed." Not that she cared one way or the other, except for the effect it would have on her mother's temper.

As Mrs. Hart straightened, maintaining excellent posture even though there was no one around to see, Amelia couldn't help feeling sorry for her. Even though she didn't like the way her mother went about it, all she really wanted was to be accepted, and it wasn't fair that society kept that from her.

Mrs. White hustled into the room, carrying a tray of tea. She set it on the table to the left of the chaise that Amelia and her mother were seated on. A maid followed behind her, bringing scones with jam and clotted cream to the table beside the chaise opposite them.

"Thank you," Amelia murmured.

They both curtsied and left.

Amelia wondered who—if anyone—would be the first to put in an appearance. After last evening, she was certain that neither Lord Downing nor the Marquess of Overton would visit. She feared she'd bored them both dreadfully. A shame, when the marquess was one of only two of the gentlemen she'd danced with whom she considered appealing.

The other, the Earl of Longley, confused her. He had ever since he'd startled her while she was loitering behind the shrubbery. She didn't know what to make of him, or whether he'd been genuinely interested in her, simply humoring her, or somehow mocking her.

He was a solid man, with broad shoulders, a trim waist, and an innate gracefulness that had made him enjoyable to dance with. His square-jawed face was pleasant to look upon, and his sparkling gold-flecked eyes, smattering of freckles, and reddish hair kept him from bland handsomeness.

There was a rap at the door.

"The Earl of Winn has arrived," their butler announced.

Amelia stiffened.

Her mother, on the other hand, beamed. "Show him in, Mr. Grant."

He bowed and backed away, returning moments later with the Earl of Winn's familiar paunchy figure.

Amelia's eyebrows rose. She was surprised by how well he looked, considering he'd seemed to have had a few too many glasses of champagne the previous evening. But now, the earl stood tall, his clothing impeccable, his eyes clear. He still did not appeal to her in the slightest, but she couldn't help being a little impressed.

Both Amelia and Mrs. Hart rose to their feet. Mrs. Hart made a display of curtsying deeply. Amelia followed suit. As she rose, she noticed the earl's gaze dart away from her decolletage. Her cheeks heated. Sober or not, he was a lecher.

"We are honored you have called on us," Mrs. Hart said, sinking gracefully onto the chaise. She gestured at the one opposite them. "Please, make yourself comfortable."

"Would you like tea?" Amelia asked, knowing her role in this performance.

He nodded. "Please, my dear."

Her skin crawled, but she did her best to hide it as she crossed to the table, poured tea into three cups—for him, her mother, and herself. "How do you take it?"

"Black. No sugar." He fingered the edge of his mustache. "That's the most British way, in my opinion."

Mrs. Hart giggled. "How right you are."

Amelia fixed two black teas and one with sugar and milk,

as she preferred. She stirred, set the spoon down with a clink, and served her mother and the earl before claiming her own cup and returning to her seat.

They sat in silence. It dragged out for far too long. Mrs. Hart shot Amelia a look, but she didn't know what to say. She was good at recalling social rituals but less so at actually speaking to people she had little in common with.

"How are you enjoying the season?" she asked awkwardly.

"So far, so good." He sipped his tea, and she inwardly winced. It must still be very hot. "Of course, it's all about the company, isn't it? I very much enjoyed yours during our dance."

"Thank you, my lord." Remembering how he'd attempted to look down her dress at every opportunity, she'd prefer to be less polite, but her mother would be furious, and it wasn't worth the bother.

Sometimes, she thought it would be nice if Mrs. Hart wasn't quite so mercenary. She probably meant well, but Amelia had difficulty believing that her mother cared whether she married a lecherous drunkard like Winn or a handsome charmer like Longley, provided they were titled.

They continued a somewhat stilted conversation until the earl took his leave.

Soon after he departed, Mr. Grant declared the arrival of the Duke of Wight. The duke entered with a dignified gait that Amelia supposed arose from age as much as station. She doubted he could move much faster. Perhaps she would be safe married to him if she failed to bear his children. After all, she only had to be able to outrun him.

That said, the thought of him touching her made her want to fling herself off the cliff anyway.

She poured him tea, which he promptly set aside, instead helping himself to a scone laden with jam and cream. He began a conversation that didn't seem to require their participation to maintain. He kept up a constant stream of hunting stories, bragging about how many grouse he'd bagged, among other things.

Amelia did her best to hide her distaste. She understood the need to kill for sustenance, but the idea of killing for sport had always seemed unnecessarily cruel to her.

Of course, her mother flattered the duke every time he stopped speaking for even a few seconds. She probably considered that Amelia ought to do the same, but he didn't even notice her lack of interest, so what did it matter?

The duke excused himself after yet another scone, leaving his tea untouched. He scanned Amelia in the same way he had at the ball, as if she were a broodmare he was considering purchasing, then made a passing remark about seeing them soon. She couldn't tell if he was being sincere or if he'd decided she was not his best bet as the provider of his heir and they'd never hear from him again.

Despite her mother's obvious hopes to the contrary, she couldn't help but pray for the latter.

After Mr. Grant showed the duke out, Amelia and Mrs. Hart sat alone in the drawing room as the minutes ticked by.

Mrs. Hart's optimism gradually faded, and after a while, she instructed Amelia to get her needlepoint. Amelia knew better than to refuse, so she did, and they worked side by side. Her mother created beautiful artistry while Amelia struggled with a simple floral design.

Eventually, Mrs. Hart heaved a sigh. "I do not understand. I was certain we'd receive more callers."

"Perhaps they will come soon." But Amelia wasn't surprised. No matter how much her mother tried to foist her onto society, the only men who'd consider marrying her were either fortune hunters or less desirable for some other reason, such as the Earl of Winn and the Duke of Wight.

"Perhaps." But Mrs. Hart didn't sound hopeful.

They resumed their needlepoint. While Amelia's fingers

tripped clumsily over the needle, and she pricked herself on more than one occasion, she allowed her mind to wander to Joceline Davies. She longed to get started on her next tale. She'd decided that Joceline would set sail for the Americas but was still fleshing out the whys and hows.

She jabbed her finger and hissed as a droplet of blood welled on the tip. She sucked it into her mouth, ignoring her mother's rebuke.

"You are not a heathen," Mrs. Hart muttered. "I know you are able to do needlepoint better than this."

She really wasn't. Amelia had never been particularly adept at any of the ladylike skills her mother had attempted to teach her, with the exception of speaking other languages. She was a passable dancer at best, had no eye for color, and would much rather have a quill in hand than a needle.

Still, she supposed it was nice that her mother cared enough to delude herself into believing that Amelia possessed some of the expected feminine talents.

"Ma'am. Miss."

Both of their faces snapped toward the door where Mr. Grant stood, his potbelly buffed out in a display of self-importance.

"The Earl of Longley."

Amelia's hands stilled. The earl had come?

She didn't have time to gather her thoughts before Mr. Grant was showing him in. Longley grinned at them with that same mischievous smile he'd worn yesterday. His hazel eyes twinkled as if he knew something they didn't, and his thick auburn hair was slightly tousled. Her stomach fluttered. He was awfully good-looking, and she liked that despite his attractiveness, he didn't seem unapproachable.

"My lord." Her mother looked utterly delighted as she placed her needlepoint in a basket near her feet and rose. "We so hoped you would grace us with your presence."

Longley held his palms up. "Please don't get up on my account."

He bowed to her and then to Amelia, one side of his mouth curled as if he found the world incredibly amusing.

"B-but we must," Mrs. Hart sputtered, thrown off by his casual demeanor. "It is only proper."

"Do as you wish, my good lady." He strode farther into the room, glancing about and studying one of the paintings with interest.

"Would you like tea and scones?" Amelia asked, eagerly dropping her own needlepoint into the basket too.

His gaze followed the movement, and he smirked. "Tea and scones would be welcome, Miss Hart."

She gestured for the earl to sit while she went to the tables. "How do you prefer your tea?"

"With two spoons of sugar, please. Both jam and cream on the scone."

He waited while she poured a drink, stirred in sugar, and prepared a scone for him. When she'd passed them over, he blew across the top of the teacup and placed it back on the table to cool.

The earl bit into his scone, careful not to smear any cream on his face. "You have a lovely home," he said after swallowing his mouthful. "Who is the art aficionado in the family?"

"We all appreciate the arts," Mrs. Hart hedged. "But it was I who selected the paintings for our walls."

"You have excellent taste."

Amelia watched the interplay, baffled. When he'd said he would call today, she'd assumed it was a polite overture that would not be followed up on. Yet here he was.

She didn't understand. What possible interest could a rich, charming, and titled man have with a plain merchant's daughter he'd found hiding behind a plant?

Mrs. Hart preened and sent Amelia another pointed look. She reminded Amelia of a cat with a mouse in its sights.

"We need more tea," she said, standing and brushing off her skirt. "I will speak to Mrs. White. I'll be just a moment." She widened her eyes meaningfully and sashayed out of the drawing room.

Amelia cocked her head, confused. Her mother could just as easily have called for Mrs. White to come to her. It was unlike her to go in search of the servants herself. She considered that kind of behavior beneath her. Not to mention the fact that she was leaving them alone together, which was most improper.

Then it struck her. Mrs. Hart must have realized that Amelia wasn't as repulsed by him as she had been by the others, and that therefore the earl was her best chance thus far of marrying into the aristocracy. Perhaps she hoped that something scandalous might occur between them while she was gone to force the issue.

Amelia looked at the earl.

He looked back.

She pursed her lips, uncertain what to say. She decided the direct approach would be best. "What is it that brings you to our home this morning?"

His forehead crinkled. "The pleasure of your company. It is rare that I find a woman who sparkles the way you do."

She narrowed her eyes. Was that supposed to be a reference to her looks? Her clothing? Or perhaps the expensive jewelry her mother insisted on dressing her in.

"Whatever do you mean?" she asked.

He tilted his head and eyed her quizzically, then changed tack. "In all honesty, I found you to be the most interesting woman I was lucky enough to meet yesterday. I'm not one to deny myself that which interests me, so here I am, eager for more of your company."

Against her better judgment, she smiled. Considering

how they had met and the unconventional encounter that had followed, she could believe he'd found her interesting more easily than that he had been struck senseless by her beauty.

"You are an unusual man," she observed. "Yesterday, you asked me to tell you something about me, and I did. Now, I'd like to know something about you. All I know is that you're an earl and my mother is impressed by you."

He grinned, and her insides fluttered again. "What else do you need to know?" He ate another bite of scone while he thought. "I have one sibling. A younger sister. Do you have any siblings?"

Amelia's chest squeezed. "No. I should have liked a sister."

"They're pests of a thing," Longley teased before growing serious. "But I love her dearly anyway."

"What's her name?"

"Katherine. We call her Kate."

"And how old is she?"

"Eighteen. We intend to introduce her to society next season."

"I am sure she will have every success she wishes for." The words held a hint of bitterness, and she hoped he didn't notice. It was just that it would be nice to have someone care about her as Longley cared for Kate. She could already tell that he was a protective older brother.

"I have returned," Mrs. Hart declared, striding into the room with Mrs. White close behind her. When she spotted Amelia and Longley still sitting on opposite chaises, her face fell.

Amelia resisted the urge to roll her eyes. What had she thought would happen? Amelia was hardly the sort to seduce a man in her parents' drawing room.

Mrs. White set a fresh teapot on the table and removed the other. She left without a word.

Mrs. Hart joined Amelia on the chaise. "My lord, Amelia

and I would love to hear about Longley Manor. It is in Suffolk, is it not?"

The earl popped the remainder of the scone into his mouth, wiped his fingers on his handkerchief, and started to tell them a little about his country home. Amelia listened, eager to learn more about a part of the country she had not yet visited.

Unfortunately, he didn't get far before her mother took over the conversation. As she listened to Mrs. Hart's chatter, Amelia wished she'd had more of a chance to learn about who Longley was as a man.

When the earl finally glanced at the clock and said he had best leave, Amelia still could not make heads or tails of his intentions toward her. She couldn't imagine that a man like him would court her without an ulterior motive, but he did seem sincere.

She and her mother escorted him to the door. He turned toward her.

"May I call on you again?" he asked.

She inclined her head. "Of course. We would be delighted."

Although what would please her even more was if she knew exactly what the man was up to. She wanted to believe that he was simply interested in her as a prospective bride because he found something about her intriguing, but her instincts told her there was more to the story than she was seeing.

She feared that if she did not uncover his true motives soon, she might allow herself to fall for his flirtation.

That could only end poorly.

CHAPTER 7

Andrew straightened his back, donned his most charming smile, and knocked on the Harts' front door. It opened instantly, as if the butler had been waiting on the other side for him to overcome his nerves.

He raised one fluffy gray eyebrow. "Can I help you, sir?"

Andrew cleared his throat. "Please advise Miss Hart that the Earl of Longley is here to call on her."

The butler inclined his head. "Very good, sir. Please enter." He stepped aside to grant Longley entrance and then closed the door behind him. "Wait here. I will return momentarily."

Andrew watched as he climbed the stairs slowly enough that he was tempted to dash up them himself in search of Miss Hart. Alas, that was a surefire way to end up trussed at the altar.

Although… wasn't that his aim? Would it be so bad to push the matter?

Yes.

He sighed. She deserved the opportunity to turn him down, if she so desired. He hoped she wouldn't, but she ought to have the choice. He was especially reluctant to press the matter considering the fact that her mother already seemed to be trying to do so, having previously left them alone together when it wasn't entirely proper to do so.

After a few minutes, the butler reappeared with three women in tow: Miss Hart, Mrs. Hart, and a maid. He forced his smile to remain in place, silently praying the mother did not intend to accompany them. Miss Hart was so much easier to converse with when Mrs. Hart was not present.

"Good afternoon, ladies." He bowed and offered his hand to Miss Hart to help her off the bottom step.

She murmured a greeting in return, her sky-blue eyes meeting his with a hint of curiosity. Why was it that she always seemed so surprised when he did the things he said he would?

"How lovely to see you again, my lord." Mrs. Hart beamed at him. She was attractive, for a woman of her age, although there was little resemblance between her and her daughter other than those piercing eyes.

"Are you ready to leave?" he asked Miss Hart. His carriage was waiting outside to bear them to Hyde Park. Promenading was definitely an expected courting activity that he ought to cross off his list, and it was also an excellent way to be seen together.

The last thing he needed was for another gentleman to sweep Miss Hart off her feet. He hoped that if his acquaintances knew he was pursuing her, they would leave her alone. Of course, there was always the possibility that they would wonder what the appeal was and decide to learn more about her themselves, but he had to take the risk.

"I am." Miss Hart's lips were slightly pinched. "This is Mary. She will be accompanying us as a chaperone."

"Of course." Thank God it wouldn't be her mother. His gaze skimmed down Miss Hart's body. "You look very fetching today."

It was true. The pale sage color of her dress suited her

complexion far more than the ruffly white contraption she'd worn at the Wembley ball. Although, he rather thought that most outfits would look better on her than that.

She frowned—not the reaction he'd expected. "Thank you, my lord."

Why did he get the sense that she didn't believe him?

He turned to Mrs. Hart. "I shall have her home at a respectable hour."

"I am certain you will." A fact she sounded disappointed by.

"Shall we?"

Miss Hart nodded, so he escorted her out the door, with Mary trailing behind. A breeze stirred his hair as they emerged, but it wasn't cold. Considering the season, it was a pleasantly mild day. There was certainly no need for heavy coats or gloves.

His driver opened the carriage, and Andrew took Miss Hart's hand to help her inside. Her grip was surprisingly firm for a woman. He assisted Mary, too, and then climbed in and sat next to Miss Hart on the forward-facing bench seat.

"So, how long have you lived in London?" Andrew asked as the carriage rumbled into motion.

"About three years," she replied without turning toward him. "Prior to that, we lived in a country home in Northumberland."

He whistled. "That's quite a change."

"It is."

"Do you like the city?" He always had, although he did enjoy spending a few months of the year in Suffolk too.

She considered his question. "I like the access to interesting places we have in London. Northumberland is far less populous, and therefore, there are fewer opportunities for diversion."

He almost laughed, impressed by how she had managed to answer his question yet say very little. He now knew that she liked some parts of London, but he had no idea what those parts were or whether she preferred the city, on the whole, to her family's country home.

"What sort of places?" he asked. While he admired her evasion tactics, he needed to know more about her if he intended to make her his wife.

She opened her mouth but then promptly closed it. She remained silent for several seconds. "The beautiful homes, perfect for balls, and the theater."

He pursed his lips, disappointed that she'd stopped herself from saying what she actually wanted to rather than what she'd been trained to.

He could hardly hold her cautiousness against her. She'd no doubt experienced many shades of rejection since debuting last season, so it was understandable she'd want to avoid saying anything that may mark her as different from her peers.

But damn, he felt a connection between them, and he was excited that his hunt for a well-dowered wife may not have to result in a marriage that he'd regret. He wanted her to be truthful.

They arrived at the park, and the driver stopped the carriage for them to disembark. Andrew got out first and helped the women down. He linked arms with Miss Hart and led her onto the pebbled path into Hyde Park.

Half the ton had come out for the fresh air. He and Miss Hart wandered along the path, deeper into the park. The river babbled along beside them, and he couldn't help but notice that they were attracting stares.

As they passed courting couples and clusters of maids or older women—the chaperones, presumably—eyes followed their movements. Miss Hart must have realized this, too, because she put slightly more space between their bodies, her eyes darting around nervously.

Many debutantes would enjoy the attention, but not her.

He was getting the distinct impression that Miss Hart liked to be invisible and did not know how to respond when she was dragged into the light.

In an attempt to ease her discomfort, he asked, "Other than learning about strange places and civilizations, what do you enjoy doing in your spare time?"

She glanced at him, her eyebrows knitted together. Once again, he felt that she had an answer but was choosing not to give it, instead thinking of something that he, or perhaps society, would find more acceptable.

"What about needlepoint?" he prompted. "You were working on a design when I visited, were you not?"

"Needlepoint is a useful feminine skill." The words were completely toneless. She may as well have been reciting her letters.

Frustration nipped at his heels. Her avoidance of a real answer was deucedly annoying. He wanted to get to know who she really was, but she was making it difficult to do so. He just wanted another glimpse at the woman he'd seen when he'd startled her at the ball, or when her mother had briefly left them on their own during his earlier visit.

Perhaps it was the company that was making her hedge. The maid was far enough behind that he wasn't certain whether or not she'd be able to hear their conversation, but maybe Miss Hart feared she could and was worried she would report back to Mrs. Hart if she said anything out of order.

"You seemed very skilled," he said for lack of anything more meaningful to contribute.

She snorted and shot him a skeptical look from beneath her eyelashes.

He grinned. *There she is.*

So far, complimenting her hadn't worked as well as Kate had assured him it would, but at least her amusement was a genuine reaction.

Unfortunately, it lasted for only a few seconds before her expression shuttered as if the flicker of personality had never crossed her face.

Fine. He would just have to draw her out again.

He ducked his head closer to hers. "Your eyes remind me of the color of the water at a beach I once visited on the Indian subcontinent. There is a certain lightness and brightness to the shallows that you don't see in England."

Her face snapped toward him, and a wide smile spread across her lips. For a moment, he thought he'd found the secret to winning her over: compliments. But she swiftly disabused him of that notion.

"You've been to the subcontinent?" Excitement danced in her eyes.

"I have." Ah. He should have realized that her interest lay in the subject matter itself. "I spent several weeks there a few years ago."

"Can you tell me about it?" she asked breathlessly.

"Anything you'd like to know."

Grateful for the opportunity to escape the stiltedness of their previous conversation, he told her as much as he could remember of his time on the subcontinent.

He shared about the markets he'd visited. The exotic spices and the rich, flavorful food. He described the temples he'd seen and the beauty of the beaches and natural areas. She asked thoughtful questions that showed a keen interest in the topic and an attentiveness to details that he admired.

When she finally ran out of questions, he decided it must be his turn to ask them.

"Where did your fascination with other countries and societies arise from?"

Her expression closed off immediately. "I'm sorry. I've been terribly rude, dominating the conversation."

"No, you haven't," he huffed, irritated at losing the ground he'd made with her. "I—"

"My lord!"

A young woman appeared in front of him, and he stopped abruptly, barely managing not to walk into her.

Miss Hart caught him as he stumbled, and the brief press of her side against his sent a flash of awareness through him. The faint scent of peppermint tickled his nostrils. He wanted to lean closer and bury his face in her hair to see where it originated from.

"Oh dear. You caught me by surprise. Are you all right?" he asked the woman, who he now recognized as Miss Wentham.

Her eyelashes fluttered, and she bobbed a curtsy, her pink skirt brushing the ground. "I am fine, thank you, Lord Longley."

She glanced at Amelia, then looked back at him. "When my mother spotted you, I knew we simply must say hello." She gestured at the two women behind her. "This is my sister, Mrs. Cordover. I do not believe you've met."

Andrew nodded to both women. "Charmed, Mrs. Cordover. Mrs. Wentham. Do you know Miss Hart?"

"They've met," Miss Wentham said briskly, not giving either her mother or sister the opportunity to respond—not that they seemed inclined to. "May we walk with you, my lord?"

He sneaked a look at Miss Hart, who had withdrawn back into herself, although he couldn't say whether that was a result of the Wenthams' presence or his own bungle.

"I have been enjoying Miss Hart's company," he said. He didn't wish to be rude, but how many men would want to be stuck between two potential future partners?

Not him, that was for certain.

"She will continue to accompany us, of course," Miss Wentham demurred. Studying her expression, no one would ever know the disdain she'd shown toward Miss Hart previously.

"I'm afraid we cannot dally long. I must return Miss Hart to her parents before the hour is up." That wasn't true, but he couldn't think of any other excuse that would not be impolite.

"And so you shall." Miss Wentham didn't seem at all put off. "Let us walk, then."

Casting a quick apologetic glance at Miss Hart, Andrew fell into step with the other women. He kept Miss Hart tucked against his side, but though she was physically close, she didn't speak a word, and it felt as if there may as well be a chasm between them.

He tried to include her in the conversation, but Miss Wentham was adept at monopolizing his attention and steering away from any subjects on which Miss Hart may be willing and able to contribute. The more she chattered away, the further Miss Hart faded into the background.

At first, he thought perhaps she was just shy, but as time moved on, he began to notice the firm line of her mouth and the tension at the corners of her eyes.

She was miserable.

"Where did you get that dress?" Miss Wentham asked her, smiling slyly.

Miss Hart glanced down. "From Madam Baptiste."

Miss Wentham pouted with faux sympathy. "Last season? The cut is a little outdated."

"I think it suits her," he said, refusing to allow anyone to denigrate her in his company.

"Perhaps it does." Miss Wentham seemed amused, as if her casually cruel comments were the height of witticism.

He stopped walking and checked his watch. "My apologies, but we really must be off." He tugged on Miss Hart's arm and guided her away from their companions. Mary hurried behind, shooting a nasty look at Miss Wentham.

"Well, that was lovely," Miss Hart remarked when they were far enough away not to be overheard.

"I'm sorry. I shouldn't have entertained the notion of walking with them when she was clearly out to make trouble."

Miss Hart seemed startled by the apology, which only irritated him more. People should expect common decency.

"Don't think on it," she said. "No harm was done."

"No one has the right to make anyone else feel inferior," he growled.

Her eyebrows rose. "I'm not sure if you realize this, but as far as most of the ton is concerned, I am inferior. I'm the daughter of a merchant and a social climber. Even if not for that, I am something of a wallflower, which would earn me disdain in my own right. When the two are combined, I am a crime against the aristocracy waiting to happen, and everyone knows it."

He stared at her, stunned by the eloquence with which she had spoken. Miss Hart may be slightly awkward and unwilling to open up most of the time, but she was clearly an intelligent woman who felt passionately about the things that mattered to her.

He looked her in the eyes. "If I may speak bluntly?"

She nodded. "Please do."

"Anyone who doesn't take the time to see that you are more than all of that is missing out."

Her mouth fell open. "I…." She trailed off, confusion stamped across her features.

"The carriage is this way." He nudged her forward. She could dissect his words all she wanted in the privacy of her own mind. He didn't need an immediate response.

Once they were back inside the carriage and trundling along the street toward her parents' townhome, he closed his eyes, inwardly seething. It was unlike him to be angry, but Miss Wentham had touched a nerve by treating Miss Hart the way she had.

Andrew despised bullies. He always had. That was one of

the reasons he was so close to Ashford. Children could be cruel, and even at a tender age, Andrew had realized that Ashford needed protection from them. His name and wealth would only go so far when he was quiet and prone to bouts of anxiety.

Andrew had helped him forge a place among their peers, and in return, he'd earned the truest, most loyal friend he'd ever had.

They arrived at the Hart residence, and he helped both Miss Hart and Mary out of the carriage. The double doors opened, and Mrs. Hart glided down the stairs, practically giddy with excitement.

"When might I see you next?" he asked Miss Hart before her mother had the chance to whisk her away.

Miss Hart cocked her head. "You wish to see me again?"

"Of course." Had he not made his interest abundantly clear? Perhaps, next time, he ought to bring flowers.

"We will be at the Latham ball," Mrs. Hart said. "Isn't that right, dear?"

"Yes," Miss Hart agreed.

"Excellent." He stepped backward. "I look forward to seeing you then."

He returned to the carriage, the prickle of the hairs on the back of his neck reminding him that Miss Hart was watching. He gave his driver the signal to move and sat back to mull over their encounter with Miss Wentham.

It bothered him. But why the hell was he so worked up on behalf of a chit he hardly knew?

CHAPTER 8

Excitement fluttered in Amelia's stomach as they moved on from the greeting party at the Latham ball and entered the ballroom proper. She'd tried her best to deny it all day, but the truth was, she was eager to see the Earl of Longley again.

It was ridiculous, and she was annoyed with herself for being gullible enough to fall for his charms when there must be a sensible reason why he was showing interest in her—beyond simply finding her amusing—but she couldn't seem to convince her heart of that. It found his attention intoxicating and whispered that maybe he was sincere.

As if a handsome earl would ever genuinely be attracted to a lowborn bluestocking without some other motivation.

He must have an angle. She just hadn't deduced what it was yet.

Mrs. Hart guided her around a Roman-style pillar toward the dance floor. The room was beautiful, with cream walls, ornate gold edging, and pockets of greenery. A quartet played uplifting music, and a floral aroma emanated from the plants. It might have been overpowering if not for the hint of perspiration and alcohol overlaying it.

Amelia glanced over her shoulder. Her father had already disappeared into a corner, no doubt to chat with a friend while her mother did all she could to ensure that Amelia became the next Countess of Longley.

At least the earl's apparent interest had reduced Mrs. Hart's desperation to foist her upon every eligible bachelor of the ton.

Her mother turned to her and spoke quietly. "Whatever you are doing to attract Lord Longley, keep doing it. I'm sure I don't need to impress upon you the importance of not losing his favor."

"I understand." Not that Amelia had any idea what she was doing to capture his attention in the first place. "Should I dance with the Duke of Wight and the Earl of Winn too?"

She didn't want to, but she'd also like to avoid a lecture after the ball.

Her mother hummed thoughtfully. "If they approach you, then you must, but don't seek them out. We don't wish to discourage them, but we also don't want to put off Longley. I'm uncertain whether he's the sort of man who thrives on competition or avoids it."

"All right." Amelia decided right then that she would do all she could to be invisible to Wight and Winn. She didn't want to be pushed into a marriage with either of them, and if her mother wouldn't be upset by it, then the best way forward was to hope they forgot about her.

She kept her head down except for the occasional survey of the room. No one approached them, and she could easily become part of the wallpaper. This was how her last season had passed and how this one likely would have begun if not for her mother deciding that Amelia could obviously not be trusted to find her own suitors.

She couldn't let herself forget that this was where society thought she belonged.

None of the men who'd shown interest in her this season

would have done so without Mrs. Hart's persistence and the Hart family fortune. If she were a simple untitled miss of average means with timid parents, no one would look at her twice.

She had no charms of her own, which only made her more certain that the Earl of Longley must be up to something.

Mrs. Hart jostled her shoulder and jerked her chin toward the entrance.

Speak of the devil.

He stood tall in a simple black suit of elegant cut just inside the entrance. The suit fit his broad shoulders perfectly and tapered inward to his waist. He was taller than many of the gentlemen present, although not the tallest man in attendance. He lifted his hand to push his richly colored hair away from his face, and her heart gave a little sigh.

She frowned.

No. She could not afford to find him handsome. He was manipulating her, and she needed to know why. It wasn't as if he could possibly have taken one look at her hiding behind a shrub and decided that she was his future countess. Therefore, she could not trust him.

But when he caught her eyes and grinned, the full force of his warm, sparkling gaze hit her, butterflies flooded her stomach, and it was difficult to remember that. He excused himself from his conversation and made his way through the revelers toward them.

"Excellent," Mrs. Hart murmured.

"Fancy seeing you here," the earl said as he came to a stop several feet away.

"What a surprise," Amelia said dryly. "It's almost as if we told you we would be in attendance."

Mrs. Hart discreetly sank her elbow into Amelia's ribs, and the breath wheezed out of her lungs.

The earl cocked his head. "Are you all right, Miss Hart?"

"Fine," she gasped. "My apologies. I had a tickle in my throat."

He looked concerned. "Nothing bad, I hope?"

"No, no." She forced herself to smile more widely even as her eyes watered. "I'm quite all right."

"I'm happy to hear that." He glanced from Amelia to Mrs. Hart and back. "May I ask to save a dance?"

She nodded and offered him her card. He jotted his name beside her next dance… and then to another dance later in the evening. Eyes wide, she stared at him. Everyone knew that claiming two dances was as good as declaring a courtship. What on earth was Longley doing?

Beside her, Mrs. Hart muffled a high-pitched sound of excitement. "You honor us, my lord."

He released Amelia's card and straightened. "The honor is all mine. Miss Hart, I believe our waltz is about to begin. Will you join me?"

A waltz?

Her gut flipped over, and a fizzle of pleasure burst inside her. Damn her naive, optimistic heart. It yearned to believe he was genuinely interested in her.

Whatever his motivation, she could no longer deny that he was courting her. There were few more public ways he could make his intentions clear.

She took his hand, and he guided her onto the dance floor. As the first chords of a new song rang through the assembly, they began to move. She'd never enjoyed the waltz. Being so close to someone didn't appeal to her. The pressure to perform made her uncomfortable, and she feared making a misstep.

With the Earl of Longley as her partner, she practically glided across the dance floor. Every time they brushed against each other, the silk of her skirt whispered, and the heat from his body cocooned around her.

Her feet moved instinctively. Fleeting touches made her shiver.

She was unaware of anything but him.

The square line of his smooth-shaven jaw. The way his eyes seemed to change color as they caught the light. His full lower lip, so ready to smile.

And then it ended.

He gazed at her, his breathing slightly ragged. "That was…."

"Wonderful," she murmured.

He dipped his head. "I couldn't have said it better." He linked his arm with hers. "Shall we take a stroll around the room?"

"That would be nice."

Arm in arm, they circled around the party. Several people greeted Longley with a smile and friendly words. Very few acknowledged Amelia, although plenty cast surreptitious looks at her.

He then returned her to her mother, thanked her prettily, and left.

"Well?" Mrs. Hart asked when he was gone.

"I think it went well." She was reluctant to say more than that when Longley always seemed so pleased with life and was therefore difficult to read.

Mrs. Hart sighed. "You danced together beautifully."

"He's very graceful for a gentleman." Perhaps more graceful than she was. Or maybe he just had more years of practice than she did. "I'm going to get a glass of lemonade. Would you like one?"

"No, thank you." Mrs. Hart was distracted, searching for someone across the room. "I think I see your father. I'm going to speak with him."

Amelia grinned. Likely her mother wanted to dance, and her father was about to find himself cajoled into doing so with her.

She made her way out of the ballroom into the refreshments area and helped herself to a small piece of cake. Savoring the sweetness on her tongue and the fluffy lightness of the cake itself, she quickly checked that neither the Duke of Wight nor the Earl of Winn was within eyesight.

She hadn't seen them thus far, but she didn't want to let her guard down. Regardless of whether or not she trusted Lord Longley's motives, he was undeniably the most appealing of the bunch, and honestly, she didn't believe he wished her harm. She'd just prefer not to feel so blind where he was concerned.

If she knew his reasons for courting her, then she could respond appropriately.

Not knowing made her vulnerable.

She meandered between the tables and poured herself a glass of lemonade, then stood in the corner to sip it, enjoying the tang.

"Miss Hart."

She turned toward the feminine voice and scarcely hid her grimace. "Miss Wentham."

The pretty blonde wore a smirk that said she knew something Amelia didn't. She hated it. She'd disliked Miss Wentham even before she'd insulted her dress. There was just something predatory about her.

Miss Wentham lifted a delicate glass to her lips and drank. "I just thought you ought to know that someone like the Earl of Longley can only possibly want you for your family's money. There's no other reason he would tolerate your company."

The words cut. Not because they were untrue but because they too closely aligned with her own fears.

"The earl is wealthy," she said, keeping her chin high. "He has no reason to need my family's fortune."

Miss Wentham's smirk deepened, and she shrugged and sauntered away.

Try as she might, Amelia could not unhear Miss Wentham's claim. Her mind was busy turning over possibilities while she finished her drink and tracked down her mother. By the time the earl appeared for their second dance, she'd grown tired of all the "what-ifs."

As he took her hand and drew her onto the dance floor alongside him, she gathered the courage to do something that would infuriate her mother if she found out.

"Why are you courting me?" she asked quietly.

One of his reddish-brown eyebrows flew up. "What do you mean, why?"

"Exactly what it sounds like." She placed her hand in his and circled around him, keeping in time with the other dancers.

"Because you are interesting." They switched hands and circled the other way. "I like that we can have conversations together."

That could be true, a voice in her mind whispered.

Maybe so, but she was afraid to believe it.

The earl seemed to consider the discussion closed because he didn't say anything else. The dance finished. He bowed, and she curtsied.

"Allow me to walk you back to your mother?" he asked.

She accepted his arm.

He leaned closer to her. "I may be off the mark, but there is a new Roman history display at the museum. Would you like to attend with me on Sunday?"

"I'd love to!" The exclamation emerged before she had time to temper it. "I mean, I'll have to ask my parents, but I can't see it being a problem."

She couldn't help the smile that spread across her face as they rejoined her mother. Perhaps Longley was being truthful and transparent in his intentions after all. He'd shown that he enjoyed discussion of his travels, and if he was drawn to a historical exhibit at the museum, then they likely had other interests in common too.

Amelia may have been needlessly suspicious of him. She ought not to be so cynical. Sometimes things really were as they appeared.

Mrs. Hart sighed when they reached her. "You dance so well together."

"Mother, the earl has invited me to an outing at the museum on Sunday," Amelia gushed. "Please say I may go."

A tiny groove formed between Mrs. Hart's eyebrows, demonstrating her bewilderment, but it smoothed out quickly when she realized it would mean more one-on-one time between her daughter and a single earl.

"You'll take Mary as chaperone?"

"Of course."

"Then go ahead."

Longley grinned, and for the first time, she noticed that one of his incisors was slightly crooked. It was endearing. "I'll collect you at two."

"I look forward to it."

"Good job, Amelia," her mother murmured as the earl walked away. "I do hope you didn't mention your scribblings to him, though."

Amelia rolled her eyes. "I didn't. During our walk in Hyde Park, we discussed his time on the Indian subcontinent, which is likely what gave him the idea of inviting me to the museum."

Mrs. Hart side-eyed her. "You didn't pester him with questions, I hope."

"I don't believe so." She struggled to maintain a straight face. In hindsight, she probably had asked too many questions, but he hadn't protested, so she was going to assume she hadn't been "pestering."

"Do you—" Mrs. Hart broke off when the white-haired

Duke of Wight appeared out of nowhere directly in front of them.

"Ladies." He bowed. "You both look… ravishing. Join me for a dance, Miss Hart?"

It was a question, but his intonation left little doubt that a refusal wasn't possible. Amelia shot her mother a look as the duke took her hand and escorted her away.

"You must be popular tonight," the duke said as they positioned themselves opposite each other. "You were never anywhere to be found."

"I spent a while in the refreshments area." She didn't mention her dances with Lord Longley. If he hadn't seen them for himself, she'd prefer he not know about them at all. If he realized he had such stiff competition, then he might begin to pursue her in earnest.

"I do hope that was all you did."

Her jaw dropped at the muttered comment, but then the dance began. Since it was fast-paced, she didn't have the opportunity to ask him what he'd meant until the song concluded, and by that point, she decided she'd rather not know.

She got the impression he was insinuating that she might have been having an illicit affair elsewhere on the premises, and such an insult could hardly be borne. Unfortunately, he was a duke, and she was a societal outcast, so she was not in any position to cause a scene.

She maintained her composure, separated from him as quickly as possible, and quietly simmered. She really hoped Lord Longley wasn't playing games with her. Even if she didn't particularly want to take a husband, he was a far superior choice to a rude, elderly duke and a drunken lecher of an earl.

Mrs. Hart, perhaps sensing her sour mood, made their farewells soon after, and they retreated from the ballroom and called for their carriage to be brought around.

When they were shut inside the carriage and on their way home, her encounter with Miss Wentham returned to the front of her mind.

"Father?"

Mr. Hart's eyes shone in the dark as he looked across at her. "Yes, Mia?"

"Amelia," her mother griped.

He sighed. "Yes, Amelia?"

"Miss Wentham said something tonight that made me curious. Is the Earl of Longley having financial difficulty?"

"Oh, yes."

Her stomach dropped to the soles of her feet. "He is?"

Her father nodded. "It's a closely guarded secret, but I make it my business to know such things. My understanding is that his man of business defrauded him and fled the country. I don't have all the details, but I suspect that, if not for his entailment, he'd be almost broke."

An invisible vise squeezed her chest. She'd been searching for an explanation, but without having the full picture, it had been impossible to find. Now that she knew the truth, she could see exactly what was happening.

The earl had no money.

He also had a mother and a sister, whom he obviously cared for.

Social standing meant everything among the aristocracy, and he likely wanted to replenish his fortune before too many people discovered his circumstances—both to protect his reputation and to provide for those dependent on him.

As far as reasons for fortune hunting went, it was noble.

But he was still a fortune hunter.

Amelia had a sizable dowry—perhaps the largest in the ton—and she and her mother had been described as "desperate" more than once. What better way for him to refill his coffers than by marrying an heiress whose parents would be more than eager for the match?

If he made it look like a love connection, no one would ever question his actions.

Except her.

She almost wished she didn't know the truth. It was a relief, in a way, to be reassured that she hadn't simply been thinking the worst of him. But Lord, for a few brief seconds, she'd let herself believe that he might actually hold her in high esteem, and learning otherwise hurt.

She angled her face away from her father, looking out the window as a tear slipped down her cheek. It dripped from her chin, but she made no effort to dry her skin. That would only attract attention.

Instead, she cried quietly until they were two blocks from their home, and then she blinked her eyes dry and made a show of "sneezing" into her shoulder to blot any wetness away.

She shouldn't be upset. It was ridiculous. She'd known something was amiss. And yet the hurt remained.

Neither of her parents noticed anything wrong as they exited the carriage and climbed the stairs. Mr. Grant held the door open, and his gaze was fixed ahead. Amelia bid them good night and went straight to her bedchamber.

"What's the matter?" Mary asked as soon as she entered.

Amelia shook her head. "Nothing."

It was clearly a lie, but Mary didn't ask again, just helped her undress in silence, then took the discarded gown and left. Amelia blew out all the candles but one and got into bed. She lay there, staring at the ceiling, for some time, but sleep did not come.

Eventually, she got up, took the remaining candle, and used it to light the way as she wandered through the house. As she passed her father's office, she noticed a flickering orange glow beneath the door. She hesitated, wishing she felt comfortable enough to go inside and plead with him to rethink this season.

Do I have to marry? she wanted to ask him. *Must I become a sacrificial bride for you and Mother to gain entrance into the aristocracy?*

Amelia wasn't brave though. Not like Miss Joceline Davies. She pushed the boundaries, but only so far.

She drew in a deep breath and brushed her fingers over the wood of the door.

Perhaps she could. He might even listen.

Her touch wavered.

CHAPTER 9

Amelia's eyes were gritty, and her head throbbed so much, she almost didn't hear her parents' voices as she passed her father's office on her way to the dining hall the next morning after tossing and turning all night, second-guessing her decision not to approach him.

She stopped and edged closer to the door, massaging her temples in an attempt to clear her thoughts. Her mother was speaking, but for once, she was keeping her tone low, the words almost impossible to distinguish.

"... relieved she isn't persisting with that nonsense." She sighed, and Amelia could imagine her pinching the bridge of her nose. "It's not right for a girl to be so interested in books. It's much better that she's focusing on finding a husband instead."

Amelia froze. Her heartbeat quickened. For an instant, she feared it was so loud, her parents would hear, but that was ridiculous.

She waited, half expecting her father to speak up for her. After all, he'd encouraged her creativity when she was younger. He'd read stories with her and given her advice on how to improve them. Perhaps he hadn't done so in a while, but surely that didn't mean he disapproved.

He didn't defend her.

Instead, he said, "I hope you're satisfied with the Earl of Longley as a suitor."

"I'm ecstatic." There was a muffled sound. Perhaps some movement. "After last season, I never dreamed that Amelia could hook such an eligible gentleman so quickly. The only thing that would make it better is if he were a duke or a marquess, but Lord Longley has a better reputation than the Duke of Wight and is far handsomer, which makes it even more of a coup."

"You will be happy to have him as a son-in-law?" he asked.

"Delighted. No one will be able to turn a cold shoulder to us once Amelia is a countess. We will be invited to the most exclusive events. They'll have to accept us."

Amelia couldn't bear to listen anymore. She stalked back to her bedchamber, breakfast forgotten.

She'd known her mother saw marriage into the aristocracy as the ultimate prize, but not once during that conversation had she mentioned Amelia's happiness as any kind of factor.

It hurt.

She wanted to believe that her parents cared about her future happiness at least a little, but neither of them had given any indication that they were thinking of her wishes, except for that throwaway comment about the earl's handsomeness, which reflected on the family as a whole, so could it really even be counted?

They'd spoken as if the marriage was fait accompli. As far as Amelia knew, the earl had not asked for her hand. Nor had she agreed. Did they even consider her agreement necessary? Or did they believe she would go along with whatever they decided was best?

She always had before—at least outwardly. Resistance had seemed futile. More hassle than it was worth, when her mother would always get her way anyway.

This was the rest of her life, though. Hardly trivial. If anything was worth making a fuss about, it was who she married. Did they care what her opinion of the earl was? Or did they assume that because he was titled and handsome, she would have no objections?

She huffed, frustrated, as she marched into her room and yanked a pelisse out of the wardrobe. What she needed was a walk to clear her head. Right now, she was too emotional to think clearly, and if she stuck around, she would no doubt say something she regretted.

When she left the bedchamber, she summoned Mary, instructed her to get a coat, and they set off together on foot.

They didn't talk as they strode along the streets of Mayfair. Mary struggled to keep up, and Amelia's mind was occupied with how to make the best of her situation. A carriage passed by, and she inhaled, the familiar horsey scent bringing her a modicum of comfort.

She wondered whether Lord Longley had horses. She enjoyed riding, although she didn't do it often. He would have some to pull his carriages, but did he have a personal horse? Did his mother and sister? Or was he one of the men who didn't think women ought to ride?

He hadn't given her that impression, but he also hadn't given her the impression of being poor, so what did she know?

Not that his financial state was a problem. She just disliked being deceived, and it had been nice to fantasize, even for a few brief moments, that he might genuinely be interested in her rather than her family fortune. Now that she knew the truth, she couldn't pretend any longer.

She and Mary circled around and returned to the house. Mary, grateful for the respite, quickly disappeared into the depths of the home while Amelia trudged up the stairs and back to her bedchamber.

Inside, the air was warm from the remnants of a fire, and she sat at her writing desk and began to scribble furiously. She knew exactly what direction she was taking Miss Joceline Davies in.

Joceline, subject to the same emotions as any woman, would fall prey to a fickle suitor. When he let her down—as he inevitably would—she'd pick up her life and move to the Americas. She would take charge of her future. No allowing others to dictate it for her. No struggles with uncertainty.

Joceline was strong. She would take control.

Amelia's hand faltered, and she smudged ink on the paper. Cursing, she dabbed at the paper and then the side of her palm, where the ink was already drying.

Never mind that. If the fictional Joceline could take control of her own future, why could Amelia not do the same?

Perhaps she wasn't as courageous or as adventurous as Joceline, but she was determined. She had dreams and ambitions. Just as Joceline didn't have to accept the options that were presented to her, nor did she.

She pushed the paper aside and began to jot notes on a clean sheet.

What *were* her options?

She tapped her chin as she thought. Obviously, she could pretend not to know about Longley's ulterior motive and continue with their farce of a courtship. After all, if she hadn't known, she likely would have married him. He was, objectively, the best of the suitors available to her.

Failing that, she could marry one of the other men her mother considered suitable. The Duke of Wight probably didn't have too many years left in him, and she knew enough about him to be on her guard in case he attempted to do away with her.

The trouble was that she shuddered at the idea of allowing him to touch her, and honestly, she'd prefer not to spend years of her life paranoid that her husband might try to get rid of her.

The Earl of Winn was not an option she could countenance. She would be miserable with him—potentially for decades to come. But perhaps there were other men she could win over. Surely there was more than one impoverished aristocrat desperate to replenish his coffers. Would any of the others appeal more than Longley?

She didn't know.

Her third option was to refuse to marry and hope her father was willing to provide a living for her. She could move to a cottage in the country and write her stories in peace. There would be long walks, starry skies, and fresh air.

But all of that relied on Mr. Hart being willing to override her mother's wishes. If she were honest with herself, she didn't believe he would. Not even for her.

She could run away to the Americas like Joceline. She could easily sell some of her jewelry, buy a ticket on the next ship to depart, and begin anew in a foreign land.

Unfortunately, while Amelia loved to write adventure stories—and to read them—she wasn't certain that she'd enjoy living in one. She liked comfort. A warm bed, regular meals, and a reliable supply of books. Not to mention privacy. Aboard a ship, she may not get that, let alone in a strange place she'd only ever read about.

All right, so not that option. Nor was she willing to rely on her father's good graces.

As long as she was unmarried, she would be under her mother's thumb because her father would never stand up to her on Amelia's behalf.

Ergo, she required a husband.

But then she would be under her husband's thumb.

Unless, of course, she had leverage to ensure he couldn't control her.

A slow smile spread across her face. She did have leverage. A temptingly large dowry.

Perhaps the most pragmatic course of action was to beat the men at their own game. They wished to wed her, either for her money or her childbirthing ability, and she needed to wed in order to chart her own course.

Two of her three prospective suitors could likely not be wooed by money, but the third could.

Her smile grew.

She would propose a marriage of convenience to the Earl of Longley. If he agreed to her terms, he'd gain access to her dowry. She wanted freedom, and as her husband, he would be able to grant it to her.

Right now, she was in the best possible position to negotiate. After all, she could still refuse to marry him, and then he'd have to start over with another heiress. Certainly, another heiress would accept him, but for whatever reason, he'd decided on her, and if he were willing to make a few concessions, she would make it easy for him to get her.

Would it hurt to marry a man she'd come to admire, knowing he had no feelings for her?

Possibly.

But she could live with injured pride—especially when the earl was an otherwise agreeable man. He didn't seem to be cruel—or at least, if he was, he hid it well. He had good hygiene and nice hair and eyes. She doubted she could do better.

"Amelia!"

She flinched, caught off guard by the shout outside her bedchamber door. Hurriedly, she hid her scribbled notes and the beginning of a scene she had written for Joceline's next story. She considered pulling on a pair of gloves to hide the ink smudge on her hand but didn't want to ruin them, so instead she held her hands by her sides, angled away from the door, as she stood.

"What is it?" she called.

Mrs. Hart pushed the door open and swept inside on a wave of jasmine-scented air. Her eyes narrowed, as if she sensed that Amelia had been doing something she disapproved of, but she couldn't quite put her finger on what.

"You've been shut in here for hours." She crossed her arms, radiating displeasure. "We are attending the opera tonight, or have you forgotten?"

Amelia glanced at the clock, surprised to see that it was now midway through the afternoon. Her stomach growled, reminding her she'd yet to eat.

"I'm not feeling well," she lied.

Mrs. Hart looked dubious. "How do you know that if you haven't ventured beyond the confines of this room? Perhaps a little fresh air will do you good."

"I went outside," Amelia admitted. "This morning, for a walk. Mary accompanied me. I took a turn upon returning."

"Have you tried a cup of tea with honey?" Mrs. Hart was very British in that she believed a good cup of tea could cure anything.

"Yes, Mother."

Fortunately, Mrs. Hart didn't look around for the evidence. She probably assumed that one of the servants had cleared it away.

"Please let me stay home tonight," she pleaded. "You and Father can go together. I know how much you enjoy your outings." Without her to get in the way.

Her mother sighed. "Are you sure you're not well enough to come?"

Amelia nodded.

"Fine." She retreated to the door. "I'll have Mary bring you dinner."

"Thank you."

When she left, Amelia waited until the latch clicked into place before flopping onto her bed. Thank goodness her mother hadn't argued or insisted she accompany them. Amelia was really getting somewhere. She couldn't afford to be interrupted now.

She closed her eyes for a few seconds, mentally composing a to-do list; then she sat at her desk and began to work.

Over the next two hours, she wrote and revised a marriage agreement. One that was different from anything she'd ever heard of before.

She ate dinner in her room and then rewrote the contract and copied it so there were two identical versions. Once they were safely locked in her drawer, she called Mary to help her prepare for bed.

"Are you feeling any better?" Mary asked as she undid the buttons on her dress.

Amelia glanced at the door. "Can you keep a secret?"

Mary made an intrigued sound in the back of her throat. "If you ask me to keep a confidence, you can consider it kept."

Amelia grinned. "I'm not unwell. I've been working on something."

"What?" Mary asked.

"I intend to propose marriage to the Earl of Longley."

Mary gasped. "That's scandalous!"

"Only if anyone finds out." She explained her reasoning and even shared a little about the contract she'd created.

"Do you think he'll say yes?" Mary asked cautiously. "If he spreads word of your plan, it could ruin you."

Amelia stepped out of the dress and allowed Mary to slide a nightgown over her head. "If I'm correct in believing he wants my dowry, then yes. I think he will. Surely his need for money outweighs any shock he may feel as a result of the offer. Besides"—she hesitated—"I get the impression he's a kind man."

A liar, perhaps, but not an ill-intentioned one.

"I've a friend who works at Longley House," Mary said quietly. "She says he's a decent sort. A bit of a rake, but not cruel."

Amelia's chest tightened. Logically, she knew that the earl likely had no shortage of female company and that he would continue to enjoy others after they were wed. For some reason, the knowledge made her uncomfortable, but she would simply have to get used to it.

She bit her lip. "I've written the earl a note, asking for him to grant me a private interview after we visit the museum tomorrow. Can you please arrange to have it delivered?"

"Of course, miss. I'll make sure he receives it."

CHAPTER 10

Andrew's mind was alive with curiosity as he arrived outside the Harts' residence. When Boden had informed him that he'd received a note from Miss Hart, he'd been surprised. After reading her brief request to meet with him in private, he'd become intrigued.

This was not the sort of thing unmarried misses did. It wasn't the behavior he'd come to expect. But then, when it came to Miss Hart, perhaps he ought not to have any expectations. After all, she seemed to flout them at every turn.

Regardless of that, he'd spent most of last night and this morning pondering what the chit was up to. Thinking about that prevented him from dwelling on the unfortunate news he'd received last night.

The ship Mr. Smith had supposedly boarded had docked in Spain. Officers of the law had awaited him, but he hadn't disembarked, and upon searching the ship, they'd found no sign of him.

Mr. Smith had slipped away, taking the last of Andrew's fortune with him.

The bastard.

Yes, it was infinitely preferable to concentrate on Miss

Hart than on the sorry state of his financial affairs. He'd yet to break the news to his mother and sister, and he dreaded having to do so. He knew that Kate, especially, still clung to hope.

"My lord?"

Andrew jerked into motion. Good God, how long had he been sitting there, staring into space?

He stepped briskly out of the carriage, marched up to the Harts' front door, and rapped loudly on the wood. The door opened to reveal the potbellied butler.

Andrew passed him a calling card. "The Earl of Longley for Miss Hart."

"Just a moment, my lord."

The butler strode through the foyer and vanished through a door on the other side. Andrew hovered awkwardly in the open doorway until he returned with Miss Hart and her maid in tow. Blessedly, Mrs. Hart was nowhere to be seen.

He bowed and took Miss Hart's hand. "You look especially fetching today."

Once again, she was wearing a dress of simple design. It was a muted shade of blue and paired well with the sapphire resting at the base of her throat. Attraction sizzled low in his gut. If they married, he would very much enjoy kissing the length of her long, pale neck and sucking marks onto her delicate collarbone.

He drew in a shallow breath.

Get a grip.

He forced himself to lift his eyes to her face, only to see she was frowning. He thought back over his words. All he'd said was that she looked fetching. He didn't know how that could have upset her. Perhaps something else was on her mind.

"Are you looking forward to the exhibit?" he asked, drawing her alongside him and out the door.

"Yes, thank you."

Now, it was his turn to frown. Something was definitely not right with her. On Friday, she'd been excited to learn and see everything she could. What had changed between then and now?

He assisted her into the carriage, did the same for her maid, and got in himself. Rather than leaving him the seat beside her, as she'd done when they visited Hyde Park, she'd sat alongside Mary, forcing him to take the bench opposite.

"How much do you know about it?" he asked.

"A little. Not much."

He grimaced. She wasn't giving him a lot to work with. He'd had the impression that she was the sort of person who researched everything ahead of time, but if that was the case, she didn't seem inclined to share.

She didn't even seem to want to engage with him. She was staring ahead. Not at him, but somewhere above and to the left of his shoulder.

"From what I understand, the exhibit is focused on the period from 753 BC to AD 324 and covers the foundation of the Roman Empire," he said.

One of her eyebrows twitched. Her eyes darted his way. He got the feeling she wanted to comment but was forcing herself not to. Why?

"There are several key historical pieces within the exhibit, including a collection of tablets that detail the everyday lives of people from that time period. Those are mostly dated between AD 50 and AD 200."

Another facial twitch.

"I have heard of the tablets," she murmured.

He grinned. A response. That was progress. "What else have you heard of?"

She pursed her lips and seemed to be considering whether or not to answer. "I've heard that there are items retrieved from some of the sites that the museum will not display because of their startling nature."

At that, he laughed. "Indeed."

He was surprised she'd mentioned it. They couldn't discuss the nature of such discoveries now, but perhaps if they were married....

The idea appealed more than it ought to.

The carriage stopped outside the museum gates. Andrew waited for the door to be opened and got out, then offered his hand to Miss Hart and then her maid to help them down in turn.

He linked his arm with Miss Hart's, and together they passed through the gates. She stopped walking just inside and stared at the building rising before them. Andrew guided her to the side, out of the way of other visitors, so she could admire the view without being disturbed.

"I haven't ever visited the museum," she breathed without looking away. "It's beautiful."

He followed her gaze and considered her words. He supposed it was a rather impressive building, with its Roman-style marble columns and dozens of ornate carvings set into the facade.

"Given your interests, I'd have thought you'd have been here before," he said.

She sighed. "When I was young, my father considered it too risky to take me in case I damaged anything. As I grew older, my mother decreed it an inappropriate place for young women to occupy themselves."

He didn't understand. How on earth could a museum filled with years of world history possibly be considered inappropriate?

"Yet she allowed you to come with me," he mused.

She shot him a sidelong look. "Of course, my lord. You're an earl. She would gladly put aside her own opinions if they differ from yours."

"In that case, I will insist you simply must visit every time there is a new exhibit."

She turned toward him, her eyes sparkling. "That would be most welcome."

He nodded toward the entrance. "Shall we?"

She inclined her head in acceptance, and they crossed to the doors together. Andrew paid their admission and accepted a sheet of paper with a map of the exhibition printed on it.

He passed her the map. "Where would you like to start?"

Her eyes widened momentarily, and then she focused on the map, starting at one side and working her way across to the other. "There are so many fascinating things to learn. Can we not just set off in one direction and loop through all the rooms?" She deflated slightly. "Perhaps we haven't the time?"

His stomach swooped. "We have all the time you need."

How could he possibly deny her when she was so adorably eager?

He gestured toward a door on their left. "Shall we begin through there?"

"Yes, please."

Slowly, they worked their way through rooms containing collections of books, medals, and other historical items.

He realized he'd severely underestimated Miss Hart's interest. She read the information attached to every single display. It made progress slow, but he loved to watch her face as she took in everything around her. Her expression hid nothing.

When they reached the statue hall, her pretty pink lips parted, and she made a sound of delight. She rushed to the one closest—a statue of a man carved from marble, wearing a toga and a laurel crown.

"It's incredible," she breathed. "The detail is exquisite."

She hurried to another and reached out as if to touch it,

only dropping her hand at the last minute. She looked around, perhaps expecting someone to chastise her, but when no one did, she cocked her head and studied the figure of a woman in a dress clutching an infant to her chest.

Warmth blossomed in his chest as he watched her scurry to another statue, her eyes alight, her cheeks pink with pleasure. Attraction simmered in his lower abdomen, and he was struck by the urge to kiss her.

Her obvious passion rendered her incredibly enticing.

A voice in the back of his mind told him that he didn't really want to kiss her. It was just that doing so would move their courtship forward. After all, he'd never have looked at her twice if not for his somewhat unfortunate financial situation.

But he wasn't quite sure he believed that.

"I say. Longley, is that you?"

Andrew turned slowly, a pit of dread in his gut. Mr. Norton Falvey stood behind them, smirking as if he'd caught Andrew stealing cookies from the kitchen.

"Hello, Falvey," he said levelly. "I didn't expect to see you here."

Honestly, the only place he usually encountered the man was at their club, the Regent, although he knew Falvey also spent a great deal of time at the horse races.

Falvey glanced at Miss Hart, who'd abandoned her study of the statue to join them. He inclined his head in a way that would have been respectful if not for the slight curl of his mouth. "Miss Hart."

She dipped into a curtsy far more respectful than he deserved. "Mr. Falvey."

Falvey returned his gaze to Andrew. "I heard rumors you were bound for the parson's noose, but I didn't believe it. Perhaps I dismissed the rumors too swiftly, though?"

Andrew gritted his teeth. How dare Falvey make such a

comment in front of Miss Hart? She deserved better than to be referred to in such a way.

"I intend to wed this season," he said, sidestepping Falvey's insulting terminology. Perhaps once, he'd have used the same phrase himself, but never in front of a marriageable miss.

"It seems you've been quick off the mark." Falvey's gaze swept over Miss Hart from head to toe. "Perhaps a little too quick?"

Andrew crossed his arms. "Now isn't a good time. I'll see you in the Regent."

Falvey chuckled and sauntered past them, heading through the statue hall and out the other side.

Releasing a long breath, Andrew hoped Falvey hadn't ruined this for him. "I'm sorry about him," he told Miss Hart. "He was completely out of line."

To his surprise, she just shrugged. "Don't worry yourself over it. I'm well aware of how some men view marriage."

His eyebrow rose. He'd expected a more negative reaction. Regardless of his reason for pursuing a courtship, he doubted any woman wished to be made to feel unwanted or inadequate compared to her peers.

"Are you sure? I can—"

"Quite," she cut in firmly. "Let's continue."

She resumed her study of the exhibit. As they moved through the hall and into the next room, he observed her for any indication that she was bothered by the exchange with Falvey, but she seemed to have put it completely out of her head.

Eventually, he allowed himself to do the same. He chatted with her over the ancient tablets, wondering out loud about the people who'd created them and the lives they'd lived. The maid had long since stopped staying close to them, instead opting to sit on a bench and watch until it was time to shift from room to room.

They didn't emerge from the museum until hours later. He summoned his carriage and waited while the footman helped both women into the back. He asked the driver to deliver them first to the Hart residence.

During the drive, Miss Hart's earlier reticence returned. He couldn't help but wonder if it was related to whatever she wished to speak to him about. He tried to engage her in conversation to no avail, so he settled for watching London pass by the window.

When they came to a halt, Miss Hart turned to him. "Will you come in so we can speak in private?"

"What is it regarding?" He'd go with her whatever the case, but he'd prefer to have at least a couple of minutes to mentally prepare himself for what was to come.

She shook her head. "I'll explain inside."

"Very well, then."

They disembarked and approached the house. He knocked, and after a moment, the butler held the door open for them to enter.

"Come this way." Miss Hart led him past a staircase and the drawing room where he'd called on her previously, then into another drawing room. This one was painted predominantly yellow, with a green door, green boards above the fireplace, and a massive bookshelf along one wall. "Have a seat. I'll be just a moment."

He sat on a comfortable brown leather chair. Mary hovered in the corner, keeping her head down so as not to engage with him while her mistress was gone.

Miss Hart returned only a minute or two later with a sheaf of papers clasped in front of her. She kept the papers against her skirt, a blank side toward him, as she claimed another brown leather chair and angled it toward him.

She cleared her throat. "It has come to my attention that you're seeking a bride with a substantial dowry."

His chest squeezed, and blood rushed to his head. "Excuse me?"

She frowned. "A dowry. You need a wife with a large one."

"N-no," he stammered, completely caught off guard.

Her nostrils flared. "Don't deny it. I know that is the reason you are... courting me. If that's what this is. I have money, and you need it."

Guilt curdled in his gut. He'd never intended for her to know that. Whatever his reason for pursuing her, he liked her as a person too. He didn't want to hurt her.

"You have plenty of attractions beside your wealth," he protested.

Her mouth pressed into a grim line. "Please be honest, Lord Longley."

She passed him the sheaf of papers. He read the top line and froze. The document was entitled "Marriage agreement between Andrew Drake and Amelia Hart." He skimmed down the page. It was handwritten and looked like a legal contract.

His brows knitted together. "What is this?"

She rearranged her skirts, and the scent of peppermint wafted toward him. "My parents wish me to marry into the aristocracy. You are an aristocrat. You need money. I have money. Or, at least, my future husband will. Rather than endure a farce of a courtship, I'd prefer to come to an agreement."

He lifted the papers. "You want to marry me?"

She looked down at her hands. "For convenience only. Although I will, of course, do my best to provide an heir."

He tried to ignore the flare of interest that statement roused in him. He could scarcely believe this was happening. He'd been prepared to go through the usual courtship rituals with her, and strangely enough, he felt robbed of the opportunity to do so. Yet she was offering him everything he wanted. He should be pleased.

She shifted closer and tapped the top paragraph of the agreement with her forefinger. "These papers set out the conditions of our potential marriage. I advise you to review them carefully and perhaps have your solicitor do the same. Essentially, I will agree to wed you and ensure you receive my full dowry provided you meet my terms."

He leaned toward her, intrigued. "What are your terms?"

She sat back, creating more space between them. "Read the agreement. We can discuss them after. I would prefer for you to take it home to review at your leisure rather than doing so here. I haven't mentioned this to my parents, and your prolonged presence is likely to draw their attention."

Andrew gaped at her. First, she'd absolutely stunned him with this cold-blooded offer of marriage, and now she was effectively dismissing him from her presence. He didn't know whether to be offended or impressed by her sheer audacity.

He stood, careful not to stumble. "I'll see myself out."

She nodded. "I appreciate your cooperation."

Cooperation?

He doubted he was intentionally cooperating at all. He was simply too shocked to do or say anything else. The world spun around him as he walked back to the house's main entrance and let himself out.

His carriage was waiting for him.

Good gracious. Miss Hart really had thought this through.

Amelia.

That was the name she'd used on the contract. He rather thought it suited her. Nothing as plain as Jane, nor as fanciful as Lydia. It was strong, but a little unusual.

He climbed into the carriage. During the drive to Longley House, he tried to focus on the papers that Amelia had given him. The text was very official. Had she written it herself, or had someone else prepared it? He suspected the former. She was, after all, a very intelligent woman.

As far as he could tell, she had few major stipulations. First, he must provide her with a weekly stipend. He'd always intended to do that for his wife anyway.

Second, he was never to use violence against her. The fact that she felt the need to make that a condition of their marriage rocked him. Did she believe him capable of violence?

He wasn't naive. He knew that certain members of the ton were reputed to raise their hand against their wife, but that wasn't him. He didn't even like to squash bugs unless he had to.

Thirdly, he was not to attempt to control her behavior. This made him curious. At first, he thought it might be a general clause because some husbands treated their wives like servants, but in conjunction with the fourth clause, he suspected there might be more to it than that.

What did she mean by "the husband agrees to allow any and all personal literary endeavors undertaken by the wife"?

Did she intend to start a book club? Write poetry? Or did she just wish to spend all day reading and not participate in any social outings he might arrange for them?

He would require clarification.

Unfortunately, the fifth and final clause required no clarification.

"The husband will employ a new man of business who meets the approval of the wife's father, Mr. Walter Hart."

That single phrase bruised his ego until it was black and blue. Clearly, Miss Hart had no confidence in his financial acumen. But then, why should she?

He rubbed his temples as the carriage slowed. What on earth had he gotten himself into?

CHAPTER 11

A SHARP KNOCK ON HER BEDCHAMBER DOOR STARTLED AMELIA, and she clapped her hand to her chest. "What is it?"

"Miss Hart." Mr. Grant sounded miffed that she had not rushed over. "The Earl of Longley is asking to see you."

"Oh." She jolted upright, almost knocking over her inkwell. "Tell him I will be there soon. Can you please send Mrs. White up?"

"Yes, miss."

She heard his footsteps retreat, and she quickly tidied away her papers. She'd been working on more of the story where Miss Joceline fled to the Americas, driven to desperation by the fickle attention of a suitor who wasn't worthy of her.

She looked at her hands and grimaced. There were two particularly obvious ink smudges. She didn't have the supplies to clean her hands properly, so instead she donned one of her least favorite pairs of gloves—so as not to ruin one of the pairs she actually liked—and inhaled deeply, attempting to pull herself together.

It had been two days since the earl had departed from her family's house with the marriage agreement in hand, and she hadn't heard from him since. She'd tried not to tie herself in knots worrying over what his response might be or, God forbid, whether he'd tell her parents about her proposition, but it was difficult not to when faced with such a large unknown.

She steepled her fingers and closed her eyes, doing her best to gather herself.

"Miss Hart?"

Her eyelashes fluttered open, and she blinked as her vision cleared. "Mrs. White. Thank you for coming. Would you be able to arrange for tea and cakes to be sent to the yellow drawing room, please?"

Mrs. White nodded, her cheeks ruddy. "I'll get on that right away, and I'll ask Mary to join you."

She bustled away without waiting for Amelia to dismiss her.

What would the earl say? Would he agree to her proposal?

With a sigh, she strode out of the room. The only way she'd find the answers to those questions was by asking him herself.

As she hurried down the stairs, she thought to check her dress to make sure it was acceptable for interacting with an earl. It was probably a little plain, and the skirt was slightly crumpled from sitting for so long, but it would have to do.

She shivered as she reached the ground floor. It was cooler than on the second floor—especially her bedchamber, which was flooded with midafternoon light.

She rounded the corner into the drawing room and forced a smile onto her face.

"My lord." She swept into a curtsy. "How lovely to see you."

He grinned at her from where he stood in front of the bookshelf, flashing his crooked incisor. For some reason, the sight of it felt oddly intimate. "And you too."

She glanced at Mary, who stood in the corner with her hands folded over her lap and her head down.

"Our housekeeper will be in with tea and cake. I assume you've come to discuss my proposition?"

He opened his mouth, but before he had a chance to respond, Mrs. Hart glided through the doorway and into the drawing room. She beamed at Lord Longley and shot Amelia a disapproving glare.

"What a surprise to see you, my lord," she said. "Do forgive my lateness. I wasn't informed that we have a guest."

His mouth quirked up on one side. "That's perfectly all right, Mrs. Hart. You're here now."

"I am indeed. Would you like some tea?"

Longley met Amelia's gaze. "Miss Hart just finished telling me that tea and cakes will arrive momentarily."

Mrs. White hurried in, faltering slightly when she spotted Mrs. Hart, but she covered the brief hesitation and set the tea tray on the side table.

"Amelia?" Mrs. Hart said.

"Yes, Mother?"

"Won't you be a dear and fix the earl a cup of tea?"

Amelia struggled not to laugh at Mrs. Hart's attempt to show off her domestic skills in front of a potential husband. She poured him a cup, grateful she could recall his preference from last time. Sugar, but no milk. She passed it to him, then prepared a cup for her mother and then herself.

Her mother accepted the saucer and perched on the edge of a brown leather chair.

"Why on earth did you see fit to receive a caller in this room?" she asked Amelia. "The blue drawing room is far more suited to such things."

Yes, and she'd thought being in the yellow drawing room was less likely to attract her mother's attention, but look how that had worked out.

Unfortunately, Mrs. Hart was right. The yellow drawing

room had fewer chairs, so unless Amelia wanted to sit at the desk, she had to either remain standing and allow Longley to take the other chair or claim it herself. She couldn't decide whether her mother would prefer for her to abide by society's dictates and sit or show graciousness by offering the earl her seat.

Fortunately, he saved her from making the decision.

"Miss Hart, please take a seat," he said, gesturing at the chair with his free hand. "Don't feel the need to stand on my account."

Relieved, she did as he said, arranging her skirts around herself and holding on to her teacup and saucer.

"What brings you here on a day as cold as this one?" Mrs. Hart asked. "I'd have thought everyone would be eager to stay home."

He glanced at Amelia, and she did her best not to let him know she was quietly panicking. He wouldn't sell her out, would he?

He smirked. "I simply couldn't stand the idea of going another day without Miss Hart's company. After our visit to the museum, she suggested I read a particular paper of interest to her, and I wanted to give her my thoughts on it."

Her chest tightened. He must be referring to the marriage agreement she'd given him.

Mrs. Hart's eyes narrowed. "Nothing too academic, I hope?"

The earl waved dismissively. "No, nothing like that. It was an article about women's fashion through the ages."

Thankfully, her mother was satisfied by that explanation, and the tension gripping Amelia eased.

"What did you think of it?" she asked, knowing he referred to their agreement, since there had been no fashion article.

He cocked his head, and a hint of a smile tugged at his mouth. "I definitely thought it was worthy of further discussion. It raised several interesting points, and I'd like to learn more."

Her stomach fluttered. Surely that must mean he was interested in taking her up on the offer.

She hesitated. "There's a tome in our library that may be of interest. I'm sure Father won't mind if you'd like to borrow it."

Mrs. Hart's nose crinkled, and she looked between them, clearly uncertain whether to steer the conversation in a direction she deemed more appropriate or whether to go along with it, since the earl hadn't expressed any dissatisfaction.

Her lips twisted wryly. "You may borrow whatever book catches your eye, my lord. I'll leave you two to peruse the library in peace, but before you go, may I inquire as to the next ball you will be attending?"

Longley nodded. "I will be at the Studholme ball on Thursday."

Mrs. Hart deflated. "Ah."

Amelia understood her disappointment. The Harts had not secured an invitation to the exclusive Studholme ball.

The earl, noticing her dejection, said, "Won't you come as my guests?"

Mrs. Hart's head shot up, and her mouth fell open. "We would be thrilled to accept. That's so generous of you."

"Excellent. I shall have the arrangements made." He turned to Amelia. "I hope you will save me two dances."

She grinned, her heart lifting. That sounded promising. "I will."

He emptied his teacup in a few mouthfuls, and she did the same. He took it from her and set both cups on the table; then he offered her his arm. She stood and took it.

"A pleasure, as always," he said to her mother and led Amelia out of the room. "Which way to the library?"

"Up the stairs and to the right."

They climbed the stairs and headed down the corridor, only stopping when Amelia gestured at a closed door. Lord Longley turned the handle and pushed it open. The library was dim, muted light coming through a small window on the far wall. The darkness helped preserve the integrity of the books, many of which were old.

"This is quite a library for a family like yours," he remarked.

She laughed. "Common?"

He pulled a face as he released her and strolled over to read the spines of the books on the shelf closest. "I mean no offense. But a family that has a history such as mine accumulates books over many generations, whereas I assume all of these were purchased by your father?"

She inclined her head in acknowledgement. "You would be right about that. My father is an avid reader of business, science, and mathematics texts. The fiction, I must admit, he bought solely to entertain me. I also enjoy factual texts, but in my opinion, they're best when interspersed with stories that give them context."

He looked over his shoulder at her, something calculating in his gaze. "You are quite a reader?"

"Indeed." Not that her mother would be pleased she'd admitted as much. Still, if they were to wed, then it was best he knew that now. "Is that a problem?"

"Not at all." He trailed his finger down the spine of a book, withdrew it from the shelf, and opened it to the first page. "I must confess, I'm curious. In your agreement, you reference literary pursuits. What did you mean by that?"

She pressed her lips together and closed the door to ensure no one could overhear them. "I've already told you that I like to read."

He nodded, still looking down at the book rather than at her, as if he knew that would make it easier for her to continue. She debated how much to tell him. She needed to share enough to allow him to make a reasonably informed decision, but she was also afraid that being wholly truthful might put him off.

"I also like to dabble in writing," she said finally. It was true, but also somewhat of an understatement. "Letters, scenes from fictional situations. Whatever catches my fancy. It would make me miserable if my husband were to interfere with my ability to do that."

His shoulders relaxed. He returned the book to the shelf and turned toward her. "As far as hobbies go, I cannot imagine it is a particularly dangerous or expensive one. I see no reason you couldn't continue if we were to wed."

Her soul lightened. It felt as though a weight she had been carrying for years had finally lifted. "Thank you, my lord." He had no idea how much this meant to her. "Does this mean you are willing to agree to my terms?"

He raised a finger. "I have two other questions."

She bit her lip. Of course it would not be so simple. "Ask them."

He took a step toward her, and her heart rate increased. "First, you do not want your husband to attempt to control your actions. Please explain exactly what you mean by that."

Amelia twined her fingers together and drew in a calming breath. "Just what it sounds like. I don't want a husband who will tell me what I can and can't wear, or eat, or read. If I feel like writing a story or going for a walk in the countryside, I don't want anyone to stop me. If I find a particular person or event unpleasant, I'd like to be able to leave without being chastised later."

Something flickered in his eyes. "That's perfectly reasonable."

The knot in her gut loosened. "Thank you."

"But," he added, "if we were to marry, I hope you would take your husband's thoughts and feelings into consideration. Say if you wanted to walk outside when a storm was approaching. I might advise against it. Not for the sake of controlling you, but to keep you safe. Of course, the end decision would be yours, but I hope you would at least consider my opinion."

Nibbling on her lip, she searched for issues in what he'd said but found none. He was right that it would be respectful to consider her husband's wishes even if she ignored them in the end.

"I can agree to that," she said. "What's your second question?"

He stepped even closer, and warmth pooled inside her. "What do you get out of this arrangement?"

She frowned, the warmth dissipating. "I don't understand."

He moved forward again and reached for her hand. She allowed him to take it, ignoring the zing of sensation his touch elicited.

"You said that your parents would like you to wed an aristocrat, but that's not a benefit to *you*. It's one for *them*."

"Oh." Her voice was small. She hadn't expected him to ask. Most men wouldn't. She studied the firm set of his mouth, which contrasted with the warmth of his hazel eyes. "Marriage to you would appease my mother, so I would no longer have to deal with her machinations. Also, to be perfectly blunt, I doubt I will find a better potential husband than you."

His eyes widened. "How so?"

She looked to the side. "Surely you know that most young ladies would consider you a catch."

He arched an eyebrow. "You don't strike me as the type of woman to go along with common opinion."

"Perhaps not," she allowed, removing her hand from his and striding to the small window. She needed space to clear her thoughts. It was difficult to concentrate when he touched her. "You are young. You don't seem half-witted or dull, and you have always been good-natured toward me. That's all I can ask for in a husband."

He paced along behind her, closing the distance between them once again. "But you don't trust my financial judgment?"

She glanced back at him. "Can you blame me?"

He winced but didn't argue. "For what it's worth, I think you're selling yourself short. You could have any husband you desired. Your situation is not so dire."

She turned away, doing her best to quell the little fizz of joy his claim brought her. They didn't mean anything. He was a born charmer. Sweet words no doubt spilled from his lips without any real emotion or meaning behind them.

"Never mind that." She pivoted on her heels and stuck out her hand. "Do we have a deal?"

∽

Andrew narrowed his eyes. He didn't like the fact that Miss Hart seemed to believe the only thing of value she had to offer a husband was her dowry. She was an intelligent, interesting woman—not to mention attractive, even if her style of beauty wasn't that favored by the ton, but instead the sort which grew upon a person over time.

He couldn't help but wish that he'd courted her for more honorable reasons.

If he still had his fortune, he'd have showered her with gifts so she didn't doubt her appeal. Unfortunately, this was reality, and he wasn't in a position to do that.

He shook her hand. "We do."

Some of the rigidity eased from her shoulders. "Good."

Had she really expected any other outcome? Surely she knew that the deal she offered was too tempting to resist. He suspected she'd learned negotiation at her father's knee.

She'd found something she could use as leverage and had done so to get what she wanted.

In truth, he admired her for that.

"I didn't bring the agreement." He hadn't been certain what the outcome of their conversation would be. "I will sign both copies later today and have one returned to you."

"Thank you. Please ensure it is taken directly to me and does not fall into either my mother's or father's hands."

"You have my word." Considering all that she'd risked to make this proposal, the least he could do was protect her privacy.

"I'll show you out." She marched to the door and held it open for him, then escorted him down the stairs and out of the house.

It was only as he seated himself in his carriage that he realized what this meant. He was, for all intents and purposes, betrothed.

Not even two months ago, that thought would have been enough to drive him to the Regent to drink more than his fair share of brandy, but now, it made him smile. At the very least, being married to Miss Amelia Hart would not be boring.

Once he arrived home, he retired to his office and penned a letter to Ashford. The duke had returned to his country estate, and Andrew had promised to keep him up-to-date on his search for a wife. He skimmed over the details of their betrothal, keeping it sufficiently vague and ensuring Ashford knew that it wasn't official yet.

At the end of the missive, he paused. Then, after a long hesitation, added a postscript.

P.S. I have a query for Lady Emma. Theoretically, how would I go about ensuring my future wife knows that I value her for more than her dowry?

CHAPTER 12

"You seem rather anxious," Lady Drake observed as their carriage stopped outside the Harts' residence.

Andrew adjusted his cravat, which felt far too tight around his throat. "It's not every day that I introduce my mother to the woman I intend to marry."

She tilted her head. "You're sure about this?"

"Yes." He cleared his throat. "You'll understand when you meet her. Wait here. I'll collect Miss and Mrs. Hart."

He exited the carriage and hurried up the stairs with a sense of haste most would probably consider unbefitting of an earl. Tonight, he wasn't just an earl. He was a man.

The doors were already open, and as he stepped into their frame, his gaze landed on the two Hart women standing in the center of the foyer. They both looked up. Mrs. Hart beamed at him, but it was Amelia's gentler smile that turned him inside out.

He bowed. "Good evening, ladies. Your conveyance is here."

Mrs. Hart thanked him effusively, and he took a quick moment to study their attire. She wore a gown of deep blue and a matching headpiece, while her daughter was clad in a frilly white contraption similar to the one she'd had on the evening they met.

She caught him looking at it and scowled. Apparently, she knew the dress wasn't flattering. That said, he'd challenge anyone to tell him she looked poorly when her expressions were so lively and humor was constantly flickering across her face.

Ugly gown or not, he couldn't take his eyes off her.

"Are you ready to depart?" he asked.

"Yes, my lord." Mrs. Hart breezed past him, not pausing to allow him to take her arm.

He turned to Amelia instead. "May I?"

She allowed him to escort her outside at a more measured pace. "I received the papers you sent over."

His gaze remained forward. "Was everything to your liking?"

"It was. Thank you for indulging me with the agreement. I know it is… unconventional."

"Perhaps." He leaned closer and lowered his voice. "But everything about our arrangement is unconventional, so that's fitting."

She huffed a quiet laugh. "I believe you'll find I'm a somewhat unconventional person. I hope that won't be a problem."

"Not at all." In fact, he looked forward to learning more about the way she viewed the world.

They reached the carriage just as his footman was assisting Mrs. Hart inside. The footman stepped aside to allow Andrew to do the same for Miss Hart. The mothers were seated next to each other, so he found himself alongside Amelia as they trundled toward Studholme House.

"Please allow me to make the introductions," he said smoothly, smiling at each woman in turn. "Mother, these beautiful ladies are the esteemed Mrs. Hart and her enchanting daughter, Miss Amelia Hart. Mrs. Hart and Miss

Hart, I present to you my mother, the Dowager Countess of Longley."

Amelia bowed her head respectfully. "It's an honor to meet you, my lady."

His mother's eyes sparkled. "The honor is all mine, Miss Hart. My son is quite taken with you. I look forward to getting to know you better."

"That's very kind of you."

Amelia didn't say more. A faint pink flush appeared on her cheeks. He couldn't help but wonder why. Was it because his mother had implied he was smitten?

"Have you been in London for long?" the dowager asked Mrs. Hart, and within a matter of minutes, the two were engrossed in a conversation.

Andrew met Amelia's gaze and tried his hardest to send reassuring thoughts from his mind to hers. Although honestly, he might need them as much as she did. He had the feeling that Miss Hart and his mother would be a formidable combination.

The carriage slowed as they neared Studholme House and joined a queue of their peers waiting to attend the ball. Fortunately, it didn't take long for them to progress to the front of the queue and disembark.

Their mothers took the lead, sweeping through the double doors and the foyer to the edge of the ballroom.

Andrew noticed Baron Studholme's expression waver as he saw them together. No doubt he was confused because the Harts hadn't been invited. Nonetheless, Andrew had been assured that he and his mother were both welcome, each with a personal guest, so there was nothing he could say about their presence.

Perhaps he should feel guilty for springing them on Studholme without warning, but the man was a dreadful snob, and he deserved to be shaken up a little.

The baron recovered quickly, greeting Lady Drake and

Mrs. Hart with courteous bows—although one was certainly shallower than the other—before turning to Longley.

"So good to see you, old chap." He shook Longley's hand vigorously. "And in such lovely company."

"Glad you could have us," Andrew replied cheerfully. He bowed to Lady Studholme. "You have outdone yourself, my lady. It's even more elegant than last year."

She ducked her head. "Thank you, Lord Longley. I hope you enjoy your evening."

This time, his smile was genuine. Lady Studholme was much more pleasant than her husband. "I'm certain we will."

A string quartet was playing in the corner of the ballroom. Dancers occupied the ballroom floor. Andrew guided Miss Hart to the edge of the dancing and waited for the song to end.

"I assume I get your first dance, since I was your escort," he murmured.

"I suppose so," she replied. "That seems only right, since we are to marry."

He chuckled. "Don't speak too loudly or your mother will have planned the wedding before we even leave the ball."

She peered up at him. "Would that be so bad?"

He was startled by the comment, but there really was no reason to be. Thanks to her, they both knew what this was. "I guess not. It *is* our end goal, after all."

The dancers reset their positions for the next song, and he took Amelia's hand and led her to join them. When the music began again, they moved together as if they'd danced dozens of times before. Every time he reached for her, she was exactly where he expected. He couldn't help smiling. Was this what marriage to her would be like? Always being pleasantly surprised?

If so, he was a lucky man.

"Why are you grinning like that?" she asked as she swayed closer to him.

"I'm glad we've come to an arrangement," he told her.

Her eyes widened, but she quickly schooled her expression. "As am I."

When the dance finished, he wasn't ready to leave her company yet.

"May I escort you for a glass of lemonade?"

She searched his eyes, but he didn't know what she was looking for. "I'd like that."

They made their way to the lemonade table. He grabbed two glasses—one for each of them. They stood side by side on the edge of the dancing, both content not to speak. Andrew had always liked talkative girls, but he had to admit that there was an appeal to Amelia's quiet, steady presence.

He spotted his mother and Mrs. Hart in an alcove at the end of the room. The dowager met his eyes and winked.

"Miss Hart."

Andrew jolted. The masculine voice had caught him off guard. He hadn't noticed anyone approaching.

The Duke of Wight looked down his imperious nose at Amelia. "Are you engaged for the next dance?"

She glanced at Andrew, nibbling on her lower lip, visibly uncertain of how to respond. He shrugged discreetly. They hadn't announced their betrothal yet, so it would be improper for him to intervene.

"I am not." Dread laced her tone.

"Then you must dance with me." He extended a long-fingered hand toward her. "Come."

She accepted his hand and allowed him to lead her away, casting a narrow-eyed look back over her shoulder. He liked it more than he should that she clearly didn't want to dance with the duke. It gave him a strange sense of satisfaction.

Instead of watching while they danced, he carried his lemonade around the room to where his mother now stood alone.

"Where's Mrs. Hart?" he asked.

"Speaking with Lady Bowling." She didn't take her eyes off the dance floor. "She asked about you."

"Who? Lady Bowling?"

"Mm."

He grimaced. "I suppose that's inevitable. I'll have to avoid her until the announcement of our betrothal. Lady Esther is nice enough, but my search for a wife is over."

She glanced at him out of the corner of her eye, a smirk playing at the edge of her lips. "Miss Hart is very quiet."

He scoffed. "Until you get her talking about something she's passionate about." He hesitated, then added, "I get the impression her mother told her not to speak about her interests because she doesn't consider them socially acceptable."

Lady Drake made a sharp sound of surprise. "How so?"

"Miss Hart likes to read. She is fascinated by different civilizations and other parts of the world. You should have seen how alive she became when I took her to visit the museum."

"You like her."

He didn't know why she was surprised by this. "Of course I do. I'd hardly have agreed to marry her otherwise."

He searched her out on the dance floor, only to frown when he noticed she was no longer dancing with the Duke of Wight. Instead, she was on the Marquess of Overton's arm.

Did the marquess really need to hold her so closely?

He was not her intended.

As the pair turned, Overton's hand grazed Amelia's hip. Andrew's feet carried him toward them without his consent. He forced them to stop after two paces. There was no reason for him to intervene. Perhaps Overton was being more familiar than Andrew would like with his future countess, but until their engagement was made public, he couldn't tell the other man to back off.

"That's not what I mean," his mother said, stepping up beside him. "You're bewitched by her."

"No, I'm not." That was ludicrous. He was simply possessive because Miss Hart was the key to securing his family's future.

Certainly, that was all it was.

Even he couldn't convince himself of that. He was attracted to Miss Hart, plain and simple.

As soon as Overton bowed to her, Andrew was at their side, inserting himself between them.

"The next dance is mine," he said gruffly.

She took his hand without protest, although there was no missing the puzzlement that passed across her face.

"Do you like the theater?" he asked impulsively.

She blinked rapidly, a furrow forming between her eyebrows. "Very much."

"Will you accompany me tomorrow night?" He wondered when his mouth had started making plans without his brain's permission.

"I would love to."

"Excellent." Now he would simply have to arrange to attend the theater with very little notice and ensure his mother came along so no one could accuse him of having nefarious intentions.

Damn.

∽

Amelia couldn't stop smiling as Lord Longley helped her down from the carriage and walked side by side with her into the theater. A secret part of her felt special that he'd invited her to watch a play. This wasn't something they needed to do as part of their courtship. It wasn't expected.

And yet, he'd asked anyway. She could only presume he'd done so because he knew she would enjoy it. She was especially excited because this was not only a play, but one set in

Italy. For a brief time, she could immerse herself in the story and pretend to be there herself.

Lord Longley escorted her to a box above and slightly to the right of the stage. From there, they would have a perfect view.

"Shall we sit in the front?" he asked.

"Yes, please."

They claimed chairs in the center of the box. Her father sat to her left, and her mother joined the dowager countess to the right of the earl. She was closely attuned to the earl's presence beside her, his body heat radiating across the small space between them.

"I've been looking forward to this all day," she told him softly. "Thank you for the invitation."

He smiled. "I hope it lives up to your expectations."

The show began, and gradually, Amelia became absorbed and was able to put the earl's proximity to the back of her mind—except for as a conversational partner. More than once, she found herself whispering something to him before darting a look at her mother, certain she was about to be scolded. Fortunately, Mrs. Hart paid her little attention, and the earl seemed entertained by her running commentary.

He didn't chastise her for distracting him or suggest that women were less knowledgeable about literature than men and so she ought to keep her views to herself. He treated her comments with respect and answered her questions thoughtfully.

By the time the show ended, she was giddy from the experience but also, deep inside, a little sad. She enjoyed spending time with the earl, but she couldn't forget that he didn't actually want to marry her. He'd courted her for her fortune. No matter how warmly she might feel toward him, she doubted he felt the same.

This was a practical match, not a love match, but he kept

doing and saying things that made it difficult for her to remember that.

They waited for the downstairs to empty before leaving their box so as not to be inundated by the crowd below. Once outside, Lord Longley summoned his carriage, and they all clambered in. As they started to move, the dowager countess made a comment about the superb acting, and Mr. Hart responded. Her mother was uncharacteristically silent.

To Amelia's surprise, they passed by Longley House first, and a footman escorted the dowager inside. Mrs. Hart shot her a meaningful look. Amelia tried to ignore it.

When they arrived at the Hart residence, Lord Longley waited until they had all disembarked from the carriage before addressing Mr. Hart.

"May I speak with you in private, sir?" he asked.

Mr. Hart nodded, unsurprised. "Come into my office."

Mrs. Hart raised her eyebrows at Amelia, who just shook her head. She could assume what the earl had in mind, but they hadn't previously discussed it.

As soon as they entered the house, Mr. Hart and Lord Longley disappeared into the office. Mrs. Hart gestured for Amelia to join her in the drawing room. Amelia sat on a chaise in the dimly lit space, watching in the flickering light of a solitary lamp as her mother opened a cabinet and withdrew a bottle of sherry and two small glasses.

Amelia's jaw dropped. She'd had no idea that was there.

Mrs. Hart caught Amelia's eye. "I think you and I deserve one of these."

She poured a couple of inches of sherry into each glass, returned the bottle to the cabinet, and passed one glass to Amelia.

She sat beside her and raised her glass. "To your future—and ours."

Cautiously, Amelia tasted the drink. Her nose crinkled. "I'm not sure I like that."

Her mother laughed. "It will grow on you."

They drank without speaking further. She could sense her mother's pride in what she considered to be a joint victory, but that sliver of sorrow remained lodged in her heart.

Yes, this was what she and the earl had planned, but a tiny part of her that she didn't dare acknowledge longed for more.

She'd just have to resign herself to the fact she wouldn't get it. She'd have her stories. Her career. That was all she'd ever wanted before now.

The door swung inward, revealing a man framed in the doorway. She couldn't see much of him in the darkness, but the figure was too tall and lean to be her father.

"Mrs. Hart," Longley said, his voice stirring the heavy air between them. "May I speak to your daughter in private?"

Mrs. Hart rose. "Of course, my lord."

She stole out of the room with the faintest rustle of silk.

The earl strode inside and came to a stop above Amelia. He hovered there for a moment, then lowered himself onto the seat beside her. This close, the candlelight revealed the hint of green in his eyes and the crooked incisor that made his smile so endearing.

"Miss Hart," he began solemnly. "Amelia."

He held his hands out, palms up. Hesitantly, she placed hers on them, palm to palm. She shivered. It was perhaps the most intimate exchange she'd ever shared with a man.

He cleared his throat. "I know we have an agreement, but I want to do this properly. Will you grant me the privilege of claiming your hand in marriage?"

She stared at him, stunned silent. She'd known the engagement would be imminent when he had failed to disembark at Longley House. But for some reason, it had never crossed her mind that he might actually ask her for her hand. She'd assumed he'd speak with her father and the matter would be settled. Perhaps her father hadn't responded favorably.

"What did my father say?" she asked. "Does he disapprove?"

He hadn't given any indication that he might consider the earl unsuitable, but he could be circumspect when the situation called for it.

The earl gave a strained laugh. "Is this your way of attempting to make me sweat while I await your answer?"

"No." She drew back sharply. "Sorry, I didn't mean to worry you. Of course we will marry. That was never in doubt. I was just curious what my father said when you spoke to him."

He raised her hands and kissed the back of each one, holding her gaze as he did so. She barely resisted the urge to shiver.

"That was a man-to-man conversation. However, I can tell you that he cares about you a great deal."

Her heart thudded. Even though she knew as much, it was nice to hear it out loud—especially given that she'd always been second place in her father's affections.

"Thank you," she whispered.

"No. Thank you for offering me a life raft when I was adrift." He released her hands, reached into his trouser pocket, and withdrew a small box. "This is for you."

Amelia took the box with shaking hands. It was delicately carved, an intricate design imprinted on the wood. She opened the lid and sucked in a breath. Lying on a bed of silk was an antique engagement ring, a ruby framed by diamonds and set into a delicate gold band.

"It's beautiful," she breathed.

"It belonged to my grandmother on my father's side. She gave it to me when I was young and told me to save it for my wife."

Her chest constricted and tears prickled at the backs of

her eyes. This stunning ring wasn't meant for her. It was supposed to go to the wife he chose.

The one he wanted.

She couldn't help but feel like his grandmother would be disappointed to see her wearing it.

"Try it on. I want to see how it looks on you. It may not fit, but we can have it resized immediately."

Struggling to hide how badly she was trembling, she slotted the ring onto her finger. It fit almost perfectly.

"It's slightly loose," Longley mused. "Slide it back off. I'll take it to the jeweler tomorrow."

Reluctantly, she did as he asked. For some reason, she couldn't shake the feeling that the ring wasn't intended for her, and if she let it out of her sight, she might not get it back.

Nevertheless, she forced herself to hand it over. Whether or not he returned it to her, it didn't change the fact that he wouldn't have chosen her as his wife in any other circumstance. Could she bring herself to accept that?

CHAPTER 13

*London,
November 1820*

EMPTYING THE CONTENTS OF HER WRITING DESK INTO TIDY stacks inside a suitcase, Amelia reminded herself that this was a beginning, not an end. This time tomorrow, she'd be able to indulge herself in Joceline's fictional world for as long as she wanted, and no one would stop her.

Unfortunately, until then, she had to finish packing her belongings and, well, get married.

All around her, servants were folding her clothes into cases and storing her other belongings in boxes. She wouldn't take too much with her. Only her clothes, her stories and writing equipment, a few of her favorite pieces of jewelry, and a collection of books she couldn't bear to part with.

Anything else she wanted, she could get later. Although honestly, she didn't expect to want for much. She'd be perfectly happy if all she did was eat, sleep, read, and write—perhaps with the occasional walk outside for fresh air and sunshine.

Beside her, Mary fastened a valise and pushed it at a footman, who carried it from the room.

Mary put her hands on her hips and looked around. "It's so different without your personal touches."

"I know." Her bedchamber was now as welcoming as a guest room. It no longer felt or looked like a home. She glanced at the clock. "Time to dress my hair?"

Mary nodded. "Best not be late. I can only imagine what your mother would say."

Amelia pressed her lips together so she wouldn't laugh. Her mother had been in heaven, planning their wedding. She'd insisted on having the best flowers, the most elaborate dress, and the largest guest list. Almost everyone she'd invited had accepted the invitation, although Amelia suspected that was as much out of curiosity as anything else.

Mary positioned a chair in front of the long mirror they'd borrowed from her mother's chamber. "Do you still want it the way we practiced?"

"Yes, thank you."

Mrs. Hart had suggested a number of ridiculous configurations, but Amelia had managed to persuade her that taking a classic, elegant approach would be best. She'd argued that keeping her hair simple would ensure it didn't detract appreciation from her dress.

In reality, she doubted she'd have the patience to sit through the hours of ministrations necessary to achieve her mother's vision.

She gazed at her reflection as Mary brushed her hair, tied it at the nape of her neck, and twisted it into a chignon. She pinned the hair into place using Mrs. Hart's jeweled hairpins —Amelia's concession to a subtle display of wealth.

She smiled at Mary in the reflection. After today, Mary would no longer be her maid. All the years she'd spent learning Amelia's preferences and encouraging her love of stories would be lost. She'd have to find a new maid and hope that they would be able to get along reasonably well.

With a sigh, she asked, "Are you sure you can't come with me?"

"I'm sure." Mary sent her a quick, sympathetic smile. "My place is here, with your parents and my husband."

Mary was married to Mr. Hart's valet.

"I understand. I'll miss you."

The maid squeezed her shoulder gently. "You'll be sorely missed too. We'll have to get our excitement somewhere else if there's no more Miss Joceline to keep us entertained."

Amelia laughed. "If I have my way, Miss Joceline will be coming to the world in print soon. If that happens, I'll make sure you receive a copy."

Mary didn't read, but Mrs. White did, and Amelia was certain the motherly housekeeper wouldn't mind reading aloud for the others.

There was a knock on the door, and someone entered. Amelia didn't turn her head, wary of ruining her hair, but based on the light and purposeful footsteps, she guessed it was her mother.

"Oh, good. You're almost ready for the dress." A floorboard creaked as Mrs. Hart crossed the room to the wardrobe.

Mary inserted the last pin into Amelia's hair and examined her with a critical eye. "Is she acceptable, ma'am?"

Her mother approached, her reflection appearing at Amelia's side. "She'll do."

Amelia stood and turned away from the mirror. Mrs. Hart had opened the wardrobe door to reveal her wedding gown, an extravagant lace creation with more frills and layers than any of her ball dresses.

Her mother had wanted her to wear pink, but Amelia hadn't been able to find a shade she liked, so they'd settled on a more subdued champagne fabric that wasn't entirely unflattering for her complexion. Despite the compromise, Amelia still abhorred the dress.

Mrs. Hart, on the other hand, sighed joyfully as Mary lifted it from the wardrobe and laid it on the bed. "Your wedding will be the talk of the ton. The wedding of the season. No one will outdo us."

Amelia just nodded. She wasn't particularly concerned with the wedding. It was the marriage she was looking forward to—or at least, the part of the marriage that would allow her to occupy herself as she pleased with no one to tell her that what she wanted was wrong.

As Mary loosened the strings on the back of the dress, Mrs. Hart withdrew a box from the folds of her skirt.

She offered it to Amelia. "Here. A wedding gift from your father and me."

Amelia's throat tightened and she took it carefully. "Thank you."

She'd never expected a gift. She wasn't sure what might be inside, but it was relatively heavy. Too large to contain a necklace, but too small for a book. Not that her mother would think to give her a book anyway. The last thing she'd do was encourage Amelia's bluestocking tendencies.

She lifted the dark wooden lid and gasped. Inside, nestled on a velvet pad, was a small tiara. It was formed of delicate silver, diamonds, and pearls. Surprisingly elegant and tasteful.

She looked up. "It's beautiful."

Mrs. Hart smiled. "I'm glad you like it. I would have chosen something"—she waved her hand—"more substantial, but your father insisted on this one, and he's rather stubborn when he chooses to be."

When Mary positioned the dress for Amelia to step into, she did so. The maid pulled it up and began to fasten the laces. Her mother picked up the tiara and positioned it on Amelia's head, shifting it slightly until it was stable.

"There." She stepped back and looked Amelia up and down. "You are a bride befitting an earl."

Amelia barely resisted the urge to roll her eyes. She supposed Mrs. Hart had used up her quota of sweetness for one day and had returned to the status quo, where everything was about appearances.

"How long until we need to leave?" she asked.

Mrs. Hart checked the clock. "Fifteen minutes."

Mary tied the laces and dropped her hands from Amelia's back. "All done."

Mrs. Hart nodded. "Thank you, Mary. You may leave us."

Mary curtsied and caught Amelia's eyes as she rose. She didn't say anything—likely Mrs. Hart would have considered it inappropriate if she did—but Amelia could see the silent farewell in her expression.

"Thank you for everything," Amelia murmured. "Stay well."

Once Mary had left the room, Mrs. Hart sat on the edge of the bed.

"You are fortunate to be in this position," she told Amelia, folding her hands on her lap. She wet her lips, looking uncharacteristically nervous. "Once you are married, you must lie with the earl as often as possible in order to beget an heir. You will not be truly secure until you have done so because if anything were to happen to your husband, his replacement could cast you out."

Amelia frowned. She hadn't considered that. But the earl was young and strong, so she saw no reason to be concerned. Also, in the event he were to pass away unexpectedly, surely her parents would take her in. After all, she was doing this partly to help them.

"What exactly does lying with him entail?" she asked.

She'd read books that had made reference to the act, but nothing that was particularly useful.

Mrs. Hart grimaced. "He will explain all of that to you.

Just know that once he does, you should indulge at every opportunity until you have a son."

"I understand." Although she wasn't entirely sure what to expect. Her mother didn't realize exactly how cold-blooded this arrangement was, so she had no reason to doubt what would happen.

Amelia, however, had no idea how soon the earl would want to be intimate. She had promised to provide him with an heir, but would he want to pursue that immediately, or would he prefer to wait?

Personally, she wasn't sure which option appealed most. Getting the act out of the way quickly would stop her from worrying over it, but what if she disliked doing…whatever it was? Once they crossed that line, there would be no returning from it.

"Good." Mrs. Hart stood. "Let us be off, then. It's time to get you married."

As they left the room, Amelia glanced over her shoulder, taking one last look at the place she'd spent much of her life for the past two years. It no longer felt like home, which was fortunate in the circumstances.

Her father was waiting patiently near the door as they descended the main staircase. "The carriage is ready." His gaze lingered on Mrs. Hart and then journeyed to Amelia. "You are exquisite, Mia. Do you like the tiara?"

"It's lovely."

Mr. Hart kissed her cheek. "Perfect for you, then."

Her heart squeezed. When he was like this, it was difficult to remember why she had to marry Lord Longley. But no matter how loving he was toward her, she couldn't forget that her mother's wishes would always trump hers where he was concerned. Because he was the one with the money, he got to make the decisions.

She looked away. "Which carriage are we taking?"

Mrs. Hart laughed. "The best one. I've had it decorated so it's suitable for a wedding."

"Nothing like what you and I rode to our wedding," Mr. Hart murmured.

Amelia forced herself to keep a smile plastered to her face. Sometimes it was easy for it to slip her mind that her mother hadn't had the elaborate wedding she wanted. She and Mr. Hart had been married in a small ceremony. She hadn't even been able to buy a new dress for the occasion.

While Amelia might prefer that to this performance, she supposed at least Mrs. Hart had finally had the chance to plan an extravagant wedding, even if it wasn't her own.

She was barely aware of her surroundings as they left the house and got into the carriage. The drive somehow seemed to take forever and no time at all. Before she knew it, her father was helping her down onto the pavement outside St. George's Church.

The wind whipped her skirt around her legs. She stood firm against the bluster and looked down at the ring on her finger. It still didn't feel right for her to wear a ring that had belonged to the earl's grandmother. All of this was so false. He was marrying her because she was rich, not because he wanted to.

Maybe, if the circumstances were different, she wouldn't feel like such an imposter.

She straightened her back.

Never mind. Whatever the reason, she was marrying the earl.

She was practical. She could get through this.

She marched up the stairs toward the entrance.

∽

When the organ began to play, Andrew adjusted his posture and turned toward the door. He blinked against the glare of the clouds outside and focused on the silhouette that had appeared in the doorway. He stared at her as she drew nearer until, finally, he could make out her features.

His breath caught, and he rubbed at an ache in his chest.

She was stunning.

Despite the dress that wasn't quite the right style or color for her, Amelia looked radiant. Her eyes sparkled brighter than ever, and her thick hair gleamed as jewels glittered within its dark mass.

The ache in his chest deepened, but he made himself drop his hand so no one would notice his discomfort. The damned bacon he'd eaten this morning must have given him indigestion.

Behind Amelia, her parents strode down the aisle, their chins high, expressions proud. It was unconventional for both parents to accompany the bride in such a manner, but Mrs. Hart had insisted, and since Andrew had no strong feelings on the matter, he'd been happy to allow her to have her way.

Amelia stopped in front of him, and her father took her hand and presented it to Andrew. He cupped it in his, reveling in the softness of her skin and at how the featherlight touch sent bolts of awareness zapping through him.

She met his eyes, and rather than the wide-eyed innocence one might expect of an aristocratic bride, all he saw in her gaze was determination. He grinned. His wife-to-be was strong. He gave her hand a squeeze, and the side of her mouth quirked up.

The minister spoke in a pleasant baritone, welcoming the congregation to the wedding of Andrew Drake, the Earl of Longley, and Miss Amelia Winnifred Hart.

Andrew had expected to experience either panic or relief at his wedding—he hadn't been certain which. Yet he felt neither of those emotions as he repeated his vows in front of most of the ton.

Instead, there was a gentle warmth inside him because he somehow knew he'd only scratched the surface of who Amelia was, and he looked forward to learning more.

He did experience a pang of fear when it was her time to speak, just in case she had a last-minute change of heart, but she didn't falter, her voice ringing clearly throughout the church.

The minister declared them husband and wife, and Andrew held her face between his palms and kissed her. He'd intended to pull away after a chaste brushing of their lips but found he couldn't. Her lips were the perfect pillow for his, soft and clinging.

He inhaled through his nose, and her intoxicating peppermint scent made his cock wake up and take notice. It shouldn't be arousing to be able to recognize a woman—*his* woman—by her scent alone, but it undeniably was.

She swayed closer, pressing herself lightly against his front. Her hands buried themselves in his jacket, and she used the grip to steady herself. They parted, and he opened his eyes a moment before she did.

Her eyelashes fluttered, sooty and dark against her alabaster skin. Then her eyes blazed into his, burning with an intensity that rocked him to his core. The passion in their depths shook him.

And she was all his.

Only a few feet away, the minister announced the new Earl and Countess of Longley. The wedding guests rose to their feet. Meanwhile, Andrew battled to control his eager cock. He could hardly walk out of here with an erection.

Amelia arched an eyebrow. "My lord?"

He exhaled roughly, reasonably sure he was safe for now. He linked his arm with hers and led her back down the aisle and out of the church.

A chill wind buffeted them the instant they stepped

outside, and he couldn't help being relieved. His body surely couldn't run rampant when it was so deuced cold.

His carriage awaited them, his family crest embossed on the door, which a liveried footman held open. He escorted her to the carriage and helped her in, then leaped in behind her. The footman closed the door, and the carriage began to move.

He turned to her. "You look incredible, my countess."

She raised an eyebrow dubiously. "This gown may be the height of fashion, but that doesn't mean it suits me."

He chuckled. "Perhaps not, but that isn't what I mean anyway. You are very pretty today. Not the dress or that no doubt priceless tiara. You."

Her cheeks pinked, and she angled her face away from him. Was she shy, or did she still not understand her appeal?

They rode in a peaceful quiet, both glad for the small reprieve before the wedding breakfast. Mrs. Hart had opted for a less traditional setup, which would leave guests free to circulate. It would also render him and Amelia more accessible to the nosy members of the ton.

The driver took a circuitous route to the Hart residence, and by the time they arrived, many of the wedding guests were already there. Andrew immediately caught sight of Ashford waiting out the front of the building, his stance rigid, expression detached.

The carriage stopped.

"Are you ready for this?" he asked her.

She pulled a face. "Are you sure we can't just go straight to your residence?"

"And deny your mother her day in the sun?"

"Ugh." She rose from the seat. "She'd never forgive me."

He hurried out and helped her down before she rendered him useless by proving she was fully capable of disembarking the carriage without him. She was, of course, but it was nice for a man to feel needed.

"Before we enter, there's someone I'd like you to meet," he murmured close to her ear. He drew her toward Ashford. "Amelia, this is my oldest friend, the Duke of Ashford. He's traveled from Norfolk for our wedding despite the fact he has a wife and infant daughter at home."

Amelia sank into a curtsy. "Thank you for making the journey, Your Grace. It's an honor to meet you."

"Likewise." Ashford's cool eyes warmed a degree. "I understand you like to read?"

She snuck a look at Andrew, obviously uncertain how to respond. He understood her confusion. The question had come out of nowhere, and her mother had taught her that she shouldn't mention such things.

"Her Grace, the Duchess of Ashford, is also an avid reader," Andrew explained, hoping to make it clear that the duke didn't disapprove of her habit.

Her tight features relaxed. "How lovely. I would like to meet her when it's convenient."

Ashford's mouth curled ever so slightly, which was as much enthusiasm as one was likely to see from him. "We would be happy to have you stay with us, once you're settled into your new life."

"Andrew!"

They all turned toward the dowager countess, who was hurrying toward them, grinning from ear to ear with Kate following close behind.

"Congratulations." Lady Drake wrapped her arms around him and stretched on tiptoes to whisper in his ear, "You chose well. Thank you for doing this for us."

He kissed her cheek. "Mother, Kate, allow me to properly introduce you to the new Countess of Longley."

Lady Drake pulled Amelia into an embrace. "Welcome to the family, Countess."

Amelia's eyes flew to his, startled by the physical display of affection.

"Just go with it," he mouthed.

"Thank you, Lady Drake."

His mother glanced around to make sure no one was listening. "Call me Brigid. Or Mother. Whatever you're comfortable with."

Amelia's mouth opened and closed. "Th-thank you," she repeated, then turned to Kate. "It's lovely to meet you. Would you prefer me to call you 'Katherine' or 'Kate'?"

Kate smiled. "Please call me Kate. We are to be sisters, after all."

Amelia's expression wavered. She didn't seem to know what to make of that. She blinked rapidly, and he suspected she was trying to regain control over her emotions.

"I would like that very much," Amelia said, her voice hoarse. "I'm eager to learn more about you."

Kate nodded. "And I, you. Andrew speaks highly of you."

Lady Drake gestured toward the entrance. "We can speak more later. For now, won't you come in? Your mother is eager to commence the festivities."

Amelia allowed herself to be led to the door. Andrew stayed close behind.

Unfortunately, the remainder of the wedding breakfast was not so pleasant. For several hours, they were subjected to the most intense scrutiny Andrew had ever experienced.

Everyone wanted to talk to them. Every single wedding guest seemed inclined to personally thank them for the invitation, even though it had been Mrs. Hart who'd chosen the guest list. More than one person offered well-intentioned marriage advice that made him inwardly cringe.

By the time they emerged, he was hardly capable of stringing together a sentence. Somehow, he managed to give his driver directions to take them home, and then he and Amelia piled into the carriage and collapsed onto the seats.

He stared blindly at the wall opposite them. "I like people, but that was…."

"Exhausting," she suggested, sounding as weary as he did.

His stomach grumbled. He was bloody starving. He hadn't had the opportunity to consume more than a slice of cake and a couple of tiny pastries. God forbid the groom be allowed to eat at his own wedding.

"At least it will be quiet at Longley House." His mother and sister were staying with friends to give them a few nights alone.

Amelia buried her face in her hands and groaned.

"What is it?" he asked.

She peeked at him from between her fingers. "I still have to meet your household staff. What if they don't like me because I'm not highborn?"

They damned well *would* like her because she was the reason they didn't have to seek new employment, and he was certain at least their more senior members of staff realized that. Not that he could say as much to her. He suspected she wasn't as blasé about the reason for their marriage as she'd like him to believe.

"They will respect you because you're my wife." It was the best reassurance he could offer. "If anyone makes you feel unwelcome, I want you to let me know."

She dropped her hands, her lips pursed. "It's important that I find my own way with them. I can't have you acting as an intermediary for the rest of our lives."

And that was exactly why his staff would respect her. She was a practical woman but kind.

He rested his hand on her thigh. "Trust me. It will be all right."

She sighed. "I hope so."

When they turned into the entrance to Longley House, the staff were lined up along the front of the building. Mrs. Smythe, the housekeeper, stood at the front alongside Boden, the only member of the household who might be considered slightly snobbish. At the farthest end were the stable boys, bouncing with restless energy.

Mrs. Smythe greeted them as they left the carriage, warmly welcoming Amelia to Longley House. For her part, Amelia's nerves were hardly noticeable. She was quiet and polite as Mrs. Smythe—a short, stout woman with gray hair and friendly eyes—introduced her to each member of the household staff.

That done, Mrs. Smythe dismissed the staff and offered Amelia a tour of the house.

"I'd like that," Amelia replied, smiling.

Mrs. Smythe's cheeks were ruddy, and she seemed pleased. "Excellent."

She led them inside and escorted them through the ground floor, showing Amelia the drawing rooms, the morning room, the earl's office, the dining hall, and the ballroom. They moved upstairs and made their way through the guest wing first, finally ending at the earl's and countess's chambers.

"I hope Lady Drake didn't have to move on my account," Amelia said as they paused outside her new bedchamber.

"Oh no, my lady," Mrs. Smythe rushed to reassure her. "Her ladyship has used the room up the end of the corridor on the right for years now."

Amelia's shoulders relaxed. "Good. I wouldn't want to make her uncomfortable in her own home."

"It's your home, too, now," Andrew reminded her.

Her smile turned wry. "I suppose it is."

Andrew gestured at the door. "Go ahead, Mrs. Smythe."

The housekeeper pushed the door open and held it for them to enter. Andrew gazed around the room, hoping it would meet Amelia's expectations.

The bed was large, with a rich red covering. The wardrobe, which was against the wall opposite the foot of the bed, was spacious and well taken care of despite its age.

Her dresses had already been unpacked into it, as had the rest of her belongings, and those that remained were stacked in bags and boxes against the nearest wall.

There was a small dressing table with a mirror to the right of the wardrobe, and on the far side of the room, beside windows hung with ruby-hued drapes, stood an ornately carved writing desk. He'd had it moved there from the library and furnished with a fresh supply of paper, ink, and a seal to indicate her position as the Countess of Longley.

Amelia wandered toward the desk, her gaze locked on it. "This is for me?"

"Yes. I hope it meets your needs."

She ran her finger along the wood. "It is… exquisite. Thank you, my lord."

He checked to ensure that Mrs. Smythe had left them and they were now alone. "None of that. You may call me Andrew."

She glanced back at him, a smile flitting across her lips. "Andrew is a nice name. Strong. Kind. It suits you."

His heart gave an extra thump. "May I call you Amelia?"

She nodded. "If you wish."

"I do." He moved toward her and reached for her hand. "I know this arrangement of ours is for convenience, but I hope we can be friends. I would infinitely prefer that to being strangers who live together."

She searched his eyes. "As would I."

His throat tightened, and he coughed to clear it. "Then friends it will be." He hesitated. "I'm going to leave you here to get settled, but before I go, is there anything you need or would like to know?"

She nibbled on her lower lip, all the confidence draining out of her. "Uh… will I be fulfilling my wifely duty tonight?"

CHAPTER 14

Amelia twisted her hands in her skirt, anxious to hear Andrew's response.

He blinked at her rapidly, obviously taken by surprise. "There's no rush to consummate the marriage. We can take some time to get comfortable with each other."

The tightness in her chest loosened, but a nasty voice in the back of her mind whispered that he wasn't really offering a reprieve for the sake of her comfort, but because he wasn't attracted to her.

She did her best to ignore that thought, but then another struck her. Her mother would not be pleased if she delayed the consummation of their marriage.

She gritted her teeth. Her mother didn't get to have an opinion. Amelia was married now, and according to the terms of their marriage agreement, the only opinion that mattered was her own—and wasn't that a novelty?

She smiled. "Thank you for your thoughtfulness."

"You're welcome." His eyebrows pinched together, and he opened his mouth as if to ask her something, but then closed it again, clearly thinking better of it.

"Has a maid been assigned to me?" she asked.

"Not yet." He studied her closely. "You can either share a maid with my sister, hire one of your own choosing, or select one from among the housemaids. Which would you prefer?"

She considered briefly. It would be nice to have her own maid, but she didn't intend to participate in societal events often, so any maid she employed would likely be bored most of the time if they had no other duties.

"Will it upset your sister if we share?" She didn't want to create any friction between them when they'd only just met for the first time hours earlier.

"Not at all." He tilted his head. "Kate doesn't have much cause to go out, so caring for both of you won't be too much of a burden for her maid, Margaret."

"Then I will share." At least for now. She could reassess once she had a better idea of how the household functioned.

He backed toward the door. "I'll send Margaret in."

"Thank you, Andrew."

He flashed his teeth. "You are very welcome, Amelia."

With that, he left the room, a jaunty swing in his step. She laughed to herself. Of course he was in a good mood. His family's fortune was significantly improved, compared to what it had been yesterday.

Perching on the edge of the bed, she was surprised to find the mattress much softer than her one at home.

No, not home. Her parents' house. This was home now.

She wished she could lie back and close her eyes but feared that if she tried, the dress would tear at the seams. It didn't seem the type of ensemble that would handle much strain.

Light footsteps tapped down the corridor outside, and then a woman perhaps a few years older than Amelia entered the room and curtsied deeply. She was petite, with dark hair and a freckled face. Amelia recalled being introduced to her outside, although she might not have remembered her name if Andrew hadn't mentioned it.

"My lady." She rose but kept her eyes on the floor. "His lordship said you're in need of my services."

Amelia clambered to her feet. "Thank you for coming, Margaret. I'd so appreciate it if you'd help me get out of this gown. I feel like I can't breathe properly with it on."

She turned her back to Margaret, and the maid started loosening the ties. The pressure on Amelia's rib cage eased bit by bit until the gown slipped from her shoulders. She stepped out of it, and Margaret swept it out of the way.

"Would you like your hair undone too?" Margaret asked.

"That would be lovely." Amelia padded to the chair in front of the dressing table and sat. While Margaret searched for a hairbrush, Amelia leaned closer to the mirror and carefully extricated the tiara from her hair. She set it on the table, far enough away that neither of them would accidentally knock it.

"It's a beautiful tiara," Margaret said wistfully. "I've never seen one like it."

No, Amelia imagined she hadn't. Aristocratic women only tended to wear their best jewelry for royal appearances or weddings.

"It was a wedding gift from my parents," she said.

Margaret set a hairbrush on the table and stood behind Amelia. She bent her dark head and began to remove the jeweled hairpins one by one. Locks of hair fell around Amelia's shoulders. Her scalp tingled, and she resisted the urge to scratch it.

When they were all out, Margaret brushed her hair until it shone.

"Would you like to leave it loose?" she asked.

Amelia cocked her head, examining her reflection. "Yes, I think so."

Here, there was no Mrs. Hart to chide her for failing to appear at dinner in appropriate attire. She could choose to wear her hair down or simply tie it back if she wanted to.

Margaret moved away, and Amelia pushed the chair back. "Before you leave, can you help me into a day dress?"

"Of course."

The maid assisted her into a pale blue day dress and then departed with another curtsy and a polite farewell.

As soon as Amelia was certain she was alone, she searched the room until she found her copy of the signed marriage agreement. She carried it to the writing desk, which bore a small lock with a key attached, and locked it inside.

From what she had seen of Andrew, she believed that he would honor their agreement and she wouldn't ever have to attempt to legally enforce it—if the courts would even uphold such a thing—but it was best to have it stored somewhere safe just in case.

Next, she went looking for her tidiest copy of Miss Joceline Davies's first adventure. She stacked it neatly on one side of the writing desk, sat, and penned a letter to one of the publishing companies she had previously researched.

Her new stationary was slightly different than what she was used to, and she had to rewrite the letter twice before it was neat enough to satisfy her.

That done, she tied the letter to the front of the stack of papers and wrapped them, sealing the bundle with the Longley crest and jotting the publisher's address on the front.

Then, with as straight a face as possible, she carried the package downstairs and asked Mrs. Smythe to ensure it was sent posthaste. The housekeeper didn't even question her. She just smiled, nodded, and said it would be done first thing tomorrow.

On the way back up the stairs, Amelia stifled a giggle. She felt giddy inside. Light, joyful, and years younger.

She'd submitted a work of fiction to a publisher.

There was no way she'd have been able to do that as Miss

Amelia Hart, but no one would stop the Countess of Longley.

Even if the publisher wasn't interested, she could try again. And again. If she so desired, she could choose to dedicate every day to exploring strange new worlds with Joceline.

Nobody would shout at her if she got distracted at her desk or if her hands were stained with ink. No one would make her feel inferior because of how she liked to spend her time.

She breezed into her new bedchamber, collapsed onto the bed, and grinned up at the ceiling. Her first taste of freedom was every bit as wonderful as she'd dreamed.

Closing her eyes, she finally allowed her mind to quieten. The day had been hectic from beginning to end. She'd been primped to within an inch of her life, had to speak in front of a huge audience, and then engaged in pointless small talk with dozens of people—many of whom knew next to nothing about her.

But this made everything worth it.

She had privacy, blessed silence, and at least a modicum of control over her own destiny.

With more than a little glee, she decided that it was well within her rights to pass the rest of the afternoon lying on the bed and reading a semi-autobiographical adventure novel written by a missionary who'd sailed to the Indian subcontinent and lived there for several years.

When she was called for dinner, she did not summon Margaret to dress her hair, nor did she change into a more formal gown. She took herself straight to the dining hall, only to discover that it was empty.

"There you are."

She spun around. Andrew stood behind her, clad in a long-sleeved shirt and trousers, without the many accouterments he'd worn for their wedding.

"I prefer to eat in the morning room." He grinned sheepishly. "I know it's unconventional, but we have a small dining table in the corner, and it's much more pleasant than using the formal dining hall."

A slow smile spread across Amelia's face. "That sounds perfect."

"I hoped you would think so." He offered her his arm. "My lady."

She almost glanced over her shoulder and then laughed. "That will take some getting used to."

He led her into the corridor and one door down to the morning room they'd briefly paused in earlier. Amelia hadn't noticed many of the details at the time, too overwhelmed by everything that had happened during the day, but now she paused to take them in.

The wallpaper was forest green with a gold pattern. The drapes were also green, and as Andrew had said, a square table large enough to seat four people was located in the corner of the room.

A plate of bread rolls in the center of the table gave off a yeasty aroma that made her mouth water. A covered plate was positioned on each side of the table.

Andrew pulled out the chair farthest from the wall for her, and she sat. He took the seat opposite. A maid entered the room and removed the covering from each plate. Andrew thanked her, and she left as silently as she'd arrived.

"There's more if you're hungry," he said, picking up his cutlery. "It's simple fare this evening, since we had such a rich meal earlier."

Amelia did the same. She'd been served a bowl of beef stew and a side plate of potatoes, beans, and peas. "I didn't eat much earlier, and this looks delicious."

"Mrs. Baker is a wonder in the kitchen."

She waited for him to take a bread roll before following suit. He didn't seem like an overly traditional man, but it was best not to assume such things. She broke the bread roll open, dunked it in the stew, and tore off a bite. The bread was soft and warm, the stew flavorsome.

"Oh, that's good," she murmured.

He smirked. "I told you so."

They both ate ravenously, without pausing for conversation other than mutual appreciation of their meal. When their plates were clean, the maid cleared them away and returned with two servings of rhubarb fool.

Amelia patted her tummy. She was reasonably full but could definitely make room for dessert. "You are spoiling me."

He flashed that crooked incisor. "Isn't that what husbands are supposed to do?"

"I have no complaints." She scooped out a blob of cream and rhubarb and tasted it, closing her eyes to savor the slight tartness combined with sweetness.

He made a sound in the back of his throat. "You like dessert, then?"

"Doesn't everyone?" She paused to take a drink. "I'm not addicted to sweets, if that's what you mean, but I enjoy good food in whatever form it comes."

He tipped his head toward her. "Just as you enjoy writing."

She looked at him questioningly, and he nodded toward her hand. "There's a smudge of ink. I assume you were writing something before dinner. Will you tell me more about that?"

Amelia hesitated. Technically, her letter to the publisher wouldn't leave the house until tomorrow. If she told him the full truth and he disapproved, he could stop it.

She bit her lip. Honestly, she didn't think he would interfere. The earl—Andrew—struck her as a man of honor. Besides, it might be best for him to know now rather than discover further down the track.

"I've written a novel," she told him, her pulse thundering like mad at the base of her throat. "About a young woman who gets stranded abroad in the jungle after the ship she's traveling on goes down in a storm."

He stopped eating, his lips parted in surprise, his twinkling hazel eyes focused on her. "Go on."

So she told him everything.

After a while, he began to smile, and by the time she finished, he was beaming.

"That's incredible." He shook his head. "I can't believe I married such a talented woman."

Amelia's heart lifted. "You don't disapprove?"

He frowned. "Disapprove? You've written a novel. Do you know how many gentlemen of my acquaintance have talked of doing such a thing? Yet none of them have accomplished it, and you have."

She ducked her head shyly. "It's not as if it's been published yet though. They may not be interested."

"They will be." He laid his hand on hers atop the table. "I have faith in you."

Her stomach flipped over, and the strength of her emotions made it difficult to speak. She hadn't dared to dream he would react so positively. Was this how it felt to be supported wholeheartedly?

It seemed she had gotten luckier in the marriage game than she ever could have imagined.

∽

THE FOLLOWING MORNING, ANDREW SHARED A PLEASANT breakfast with his new wife in the morning room. She served him tea, adding sugar just as he liked, and in return, he filled a plate for her with egg, toast, and sausage.

He was more at ease than he had been in weeks as he snuck glances at her across the table. Everything was coming together. Her dowry had been transferred to his account, and he could already tell that they would be well suited together. She was intelligent and ambitious—two things he admired even if he didn't share the same traits.

She was also rather pretty.

He'd always thought her nice to look at even though she didn't meet the ton's typical standards of beauty, but as she cut her toast with a secret smile on her lips and a flush on her cheeks, he'd challenge any man not to find her attractive.

"What do you intend to do today?" he asked.

Her knife chinked against the plate. "The past few days have been overwhelming, so today I intend to do nothing but read."

He chuckled. He ought to have expected as much. "You should explore the library."

Her eyes lit up. "I will. Are there any sections you would particularly recommend?"

He squinted, envisioning the library. "The fiction books are mostly along the side wall. The others are arranged by subject. They aren't labeled, but it won't take you long to work out what's what."

"Excellent. Not that I would mind the opportunity to explore anyway."

He almost laughed. Of course she wouldn't. He'd married a woman who was perfectly capable of entertaining herself. She had her own interests. Her own hobbies.

While that may make some gentlemen feel superfluous, he found it freeing because it meant her happiness wasn't dependent on him. There was no pressure on him to keep her occupied.

They chatted as they finished breakfast, and then Andrew took a carriage to Ashford House. The duke received him in his office, where they were both more comfortable than in the drawing room.

"How is married life treating you?" Ashford asked as his housekeeper poured them each a cup of tea.

"So far, so good." Andrew took the teacup and blew across the surface. "My wife is quite an unusual woman, but I like that about her."

Ashford set his teacup on the desk to cool. "I get the impression that she and Emma would get along well. I was sincere about my invitation. When you leave London, you should consider visiting Ashford Hall. I'm sure Emma would appreciate having another woman to spend some time with."

"We'll do that." He didn't know whether Amelia had any friends within the ton. He'd never seen her speaking with any other young ladies in particular, nor had she mentioned anyone during their acquaintance. "Thank you for coming. I know it must have been difficult for you to leave home again so soon."

Ashford glanced away, no doubt uncomfortable talking about anything that might be termed emotional. "I wouldn't have missed it. I can't deny that I'm eager to return, though."

"I'm glad you've found someone who makes you happy," Andrew said. His friend had spent too many years lonely. He deserved better. "Before you leave, may I ask your opinion on a few matters of business?"

Ashford leaned back in his chair and crossed his ankles. "Of course."

Andrew sipped his tea and winced. Still hot. He placed it on the desk and rested his forearms on his thighs. "I will be speaking with Amelia's father about hiring someone to manage our money, but I'd like to take some ideas to him when I do. I don't want to just take Amelia's dowry and live off it. I want to grow it."

Ashford inclined his head. "You want investment advice?"

Andrew waved his hand back and forth. "Possibly. I have some ideas I'd like to run past you. To be honest, I feel guilty at the idea of spending money that is effectively my wife's, and I want to do everything I can to make sure I don't lose it. I refuse to be a bad husband to her."

"That makes sense." Ashford eyed him in a way that made Andrew nervous. "I can understand your concern, given what happened with Mr. Smith. What are you thinking of?"

Andrew set forth his plans, beginning with the safest option: mining. Mr. Hart had made much of his own fortune from mining; ergo, it stood to reason that he would approve an investment in that area.

But Andrew was less sure whether he'd consider his second investment idea to be sensible. An inventor was working on a mechanical plow that would not require a horse to pull it. If his work was successful, it could revolutionize cropping in England. But it was a big "if."

In the end, Ashford didn't have any useful perspective to offer on the matter beyond the possible benefits and concerns that Andrew had already thought of himself. He supposed he would simply have to ask for Mr. Hart's thoughts on the matter.

He drained his tea in a few gulps and refilled his now empty teacup with lukewarm tea. "I also want to do something to show Amelia how much I appreciate her. Something that's just for her."

"Ah, yes." Ashford steepled his hands. "After we received the letter advising us of your engagement, Emma and I discussed what you could do to show her that you care about her as more than a source of wealth. The countess likes to read, correct?"

Andrew nodded.

"There's a bookshop that I once took Emma to. It's owned by a female proprietress, and Emma enjoyed her time there immensely. Perhaps Amelia would like it too."

"That's perfect." Andrew straightened. "Give me the address. It's about time I spoil my wife."

CHAPTER 15

Joceline grabbed hold of the railing, struggling not to go overboard as droplets of water stung her face and waves buffeted the side of the ship, tossing it about like flotsam. She couldn't help but recall a night like this many months ago, when...

Amelia's quill froze in place as a quiet knock interrupted her stream of thought. Irritation flared. She'd secluded herself in the library and had been deep into a scene. She was reluctant to return to the real world. Unfortunately, the knock repeated, and then the door cracked open.

"Amelia?" It was her husband's voice.

She placed the quill on its holder and angled herself toward the door. "Yes, my lord?"

His head came around the opening, and his infectious grin made it impossible for her to remain irritated. "Are you busy?"

She considered. "That depends on what you're here for."

She was enjoying the opportunity to write, but it was also important that she maintain a good relationship with him as much as possible, so she would humor him if she could.

He stepped inside, and she noted that he was dressed to

leave the house. "There is a bookshop Ashford told me about. I wondered if you might like to visit it with me."

"Oh yes, please!" She leapt to her feet. "Now?"

He chuckled. "If it suits."

"It's always a good time to shop for books. Just let me get a pelisse and put on some decent walking shoes."

He sat on one of two green chaises. "I'll be waiting here."

She hurried to her bedchamber, her heart warm as the ramifications of what they were doing completely sank in. The earl didn't have to spoil her in such a way any longer. He had her money. Yet he'd chosen to invite her somewhere she would enjoy anyway.

But then the warmth dissipated as she chose a pale blue pelisse from her wardrobe and swapped her shoes. Perhaps he wasn't doing this to please her, but rather out of guilt.

That made more sense.

He'd married her for her father's fortune, but he was a decent man and felt bad about it. Ergo, he was doing what he could to make it up to her.

She sighed. It was a nice gesture, but she couldn't help wishing it came from a different place.

She met Andrew in the drawing room, and they walked arm in arm through the foyer and out to where one of the carriages bearing the Longley crest awaited. He helped her up the step into the carriage and climbed in behind her.

"Is it far?" she asked, sitting on the bench at the rear of the carriage. To her surprise, he slid onto the bench beside her rather than sitting opposite.

"I don't think so." He turned toward her slightly. "I haven't been there before."

"That's right. You said the Duke of Ashford told you about it." She'd forgotten that, too excited about visiting a bookshop to pay attention to the details.

For as long as she'd been alive, her father had possessed enough money to buy her all the books she wanted, but it had become increasingly difficult for her to get her hands on them in recent years because her mother considered reading an inappropriate pastime for a young lady.

Now, her new husband was not only allowing her to buy books but was supporting her in the endeavor. She smiled to herself. Whether or not the shopping expedition was a product of guilt, it meant something that he was willing to indulge her. She'd chosen well when she'd asked him to be her husband.

Amelia watched the scenery through the window. They'd entered one of the more popular shopping districts and had almost passed through it when the carriage pulled over outside a stone building with a sign attached to the roof that read "Babbington Books."

Andrew got out first and assisted her down. She peered through the window as he led her toward the building. Rows of shelves ran from the front window deep into the shop.

"Are you sure I'm welcome here?" she asked.

Not all bookstores liked female patrons.

He grinned. "Quite. You'll see what I mean once we're inside."

Intrigued, she allowed him to guide her through the doorway. A bell tinkled, and a curvaceous woman with long, dark hair appeared in front of them.

"Welcome to Babbington's," she said. "May I help you?"

Amelia's jaw dropped. "Do you work here?"

The woman smoothed her hands down her dress. "This is my shop."

"It's wonderful," Amelia breathed. "I can already tell I'm going to love it."

The proprietress smiled. "I hope so."

"I'm Mi—Lady Longley," she corrected herself. "This is my husband, the Earl of Longley."

The proprietress curtsied. "A pleasure to meet you, my

lady. I'm Mrs. Babbington. Are you looking for anything in particular?"

"I love to read," Amelia admitted. "Tales of adventure, in particular."

Andrew nudged her. "You do more than just read."

Her cheeks heated, and she darted a look at him. He wasn't suggesting she disclose her writing habit, was he? He'd implied that he wouldn't be embarrassed by her behavior, but she hadn't dared imagine he'd encourage her to discuss it with others.

Nibbling on her lower lip, she tried to quell the nerves rioting through her. "I'm a writer too." The statement was almost whispered. "I recently submitted an adventure novel to a publisher. The protagonist is a woman."

Mrs. Babbington's face lit up, her dark eyes dancing with excitement. "How wonderful. I hope they accept it. I would love to read it."

Amelia shifted her weight. "Really?"

Mrs. Babbington nodded. "So many adventure stories are for men. It's about time we women had one, isn't it?"

"Exactly my thinking!"

"Tell me more about your story."

Amelia launched into a recounting of the highlights. Mrs. Babbington peppered her with intelligent questions, her eyes gleaming with interest.

Before she realized it, an hour had passed, and they were still hovering in the aisle between the shelves. Andrew stood silently beside them, having uttered very little since their conversation began.

Oh dear. They'd probably bored him out of his wits.

"I'm so sorry," she said, turning to him. "I'm afraid that time got away from me."

Mrs. Babbington's eyes widened as she also checked the clock. "I've monopolized you terribly. My apologies, Lord Longley."

But Andrew just shook his head, his expression completely unbothered. "I've enjoyed listening to you. Please don't rush on my account."

Mrs. Babbington's skirts swished as she paced farther down the aisle. "Let me show you some books I think you'll like."

With a quick glance to make sure that her husband wasn't upset, Amelia followed her.

Once again, it was all too easy for them to get lost in discussion of their favorite books. When she and Andrew emerged into daylight a while later, he was carrying a stack of books that were wrapped in paper for the journey, including her own brand-new illustrated world atlas, since she'd had to leave her parents' one at their home.

They'd declined having them delivered because she simply couldn't bear to part with them. Even though she knew her own money had bought these books, she still felt spoiled as Andrew stacked them on the bench in the carriage and rested his hand atop them to ensure they didn't fall over during the ride.

"Can I interest you in getting a piece of cake and a cup of tea before we return home?" he asked, linking his arm with hers.

She gazed at him, noting the light spattering of freckles over his nose and the flecks of green in his eyes. "Haven't I taken up enough of your time?"

"Not at all." He flashed his teeth at her. "Besides, I find myself hungry for something sweet. What do you say?"

She hesitated, then nodded. "I'd like that."

He knocked against the wall and leaned out the window to call something to their driver. When he sat back again, the tip of his nose was slightly pink from the chill outside.

"So, you adore bookshops," he said, his knees spreading as he got comfortable. "What else do you like to do?"

She side-eyed him. "I'm afraid I'm not complicated, my lord."

"Andrew."

"Andrew," she repeated. "As I've said, I like to read, write, and learn. Anything that facilitates those pursuits is something I'll enjoy."

"Hm."

He didn't ask her more, and as they rode in a comfortable silence, she couldn't help wondering what was preoccupying his mind. He never reacted as she expected, which meant he must think differently too.

Before long, they stopped outside a teahouse in one of Mayfair's busiest streets. Through the window, she could see well-dressed ladies and gentlemen seated at the small, round tables inside. She'd been here before with her mother, and it was definitely a place to see and be seen.

Thankfully, they also made a delicious lemon cake.

Andrew escorted her inside, and a server hurried to seat them near the window. Amelia hid her smile. She was accustomed to being seated near the back. Now, as a countess, she was someone to be flashed in front of others to entice them in.

Andrew pulled out her chair and waited for her to sit. They each ordered tea and a slice of cake—lemon for her and a vanilla sponge for him.

His hand brushed hers across the table, and sparks skittered up her arm. She allowed her fingers to rest against his, although the display of affection didn't come easily. At least, not to her. He seemed perfectly content to shower her with casual touches that left her nerves alight and eager for more.

Was it intentional?

It was impossible to know for sure, but the more closely she paid attention to him, the more she realized that he didn't even seem to notice that he was doing it. Physical affection was simple for him. It didn't require careful planning or consideration of the reasons why it may or may not be a good idea. It's just how he was.

She wasn't sure whether to like that or mistrust it. On the one hand, she couldn't deny that his touches felt good. She liked them too much for her own peace of mind. But on the other hand, if he was comfortable casually brushing up against women, did that mean he'd done it so many times in the past that he was immune?

He had a bit of a reputation as a charming rogue—although his reputation was far from the worst among the ton. At least he'd never led any debutantes astray. But how many other women had he been intimate with?

Stop it, she scolded herself. *It's none of your business. Fidelity is not part of your agreement. You have no right to question him on such a matter.*

The server returned with a gleaming silver tray, which she set in the center of the table. With steady hands, she poured tea for each of them and doctored it to their preferences; then she placed a slice of cake in front of each of them.

"Thank you," Amelia murmured.

The server dipped her head and backed away.

Amelia used a fork to separate off a morsel of cake and popped it into her mouth. The delicious combination of sweet and tart flavors danced on her tongue, and she closed her eyes to savor them. Once she'd swallowed, she opened her eyes and found Andrew's gaze burning into her, his eyes darker than usual.

She blinked, surprised. "I—"

"If it isn't the Earl of Longley."

Amelia jerked in her seat, her heart leaping. She'd been so absorbed that she hadn't noticed the woman approach. She spun toward her so quickly, the seat squeaked against the floor.

"Miss Giles." Andrew's tone was uncharacteristically cold as he looked over Amelia's shoulder. "What a surprise."

The woman smirked, her plump lips twisting in a way that unsettled Amelia. "I imagine it is. I could hardly believe my eyes when I looked up from my scone and saw you sitting mere yards away."

"I'm afraid I didn't notice you when we entered," he said. "Otherwise I would have taken my wife elsewhere."

Amelia frowned. That wasn't very polite. "Hello. I'm Lady Longley. And you are…?"

The woman's dark blue eyes flitted to Amelia, and her smirk deepened. "I'm Miss Florence Giles." With one elegant hand, she brushed a strand of wheat-blond hair off her forehead. "An old friend of Andrew's."

"It's a pleasure to meet you." Amelia forced herself to smile. "Did you grow up together?"

Because despite what Miss Giles said about them being friends, Andrew obviously wasn't pleased by her presence. In fact, she'd go as far as to say that he wished her gone. Yet Miss Giles was familiar enough to call him by his given name.

"Something like that." Amusement shone in her eyes. "I'll leave you to enjoy your cake."

With that, she sashayed away.

Amelia no longer felt like eating cake. She tried another bite, but chewing was difficult, and swallowing proved almost impossible. Andrew, too, had lost his appetite. They departed soon after.

When they were alone in the carriage, she allowed the question burning in her chest to come out. "Who was that woman?"

She studied his face closely. His mouth tightened almost imperceptibly, and a slight furrow formed between his eyebrows.

"No one you need to worry yourself about."

ANDREW STEWED IN SILENT RAGE THROUGHOUT THE REST OF the day. He could tell Amelia knew something was wrong and that it was connected to Florence, but she hadn't pushed him to talk about it after her initial question.

By the time they'd finished their dinner, he'd had a very disapproving Boden obtain Florence's new address. He was beyond ready to let her know exactly how angry he was with her.

He took a carriage to her apartment, inquired as to her floor, then marched up and rapped on her door. It took forever for her to answer, and when she did, she didn't bother speaking. She grabbed him by the lapel, tugged him into the room, and tried to kiss him.

He dodged and extricated himself from her grasp briskly but not roughly. No matter how furious he was, he wouldn't hurt her.

She pouted. "No kiss for me?"

He exhaled sharply. "What the hell were you thinking today? You approached me when I was out with my wife. My wife."

"Wasn't it fun?" she asked, a mischievous smile flitting around the corners of her mouth. "I know you enjoyed having me right under her nose."

He felt sick. "I can tell you with one hundred percent certainty that I did not enjoy it."

She slunk toward him, and he backed away, putting a chaise between them.

Her upper lip curled. "Don't be so miserable. It's not as if she had any idea who I was."

"But what if she did?" His heart squeezed. The possibility that Amelia might have guessed how he knew Florence made his stomach roil. She'd given him so much. She deserved better than having his former mistress flaunted in front of her.

She shrugged. "Aristocratic wives expect their husbands to stray."

"Not two days after the wedding." For the love of God, did she not see how wrong her behavior was?

She crinkled her nose. "You're being unusually sentimental. Don't forget, I know how the ton operates better than most. Or have you forgotten the circumstances of my birth?" Her tone was bitter. "Besides, it's not as if it was a love match."

Guilt sank its claws into him.

"Perhaps not," he said stiffly. "But I care about her."

She laughed incredulously. "That plain little mouse?"

"Watch your tongue, Florence."

Her hips rolled as she sauntered to the end of the chaise, attempting to round it to get to him. "Surely you don't desire her. Your timid wife can't do the things to you that I can."

He bit the inside of his lip to rein in the retort that immediately came to his tongue. He did desire Amelia. He may not love her, but he liked her, and once she was ready, he looked forward to bedding her.

Telling Florence that would help nothing. She was motivated by competition, not put off by it.

"Our affair is over." His tone brooked no argument. "I made it clear that you need to seek protection elsewhere."

Her eyes widened as if he had genuinely surprised her, but she hid it quickly. "You're married now. You have money. We can continue as we were."

Andrew pursed his lips. The heat of his anger had faded, although the frustration remained. He couldn't help but feel that this was partly his fault. Perhaps he hadn't been firm enough with her when he ended their arrangement. He hadn't wanted to hurt her, just as he didn't want to hurt her now.

Whatever their reasons, they'd been intimate with each other, and he'd enjoyed her company. He hated the idea of causing her pain. But he had to put Amelia first.

"I won't use my wife's dowry to pay to keep a mistress." He straightened his back. "It wouldn't be right. She deserves better."

"I deserve better," she interjected. "You used me and cast me aside when you were done with me."

The blade of guilt twisted. It was an accurate, if somewhat unfair, accusation.

"I'm sorry for that. But you knew from the beginning that what we had wouldn't last. I enjoyed it, and perhaps you did, too, but it's over now. If you need a one-off payment while you get back on your feet, I'll consider it, but tell me now, and then don't approach me again."

She gritted her teeth. "You're actually choosing her over me?"

"She's my wife." Surely, that should say it all.

"Keep the mouse's money." She turned her back on him. "You can see yourself out. But just know, you'll regret this."

CHAPTER 16

"May I join you?"

Amelia glanced toward the library entrance, where Kate hovered, gripping the handle of a small basket. "Please do."

Kate padded through the doorway and sat on a chair beside one of the small windows. "Will it bother you if I do needlework while you read?"

"Of course not." Amelia marked her page with a blue ribbon and closed the book. "What are you making?"

Tucking a loose lock of reddish-blond hair behind her ear, Kate offered a tentative smile. "Last time we were in Suffolk, I painted a watercolor of the front garden at dusk. Now, I'm re-creating the image as a needlepoint design, which will last longer, if I can get it right."

"I'm certain you'll do it justice," she said, debating whether or not showing more interest would make Kate uncomfortable. "May I see the painting?"

Kate reached into the basket, withdrew a leatherbound volume and opened it, carefully withdrawing a slip of nearly translucent paper from within. She carried it across to where Amelia sat and offered it to her.

Amelia's breath caught. "It's stunning."

Kate had perfectly captured the play of golden light and shadows over the flowers while maintaining a sense of the ethereal, as if the scene had been too beautiful for this world.

"You are very talented." She could scarcely tear her eyes from the painting, but managed to do so just in time to see a blush form across Kate's cheeks.

Kate ducked her head. "I'm passably good."

"No." Amelia's tone was firm. "This is gorgeous. You have real skill, and an eye for how to make colors work together."

Personally, she'd never been particularly good at anything artistic, but she recognized genuine talent when she saw it.

Kate slid the painting back between the pages of the book and gently closed it. "Thank you." She fidgeted, as though uncomfortable with the praise. "I've always liked working with colors, whether it's painting, needlepoint, or pairing different fabric types for new outfits."

"You do have an exceptionally smart wardrobe." Amelia had thought the credit for that could be laid at Lady Drake's feet—or perhaps their modiste's—but now she began to wonder.

"Thank you." Kate brightened and raised her head, excitement gleaming in the pale gray of her eyes. "I enjoy following fashion. Mother often allows me to choose which fabrics to pair, and how to accessorize my dresses, but sometimes she refuses to allow me to select a certain combination because it would be too daring or bold for someone who is not even out in society yet."

Amelia grimaced. She understood Lady Drake's reluctance to allow anything that may attract unwanted attention to her youngest child. Still, women had so few choices that she sympathized with Kate's desire to choose what to put on her own body.

"One day, you will be able to choose whichever fabrics you like," she said. "For now, you must listen to your mother. I'm sure she has reasons for her decisions."

Kate cocked her head. "But once I'm married, won't my husband make those choices?"

Amelia felt a pang. For so many women, that was true. "Then you'll have to make sure to marry someone who values your happiness."

"Like Andrew values yours?" she asked, her wide eyes innocent.

Another pang. While it was true that Andrew did his best by her, their marriage wasn't exactly what she would wish for Kate.

"A letter has arrived for you, my lady."

She spun toward Boden, her hand flying to her chest. She hadn't heard him arrive. She drew in a deep breath to calm herself, and some of the tension eased from her shoulders. He may have startled her, but he'd also saved her from answering a question she didn't feel entirely qualified to address.

She rose, crossed the room, and took the letter from him. "Thank you, Boden."

"My pleasure, my lady." He bowed and backed out.

She carried the letter to the chaise and studied the seal on the back. She didn't recognize it.

"Who is it from?" Kate asked, setting aside the leather-bound volume containing her painting and sitting on the other end of the chaise.

"I'm not certain." She didn't usually receive mail, since she rarely sent correspondence, so her insides were alive with curiosity as she broke the seal and opened the letter.

She unfolded the paper and read.

To the Countess of Longley,

Many thanks for submitting your manuscript, Stranded: Part 1 of the Adventures of Miss Joceline Davies, for consideration.

After much deliberation, we have decided to accept your submission—provided we come to an agreement on some minor editorial changes.

If you wish to proceed, please write back to advise us of your availability to meet and make arrangements for the publication of Stranded.

We are also interested in procuring further parts of Miss Davies's adventures, if you have them available. We can speak on the matter when we meet in person.

Sincerely,

Mr. Thomas Newton, Editor in Chief

Oh heavens.

Her breath hitched, and she hurried to reread the letter.

"What is it?" Kate asked urgently.

Amelia squealed, gripping the edges of the paper so tightly, they crumpled. "They said yes."

She could hardly believe it. She'd dreamed—fantasized, really—but deep down, she'd feared she'd spend her life scribbling for the entertainment of no one other than herself. Not that doing so would be terrible, but this was infinitely better.

"Who did?" Kate sounded confused.

Amelia beamed. "Joceline's stories are going to be in print."

Other women would be able to read them. She could inspire them to wonder about the wide, wide world. Her jaw ached, and she realized she was grinning so widely, it hurt. Clutching the letter, she jumped up and danced on the spot.

"Really?" Kate rose, a smile stretching her mouth.

"Really."

She was going to be a published author.

Her.

Boring old Amelia, with rich parents but nothing else to recommend her. It was incredible.

"That's wonderful!" Kate reached for her, as if to hug her, but hesitated.

With no such qualms, Amelia drew her into an embrace,

bouncing on the balls of her feet, her heart so light, she felt as though she could float away.

"One of my stories is going to be a book," she cried, releasing Kate.

Kate giggled, her face alight with glee. "Congratulations. I don't read a lot, but I want you to tell me all about it."

"Soon. First, I must tell the earl." Amelia skipped away from Kate and into the corridor. She bounded down the stairs and around the corner to Andrew's office. There were no footfalls behind her, so she assumed Kate had gone to break the news to Lady Drake.

She paused at the door, suddenly realizing he might not want her interrupting him in the midst of his work. They'd been getting along well over the previous month, but she couldn't take anything for granted—especially not something that would have sent her mother into a fit of vapors.

Just because Andrew had been supportive thus far did not necessarily mean his attitude would continue.

"Come in," he called before she'd even decided whether to knock. "I can hear you out there. You weren't very quiet as you came down the hall."

Rolling her eyes at her own silliness, Amelia pushed the door open and stepped inside. However he reacted, Andrew needed to know. There was no point putting it off.

"I have news," she declared, her jaw still aching from the constant smile. It hadn't wavered even in the face of her nerves.

He cocked his head. "Good news, I take it?"

"The best." She couldn't resist wiggling on the spot. "My novel is to be published."

He smiled and got to his feet. "Congratulations. I agree, that is the best news we could have received."

He took a few steps forward and folded her into an embrace. She froze, painstakingly aware of every single place where they touched.

This was the first time she'd been this close to a male body—other than her father's. Awkwardly, she circled her arms around him and hugged him back.

His lips brushed her temple. "I'm so proud of you. You've worked hard for this."

"Thank you," she whispered, tears of joy stinging her eyes.

It meant everything that his support didn't waver when her dreams became reality. Lord, she'd been so lucky to end up married to him. She'd never have received such acceptance at her parents' home.

She melted against him, reveling in the firmness of his chest and the way his subtle masculine scent—a combination of bergamot and cinnamon—wrapped around her.

A laugh rumbled from him. "What are you thanking me for? You're the one who put in all the time and effort."

She pressed her lips together, fending off a wave of tenderness toward him. She couldn't afford to feel too much for him. That would only end in heartache.

"You haven't asked me to stop," she murmured, drawing back reluctantly. If she indulged in him too much, she'd never be able to control herself around him. "You haven't belittled me or made me feel like something about me is wrong. You just accept me as I am."

His family did too. Or at least, they didn't treat her as though something was wrong with her because of her dreams and ambitions, or how she liked to spend her time.

He pulled her into another quick, firm embrace. "I happen to like who you are. I don't need any kind of thanks for that."

Butterflies fluttered in her stomach, and she warmed inside. Why did he have to make it so difficult to remember that they were, at best, friends who'd married for the sake of convenience?

"They want more too." She couldn't dwell on her

simmering attraction to her husband. "They've asked if I have more stories about Joceline."

"And do you?"

"Nothing quite as long as the one I sent them, but I have a few, and I'm working on another." How exciting would it be if she had not only one book published but a multipart collection of Joceline's adventures?

"Excellent." He looked down at his hands, his expression turning uncharacteristically shy. "I'd like to read them sometime, if that's all right with you?"

She sucked in a breath. "Really?"

She'd never imagined he'd be that interested in her work.

"Of course." He frowned as if the question was ludicrous. "You were willing to make a massive life change to dedicate yourself to pursuing your craft. Why wouldn't I want to know more about something that means so much to you?"

Her heart couldn't take this. Honestly. Why did he have to be so thoughtful?

"Very well," she said quietly. "I have a copy in my bedchamber that you can read. I'll get it for you."

"You do that." He grinned. "And then you and I are going to Babbington's. This calls for a celebration."

~

That evening, Andrew was sprawled on a chair in the library, reading Amelia's manuscript—and being entirely impressed by her talent and thoroughness—when Boden announced that Mr. Fisher was waiting to speak with him in the drawing room.

His gut flipped over. He had no idea whether Mr. Fisher's visit was a good sign or a bad one. Perhaps Mr. Smith had been apprehended. Or perhaps there were yet more catastrophes waiting to be uncovered.

"I'll be there momentarily." He marked his page, placed

the manuscript carefully on a small table, and stretched. His muscles protested the movement after being locked in place for so long.

With his heart in his throat, he made his way down the corridor to the drawing room. One of the maids had lit the candles in their sconces, but the flickering light did little to alleviate the dimness. The walls were such a dark shade of blue that they seemed to absorb the light.

Mr. Fisher stood in the center of the room, his posture perfectly straight, a stack of papers in his hands and his eyes weary. He bowed. "My lord, I'm afraid I bear unwanted news."

His heart sank. "Mr. Smith has not been captured?"

"No, and it seems he participated in even more ill dealings than we were aware of. Over the past week, I've received several bills and notes for collection of funds owed that he signed for on your behalf."

Andrew buried his face in his hands. Dear God, when would it be over?

"How much?" he asked dully.

"Not a lot, all things considered." Mr. Fisher shifted uncomfortably from one foot to the other. "In the order of several hundred pounds."

"Damn." He didn't know how to feel about that. While the situation certainly could have been worse, this was still more debt he hadn't anticipated. He'd hoped that Amelia's dowry would fix everything, but Mr. Smith's actions continued to hang above his head like the sword of Damocles.

Not that he didn't deserve it. This hell was of his own making. He should have paid more attention to how his estate was being managed. If he'd only taken a more active role in handling the Longley financials, this might all have been avoided.

"Here." Mr. Fisher passed him the stack of papers he held.

"I am sorry, my lord. I can assure you that steps are being taken to ensure this never happens again."

Andrew clenched his jaw and tried to get his breathing under control. There was no point losing his temper at Mr. Fisher. They were equally to blame. Mr. Fisher should have noticed that his partner was involved in fraudulent activities, and Andrew should have noticed that he no longer owned two damn properties and most of his fortune.

"I'm sure you'll understand that I will be hiring someone else to manage my finances in future," Andrew said.

Mr. Fisher nodded, clearly unsurprised. "Just let me know the details, and I will ensure that all the necessary documentation is taken care of."

"Thank you."

Mr. Fisher bowed again. "I'll take my leave."

As he showed himself out, Andrew collapsed onto a chaise and looked at the paper on the top of the stack. He shifted it to the bottom and read the next one and then the next.

Exhaustion settling into his bones as he finished, he hauled himself to his feet and set about arranging payment to all the relevant parties.

Once that was done, he knew he could no longer delay. It was time he honored his agreement with Amelia, and that meant facing up to her father and asking for his help.

He summoned a carriage, donned his coat, and rode in silence, tugging the neck of his coat higher in an attempt to keep his ears warm during the short journey. Perhaps he ought to have waited until hot bricks could be added to the carriage to heat the air, but he'd really rather have this job over and done with.

The carriage stopped outside the Harts' residence, and he got out without waiting for his footman to open the door. The sooner this was over with, the better. He had nothing against Amelia's father, but there was very little he'd less like to do than admit his failure to a man as successful as Mr. Hart.

Ridiculous, really. Mr. Hart must already have known of his financial situation prior to marrying Amelia. He could think of no one else she could have learned the truth from. But knowing he knew it and speaking to him about it were two very different things.

Buck up, he told himself. *Time to do the right thing.*

He knocked on the door. After a brief delay, the butler opened it and showed him through to the blue drawing room. Only minutes later, the butler returned.

"Mr. Hart will see you in his office. This way, please."

Andrew followed him, then waited while the butler opened the door and announced his presence to his father-in-law. Summoning his courage, Andrew entered.

"My lord." Mr. Hart nodded respectfully from behind his desk. He gestured to the chair opposite him. "Feel free to sit."

"Thank you." Stiffly, Andrew sank onto the chair.

"Brandy?" Mr. Hart asked.

"No, thank you." He needed a clear head for this conversation.

Mr. Hart's expression was approving. "Good man. Mr. Grant, please bring us a pot of peppermint tea."

"As you wish, sir."

The butler left, and then they were alone.

Mr. Hart studied Andrew across the desk. His gray eyes seemed to notice everything, and his mustache twitched as Andrew adjusted himself in an attempt to feel less like an exhibit in a museum.

"What brings you here?"

Andrew braced himself. "I assume you know a little about what happened with my former man of business."

Mr. Hart nodded again.

"The fact is, I can't allow something similar to happen

again. I need to know who I can trust with my money and how to invest it to rebuild my fortune. Will you help me?"

Mr. Hart kicked his legs out and leaned back in his chair. "Have you thought about what you might like to invest in?"

"I have." Right now, he was extremely grateful for that fact.

He broke down his thoughts about safer investments and then delved into the more experimental agricultural technology he was interested in.

The housekeeper brought in tea, and they drank while they talked.

Mr. Hart commended him on his willingness to commit to a more stable option first, but pleasantly surprised Andrew by suggesting he invest in the mechanical plow too.

"Don't invest heavily," he cautioned. "We don't know whether it will pay back. I agree with you that if it does, it has the potential to create a windfall unlike anything you'll get with mining. But only risk what you can afford to lose."

"I will," Andrew assured him.

"As for an agent to manage your finances, you can use my own." He smiled kindly. "I'd trust him with everything I have."

"That's quite an endorsement."

He inclined his head in acknowledgement. "But well-deserved."

Andrew stood. "Thank you for your time. I want to provide the best future I can to Amelia, and I appreciate your assistance to do that."

"It's not a difficulty." Mr. Hart stood too. "I'm always here if you need a second opinion on a matter of business."

Andrew truly did appreciate that, but as Mr. Hart walked him out, he couldn't help but wonder: how could he expect his mother, Kate, and Amelia to rely on him financially when he didn't even trust himself?

CHAPTER 17

As Amelia and Andrew entered Longley House after attending a ball hosted by the Duke and Duchess of Arundel, he didn't say a word, and she could no longer deny that something was bothering him. Nevertheless, she didn't want to raise the issue in front of others. She'd have to wait until they were alone.

"Well, I am exhausted," Lady Drake declared, turning to face them as Boden locked the door. "I'll check on Kate and then go to bed. If I'm not up for breakfast, please don't rouse me. After such a crush of a ball, I feel like I could sleep for hours."

"We'll let you sleep," Amelia assured her. "Good night, Brigid."

Lady Drake patted her shoulder. "Good night, dearest. Sleep well."

While Andrew's mother traipsed up the stairs, Amelia took Andrew's hand and tugged him around the corner, into the corridor.

"What's wrong?" she asked quietly.

Andrew frowned. "What do you mean?"

She nibbled her lower lip, uncertain how much to say.

She knew some men didn't like to be questioned, but he didn't seem the type to get angry with her if she pried.

"You haven't been yourself since yesterday afternoon." She was really hoping his mood had nothing to do with the fact her book was being published.

He'd seemed genuinely happy for her, but had it been an act? If so, did she even care? She wouldn't let it stop her. But truly, she didn't want him to be unhappy.

"You don't have to tell me," she said, "but I'll listen if you'd like to talk."

He gazed at her for a long moment, and disappointment settled in her gut at the realization he'd likely brush off her concern. But then he sighed and squeezed the bridge of his nose.

"Join me in the office for a nightcap?" he asked.

"Of course."

He led her to his office, opened the door, and gestured for her to sit on the worn leather chair in the corner. He lit three candles on the desk, then opened a cabinet beneath the shelf his ledgers were stored on and withdrew a decanter of brandy and two crystal glasses.

He poured a generous portion of brandy into one glass and a slightly smaller amount into the other, then returned the decanter to the cabinet and offered her the smaller one. When she accepted the glass, he pulled over the chair from behind his desk and sat a few feet away from her.

"Have you ever tried brandy?" he asked.

"No." She sniffed the brown liquor and wrinkled her nose at its sharp scent.

Andrew laughed. "Take a small sip. It's quite strong, but once you get past the sharpness of the alcohol, it's quite sweet and fruity."

She eyed the drink dubiously. She wasn't sure she'd find it either sweet or fruity. Nevertheless, she was willing to give it a try. She raised the glass to her lips and tipped it back slightly, then sputtered as soon as the brandy hit her tongue.

"You like this?" she gasped, swallowing in the hopes she'd get the taste out of her mouth as quickly as possible.

His eyes gleamed with amusement, but it was good-humored, not cruel, and she couldn't help but be pleased that he'd at least partly broken the hold of whatever was causing his uncharacteristically somber mood.

"I do," he said. "If you drink it often enough, you develop a taste for it. Although one must be careful not to develop too much of a taste for it."

She grimaced, eyed the brandy, and contemplated setting it aside. But she knew she was in no danger of becoming a drunk from one drink, and she was determined not to shy away from new experiences, so she braced herself and tossed back the rest. It burned down her throat and heated her gut.

Andrew's eyes widened. "That's one way to do it."

"Mm-hmm." She placed the glass on the floor and folded her hands on her lap. "So, is there anything you'd like to talk about?"

He sipped his brandy, and not a single reaction showed on his face. "This stays between us."

She nodded. It wasn't as if there was anyone else she'd tell.

He rubbed his jaw and shifted his head from side to side, stretching his neck. "I'm worried about my ability to provide for you, Mother, and Kate."

The confession rushed from him on a single breath.

"Why?" she asked softly.

He shot her a look that made it clear he thought the answer was obvious. "I was careless with money once before, and we lost almost everything because of that. I'm afraid of making the same foolish mistake. You all deserve better."

An ache formed in Amelia's throat. Feeling awkward, she reached out and touched his forearm.

"I've never thought you foolish." She kept her gaze locked on his as the candlelight played across his features, highlighting them with gold and shadows. "You have a kind heart, and you trusted someone who let you down. Being kind and trusting isn't a shortcoming."

He scoffed.

"It's not," she said firmly. "But if you're truly concerned, you know my father can help."

He stared down into his glass. "I've already sought his advice, and I've made plans to shift my estate into the management of his personal man of business."

She gave his arm a gentle squeeze. "Then you're already doing plenty to ensure that history doesn't repeat."

He didn't respond, and she could see doubt etched in the lines of his face. In the dimness, the splotches beneath his eyes appeared darker, and she was struck by the unusual urge to wrap her arms around him and comfort him.

Finally, he raised his eyes. "How can you trust me not to lose your dowry when I've proven myself unable to hold on to money?"

Her heart thudded rapidly, and she searched her mind for the right answer, determined not to say the wrong thing and make this worse.

Carefully, she slid her hand into his free one. "Even when I didn't know you well, I trusted you to keep your word with regard to our agreement even though I doubt any court would uphold it because I am a woman and therefore considered your property, not an equal able to stand on my own feet. You're a good man."

His eyes searched hers. "You really trust me?"

"Yes." She intertwined her fingers with his. "With my dowry… and with myself."

His forehead furrowed. "What do you mean?"

Amelia's throat was suddenly dry. She'd shocked herself

with that last claim, but now that she'd said it, she wasn't about to take it back.

"I...." She summoned her courage. This ought not to be so hard. The man was her husband, after all. "I would like to lie with you."

As he stared at her, a wave of embarrassment washed over her, and her insides churned uncomfortably.

"Only if you want that too," she hastened to add, her embarrassment growing with every passing second.

"I would." His generous mouth curved. "But only if you're sure you're really ready."

"I am."

They'd been married for nearly a month. She knew Andrew by now. He was, as she'd said, a good man. One whose charming smile and twinkling eyes never failed to take her breath away. She trusted him to make this enjoyable for her. Or at least, as enjoyable as it could be. She didn't know exactly what the marital act entailed.

He drained his brandy far more smoothly than she had, stood, and drew her to her feet. "Your bedchamber or mine?"

"Yours." She hadn't seen much of the earl's chambers yet. Theoretically, she knew she could enter whenever she liked, but it hadn't felt right to simply go in and snoop around to satisfy her curiosity.

She and Andrew walked hand in hand up the stairs. She'd expected to feel nervous when this time finally came, but all she experienced was a faint twinge arising more from a lack of knowledge than anything else.

Amelia didn't like to be unprepared, and in this case, she very much was.

When they reached his bedchamber, he opened the door and held it for her. She stepped inside and looked around. Candlesticks burned on the nightstands, and there was a fire in the grate opposite the bed. The drapes were drawn, and the bedcovers were pulled up.

The walls, floor, and bed frame were polished wood. The red drapes and red-and-black mat made the room feel warmer than it otherwise might.

She turned to Andrew. "I don't know what to do."

He pushed the door shut and latched it, then smiled warmly as he approached. "Relax. I'll tell you everything you need to do. Don't worry about failing. There's absolutely no way you ever could."

She exhaled shakily. "All right."

"Good."

He drew closer until his chest brushed hers and their legs would touch if either of them swayed toward the other. He rested one of his hands on her hip and lifted the other to cup the side of her face.

Instinctively, she closed her eyes and turned her face into his palm.

"You are beautiful, Amelia."

She stiffened and lifted her face from his hand. She wasn't beautiful. Not in the slightest. "I don't need you to tell me that."

He put his finger to her lips. "Ah, but I do. So don't argue. I'm going to kiss you now. Is that all right?"

"Yes," she whispered, suddenly eager to experience a repeat of the kiss from their wedding. He hadn't kissed her on the lips since then, only on the cheek or her forehead, and she couldn't help but feel that she'd been missing out.

He cupped her face between his palms and touched his lips to hers. Her eyelids grew heavy, and she closed them, breathing in his sweet and spicy scent as he increased the pressure on her mouth. She gasped when his tongue brushed against the seam of her lips.

"Open for me, darling," he murmured.

She parted her lips, uncertain what was happening, but confident that she would like it.

His tongue slipped into her mouth and stroked hers. Heat

pulsed between her legs, and her breath caught. What on earth was that? How could a kiss make her throb at that secret place at the apex of her thighs?

Instinctively, her tongue twined with his. He groaned, and satisfaction coursed through her. She had been the one to make him feel good. She repeated the movement, eager for more. He grabbed her by the hips and pulled her against his body. Something was different from when they'd embraced before. Something hard and hot.

She drew back, her eyes wide. "What's that?"

"That's my cock. When we lie together, I'll put it inside you." He slipped his arm between them and cupped her secret spot. "Right here."

Her hips rocked into his touch, and fireworks exploded in the backs of her eyes. "Why does that feel so good?"

His smile became sinful. "If you think that's good, just wait. I'm going to make you scream."

She laughed nervously. Was that supposed to be reassuring?

"Stand in front of the bed," he ordered.

She did so, and he immediately started unbuttoning the back of her gown. His fingers moved deftly—he was clearly almost as comfortable with this task as a maid would be. When he reached the bottom, the gown slid off her shoulders and pooled around her waist.

A gentle touch landed on her upper arm, and she jumped.

"Shh," he murmured. "Let me kiss you."

She shuddered as he trailed more kisses along the top of her shoulder and up the side of her neck. Every single nerve in her body sang.

"Step out of the dress," he urged.

She shimmied the gown to the floor and hesitated. Clad in only her undergarments, she felt quite bare.

"Look at me."

She did so.

He kissed her. "You are temptation incarnate. May I remove your clothes?"

"All right."

He kissed her once more and loosened the ribbons at her back. The soft cotton caressed her skin as it slid down her body. Next, he removed her chemise and stays, until she stood before him, her upper body nude. His gaze skimmed over her, his pupils dilated.

"Stunning," he murmured.

She bit her tongue to stop the protest that had already formed. She wasn't beautiful or tempting or stunning or any of the other things he'd called her, but if he wanted to insist she was, she wouldn't argue. It would be nice to pretend.

He knelt and peeled down her drawers. She kicked them off and removed her silk slippers too.

Now, she was truly nude.

And he was looking at her as though she were a delicacy he wanted to sample.

He stood and wrapped her in his embrace. She shivered as the cool fabric of his suit scraped against her sensitive skin. Heat pulsed at her groin again. There was something awfully scandalous about being completely nude with a fully clothed man.

He removed his jacket and hung it over the back of a chair in the corner. "Lie across the bed, but keep your feet on the floor."

She perched on the edge of the bed and shuffled backward until only her toes touched the floor, then lay flat on the mattress. He moved, and the air shifted over her nakedness. She shivered, feeling exposed. This was an unusual position. What did he have in mind?

He knelt between her knees and rested one arm over each of her thighs. "Let me bring you pleasure before I take mine."

She bit her lip and nodded, not quite knowing what he meant but certain that whatever it was, she wanted it. Eyes closed, she waited for whatever came next. When a wet heat settled over her nether regions, her eyes shot open, and she bolted upright.

"What are you doing?" she asked breathlessly.

He lifted his mouth from her, his eyes burning into hers. "Pleasuring you."

"There?"

He grinned rakishly. "Yes. There. Now lie back and tell me if I do anything you don't like."

"A-all right."

She wasn't sure how she felt about it, but he knew better than she did when it came to matters such as this, so she lay back down, feeling a slight tension through her core that wasn't there before.

This time, when he put his mouth on her, she didn't startle or push him away. Instead, she caught her lower lip between her teeth and paid attention to how his touch made her feel. His tongue delved into the softness between her legs the same way it had entered her mouth earlier.

She gripped the bedclothes. Surely this wasn't normal. But oh, as he licked down her center and teased the bud at the top of her feminine parts, it felt good. He moaned against her flesh, and she shuddered as pleasure rippled through her.

He kissed the top of her mound. "You like that?"

"I do." She parted her thighs wider to give him better access.

He made a sound in the back of his throat and buried his face between her legs. Despite his obvious enthusiasm, he wasn't rough. He continued to tease her with his lips and tongue until the pulses of heat she'd experienced earlier were thrumming through her constantly.

He moved his arms from over her legs, and she almost groaned in disappointment. There was something delicious about him pinning her down. But then he slid his arms beneath her thighs and angled her body toward him so that he could better taste her.

She rose onto her elbows and gazed down at him. His hair was slightly mussed, his eyes the darkest they'd ever been. He looked debauched in the best possible way, and despite holding her gaze, he didn't stop lapping at her for a single second.

Her hips twitched as an involuntary shudder rolled through her. His clever tongue nudged her bud and drew tight circles around it. Her lower body clenched, and she almost dropped onto her back, but she managed to hold herself there. She wanted to see this.

Something was building within her, winding tighter and tighter. She stared into Andrew's almost black eyes and wondered what he saw when he looked at her.

His bluestocking wife?

A wanton woman?

Lord, like this, she could almost believe herself a seductress.

"That's it," he murmured against her as her hips began to tip back and forth. "Ride my tongue."

Oh God.

Her mouth opened on a silent scream as the most intense pleasure she'd ever known barreled through her. She shuddered and whimpered and somehow managed to look into Andrew's eyes until he'd wrung every last ounce of sensation from her.

She floated in a haze of sated desire, hardly aware that he was climbing over her. She didn't fully return to herself until he kissed her and she tasted something unusual on his lips. Was that from her?

"So beautiful." He shifted her around until she was lying lengthwise on the bed with him pressed along her body. He kissed her again, then nuzzled the side of her neck. "This next part might be a bit uncomfortable."

She blinked up at him, in a daze. "I trust you."

He dropped a kiss on her forehead. "You have no idea how much that means to me."

One of his hands cupped her, similar to the way he had earlier, but this time, he didn't stop there. One finger pushed against her entrance and slid inside.

Amelia gasped. It didn't feel bad, just... strange. She wasn't used to having things up there, and it was tight. If it was this tight with one finger, hopefully the part of him he needed to insert wouldn't be much larger.

"Breathe out," he urged. "Relax your muscles. The more relaxed you are, the more comfortable it will be."

She exhaled slowly, doing her best to relax, but it was awfully hard to do so on command.

He speared her with another finger.

"You're so tight." His voice was thick. "No one else has ever had you before. You're all mine."

Maybe. But was he all hers?

She cast the thought aside as he added a third finger. She tensed automatically at the pinch of pain.

"Shh." He kissed her, tangling their tongues again.

Bit by bit, the tension eased from her body. He pressed his palm flat against that magic nub, and she whimpered.

"I'm going to fill you now," he whispered. "All right?"

"Uh-huh."

He got off her and, with rapid movements, removed his shirt, trousers, and drawers. Amelia drank in the sight of him as he approached. His abdomen was flat, his nipples pink, and his torso was dusted with reddish-brown hair. His legs tensed with each step, more muscular than she would have expected, and then there was the thing between his legs.

His cock.

She gulped. It was definitely longer and thicker than his fingers, and with its dusky coloring and the way it jutted forward, she worried it might be more than she could handle.

She inhaled slowly. "That's a lot."

He looked oddly pleased. "You can take it. Your body was made for me."

As he settled over her, she tried to focus on how wonderful he'd made her feel before rather than how uncomfortable this might be. His thumb found her nub and circled gently—just enough to make her hips twitch and heat pool in her core.

"Trust me?" he murmured, holding her gaze.

"I do."

She rose off the bed and kissed him. As their lips clung together, he notched his cock against her entrance and pushed in. At first, she clenched against the intrusion, and when he continued to inch forward, she had to grit her teeth against the urge to push him away.

But he deepened the kiss, and her body grew languid. As it did, the discomfort eased. When he was fully inside her, he didn't move.

"Is that it?" she asked. "Is it done?"

He laughed, but a muscle in his jaw ticked. "No, I'm just giving you time to get used to me."

"Oh." Grateful he wasn't pushing her, she tilted her head to look down between their bodies. At the sight of his cock disappearing inside her, the heat in her core blossomed into more. It was oddly stirring.

Slowly, he eased out, then thrust back in. He threw his head back, and a pained sound rumbled from him.

The more he moved, the more consuming the heat inside her became. He stoked the flames of her sated passion until she was desperate for more all over again.

All the while, he kissed her. She couldn't get enough of the taste of him. She silently pleaded for more, and he gave her everything she desired.

The tension drew taut inside her, and she knew now that it meant that exquisite overload of sensation was nearly upon her. She clutched his shoulders and hooked her feet around his legs so that he kept entering her at just the right angle.

A groan tore from him.

"It's so good." She rubbed herself against him shamelessly. "I'm almost there. Please, Andrew. Please."

"I've got you, sweetheart."

He didn't falter until she broke apart, crying her pleasure. Only then did his thrusts become erratic. He stiffened and pulsed inside her, his face buried against the side of her neck.

He collapsed on top of her, and even though he was heavy, she didn't have the wherewithal to push him off. Instead, she just lay there with his warm weight pinning her down, wondering why on earth they'd taken so long to do this.

After a while, Andrew stirred. He got up and retrieved a cloth from one of his cupboards, then brought it over.

"Let me clean you up."

She squirmed, self-conscious as he dabbed between her legs. It came away speckled with red. She gasped, but he didn't seem concerned.

"There's often a little blood the first time a woman is with a man," he told her. "It's nothing to worry about, and it shouldn't happen again."

"Oh. That's good. I thought…." Well, she wasn't sure what she'd thought. Perhaps that her monthly cycle had arrived early. Wouldn't that have been mortifying?

He wiped himself with the cloth and tossed it on the floor. "How do you feel?"

She tested each of her limbs. There was a faint soreness between her legs, but that was all. "I'm well."

"I'm glad to hear it." He gave her a mischievous smile. "That was my first time being someone's first."

She carefully kept her face blank even though she wanted to scowl at the thought of him lying with anyone else. "This is how women become with child?"

"Yes." A pink flush appeared on his cheeks as he lay down alongside her. "When a man comes—that's what it's called when you feel that intense pleasure—he ejaculates his seed into the woman, and sometimes, that seed takes root and forms a baby."

"But not always?" she clarified, recalling what her mother had said about lying with her husband as often as possible to ensure the job got done.

"No." He looped his arm around her waist and pulled her closer. "Sometimes it takes, and sometimes it doesn't. Some couples are very fertile together, and others aren't. It's impossible to know what the case will be for us."

She nodded, grateful for his explanation. It was difficult to be a woman and not know what may or may not be happening within her own body. At this very minute, a baby might be being created inside her.

Would she like being a mother?

It wasn't something she'd ever thought about much, since it was generally considered a foregone conclusion that all women would have children. Amelia had no experience with babies, but it might be nice to introduce a miniature version of herself and Andrew to the joys of reading or to explore their new country home together.

She rested her head on Andrew's chest and closed her eyes. Her mind replayed Andrew's comment about this being the first time he'd been with a maiden. It certainly wasn't his first time with a woman in general. Based on how skillfully he'd pleasured her, she suspected he'd had many lovers.

Had he ever made love to any of the women who'd been at the ball they'd attended tonight? She wasn't sure. She knew many women of the ton conducted affairs—usually after they'd borne children.

Many of them were more beautiful than Amelia. More sophisticated. Had they brought him more pleasure than she had?

If she knew she could expect fidelity from him, it may bother her less, but the fact was, she had no idea whether he would be faithful. It hadn't been part of their agreement.

Eventually, he'd probably grow bored with her, and she wasn't sure how she'd handle it when he did.

CHAPTER 18

*London,
November 1820*

"How are things going in there?" Andrew called through the connecting door between his bedroom and Amelia's.

They were due to leave for the Hertford ball shortly. He was more or less ready, but he knew women often took longer to prepare.

"I'll be ready soon," Amelia called back. "Are you sure Brigid doesn't wish to join us?"

"Not this time." His mother and wife got on startlingly well, so he could understand Amelia's surprise, but his mother had pleaded off, citing a headache.

He tweaked his cravat and headed through the doorway, coming up short at the sight of his wife being buttoned into a dark blue gown by her maid. The silken skin on the back of her shoulders slowly disappeared from view as Margaret moved upward.

Damn, his wife was stunning. If he didn't know how much effort went into dressing her for a ball, he'd insist on stripping every last item of clothing from her body, making love to her, and starting over. Instead, he sat on the bed and watched Margaret fuss over her.

"She looks pretty, doesn't she?"

He flinched. He hadn't seen his sister standing near the wall just inside the bedchamber. "She does."

Kate's impish smile made his cheeks heat. "Blue is an excellent color for her complexion."

He glanced at his wife again. She often wore shades of blue, but the lacework and varying shades of this one differed from what she usually chose. "Is this your doing?"

Kate nodded, obviously proud. "I chose the fabrics, and Madam Baptiste designed the gown."

He nudged her shoulder with his. "You have a good eye."

She looked at the floor, but he could still make out the corners of her smile. "Thank you."

They both returned their attention to Amelia and Margaret. It was difficult to tell because of her stern demeanor, but he suspected that Margaret quite liked getting to dress a woman who would be seen and admired by the ton. As yet, Kate wasn't out, so dressing her didn't carry the same weight.

Margaret stepped back. "There you are, my lady. All done."

Amelia looked over her shoulder. "Thank you, Margaret. You may be excused."

The maid bobbed her head and scurried out.

"I'll leave too," Kate murmured. "You look like you're about to say something terribly sappy."

He couldn't deny that.

He waited until Kate had gone, then rose and erased the distance between him and Amelia. "This dress makes your eyes sparkle like sapphires."

A shy smile curved her lips. "Thank you."

With two fingers, he tilted her chin up. He wouldn't let

her hide from him. Perhaps a week of lovemaking wouldn't convince her of her appeal, but he wouldn't give up. They had a lifetime together, after all.

"In fact." He pecked her lips. "I find myself quite unable to resist you."

As he sank to his knees, her eyebrows flew up.

"Andrew?" Her voice trembled.

"Stay very still. We mustn't crease your skirt."

He lifted the hem and ducked underneath it. The fabric mussed his hair, but he didn't care. He made his way beneath her petticoats until he was between her legs.

"What are you doing?" she asked, although surely by now it must be obvious.

"My wife," he replied, unfastening her drawers to bare her to his gaze.

His mouth watered. Her pretty pinkness was right there, waiting for his attention. He leaned close and blew over her. She shivered. He nuzzled into the vee of her thighs, and she began to tremble.

"That's it, darling." His tongue darted out to taste her. *Mm*. Sweet and intoxicating. He repeated the movement more slowly, dragging his tongue along the seam of her, reveling in the soft catches of her breath.

Gently, he teased her with his lips and tongue—kissing, licking, and humming his approval against her skin. While careful not to rumple her too much, he was determined that his wife would enter the Hertford ball satisfied because of him. There would be no other men eyeing his countess.

She was his.

He made love to her with his mouth until she stiffened and her delicate muscles contracted around him; then he kissed her once and scrambled out from beneath her skirts.

She stared at him, lips parted, cheeks flushed, eyes wide. "I can't believe you did that."

He kissed her forehead, then used her mirror to straighten his hair. "Didn't you enjoy it?"

"Yes," she admitted. "But we have a ball to get to."

He sighed and offered her his arm. "Then I suppose we'd better go."

"Just like that?"

He winked. "Just like that."

~

As Amelia and Andrew passed through the house and out the front door, she couldn't help but feel like everyone who saw them knew exactly what they'd been up to only minutes earlier.

She'd learned a couple of days ago that the marital act didn't have to be confined to the bedroom, but when he'd been under her skirt just now, all she could think was that Kate had left the door ajar and anyone could happen upon them. That had simultaneously excited her and made her anxious. She wasn't quite sure how to feel about it.

Improper?

Yes, certainly.

But also strangely decadent.

"Amelia?"

She looked around and realized that Andrew was waiting to help her into the carriage. "Sorry, I was woolgathering."

He grinned wickedly, took her hand, and guided her inside. She got the impression he knew exactly what had been running through her mind. She supposed she should expect that. He was accustomed to dalliances. She, on the other hand, was new to all of this.

She adjusted her skirts as she sat on the carriage bench. How long would it be until he grew weary of her? Perhaps for now, he found it thrilling to introduce her to new intimate acts, but eventually they'd run out of new things to explore, and he'd want to move on to someone else. How much time did she have?

She pondered the question as they drove. Too soon, they arrived at the ball, and he escorted her inside. Through it all, Amelia felt detached, as though she were an onlooker watching her life from a distance.

She only jerked into reality when she stood opposite Andrew on the dance floor during the opening bars of a quadrille.

"Everything all right?" he asked, apparently sensing her discomposure.

"Fine," she assured him.

It was fortunate she'd practiced the quadrille many times, because it meant she was able to follow the steps without engaging much of her brain. By the time they were finished, she desperately needed a drink.

"Champagne?" he asked, as if reading her mind.

"Yes, please."

He escorted her to the drinks table, and she'd just picked up a glass when her mother appeared out of nowhere.

"Amelia!" She beamed. "I was wondering if I could steal your husband away for a dance?"

Andrew met Amelia's gaze and arched an eyebrow. She nodded, and he took her mother's arm.

"I'd be honored, Mrs. Hart. Shall we?"

Amelia sipped champagne as she watched them go. She wanted to be annoyed by her mother's obvious inclination to use her connection to Andrew to further her social climbing, but she could hardly bear her too much ill will when the situation had worked out well for her thus far. Perhaps if she'd been married off to the Duke of Wight, she'd feel differently, but she'd been lucky enough to escape that fate.

"You did well for yourself."

Amelia's hand flew to her chest, and she spun toward the voice. "It's you."

The woman smiled impishly. She was the redhead Amelia had encountered in the powder room at a ball several weeks ago—and to whom she'd felt a strange connection.

"Miss Helena Steele. We haven't been officially introduced. But then, people rarely bother to meet the wallflowers."

"I find it difficult to believe you're a wallflower," Amelia said, being perfectly honest. Miss Steele may not be conventionally pretty, but there was something about her that demanded attention, and she certainly did not seem shy.

Miss Steele shrugged. "I'll admit, I'm a wallflower by choice. Most of the people you meet at these events are dreadful bores, and I can't fathom pretending to be interested in them."

"You seem rather jaded."

Miss Steele snorted. "This is my seventh season. I believe I'm entitled to be. I'm just waiting for my father to realize that it's easier for him to settle some money on me and let me go my own way rather than trying to marry me off."

Interesting. Their situations were not so different.

"I might have tried the same, but my mother was determined I would wed an aristocrat, so it seemed practical to just choose the best of the options available."

"An earl." Miss Steele raised her glass. "I'm impressed, and let me tell you, that's not an easy feat."

No, she didn't imagine it was.

The other woman glanced behind her. "Your husband returns. No doubt I'll see you again."

She slinked away seconds before Mrs. Hart and Andrew rejoined Amelia. Her mother was in raptures over their dance, giggling and fanning herself like a woman half her age. It was almost… heartening. In an unusual way.

"Countess." Mrs. Hart practically purred as she said the word. "I've just been telling the earl that you simply must host a ball to officially announce your marriage to the ton."

Just like that, Amelia's good cheer faded.

"Wasn't that the purpose of the wedding?" she asked.

Mrs. Hart laughed and waved at someone passing by. "If you want to be a renowned hostess in London, then now is the time to make that clear."

Amelia groaned. "I have no aspirations of being a popular hostess."

Her mother blinked at her as if that simply didn't make sense. "But don't you want to throw the most lavish, exclusive society parties?"

How on earth could she possibly believe that? She'd known Amelia for her whole life, and she was quite certain she'd never once given anyone cause to believe she might enjoy attending parties, let alone planning them.

Socializing was not her forte.

Books were.

She was more comfortable scribbling in a library with ink-stained hands than wearing a diamond necklace at a ball.

Andrew detached himself from her mother and wrapped his arm around her. His lips brushed her ear as he said, "We probably should organize a ball, just to make sure everyone acknowledges your rightful place among us."

She tried to glare at him, but it was difficult when he was holding her like she mattered. "Must we?"

"Only once," he said.

She huffed. "That had better be a promise. I'm not making this an annual occurrence."

He kissed her. "It won't be. And don't worry, the servants can do most of the legwork. I can even have Mrs. Smythe make the decor choices if you'd like."

"But—" Mrs. Hart began to protest, but he cut her off with a hand gesture.

"It won't interfere with your writing time," he told her, proving how well he was coming to know her.

She sighed. "Fine. But, Mother, this will not be happening again."

Mrs. Hart clapped, obviously delighted. Amelia wasn't sure she'd even heard the warning.

"I'll be in touch about the planning." She whirled around. "I must find your father and let him know."

Amelia turned to Andrew. "Now you've done it."

He flashed that effortlessly charming grin that seemed to get him out of everything. "It doesn't have to be a big fuss. One evening of your life and a few minutes to make decisions before then. That's all."

"Uh-huh." It had better be so simple.

He chuckled and linked her arm with his. "Come. I see one of my acquaintances over there. Let me introduce you."

Unfortunately, they hadn't made it halfway across the room before a ruddy-cheeked gentleman with a slightly crooked cravat stepped into their path.

"Longley." He wobbled slightly. "Congratulations, old chap. Didn't expect you to tie yourself down this season. Lost a chunk of change to Falvey because of it. I should have known that weasel knew something I didn't or else he wouldn't have been making a bet in the first place."

"Mr. White," Andrew said stiffly, glancing at Amelia in a way that told her he'd rather not spend time with this man. "Have you met the Countess of Longley?"

Mr. White took Amelia's hand and dropped a slobbery kiss on the back of it. After reclaiming her hand, she subtly wiped it on her skirt.

"Charmed, my lady," he said. "You must be something special to tempt Longley here into marriage."

Yes. Rich.

She grimaced at the thought. What would Mr. White say if he knew exactly why Andrew had married her?

Except for an initial shock at the fact the earl had been defrauded, she doubted he'd be surprised.

"Nice to meet you, Mr. White." She looked around, wondering if they might extricate themselves from this conversation. Her gaze fell on a woman standing alone in a scandalously low-cut dress.

Recognition hit. It was the woman from the teashop. The one who'd called Andrew by his given name.

He followed her gaze and immediately paled. "Well, it was good to see you, as always, but the countess and I must be off. We are due elsewhere."

"What?" Mr. White blustered. "But—"

Andrew tugged Amelia away from him and toward the door.

"What is happening?" she asked, but he didn't answer.

As they made their farewells and stepped out into the cool night air, she couldn't help but wonder: who was that woman, and why was Andrew avoiding her?

CHAPTER 19

"How is my Mia?" Mr. Hart asked as Andrew settled onto the chair in his office.

They'd met to discuss business, but it was a pleasant surprise that Mr. Hart chose to begin by discussing his daughter. Andrew had gotten the feeling he wasn't particularly involved in her life.

"Mia," he mused. "That's a sweet name for her. She seems content. If she's unhappy, she hasn't said anything to me about it."

Mr. Hart nodded. "Nor I or her mother."

He stood and poured tea for himself and Andrew from a teapot positioned on the end of his desk. "Sugar or milk?"

"Sugar, please."

He added a spoonful of sugar to one cup and stirred it in. "Mia prefers hers sweetened too. My wife doesn't, so I got out of the habit."

Andrew accepted the cup and saucer and placed it in front of himself to cool. "Yes, Mrs. Hart made her preference clear. Black tea is the most British tea, if I recall correctly."

Mr. Hart laughed. "That sounds like something she'd say." He hesitated, and for a moment, Andrew thought it was time to move on to business, but Mr. Hart surprised him once again. "I'm glad Amelia is content. I worried she would be unhappy in marriage."

Andrew raised an eyebrow. "Yet you allowed her to marry anyway?"

"You don't allow Amelia to do anything. If she wants something badly enough, she makes it happen. She chose you, and you seem a decent sort despite your financial troubles, so I didn't see any harm in the match."

The man had a point there. He may not have known Amelia for long, but he could already tell that she was resourceful and determined.

"I've been very impressed by Amelia over the past weeks. Particularly by her writing. Did you know what a talented storyteller she is?"

Mr. Hart sipped his tea. "She's always had a way with words. At least, on paper. Unfortunately, she couldn't see how difficult it would be to make a career from her writing without a husband's support."

Biting the inside of his cheek, Andrew swallowed his immediate response. He didn't want to anger the man who was helping him. Yet he felt the need to stand up for Amelia.

"Forgive me if I'm mistaken, but wouldn't she have been able to have a flourishing career without getting married if you'd made it clear you were willing to provide for her?"

To his relief, Mr. Hart wasn't upset by the remark. He placed his teacup down and leaned back in his chair. "That may be true to a certain extent. My wife was determined that Amelia would marry an aristocrat. My daughter herself had no such aspirations. I'm not blind to that fact. But every man has his weakness, and my wife is mine. There's little I wouldn't do to please her."

Andrew understood that. He was beginning to suspect that his wife may also be his weakness. But it still seemed to him that if a couple created a child, they owed that child a certain level of care.

"Would you have allowed a union between Amelia and a man who was ill-suited to her?"

Mr. Hart's lips twitched. "If Amelia had been truly miserable and came to me for help, I'd have put a stop to it. Luckily for us both, that didn't happen. The so-called marriage mart was simply another obstacle that Amelia needed to conquer."

Pressing his lips together, Andrew stayed quiet. While he may not necessarily agree with the way Mr. Hart had handled the situation, he couldn't deny that he was grateful for the outcome, and he liked to believe Amelia was too.

He wondered whether to break the news that one of Amelia's stories had been accepted for publication. She'd already met with the editor and agreed upon a few changes. He decided against it. If she wanted to share with her parents, she could do that when she felt ready.

"Shall we move on to other subjects?" Mr. Hart suggested, sliding a sheaf of papers across the desk toward Andrew. "These are the investment opportunities you asked me to review."

Andrew leaned forward, mentally preparing himself for a long and exhausting conversation.

When he made his way out of the Hart residence an hour later, his money woes were lighter on his shoulders. He took his carriage back to Longley House, pausing along the way to buy a flower from a girl on a street corner. He gave her a silver coin that had her eyes turning to saucers and doffed his hat at her before returning to the carriage.

At Longley House, he breezed inside and went in search of his family. The sound of women's voices led him to the drawing room, where Amelia, Lady Drake, and Kate were squashed onto one chaise, their heads close together as they talked.

He knocked on the doorframe. Three faces turned toward

him. His mother spotted the flower, and her expression softened. Kate spared him only a glance before refocusing on a set of ribbons laid across her knee.

"Amelia?"

His wife's head cocked curiously, and she rose and came toward him.

He presented her with the flower and bowed. "A rose for my English rose."

She laughed but took it from him carefully, and a faint blush proved she wasn't immune to the gesture. "Thank you."

He kissed her cheek. "You're very welcome. What trouble are you three getting yourselves into?"

"We're planning your first ball as the Earl and Countess of Longley," Lady Drake said.

He frowned and turned to Amelia. "It isn't proving too much for you, is it? I didn't intend for it to become a big to-do."

"All she has to do is make decisions," Kate piped up. "Mother and I are giving her choices, and then Mother will get Mrs. Smythe to make the arrangements."

He looked at his mother. "And that's all right with you?"

She inclined her head. "It will be nice to play hostess again even if the role isn't really mine."

"We can share the role," Amelia said firmly. "This has been your home for much longer than it's been mine."

Andrew's heart warmed. He loved how thoughtful Amelia was and also how well she was making a place for herself in their family. His mother already adored her, and it did Kate well to have a role model with ambitions beyond marriage and children.

He pulled Amelia close and planted a kiss on her lips. Behind her, Kate and Lady Drake exchanged a knowing glance. He ignored them.

"I will be in the office if you need me," he said, kissing her once more.

She nodded, slightly dazed. He hurried out of the room before his arousal became obvious. That was the last thing he wanted to happen in front of his mother and sister.

∽

AMELIA WAS LYING ON HER BED, READING A BIOGRAPHICAL account written by a cleric who'd traveled to Australia on a ship full of convicts when Kate rushed in, clearly distressed.

"What's wrong?" she asked, sitting up and marking the page so she could return to it later.

"Mama is unwell." Kate stopped beside the bed, wringing her hands. "She cast up her accounts after dinner, and now she's clutching her head and her skin is hot to the touch."

Her gut tightening, Amelia got up and strode toward the door. "Is she in her bedchamber?"

"Yes." Kate hurried along behind her.

"Have you told Andrew?"

"No, I wanted your opinion first."

Amelia reached the end of the corridor and turned into Lady Drake's bedchamber. The curtains were closed, and a lone candle flickered on the nightstand. Lady Drake lay on top of the covers, curled on her side with her face in her hands.

"Brigid, can you hear me?" Amelia asked as she closed the distance between them.

Lady Drake murmured something.

"I'm going to touch your forehead," Amelia told her, then pressed her fingertips just below Lady Drake's hairline. "You're too warm. Probably not feverish, but that might be yet to come. We need to get you into bed. Can you stand?"

Lady Drake rolled closer to the edge of the bed, slung her legs off the side, and rose, swaying slightly.

Amelia steadied her. "Kate, I need you to pull back the

covers and undo the back of her dress so we can make her comfortable."

Kate instantly did as she was told, pulling the purple bedcover and crisp white sheets down so that Lady Drake could slide between them more easily. Amelia shifted her mother-in-law to make it easier for Kate to access her back.

With shaking hands, Kate undid the buttons and pushed the fabric off her mother's shoulders so that it dropped to the floor. She loosened the ribbons on the undergarments, unlaced her stays, and slid those down too, studiously avoiding looking at any body parts.

Amelia supposed that Kate didn't ever have reason to see her mother in a state of undress, so it might be uncomfortable doing so now. Perhaps she should have called for a maid, but it had seemed more important to act quickly.

"Where's your nightgown?" she asked Lady Drake.

She gestured listlessly toward a dresser in the corner.

Kate headed straight over, dragged a drawer out, and pulled out the first nightgown she laid eyes on. She held it up. "Is this all right?"

"Perfect," Amelia told her. "Bring it here."

Together, they managed to get Lady Drake into the nightgown and into bed.

"Can you sit with her and remove her hairpins?" Amelia asked Kate. "She might not notice if they're uncomfortable now, but she certainly will later."

Kate nodded. "Of course."

While she did that, Amelia rang for a maid. "When they get here, I want you to ask for cold water and a cloth. Put it on her forehead and refresh the cloth whenever it warms."

"I understand."

After a brief hesitation, Amelia left them. She knew Kate would take care of her mother. It was just hard for her to leave when Lady Drake had gone downhill so quickly. She'd been fine when they were planning the ball only hours earlier.

She knocked on Andrew's door.

"Come in," he called.

She opened the door and stepped through. He lay on the bed, propped up against a pile of pillows, his feet crossed at the ankles.

"Is something the matter?" he asked, reading her expression.

"Your mother has taken ill." She clasped her hands behind her back, hoping he wouldn't notice how nervous she was. "I think you should call for a doctor."

He slid off the bed and ran a hand through his hair. "It's that serious?"

"According to Kate, she's vomited at least once. Her head appears to be troubling her, and she's overly warm." She'd summed up the situation as succinctly as she could in the hope that he'd come to the same conclusion that she had.

After a moment, he nodded. "You're right. I'll have Boden send word to our usual physician. I'll be there momentarily."

Amelia returned to Lady Drake's chambers. Kate sat beside Brigid, mopping her forehead with a wet cloth.

"She's shivering," Kate said quietly. "Ought we to be concerned? I don't want to make her too cold."

Amelia bit her lip. "Your brother is calling for a doctor. I think that the cool cloth is fine because her temperature is high, but they'll know better than I do."

There was a chair in front of the dressing table, so Amelia dragged it over beside the bed and sat. She watched Lady Drake carefully, looking for any changes that could be cause to worry.

A few minutes later, Andrew joined them, standing near her shoulder. "Dr. Tanner will be here soon. I offered him a bonus to ensure it."

"That was clever."

"Is there anything else we can do for her in the meantime?"

He sounded frustrated, and she understood. It was difficult to sit around and do nothing when Lady Drake was obviously unwell.

"I don't know." She wished she had another answer for him.

A while later, Boden let them know the doctor had arrived, and Andrew went to meet him. Their greetings must have been swift, since he returned scarcely a minute after leaving.

Dr. Tanner rounded the bed to the side opposite Kate and bent over Lady Drake. He was a tall, lean figure with salt-and-pepper hair and kind eyes. He pressed his hand to Lady Drake's forehead and then to the side of her neck. Ducking closer, he examined the insides of her ears and lifted one of her eyelids.

"Hmm."

"What is it?" Andrew demanded.

"Difficult to say," the doctor replied, unhurried. "I can see why you sent for me, but I don't believe that Lady Drake is in immediate danger. Let her sleep through the night and try to feed her broth in the morning. As long as she remains abed, I imagine she will heal in a couple of days."

Andrew crossed his arms. "And if she worsens?"

"Then send word, and I will come straight away."

He didn't seem concerned, and Amelia couldn't help but be impressed by the doctor's unwavering gaze as he met Andrew's eyes.

"Should someone stay with her during the night?" she asked.

The doctor considered this and then nodded. "It's likely unnecessary, but it would be a wise precaution if you're worried she may take a turn for the worse."

"I'll stay with her," Kate said.

Andrew rested his hand on Amelia's shoulder. "Are you sure?"

"Yes," she said. "I won't be able to sleep anyway."

"Then that would be much appreciated." He gave Amelia's shoulder a slight squeeze.

Perhaps it was selfish of her, but she was pleased that she'd be able to share a bed with him tonight. His presence was always comforting.

Andrew walked the doctor out, and then he dragged a chaise in from the library, and Amelia brought Kate a pillow and blankets so she could be as comfortable as possible while Lady Drake slept.

Andrew and Amelia made their way to his bed soon after. They didn't make love that night, but they did hold each other until they drifted off to sleep.

When Amelia woke, the gray light of dawn was upon them. Andrew was still sleeping soundly beside her, so she slipped out from beneath the covers, doing her best not to wake him, and padded down the corridor to Lady Drake's chambers.

As soon as she entered, she knew something was wrong. Not with Lady Drake, but with Kate. Only her face was visible from within a nest of blankets on the chaise, and it was flushed, with beads of sweat at her hairline. Shudders racked her body, and she was whimpering quietly.

Whatever had made Lady Drake sick must be catching.

Amelia summoned Margaret, and together they got Kate to her bedchamber and into bed. Torn between whether to start a fire to warm Kate or open the window to cool her, Amelia chose to do neither until Andrew was awake to act as a sounding board.

Margaret stayed with Kate, dabbing her forehead with a cold compress while Amelia went to check on Lady Drake. The older woman was in better condition than she had been last night. While she remained unconscious, she wasn't shivering or sweating, didn't seem to be in any pain, and her temperature had come down a little.

Perhaps Dr. Tanner had been right that this illness would resolve itself within a couple of days.

Amelia ran her fingers over the sheets and, finding them damp, requested a new set from a maid. Together, they changed the bedding, shifting Lady Drake from one side to the other to allow them to work around her.

When Andrew ventured out of his bedchamber, she broke the news, and he insisted on summoning the doctor to check on both women.

Unfortunately, the doctor didn't have anything new to offer. He was optimistic about Lady Drake's recovery and believed that Kate would also begin to heal soon.

Amelia split her time between Kate's and Lady Drake's bedchambers. She made sure they remained at a pleasant temperature, that their bedding was clean and dry, and attempted—unsuccessfully—to feed them broth.

By the time evening came around, she was exhausted. As usual, she ate dinner with Andrew in the morning room, but she struggled to keep up a lively conversation. Her head dropped every now and then as sleep tried to claim her. Andrew moved around to her side of the table and spoon-fed her sticky toffee pudding.

"Sorry," she murmured.

"Don't be." He kissed her temple. "I appreciate you being so attentive to them all day. Taking care of you is the least I can do."

A glow started somewhere inside her, and she smiled tiredly. "Thank you."

"What say we get you to bed?" he said.

"That sounds lovely."

He wrapped one arm around her shoulders and helped her to her feet. They made their way up the stairs slowly, one step at a time.

As soon as they were in her bedchamber, she hurried straight to the bed and flopped onto it face down. Fingers brushed her back, and she realized he was undoing her dress. Much as she'd helped Lady Drake last night, he assisted her in undressing and climbing into bed.

He pulled the covers up to her chin, and as she dozed off, she could have sworn she heard him say, "When I went looking for a wife, I never expected to find one like you."

All she had time to think was: is that a good thing… or not?

CHAPTER 20

"Are you sure you're up to this?" Andrew asked his mother for the second time that night. "It was only days ago you were laid up in bed with a fever."

Lady Drake rolled her eyes. "I'm fine. Besides, if we're to host our own ball, we need all the inspiration we can get."

"I can take notes," Amelia told her. "I'll pay attention to the music, the food, the decorations. There's no need for you to go."

Lady Drake huffed. "Amelia, darling, you may be excellent at details when it comes to your stories, but social events are not your forte. I'll be all right. I haven't had any symptoms yesterday or today. There's no reason to worry."

"Are you sure?" Amelia persisted.

"Quite." She eyeballed them both. "And the next person who asks me whether I'm sure can expect to walk to the Winston ball."

Andrew hid a laugh. Amelia may be stubborn, but his mother could be, too, in her own way. The two women sized each other up for a long moment, and then Amelia nodded.

"Take a shawl," Amelia said. "We want to make sure you keep warm."

With a sigh, Lady Drake summoned her maid and sent her upstairs to fetch a shawl that would match her dress.

Once the maid returned, Andrew took his mother's arm and guided her through the front doors and down to the carriage. Usually, he'd escort Amelia, but he worried that Lady Drake wasn't quite as recovered as she'd have them believe.

The ride to the ball took a while, since Winston Manor was on the other side of Mayfair from Longley House. They joined the line of carriages waiting outside and disembarked when they reached the front entrance. Andrew got out first and helped both women down, then linked one of his arms with each of them to walk up the stairs.

Winston Manor was a grand old building—slightly outdated but in a way that made it seem regal rather than worn out. They passed through a marble-floored foyer and reached another set of stairs that would descend into the ballroom. Their hosts stood in a row in front of the stairs to greet guests.

"Welcome, Lord and Lady Longley," Lord Winston said. "And Lady Drake, it's always a pleasure."

Andrew bobbed his head in greeting to Lord and Lady Winston. "Seems like you've got a crush on your hands."

Lady Winston grinned. "It's too soon to know for sure, but I do hope you're right."

More guests arrived behind them.

"Please enjoy yourselves," Lord Winston said, dismissing them so he could greet the newcomers.

Andrew stayed arm in arm with both his mother and his wife as they strolled down the stairs to the ballroom floor. On his left, Amelia was slightly stiff, as she often was at social events. On his right, his mother was also alert, but she was scanning their surroundings with interest, her sharp gaze cataloging everything she saw.

As they reached the bottom, a song ended. Perfectly timed.

He released them both, turned to Amelia, and bowed over her hand. "May I have this dance, wife of mine?"

Amelia blushed, then glanced at Lady Drake as if seeking confirmation.

"Go ahead," his mother said. "I can occupy myself."

"All right, then."

They joined the dancers, and his heart lifted as he realized the dance was a waltz. He would get to keep her close, just as he preferred.

They moved into position, hands together, arms around each other. He leaned closer and breathed in her familiar scent.

"My lord," she murmured, "you're far too near to be decent."

He winked. "Haven't you heard? I'm not a particularly decent sort."

She snorted. "You have a slight reputation, but nothing particularly scandalous. If you did, do you think I'd have married you?"

"Shh. Let me pretend that my wife believes me to be a rogue," he teased.

The music began to play, and he swept her around the dance floor, expertly navigating around the other dancers. He kept his hand at a perfectly appropriate height, although he may have been holding her slightly closer than necessary. Surely no one could begrudge him that. She was his wife, and he wanted her near.

As he turned her, a flash of red silk on the opposite side of the ballroom caught his eye. He sought it out, curious who had been bold enough to wear such a daring color, but when he found her, his stomach hardened.

Florence.

"What's wrong?" Amelia asked.

He looked down at her, caught off guard. "What?"

"You look like you saw a ghost." She frowned. "Is it your mother? Did something happen?"

She craned her neck, searching for Lady Drake.

"N-no, nothing like that," Andrew assured her. "I just felt dizzy for a moment. It passed, and I'm fine now."

That was a lie. He didn't think he'd be all right until he'd ensured that Amelia's and Florence's paths would not cross again. He'd assumed they'd be safe at society events, but he'd forgotten that Florence did have legitimate connections to the ton on her mother's side, even if her father had never claimed her.

He considered how to get Amelia out of here quickly. They'd only just arrived. If he tried to leave, she'd question him. He could ask Florence to leave, but he doubted she'd do so. At least, not without making a fuss.

The fact that she was here after he'd told her that everything was over between them filled him with dread. She thrived on drama, and with her reputation being what it was, any trouble she caused would reflect more on him than her because he had more to lose.

The dance ended, and relieved, he led Amelia back to Lady Drake.

"Wait here," he said. "I'm going to fetch us some drinks."

"Do you need help?" Amelia asked.

"No. But thank you for the offer."

He wove between people to the drinks table and collected a glass of champagne in each hand. He'd prefer brandy, but that wasn't an option tonight.

"Lord Longley."

Damn.

His chest tight, he turned toward the speaker. "Miss Giles."

Florence pouted her rouged lips. "Dance with me?"

"No." He wasn't playing her games tonight.

She cocked her head. "Not for nostalgia's sake?"

"I said no."

Her eyes narrowed. "Yes, you did. The problem is, I'm the one who decides when things are over, not you. So now I'm giving you a choice. Dance with me, or I'll create such a scene that your little mouse will never dare show her face in the ton again."

He stared at her, astounded. "Why are you doing this?"

It couldn't be because of any tender feeling she had toward him. She'd been a good companion, but they had always been clear that no deeper emotions were involved.

She raised her chin. "I told you. I'm supposed to be the one who ends affairs. You took that away from me."

Andrew glanced back toward his mother and Amelia. He didn't have a good view of them from here, so hopefully they hadn't noticed who he was talking to.

"Fine. One dance. Then you leave me alone."

She shrugged. "Perhaps."

"No 'perhaps' about it. Those are my terms."

A laugh burst from her. "You're not in control here, Andrew. It's high time you realized that."

With gritted teeth, he set the glasses of champagne down and escorted her onto the dance floor. They lined up with the other partners, facing each other down like adversaries. The music began.

Fortunately, the dance was fast-paced, and he was able to keep his distance despite Florence's repeated attempts to get close to him. As soon as the song ended, he cut a line directly back to Amelia and Lady Drake, but Florence grabbed his arm and stopped him before he could reach them.

"Tut-tut." Her eyes twinkled with mischief in a way he might have found attractive once. "Here's what's going to happen. You're going to take me back. You'll continue making payments to me until I decide we're done."

He straightened his back. "And if I don't?"

"Then all of London will find out how you foolishly lost your fortune."

His insides turned cold. Among the ton, reputation was everything. He'd managed to cling to his, but if she whispered a few well-placed words, it would all be for naught. Not to mention how upset Amelia would be if people started gossiping about their marriage.

"Why are you doing this?" he asked, at a loss. "You could easily find someone else."

"You just don't understand, do you?" She put a hand on her hip. "It's the principle of the thing. Women like me don't get a lot of choices. I chose you, and I won't have you cast me aside for the sake of a plain little wallflower."

He growled under his breath. "For fuck's sake, Florence. First off, don't speak about my wife that way. She isn't plain, and she deserves respect. Secondly, I didn't leave you because I was tired of you. I left you because I was broke. Surely that appeases your pride."

She shrugged delicately. "You are no longer broke, and I've presented you with your options. Now, you simply have to choose."

∽

What on earth was taking Andrew so long to get their drinks?

Amelia looked around impatiently, searching the crowd for him, but Lady Drake's face appeared in her line of vision.

"What do you think of the choice of shrubbery over flowers?" she asked, shifting to remain directly in front of Amelia when she tried to look around her. "Would you prefer more of a focus on flowers? Of course, it can be difficult to source a large variety at this time of year, but I'm sure we can make arrangements if you'd like."

"I have no preference." Amelia looked sideways, and her heart skipped.

There he was.

Standing with the same woman who'd approached them at the teashop and whom he'd then avoided at a previous ball. The beautiful blonde clad in a scandalously red dress. She was leaning close to him, speaking rapidly.

"Who is that woman?" she asked Lady Drake.

Lady Drake glanced around without looking anywhere near her son or the woman in red. "What woman?"

"The one speaking to Andrew," she gritted out. "In the flaming red dress. You can't possibly miss her."

"Oh." Lady Drake deflated. "That is Miss Florence Giles. Daughter of the former Viscountess of Bellingham."

Amelia tried to swallow her frustration. "I know her name, but…"

But that didn't tell her everything she wanted to know. Why was the woman conversing with Andrew so intensely? Why did she keep turning up? And why did Andrew seem determined to avoid discussing her?

"But?" Lady Drake prompted. Something in her gaze made Amelia think she knew more than she was letting on.

Amelia sighed. "Never mind."

Whatever she wanted to know, she was better off asking Andrew. She glanced back at the pair and considered approaching. She wanted to know the truth, but she couldn't quite bring herself to interrupt.

She stalked to the drinks table, picked up a glass of champagne, and drained it in a few gulps, then grabbed another. This time, she sipped more leisurely.

"You ought to be careful drinking so much in public or rumors will spread," a snide voice said from a few feet away.

Amelia slowly turned toward the voice. "As it was my first drink of the night, I hardly think there's cause for concern, Miss Wentham."

Miss Wentham smirked. "You're rarely concerned when perhaps you ought to be."

Amelia frowned. "What are you talking about?"

The other woman raised a glass of lemonade to her lips, her expression as predatory as ever. "Simply that it's irresponsible of you to allow your husband to be seen with his mistress in front of so many people who matter."

"W-what?" Amelia placed her drink down and patted her chest, her throat constricting involuntarily.

"Oh dear." Miss Wentham pursed her lips. "Didn't you know?"

"You're lying." Her voice wavered, and she didn't sound as certain as she'd like to. After all, she had just been wondering about the relationship between him and the beautiful blonde. If she was his mistress, it would certainly explain the tension, and why he'd been so displeased when she approached them while he and Amelia were out together.

Perhaps she'd secretly feared making this exact discovery, even if she hadn't been brave enough to admit it to herself.

Her heart sank. No matter what she might want to believe, her gut told her that there might be some truth to Miss Wentham's claim.

"Why would you think that?" she asked.

Miss Wentham lifted one pink-clad shoulder and dropped it again. "Miss Giles is a cousin on my mother's side. Not exactly the type of relative one is proud of, but she has her uses, nonetheless. She is an excellent source of information."

Amelia shook her head. She wanted to squeeze her eyes shut and insist it wasn't true. That Andrew wouldn't disrespect her so blatantly by engaging with his mistress in public, especially not when they were….

Well, what were they, exactly?

Married, to be sure, and she'd thought there was more growing between them than that, but really, all they'd done was fulfill their duties to each other. He'd supported her and not stood in the way of her career, and she'd provided him with the opportunity to obtain an heir and enough wealth to get back on his feet.

If she'd read more into their situation than was warranted, that was on her.

She turned away from Miss Wentham and blinked rapidly, refusing to let that vulture see the tears that wanted to fall. She felt violated but couldn't even explain why. No one had broken any agreements. Andrew had not betrayed her. At least, not technically.

Yet, she felt as though he had.

She drew in a breath, struggling to fill her lungs, which were growing tighter by the second. Of course Andrew would have a mistress. She couldn't possibly compare to the beautiful, more experienced women he was used to. He was with her by necessity, not choice.

Amelia gathered herself enough to cross the room to Lady Drake.

"I'm afraid I am not feeling well," she told her. It was the truth, even if not all of it. "I am going home."

"But—"

"I'm sorry." Amelia didn't wait to hear her protests. She hurried up the stairs, across the foyer, and sent for the Longley carriage. As soon as it arrived, she clambered in and called for the driver to go.

They rumbled down the street, and her mind flitted back to the intensity between Miss Giles and Andrew during their exchange inside the Winstons' ballroom. She didn't want to believe them to be lovers, but honestly… she could.

Their conversation had obviously been heated, and Miss Giles was far more the type of woman she'd expect to attract him than she herself was.

She massaged her temples. Perhaps the situation wasn't what it seemed. Miss Wentham could have said what she did simply to be spiteful. That wouldn't be out of character. Or perhaps they truly were old friends and the friendship had ended on a sour note. Although that didn't quite ring true to Amelia.

She'd have to ask Andrew. But not tonight.

Honestly, all she wanted tonight was to tell the driver to set a course for the countryside and keep going until she'd outrun the bloody aristocracy and all their rules and double standards.

But she couldn't. He was Andrew's driver, not hers. Perhaps if she were Miss Joceline Davies, she'd know how to persuade him to save her from this wretched night, but if Amelia was honest with herself, she would always fall short of Joceline's courage. She'd never minded being practical, but now, she wished she wasn't. It would be awfully satisfying just to run off.

Although, if she did that, she wouldn't uncover the truth, and she'd always wonder. She briefly considered fleeing to her parents' home to put off the inevitable for a few nights, but she couldn't stomach the notion of allowing her mother any sort of control over her life again.

You're being ridiculous, Amelia told herself. *You never asked for fidelity, so you can't expect it. Just because you're falling for him doesn't mean he feels the same for you.*

She should have known better than to think she could keep things businesslike with Andrew. Even when she'd first met him and had been suspicious of his motives, he had been difficult to resist.

She was asking too much of herself.

The carriage stopped outside Longley House, and she rushed to knock on the door before the footman could do it and waited for Boden to open up.

Boden's forehead was furrowed with confusion, but he stepped back to allow Amelia to enter.

"Where are Lord Longley and Lady Drake?" he asked.

"They remained at the ball. I don't feel well and wish to retire early." The lie rolled off her tongue easily.

"I'm sorry to hear that. Do you need help getting to the bedchamber?"

"No, but I would appreciate it if you could send Margaret to assist me."

"Of course." Boden locked the door behind them.

Amelia made her way up the stairs, her heart heavy. She let herself into her bedchamber, went straight to the door connecting her room to Andrew's, and locked it from her side.

Margaret arrived to help a couple of minutes later, and they barely spoke as they readied Amelia for bed. When her head hit the pillow, she hoped she'd fall asleep immediately, but she wasn't that lucky.

Instead, she lay awake for long enough to hear Andrew moving around in his bedchamber. She listened as he approached the connecting door and tried the handle.

She held her breath as he knocked, and pretended to be asleep.

He didn't try again.

CHAPTER 21

Andrew stood outside Amelia's bedchamber door, poised to knock. Last night, he'd been willing to believe she'd slept through his knocking—especially if, as his mother had said, she was feeling unwell. However, this was the second time he'd knocked this morning, and still, all was silent within.

The fact that she was ignoring him made him fear there was more to the story than her simply coming down with a headache or some other malady. If that had been all there was to it, surely she'd have sought him out to tell him she'd like to leave the ball, yet she'd slunk off like a thief in the night.

He was afraid she'd seen him with Florence. He already knew she had questions about his former mistress, and Amelia wasn't one to forget a face or a name. If she'd seen them together, he had no doubt she'd remembered their previous interactions and possibly even asked his mother about their relationship.

He'd never mentioned Florence to Lady Drake, but he had no doubt she knew about her. His mother knew far more of what went on in his life than he'd have liked. The question was whether she'd have admitted as much to Amelia.

He should have asked last night. He hadn't asked because he'd wanted to avoid drawing attention to Florence's presence if his mother hadn't already noticed her, and because he'd hoped his worries were an overreaction. Now, he was beginning to wonder if that might not be the case.

He knocked again. When there was no response, he tried the handle. This couldn't continue. They had to discuss the matter.

But when the door swung open, the bedchamber was empty. The bed was neatly made, the desk was clear, and only the lingering scent of mint showed she'd been there recently.

Damn.

He pivoted and hurried down to the morning room, hoping he'd find her there. It was empty.

He huffed, frustrated. His mother and Kate were both still abed, so he sought out Mrs. Smythe, finding her in the kitchen, her portly form bent over the countertop.

"Have you seen the countess this morning?" he asked.

She jolted upright, and her hands flew to her chest. "My lord, you startled me."

He winced. "My apologies, Mrs. Smythe. I thought you'd heard me approach."

"Never mind. I must not have been paying proper attention." She adjusted her stance and dipped her head. "You're looking for the countess?"

"Yes, that's right."

"She left the house a little while ago. Perhaps twenty minutes or so."

Double damn. He'd missed his opportunity to speak with her before she started her day.

"I don't suppose she left word as to where she was going?" Unlikely, but it was worth a chance.

But Mrs. Smythe shook her head. "No, my lord. She took Margaret with her, though."

At least that was something. Not that he was concerned for her safety, but she might be upset, and if that was the case, it was reassuring to know she wasn't alone.

"Thank you. I'll be visiting the Regent this morning. Can you let me know if she returns before I do?"

"Of course." Her forehead furrowed. "Is everything all right?"

"Just fine." His tone was so falsely jovial, he doubted she believed him, but she just nodded as he left.

He sent for a carriage, then grabbed his coat and hat and headed out to meet it.

"To the Regent," he told his driver, climbing on board the carriage without waiting for the footman to assist him, although he heard a thud as he leapt aboard.

He gazed out the window. The sky was depressingly gray this morning, much like his mood. He curled his fingers into his palms to warm them and settled into his seat until the carriage stopped and the footman knocked to signal that they'd arrived.

For a few seconds, he sat still, steeling himself. He knew he needed to ask around about Florence and find out exactly what she was up to, but raising the matter would be blasted uncomfortable.

"My lord?"

With a sigh, he called for the footman to open up. He got out of the carriage and greeted the doorman, who bowed low and opened the main entrance for him.

The Regent was quiet at this time of day. Many late-night revelers would still be at home, nursing tender heads. The gentlemen who'd ventured out this morning were those more like Ashford. Or at least, he hoped that would prove the case. He rarely came here before noon himself.

"Are there any card games afoot?" he asked one of the servants.

"Down the corridor, third door on the left," the man replied.

"Thank you."

He removed his coat and hat and handed them over, then made his way down the corridor to the open doorway the servant had mentioned. A group of men sat around a table, playing a game of what looked to be whist. Andrew grimaced when he spotted Mr. Falvey among their number. He'd assumed it would be too early for the other man.

"Longley," Falvey called. "Join us."

Andrew pulled over a chair. "Deal me in the next time it's convenient."

"Of course, of course."

He looked around the other faces at the table. Mr. Chautner, a degenerate gambler who very well might have been here all night, judging by his bloodshot eyes and drooping head. Mr. Daniels, a smart fellow who'd likely only stopped in for a short bout of socialization before spending the rest of the day in his library. Baron Winthrop, a dapper gentleman with a sharp tongue. And lastly, Mr. Thompson, the third son of a viscount.

"Who's winning this morning?" he asked, wondering how best to raise the subject of Florence.

Mr. Falvey laughed. "Based on the events of last night, I'd hazard a guess that you've gotten luckier than any of us. How come you're here instead of with the lovely Miss Giles?"

Andrew stiffened. "What do you mean?"

Mr. Falvey took his turn before answering. "Your wife left the Winston ball early yesterday, and you were seen in quite an intense exchange with Miss Giles. I can only assume you've taken back up with her, and I can't blame you. She's a beauty, all right. I tried to tempt her with a little fun, but she told me firmly she wasn't done with you yet. Lucky sod."

Andrew groaned. It was even worse than he'd thought. Obviously, the gossips had been busy. There was every chance that Amelia would discover the truth, if she hadn't already.

"You're stepping out on your new wife already, Longley?" Where Mr. Falvey's voice had been full of admiration, Mr. Daniels's was disapproving. "The ink isn't even dry on your marriage certificate."

"I'm not." Andrew glanced at Chautner's half-drunk brandy, wondering whether he'd notice if it vanished. He could use a bloody drink. "Miss Giles should not have approached me in public like that. I don't have any sort of attachment to her, nor do I intend to form one. I'm quite enjoying married life."

Falvey snorted. "You'd better be careful or you'll become as tiringly proper as Ashford."

Mr. Thompson dealt Andrew a hand.

"I'll take that as a compliment," Andrew said, ignoring the fact that it certainly hadn't been intended as such. "Ashford is my closest friend, and I admire the man greatly."

Falvey shook his head. "Another good man falls afoul of marital bliss. Don't say I didn't warn you."

"I don't think anyone here can claim you haven't warned them," Winthrop muttered. "One would think you're utterly besieged by marriage-minded mamas and giggling misses, the way you go on."

The two men traded barbs for a few minutes until they settled into the game.

Andrew only stayed long enough not to make it obvious that he'd been on an information-gathering mission before he said his goodbyes and departed. He'd just crawled out of a bad financial situation and had no desire to tempt fate by betting on card games.

When he arrived home, Mrs. Smythe quietly let him know that Amelia had returned only a few minutes earlier and could be found in the library. He headed straight there, wanting to reduce her opportunity to escape unnoticed.

Gray light streamed through the windows, and the air smelled faintly musty. He made a mental note to ask Mrs. Smythe to air it out at the next suitable opportunity.

Amelia was stretched comfortably along a sofa in front of the window, reading a book he hadn't seen before. Perhaps she'd been to the bookshop. When she saw him, she swung her legs off the cushion and placed her book face down on the table.

"Don't trouble yourself to stand," he said, all too aware of how stiff he sounded. "I'll join you."

She bit her lower lip. "I'm happy to go elsewhere. I don't want to intrude on your privacy."

"If you were to go elsewhere, then I'd have to follow," he told her. "I'm here to speak with you."

"Oh." She seemed uncertain how to react. "I'm sorry for disappearing last night. A headache came on quite suddenly, and I couldn't bear the noise."

He stalked toward her, noting the slight flare of her nostrils and the widening of her eyes. "Is that what happened?"

"Yes." She raised her chin. "I'm feeling much improved now, though."

He sat on the end of the sofa and crossed his legs. "You see, I was afraid that perhaps someone had said something to make you uncomfortable."

Something flickered across her expression, but it was gone so fast, he couldn't put his finger on exactly what it was.

"What would anyone have said to make me uncomfortable?" she asked with an edge of defiance.

His heart sank. Someone *had* said something. Either that, or she'd noticed his preoccupation with Florence. He couldn't forget how observant she was.

Internally, he debated what to say. He'd prefer not to come straight out with it, but ignoring the matter wouldn't help either. If he didn't tell her where things stood, then she was free to wonder, and he already knew she had quite the imagination.

He reached for her hand, grateful when she let him take it. "Perhaps someone might have mentioned my... friendship... with Miss Giles?"

The corners of her mouth tightened. "Your 'friendship' with Miss Giles is none of my concern."

His gut clenched. Did she really believe that?

"You aren't breaking our agreement," she continued, gazing somewhere past his shoulder. "You're allowed to conduct your private affairs however you see fit."

He felt a pang. Perhaps he wasn't breaking their agreement, but she was breaking his heart. "Would you really not care if I had a mistress?"

She pulled her hand away and clasped it on her lap with her other one. "It's not my place to have an opinion." Her voice was thick with emotion, making a liar of her. "However, I would appreciate it if you'd refrain from flaunting her —or any future mistress—in front of the ton. I don't deserve to be humiliated in such a way."

He struggled to draw a breath, instinctively reaching for her again, but she pulled back, creating more distance between them.

"I'm sorry." He wished he could take her into his arms. She was right. She deserved better than the scene that he and Florence had created last night. "I'm so sorry. I swear to you, she and I are no longer together. I haven't been with her since I met you, but she was upset when I ended things, so she's lashing out however she can."

Her breath hitched, and she raised her eyes to his. "You aren't...?"

"No." He shook his head emphatically. "I don't want her. I only want you."

For a moment, the tension left her, but then her lips thinned. "For how long?"

He frowned. "I beg your pardon?"

Her teeth scraped over her lower lip, and she tucked her hair behind her ear. "For now, I'm a novelty, but eventually, you'll tire of me."

"I sincerely doubt that will happen." Not with how obsessed he'd become with his wife. The thought of touching another woman made him ill. Why would he want or need anyone else when there was so much left for him to discover about Amelia? So many facets of her yet to explore.

"It will." Her tone brooked no argument. "At some point."

He leaned forward. "I don't think you're being fair. You can't possibly know how I'll feel or what I'll want before I even know that myself."

"Perhaps not." She stood and walked to the window, standing framed by the light with her back to him. "But I'd like to be alone now, please."

∽

The clock ticked. Amelia clung to her skirts, her heart hammering wildly despite her calm exterior. She was terrified that Andrew would refuse, and then she'd have to continue to hold herself together when everything inside her was crumbling.

Thankfully, he murmured, "Very well," and excused himself.

The instant the door clicked shut, she blinked, and a tear trickled from the corner of her eye and skated down her cheek. Another followed, and she released a shuddering breath. She forced herself to remain silent. If she made a sound, there was every chance he'd return.

She tiptoed to the sofa and flopped onto it, resting her head on its arm and closing her eyes as her tears continued to fall.

"Do not dwell on it," she hissed at herself.

She shouldn't be so upset. She'd never expected love from her husband, and even when she'd suggested their arrangement, she'd known there was a strong possibility he'd be unfaithful. Andrew was right about one thing. It wasn't fair for her to feel this way. Especially when she'd never been under any illusion about what this marriage was.

And all right, perhaps Andrew had told the truth about his arrangement with Miss Giles, and it truly was over, but for some reason, that didn't calm her.

Miss Giles was beautiful. She was brave and bold and many, many things that Amelia wasn't.

If she was the type of woman to appeal to Andrew, then Amelia would have to admit that all the passion and desire she'd experienced toward him could never be fully reciprocated. Not when she was so different from the type of woman he chose to dally with when he wasn't backed into a corner by his financial obligations.

Perhaps he was genuinely fond of Amelia, but she would always be the wife he'd had to marry, not one he'd chosen because he wanted her.

That hurt.

"Amelia?"

She jerked upright, swiping at her tear-stained cheeks. Kate stood in the doorway, her brow wrinkled with concern. Amelia had been so consumed by self-pity that she hadn't heard the door open.

"What's wrong?" Kate asked, padding inside and closing the door behind herself. "Why are you upset?"

Amelia deflated. She'd never get away with pretending to be fine after what Kate had witnessed. "It's nothing."

Kate arched an eyebrow. Her hair—a few shades lighter

than Andrew's—bounced around her shoulders as she crossed the room and perched on the other arm of the sofa.

"If it were nothing, you wouldn't be in tears."

Amelia exhaled sharply. "You are persistent, aren't you?"

Kate crossed her ankles and propped her chin on her hand. "Only when it matters."

"Fine." Clearly she wouldn't be getting rid of Kate without telling her something. "But I fear that you'll either think me foolish or be angry with your brother."

"Ah." Understanding dawned in her gray eyes. "My brother has behaved foolishly."

"Not exactly. He—"

"Say no more." Kate held her hand up to cut Amelia off. "Shall we go shopping and charge the bill back to him?"

Amelia's stomach squeezed. No matter how well-intentioned the offer may be, all it did was remind her of why Andrew had married her. So his sister and mother would be able to shop if they wished to. So Kate could have a season. Not because he was suddenly and unexpectedly smitten by an ink-stained bluestocking.

"I don't think that would make me feel any better," Amelia admitted.

"Hmm." Kate tapped her chin thoughtfully. "What would?"

Amelia cocked her head, considering. Anything related to Andrew was off-limits, as was anything that required money. But there was one thing she knew she could safely focus on.

"Would you like to hear about the book I'm currently working on?" she asked.

Kate brightened. "The second one about Miss Joceline?"

"Yes." She nibbled her lip, uncertain what Kate's response would be. She certainly didn't adore books as Amelia did, but she hadn't shown a disdain for reading either, and she'd happily listened to Amelia go on about her first book.

"I'd love to," Kate said, shuffling down onto the sofa

cushion and making herself comfortable. "Tell me all about it."

So Amelia did, starting with the end of the first book and carrying on to Joceline's more recent adventures.

"I can't help but feel that this fickle suitor of Joceline's may be somewhat inspired by my brother," Kate observed, far more astutely than Amelia had expected.

She flushed, embarrassed to have been caught out. Hopefully no one else would notice. "Not exactly, but…."

Kate patted her hand. "Andrew may be a dolt at times, but he's a good man. If you're honest with him about whatever he's done to upset you, I'm sure he will do his best to put it right."

Amelia forced herself to smile. "Perhaps."

Or perhaps if he found out that her feelings for him had grown beyond what they ought to be, he'd break her heart in a thousand tiny ways. It would never be intentional. He wasn't a cruel person. But wounds stung regardless of whether they were inflicted purposefully, and there was only so much a heart could take.

Hers had, unfortunately, attached itself to Andrew. She could only hope he never realized it.

CHAPTER 22

When Amelia strode into the drawing room, she expected to find Kate, Brigid, and Mrs. Smythe ready to make plans for her first ball. Instead, Andrew was the only one awaiting her.

He rose as she entered. "You look lovely, Amelia."

She blinked rapidly, caught off guard. "What's happening? I'm supposed to be going through options for our ball with your mother and sister."

He sauntered over to her and kissed her cheek. "Mother and Kate are quite capable of working on that themselves. You and I are going on a picnic."

She stiffened, reluctant to be alone with him. "I really shouldn't leave when they're relying on me to help."

"No need to worry about that," Lady Drake said, sweeping into the room and bringing a waft of lavender-scented air with her. "Kate and I have it all under control."

"Are you sure?" Perhaps if she pleaded with her eyes, Lady Drake would take pity on her.

Unfortunately, that did not occur. Quite to the contrary, Kate glided in behind Lady Drake with a selection of fabric samples draped over her arm.

"We can manage perfectly well," Kate assured her. "Mama and I both enjoy this sort of thing. You don't. Let us do this for you."

Amelia ground her teeth together. There weren't many things over which she'd choose to make ball preparations, but spending time with her husband when their last one-on-one conversation had centered around his mistress topped the list.

"Perfect." Andrew's palm scalded the small of her back. "Let's go, then."

"I'll need a redingote," she protested.

"Margaret is waiting with one in the foyer, and a pair of walking shoes too."

He really had thought of everything. But why? What did he hope to achieve by sweeping her away for a picnic?

She sighed. "I suppose we'd best be off, then."

She could simply tell him she didn't want to, but that would be churlish when, as she'd already reminded herself many times, he didn't deserve it.

He grinned and escorted her back through the door. As he'd said, Margaret was waiting with a redingote folded over her arm and a pair of walking shoes on the floor. Andrew released Amelia, and Margaret helped her into the redingote, then knelt to remove her slippers and slide her feet into the shoes.

When she was ready to depart, Andrew took her arm and led her to the door. "You enjoy riding, don't you?"

"I do." Where was this going?

"When we're in Suffolk, we'll have to go riding together. Today, I thought we could take my phaeton."

To her annoyance, a spark of excitement began within her. She did love to travel without being confined within a closed carriage. Carriages served their purpose and provided shelter when needed, but phaetons and curricles were much more enjoyable forms of transportation.

"I haven't seen your phaeton before," she said as he held the door open for her. She stepped out and, searching their surroundings for the phaeton, immediately spotted it parked near the bottom of the stairs.

"It doesn't get out much in autumn and winter," Andrew said, closing the door and stepping out beside her. "But today is unseasonably warm, and it seemed like Providence."

Amelia glanced up at the sky. Clouds floated across it, and the sun wasn't particularly bright, but he was right that the temperatures were unusually mild for this time of year. They walked together to the phaeton, and he offered her his hand to help her up. She sat on the far side, and he climbed up beside her and took the reins.

"Where are we going?" she asked.

If he intended to take her to Hyde Park, they wouldn't get a moment to themselves, which might be a good thing, in the circumstances.

He waggled his eyebrows. "It's a surprise."

Her heart clenched. Why must her husband be so endearing?

It simply wasn't fair.

Andrew urged the pair of black horses into motion, and Amelia gripped the side of the phaeton as they rolled smoothly out of the courtyard and onto the road. He shot her a look and encouraged the horses to go faster—although not so fast that they would be a danger to anyone around them. Despite herself, she grinned.

She wondered just how fast the phaeton could go. It was sleek and well-made. She could imagine him racing his friends with it when he was younger. She suspected that if he gave the horses free rein, they could go very fast indeed. Perhaps she'd have to ask him to do so when they were in the country.

They swept around corners, the air rushing past her face and stinging her eyes. She laughed and clutched more tightly to the phaeton. No doubt her hair was a mess, but she didn't care.

The phaeton bounced along a nearly empty road on the edge of Mayfair and turned down a private way. They traveled down the tree-lined drive for several minutes before emerging into the open air.

They were in a garden. Lush trees and shrubbery occupied most of the area, with neatly maintained grass pathways winding between them. There wasn't a lot of color, but she imagined that during spring and summer, flowers brought stunning bursts of brightness to the garden.

As they came to a stop, she closed her eyes and breathed in. Even though they were still in London, all she could smell was grass and trees. None of the usual city odors.

"It's beautiful," she said.

Andrew set his reins aside. "It belongs to a friend of mine. He's granted us private usage for the day. We're the only ones here."

"That's so generous of him." Although it did, unfortunately, mean that she wouldn't have anyone to act as a distraction if Andrew opened a subject she'd rather avoid.

He jumped down and held out his hand. She rose, laid her palm on his, and let him help her down.

"Have a look around," he said. "I'm going to set the horses loose."

Her eyebrows rose. "They won't stray?"

"Not far. They've been well trained, and since we're the only ones here, I don't believe there's any reason to worry."

She stepped off the graveled parking area onto the lawn. It was slightly damp and springy beneath her feet. Gazing around, she wandered down the nearest grass path, looking both ways when she reached an intersection.

She gasped. Down the path to the right, light reflected off the surface of a pond. She hurried along the path, which opened into a clearing on the side of the water. Willow trees fringed the clearing, and several ducks floated on the surface.

"Ah, you found the pond, then."

She jumped, her hand flying to her chest. Andrew stood behind her, a basket in one hand and a blanket tucked under the other arm.

"You frightened me," she said. "I didn't hear you coming."

"Ah, sorry." He grimaced. "I did call your name, but you didn't turn."

Her cheeks heated. "I was admiring the view and must have been too distracted to notice."

He gestured at a patch of grass in front of her. "Shall we set up our picnic here?"

She nodded. "Seems as good a place as any."

He set the basket down, unfolded the picnic blanket, and laid it on the grass. Then he placed the basket in the center of the blanket and lowered himself onto one side of it.

"Join me?"

Carefully, Amelia lowered herself down, too, extending her legs and rearranging her skirts so as not to get them dirty. As he opened the basket and withdrew a flask and two teacups, she tried not to be charmed, but it was impossible.

"This is lovely. Thank you."

He beamed. "I'm glad you like it." He positioned the cups on the flattest bits of ground he could find and filled them with tea from the flask. "It's already sweetened. I had Mrs. Baker add sugar."

"Thank you." Her heart squeezed. He really was very thoughtful. Was it any wonder she'd fallen halfway in love with him so easily?

He withdrew something wrapped in a cloth and opened it to reveal several buttered scones. "Would you like one?"

"Yes, please." She accepted a scone and took a delicate bite from the corner. It was soft and slightly warm.

"Jam?"

She glanced over. Andrew held a small glass jar of berry jam and a spoon. She finished chewing and swallowed.

"What is this about?" she asked.

Something was going on here. She had the same subtle sense of unease she'd had when he was courting her under false pretenses. Her instincts were telling her that something was off-kilter.

Andrew frowned. "What do you mean?"

She waved her half-eaten scone at him. "You're up to something."

He looked affronted. "I am not. You deserve to be treated well, and that's what I'm doing."

"But it's not..." *Part of our agreement.* She couldn't bring herself to voice the thought.

"Not what?" He cocked his head. "I care about you deeply, Amelia, and I want you to be happy."

Butterflies danced in her stomach, but at the same time, her heart sank.

She had such a sweet, kind husband. That was something to be grateful for. She was lucky to have him. But God, he made it difficult to resist him.

Perhaps sensing that she didn't know how to respond, he opened the jam and spooned some of it onto another scone.

"I heard you reading to Kate the other evening," he said, raising the scone to his mouth.

She took another bite of her own to give herself a moment to think. "I hope you don't mind."

"Not at all." He flashed her a grin. "She deserves to know that women can have dreams of their own. Too many people tell them they can't. That finding a husband is the most important thing they'll ever accomplish, and maybe some women are happy with that, but I'm glad you're showing her that she doesn't have to be."

Amelia's heart expanded. "How are you so incredible?"

When she'd married, she'd expected him to tolerate her

writing at best. She'd been fully prepared to face derision, but this unwavering support was more than she could ever have hoped for.

She leaned over the basket and kissed him. He tasted of berries and the outdoors. She closed her eyes and melted as he cupped her face and deepened the kiss.

She dropped her scone. Where, she wasn't quite sure. Andrew tossed his toward the pond, and the birds flocked around it. Then he heaved her over the basket and onto his lap. She tilted her head back, and her tongue met his. Breath eased between her lips.

His fingers tangled in her hair, and he tugged, angling her head to give him better access to her mouth. She clutched his chest, reveling in the strength concealed by his coat and shirtsleeves. They continued to kiss, slow and languid, almost drugging.

He broke free. "Wait."

"What is it?" she asked breathlessly.

He nuzzled the side of her neck. "I don't expect anything from you just because I brought you out on a picnic. You don't have to do this to make things even between us. I know how you think."

She snorted. Perhaps he knew a little of how she thought, but clearly not enough if he believed she was going along with this for his benefit. In truth, she had no hope of resisting him and had simply given up trying.

"I want to," she told him.

Kissing like this, in broad daylight in the outdoors, gave her a strange kind of thrill. It was the sort of behavior she'd expect from a mistress, not a wife, and perhaps she wanted to give Miss Giles a little healthy competition.

She and Andrew may not have agreed to be faithful as part of their contract, but now that she knew exactly how much he meant to her, she wouldn't let him go without a fight. She may not have experience or beauty on her side, but she had all the time in the world to win him over. Miss Giles, on the other hand, did not.

"Really?" One side of his mouth hitched up, his expression turning wicked. "You aren't worried about being out in the open?"

"You said we're alone here." She kissed him. "I know you'll take care of me."

"Damn right I will." He peppered her face with kisses. "No one gets to see your gorgeous body except for me."

Heat rushed to her core. Surely his possessiveness was a good sign.

"Lie back," he murmured against her skin. "Let me make you feel nice."

She stiffened. "No."

"No?" He drew back, frowning. "Sorry, did I misunderstand—"

"No." Her cheeks were absolutely blazing now. "I want you to lie down. There's something I've been wanting to try."

"Oh." He sounded intrigued, but he lay back on the blanket without any fuss.

She crawled over him and sat back on her haunches. There was absolutely no way to do this without making at least a bit of a mess. She shifted the basket aside and cleared their teacups out of the way, then gazed down at him.

He smiled lazily up at her. "I'm at your mercy, my lady."

"I like the sound of that." If he was at her mercy, then he wouldn't be anywhere near the smirking Miss Giles.

Unfortunately, the burst of courage that had driven her earlier words was waning. She hesitated, suddenly unsure whether she was about to make a fool of herself.

"What's wrong?" he murmured.

"Nothing. I'm just…." She sighed, exasperated with herself. "I'm nervous. What if you don't like it?"

He chuckled. "I assure you that I will like almost anything you do to me, and if I don't, I'll tell you so."

She nibbled on her lower lip. "Promise?"

He crossed his heart. "I give my solemn oath."

"All right." She could do this. She hadn't lied about wanting to try. Ever since the first time Andrew had placed his mouth on her there, she'd been curious whether he would enjoy it if she did the same to him.

She undid his breeches, fumbling with the laces as her hands trembled.

Andrew's thumb and forefinger encircled her wrist gently. "Easy, sweetheart. Breathe. I promise you, you have absolutely nothing to worry about."

She exhaled, long and slow, and something inside her eased. He was right. If she fumbled this time, she could just do better next time. They had their entire lives ahead of them.

She tugged at the waistband of his breeches, and he lifted his hips so she could pull them down. His drawers followed. She left them around his knees and lowered herself onto her front beside his legs. She propped herself up with one hand and wrapped the other around his cock.

Her breath hitched. He was already hard, but he stiffened further in her grip, pulsing against her palm like molten steel. She pumped him a few times and spread the liquid that leaked from the head of his cock with her thumb. He groaned, and his hips twitched.

Smiling to herself, she repeated the motion. She'd played with him like this before, although she'd never tried to make him spill his seed. After all, if he wanted an heir, it was best off inside her. She doubted mistresses ever thought about anything as practical as that, though.

Quite the opposite.

Slowly, she lowered her head and licked the end of his cock. A salty, musky flavor filled her mouth. She wouldn't call it delicious, but it wasn't unpleasant either. She licked him again, her tongue darting over his flesh, there and gone again.

"Lia…"

She stilled, and her eyes rose to his. He'd never called her that before.

"Is that not all right?" he asked.

"I like it."

The name felt special. Intimate. Similar to what her father called her, but different.

Just for them.

She swirled her tongue around his head and was rewarded with more of the salty-sweet seed. Sealing her lips around him, she sucked.

His hips bucked, and he made a growling noise in the back of his throat that did strange things to her body. She could feel herself becoming damp between her legs. By now, she knew that meant she was readying herself for him.

She spread open-mouthed kisses down the side of his cock, licking and sucking his length.

"Take me in your mouth," he pleaded.

Her eyebrows pinched together, but she sucked his cock head into her mouth and tried to take him deeper. His cock hit the back of her throat, and she gagged.

"Easy." He stroked her hair. "Just take a little at a time."

She blinked rapidly, her eyes watering, and tried again, this time only going a little deeper. She pulled off and repeated the motion, going slightly deeper again. Over and over, she continued, stopping short when she felt herself begin to gag.

Her jaw was starting to ache, but with the sounds of bliss Andrew kept making, she didn't intend to stop anytime soon.

"Stop." Andrew tugged gently on her hair, drawing her off him.

"What?" she panted.

"I'm nearly there."

"I know." She didn't see the problem.

He chuckled, and his head flopped back against the blanket. "I want to be inside you."

"Oh." The wet heat between her legs throbbed. "How do we…."

He sat up and shoved his breeches and drawers all the way down. "The ground is too hard, and I don't want to hurt you, so you'll have to, uh, straddle me."

Straddle him?

An intriguing concept.

"But first," he continued, "let me get you ready."

She looked down at her hands, her hot cheeks no doubt showing her embarrassment. "I'm pretty sure I'm already ready."

His eyebrows shot up. "You are?"

With a quick glance around to confirm that they were still alone, Amelia stripped off her underwear and lifted her skirt. Andrew slipped his hand beneath and stroked her softness. She shuddered as pleasure rippled through her.

He teased her with clever fingers. "You're so wet."

"You have that effect on me," she admitted.

His eyes darkened, and he gripped his cock and pointed it skyward. "Good. Now, straddle me and lower yourself onto me."

Amelia's face was on fire as she hurried to comply. She placed her knees on either side of his thighs, and she dropped down until his cock pushed against her entrance. She bit her lip and breathed out, doing her best to relax her muscles. Inch by inch, she took him inside her body.

When she sat flush against him, she rested her head on his shoulder and savored the connection. "I didn't know it could be like this."

His arms came around her. "It can be however we want, my Lia." He thrust up, then, with his hands on her hips, guided her to rock back and forth, pleasure zipping through her over and over again. "Just like that. Damn, sweetheart. You make me crazy."

Yes. I want to make him lose his mind so he never looks at another woman.

She rode him in the way that felt best for her, since he seemed to like it, whatever she did. Pleasure built within her, growing steadily until she couldn't stand it anymore. She threw her head back and cried out, her channel tightening around him.

He grabbed her hips and pushed up into her, his movements erratic, then stiffened and pulsed deep inside her. She rested her forehead against his, and their lips met in a soft kiss.

He cupped her face and kissed her again. "That was incredible."

"It really was."

She eased off him and reached for her undergarments, but he gestured for her to wait. He grabbed the basket and pulled out a cloth, which he dabbed between her legs.

"Mrs. Baker always includes a cleaning-up cloth in picnic baskets," he told her with a grin. "Although I doubt she intended it to be used this way."

A laugh burst from her, and she clapped her hand to her mouth, mortified at the thought. "She won't know, will she?"

He shook his head. "I'll dispose of it myself."

"Good." Obviously, their household staff must be aware of the activities they engaged in, but she'd rather pretend otherwise and have them continue to do the same. She may be willing to act the wanton, but only when it was just her and Andrew alone together.

She pulled up her drawers, and he wiped his cock and tucked himself away inside his own drawers, then buttoned his breeches.

She stretched out on the blanket, savoring the tenderness in her body. "I like picnics. We should have more of them, especially in summer." She slid her gaze sideways. "And especially if they end like this."

He chuckled. "Your wish is my command." He intertwined his fingers with hers, and his expression turned serious. "I am going to do everything I can to ensure your happiness."

Unease slithered through her.

His words were no doubt intended to be reassuring, but the way he said them made her think he had reason to believe there was a threat to her happiness.

And that meant he was keeping things from her.

CHAPTER 23

"I'll be back soon," Andrew said later that day, bending to kiss Amelia's cheek as she sat behind her writing desk. "I have business to attend to."

She frowned. "In the evening?"

"It was the only time the person I'm meeting was available." He couldn't bring himself to lie and say it was a man. He was already stretching the truth to a degree he felt uncomfortable with.

"Then come home soon." She smiled at him, but there was something dark behind her eyes. "I have plans for you."

A shaft of guilt lanced through him. She wouldn't tease him so sweetly if she knew he was going to visit his former mistress.

"I'll return as fast as I'm able." He kissed her again, closing his eyes and savoring her faint minty scent. He drew back. "You'll be so busy writing that you won't even notice I'm gone."

She didn't laugh, and for some reason, her smile continued to not quite ring true. "Be safe."

"Always." He swept out before he could second-guess

himself. He'd made his choice, and it was time to tell his blackmailer what it was.

A plain carriage was waiting for him out the front of Longley House. He passed Boden, whose expression was etched with disapproval, and hurried down the front steps.

The sooner this was over with, the better.

He gave the driver the address and climbed in the back. While they traveled to Florence's apartment, he considered how best to get his message across without any chance of a misunderstanding.

He'd have to be blunt.

He didn't want to hurt her, but he also couldn't allow her to ruin the life he was building with Amelia.

When they arrived, he asked his driver to wait around the corner, and he headed to the door and knocked. He could feel eyes on him, but whoever was watching him must be hiding, because there was no one in sight.

Nobody came to the door, so he tried the handle. It was unlocked. He gritted his teeth. That wasn't safe when a building housed an unprotected woman. Fortunately, it worked to his advantage, but he'd have to remind her to be more careful.

He saw himself up to Florence's apartment and knocked. Muffled noises came from inside, and then the door opened. Florence leaned against the doorframe, her wheaten hair spilling around her shoulders. She wore only a dressing gown, and her lips were unnaturally red.

"The front door was unlocked," he informed her. "You should remind the landlord to lock it whenever they leave."

She crossed her arms and scowled. "Did you just come here to lecture me like a child?"

"No. We need to talk."

"Come in." She stepped back, and her robe gaped open, revealing a long length of neck and the swell of her breasts.

He squeezed his eyes shut before his gaze sank lower. "Please cover yourself."

"But wouldn't you like to see me?" Her voice wrapped around him like a caress. "You've always enjoyed looking in the past."

"That's over." He refused to open his eyes. "I'm no longer interested."

There was a sigh, and then she said, "Everything is decent. You may look."

Warily, he peered out between his lashes. Finding that she was telling the truth, he opened his eyes properly. "Thank you."

She rolled her eyes and muttered under her breath. "Have you come to tell me of your decision?"

"I have."

She reached for him, a smirk quirking the corner of her mouth, but he stepped away, and her hand fell to her side.

"You can spread whatever rumors you like," he said. "My relationship with the countess is more important to me than my reputation. I will not be resuming our affair."

A flicker of hurt passed over her face, but then she scoffed. "Don't be ridiculous. I can offer you more excitement than your boring, mousey wife ever could." She swayed closer and grabbed his tie before he could avoid her. "You don't have to put on an act when we're in private, darling. I know you want me."

He grabbed her wrist and gently but firmly tugged it away from his cravat. "I never set out to hurt you, Florence. I'm sorry if that's what I've done. But you must end this campaign to win me over. You won't succeed. I'm faithful to my wife."

Quick as a fox, she grabbed his cock through his breeches.

He choked on air, shocked stiff. When he regained

control of himself, he swatted her hand away and partially closed the door, putting it between them.

"Don't ever touch me like that again," he growled. "It's completely unacceptable."

"Andrew, I—"

He cut her off. "No. I've been patient with you because of our history, but let me make this perfectly clear. The only woman I want touching me is my wife. You may be accustomed to using your beauty to get what you want, but you won't have me. Never again. My heart, my body, and my soul belong to her."

"But she's so… so…," she sputtered, apparently unable to find the words she was searching for.

"She's clever," he said, "passionate, and ambitious, and she has the biggest heart. I refuse to have anything to do with bruising it."

She narrowed her eyes. "You just think I won't go through with it."

He shook his head. "Do what you think is best. It won't change my mind."

She shut the door in his face.

His shoulders slumped, and he left, unable to help the feeling that he'd failed. He'd made the right decision—he had no doubt of that—but if Florence spread rumors about his marriage, it would hurt Amelia, and it would be his fault. There was no escaping that.

He pushed the door open, strode through, and headed around the corner to where the carriage waited. He got inside without a word and buried his face in his hands as the carriage jolted forward.

How concerned should he be? Was Florence's desire for petty revenge really strong enough that she'd risk angering an aristocrat?

He sighed. He knew damn well that she wouldn't fear any

repercussions from him. She was the type of person to carry through on her threats.

Should he warn Amelia?

If he did, he'd have to tell her why this was happening, and the idea of that was sickening—especially after she'd already shown that she was insecure about Florence.

Damn. Why did it have to be so hard to know the right thing to do?

He arrived home, intending to retire quietly to his bedroom for a soak in the bath so he could consider his options in private, but as soon as he was through the door, Amelia rushed down the stairs toward him, grinning broadly.

"What is it?" he asked, uncertain what could have excited her so greatly when he'd only been gone for a short period of time.

She skipped over to him, wrapped her arms around his neck, and stretched onto her tiptoes to kiss him. "I have another story ready to send to the publisher."

"Congratulations!" He hugged her tightly, breathing in woman and mint. The smell of home. He kissed her. "I'm so proud of you."

She started to smile, but then she sniffed, and a groove formed between her eyebrows. "Are you using a new cologne?"

His heart skipped and his blood turned cold. Fuck. Florence must have left a trace of her floral perfume on him when she grabbed his cravat—or his crotch.

"Yes," he said so quickly, his tongue almost tripped over the word. "I'm trying it out. What do you think?"

She sniffed again and frowned. "It's rather feminine, but it's nice, so if you like it, then I like it too."

He grimaced. Now he felt like an utter cad. His wife was prepared to like the scent of another woman's perfume on him just because she thought it was something he'd worn to please himself.

"Have you prepared a copy of the story for submission?" he asked, desperate to change the subject.

"Yes." She let him go and gestured up the stairs. "It's in my bedchamber. I've been preparing extra copies of each section as I write them so it would be ready as soon as I was finished."

"Excellent." His wife was brilliant. "Boden!"

The butler materialized from nowhere, but his judgmental expression told Andrew that he'd heard their exchange regarding the perfume. "My lord?"

"Please arrange to have the countess's story delivered to the publisher first thing in the morning. She'll show you where it is."

Boden bowed to Amelia. "It would be my honor, my lady."

With a dirty look at Andrew, Boden followed Amelia up the stairs. Andrew wondered whether he ought to be bothered by the butler's apparent defection, but all he could feel was pleased that his people cared about Amelia.

He loped up the stairs after them and ducked into his bedchamber to anoint himself with his own cologne to cover any trace Florence had left on him before going to Amelia's room via the corridor.

Ever since he'd tried the door between their chambers and found it locked, he hadn't been brave enough to try again. He wasn't sure that he wanted to know whether or not she'd deemed him worthy of having immediate access to her. Perhaps it was cowardly, but he preferred to live in ignorant bliss.

As he entered her bedchamber, Boden was already leaving, a sheaf of papers in hand. He muttered, "My lord," as they passed each other but sounded strangely sarcastic.

Amelia sat on the edge of the bed, her legs crossed.

"What would you like to do tonight to celebrate?" he

asked, hovering in the doorway, ready to leave in the event she said she'd rather read a book or have time to herself than be with him.

She patted the bed. "It just occurred to me as I was writing the final scene, where Joceline arrives at her new home, that I know very little about your home in Suffolk. Won't you come and tell me about it?"

He relaxed. That, he could do.

He sat on the edge of the bed and bent to unlace his shoes and remove them. "May I lie down?"

She cocked her head, obviously surprised, but nodded. "Of course."

He lay back and lifted his feet onto the bed. "Lie with me."

She removed her slippers and lay alongside him. He placed his hand on her hip, urging her to snuggle up against him. She rested her cheek over his heart and pressed herself along the length of him.

He kissed her forehead, idly stroking her hip. "I spent much of my childhood in Suffolk. It was our primary residence when I was young."

"What does it look like?"

He closed his eyes, picturing it. "The design was inspired by Gothic architecture from the Continent. It's rather… dramatic."

"How so?"

"It has turrets and an impressive facade. The gardens are beautiful, too—although I say that reluctantly, as the man who designed them was French. He married an Englishwoman, so perhaps that renders him more English than French? Anyway, there's a pond with a fountain, and thousands of flowers bloom each year."

"It sounds lovely." Her tone was wistful.

"It is. There are beautiful bursts of yellow, red, and purple everywhere you look. I used to love spending time in the garden, although I got lonely. I was the type of boy who liked to be around others."

She laughed softly. "I imagine you were."

"Once I started attending school, I often brought friends home to stay during the breaks. Especially Ashford." Vaughan had always been grateful for the opportunity to escape his parents for a while. "The things we used to get up to…."

Amelia tilted her chin to look up at him, her beautiful blue eyes bright in the candlelight. "I don't believe for a second that the duke got up to mischief unless it was at your behest."

"You've got me there," he admitted. "Any trouble we created was usually my idea, but Ashford isn't quite as straitlaced as he'd like people to believe."

"I look forward to getting to know him better. Him and his wife."

"Perhaps we can visit them at Christmas." He rather liked the idea of spending Christmas with his family and Ashford's, exchanging gifts, drinking mulled wine, and singing carols.

"I'd like that." She closed her eyes. "Tell me what kind of trouble you and the duke got yourselves into."

He kissed the top of her head and began to talk. The stories spilled from him easily, and by the time he finished, she was asleep in his embrace. He smiled to himself. He could grow accustomed to holding his wife while she fell asleep.

Moving carefully, he extricated himself from her, then propped a pillow beneath her head and pulled a blanket over her. He'd return soon, but first, he had to speak with his mother.

He took a candle from the nightstand and used it to light the way down the corridor to his mother's chamber. He knocked quietly and waited. When the door opened, she stood before him in a warm robe with her hair loose, but her eyes were sharp, not hazy with sleepiness as he might have expected.

She drew herself up to her full height and crossed her arms. "I heard where you went earlier."

He winced. "Who told you?"

She arched an eyebrow. "A better question is, why would you visit that woman when you are clearly besotted with Amelia?"

He sighed and rubbed his temples. "She's blackmailing me."

Her mouth fell open. "Blackmailing?"

"Yes, and I failed to meet her terms. That's why I'm here. I need to warn you." He ought to warn Amelia, too, but that would be a more difficult conversation. Broaching the subject with Lady Drake first would ease the path.

"Warn me about what?" she demanded.

"I believe Miss Giles may intend to smear our good name."

His mother stepped aside. "You'd best come in and tell me everything."

CHAPTER 24

Andrew entered the Regent, nerves churning in his gut. It had been a week, and so far, Florence had not made good on her threat.

Unfortunately, neither had he worked up the courage to speak to Amelia about the fact that their lives may be about to become subject to public speculation. His mother was threatening to do so if he didn't hurry up. He'd intended to raise the subject last night, but she'd been in such good spirits that he hadn't been able to bring himself to do it.

Today, he'd ventured out alone in the hopes of discovering whether any damage had been done the previous evening at the first ball since his conversation with Florence. He was hanging onto a thread of hope that perhaps she'd decided not to punish him. If she'd decided to be merciful, he could avoid hurting Amelia yet again.

A servant took his coat, and another offered him a drink. He accepted the glass and made his way down the corridor, turning into the busiest room, where men sat around tables, playing card games.

Spotting Mr. Falvey at one table and knowing how much

the man liked to gossip, he pulled out a chair opposite him and sat.

Falvey met his eyes. "Are you sure you should be playing, old chap? You shouldn't gamble what you don't have to lose."

His heart sank.

So, that was his answer. Florence had indeed followed through. She must have just been waiting until the event where her actions could have the biggest impact.

"Of course he can play," Mr. White protested from the chair beside Andrew's. "He married the Hart chit, and we all know how large her dowry was."

Mr. Falvey chuckled. "How right you are. I should have known there was a reason you were so eager to settle down with someone like her. I didn't put the pieces together, though. I thought you must have seen something in her that the rest of us didn't."

Andrew gritted his teeth. He was tempted to give them all a piece of his mind and march out of there, but he couldn't afford to do that. He needed to know exactly what had been said and to whom so he could properly prepare his family.

"Deal me in," he said.

Mr. Falvey did so.

"How did you hear about my… situation?" Andrew asked.

Mr. Falvey shrugged as play began. "Henry told me."

Andrew turned to Mr. White. "And you got it from…?"

He looked uncomfortable. "I can't say for sure. It was definitely at the Benton ball last night, but it could have been anyone who mentioned it to me."

"Uh-huh." Andrew didn't believe that he'd forgotten for a second. The news of his financial downfall was scandalous enough that Mr. White would certainly remember who had told him, which meant he didn't want to admit to it for some reason.

"Well, I can recall," Chautner blustered from across the table. He was leaning back in his chair, bored with the conversation and eager for play to continue in earnest. "Several of the chits were giggling about it, including that nasty little blonde who's always got a face like she's sniffed the nearest chamber pot."

The women.

Andrew sighed. Of course Florence would choose to disperse gossip through young society misses. All it would have taken was a few words to the most loose-lipped of the bunch, and the story would have circulated within an hour. She had relatives within the ton courtesy of her late mother, so perhaps she'd started with one of those. A cousin or aunt, maybe.

"You kept it all very quiet," Mr. Falvey remarked, gesturing for Andrew to make a move. "For it to have come out now, you must have upset a woman."

He winced, not having expected the man to be so insightful. It was easy to dismiss Mr. Falvey as a gossipy toff.

Mr. Falvey's face lit up when he noticed Andrew's expression. "You did," he exclaimed. "Was it your wife? Did she not know why you married her?"

Andrew cleared his throat, ignoring the burning in his chest. "It wasn't the countess."

Mr. Falvey leaned forward, revealing his cards, which he'd apparently forgotten, more interested in whatever tidbits Andrew might be willing to share. "How can you be sure? You know there is no creature more revenge-minded than an unhappy woman."

"And how, exactly, would this situation please her?" Andrew demanded. "Our marriage will become an object of ridicule. My affection for her is being questioned. She has nothing to gain by spreading vicious rumors. Even if she did, she wouldn't. She's a better person than that."

All three men stared at him.

"Dear Lord." Mr. Falvey spoke first. "You're smitten with her."

"Why?" Mr. White sounded baffled. "She's a—"

Mr. Falvey clapped his hand over Mr. White's mouth and glared at him. "Did you not learn your lesson with Ashford? Speaking poorly of a man's wife when the fellow in question is a besotted fool will only end with you suffering another bloody nose."

Andrew's lips pressed together. "Thank you," he said to Mr. Falvey. "I'm not of a mind to listen to anyone denigrate my wife."

"Besides," Mr. Falvey added, *sotto voce*, "if the countess is not to blame, then the culprit is obvious."

Andrew pushed his chair back and stood before Mr. Falvey could continue. "Please excuse me, gentlemen." He hesitated. "If I hear that any of you have spoken of my wife with anything less than respect, you'll discover that I'm not always so easygoing."

Mr. White instinctively touched his nose.

Mr. Falvey nodded.

Chautner rolled his eyes. "Go, man. Let us get back to our game."

Andrew strode away, uncertainty consuming him. He'd now ascertained that Florence had carried through with her threat. The question was, how on earth was he going to explain this to Amelia?

∾

THE KNIFE CHINKED AGAINST THE PLATE AS AMELIA SLICED through an egg and scooped it onto her fork. She took a mouthful and glanced across the breakfast table at Kate, who'd joined her for the meal. Lady Drake was still abed, and Andrew had been gone when she'd woken.

A knock at the morning room door caught their attention.

"My lady." Boden stepped inside, his chin high, bearing

regal. "Mr. and Mrs. Hart have come to call on you."

Amelia looked at the clock. "So early?"

"I can tell them you're not at home, if you'd like, my lady," Boden offered. "But Mrs. Hart was quite insistent that they speak with you."

"What do you think it's about?" Kate asked, her head cocked curiously.

"I've no idea." But she did know that if her mother wanted something, she wouldn't leave until she got it. She ate another forkful of egg, set her cutlery down, and pushed the plate away. "Boden, can you have Mrs. Baker send tea and scones to the drawing room, please?"

He bowed. "As you wish, my lady. Shall I ask Mr. and Mrs. Hart to wait for you there?"

"No, I'll do it." If she delayed, she'd only worry about what had brought them here. If they'd called during more social hours, she might not be concerned, but it was unlike her mother to leave the house in the morning, unless it was to shop.

Boden nodded and left the room.

"Would you like me to come with you?" Kate asked.

Amelia shook her head. "Finish your breakfast. I'll be fine meeting with them on my own."

"Are you sure?"

Amelia smiled at her. For all their differences, Kate had a big heart. "I am."

She wiped her mouth and hands, rose, and walked slowly toward the foyer. Anxiety roiled inside her, making her grateful she hadn't eaten more than a few bites before Boden had interrupted. The last thing she needed was to have a full meal sitting like a lead weight at the bottom of her stomach during what could be a difficult conversation.

She rounded the staircase, and her parents came into view near the main entrance. Her father wore a stylish waistcoat that she doubted he'd chosen for himself, and her mother was dressed head to toe in lavender, as if she were in half mourning.

"What on earth?" she muttered to herself.

"Amelia!" Mrs. Hart flew toward her, and as she drew near, Amelia noticed that her eyes were red and puffy. "How could you allow this to happen?"

She frowned. "Allow what to happen?"

A sob tore from Mrs. Hart, and she covered her mouth, her eyes wide.

"Why don't we speak somewhere more private?" Mr. Hart suggested, nodding toward the drawing room.

"Please, come through."

Amelia led the way and perched on one of the chairs, leaving the chaise for her parents. Her father helped her mother sit, then lowered himself down beside her and wrapped his arm around her waist.

"What's going on?" Amelia asked, looking from her mother to her father and back again.

"I trusted you to make sure this didn't happen," Mrs. Hart whispered. "How could you?"

Amelia met her father's eyes, a silent question in them. "What have I done?"

Was this about her novel? Had they discovered she was about to be published?

She'd known her mother wouldn't be pleased, but this reaction seemed out of proportion to the situation.

"Word has spread that the earl married you for your dowry," Mr. Hart said calmly.

Mrs. Hart lifted her head, her beautiful face twisted in despair. "They're saying we bought a title. That we are sullying the earl's aristocratic lineage."

Amelia's gut tightened, but while she might wish that no one knew the truth of the situation, her mother could hardly be surprised by these claims—not when she'd insisted on such a large dowry specifically for this purpose. Perhaps, after weeks of blissful social acceptance, the gossip was hitting harder than it might otherwise have done so.

"It's not untrue," she pointed out. "Surely you knew there was a possibility this would happen."

A maid bustled into the room with a tea tray. She set it on the table and scurried out again. Amelia stood and poured tea, leaving it black and unsweetened for each of her parents and adding sugar to her own. She passed the first cup to her mother but didn't bother to offer her a scone, knowing she wouldn't accept.

Mrs. Hart took the cup and automatically raised it to her lips. Amelia passed the second cup to her father, along with a scone, and took the third cup and another scone for herself. She sat back down and munched on the scone, grateful to have something more to eat. Despite her unsettled gut, she was a little hungry, having not finished breakfast.

Her mother turned a bleak gaze on Amelia. "You haven't heard the worst part."

Suddenly, the crumbs felt like ash in her mouth. She had a feeling she wasn't going to like this.

"Tell me," she urged.

Mrs. Hart drew in a deep breath. "I was at the Benton ball last night, and I was able to trace the rumor back to its starting point."

Amelia forced herself to swallow. "Which was?"

"That harlot your husband is bedding."

The scone scraped down the inside of Amelia's throat and seemed to stick at the bottom. Tears prickled in her eyes.

"What did you say?" she whispered, unable to speak louder.

"The earl was spending time with a woman named Florence Giles. Apparently, she is the one who told the entire ton that he was broke and married you to refill his coffers."

Amelia set her cup down. The scone too. Her hands

shook badly, so she clenched them into fists, hoping no one would notice. The pain in her throat worsened.

Why did this hurt so much?

She'd known Andrew had a mistress before he'd married her. She'd even known who. He'd assured her that he wasn't seeing her anymore, but if that was so, how could Miss Giles know why they'd married?

"Mia, are you all right?"

She blinked rapidly, swallowing the emotion that threatened to overwhelm her. Hearing her father's nickname for her only reminded her of the one her husband had used, which now felt silly and false.

"Are you certain?" she asked her mother.

"Quite." Mrs. Hart looked annoyed to be questioned. But then, she had always been good at sniffing out secrets.

"What's going on in here?"

Her gaze flew to the doorway, where Andrew stood silhouetted against the gloom of the foyer. As soon as they locked eyes, a sort of knowing settled into his expression.

"You've heard," he said.

"Heard what, my lord?" She wasn't going to make this easy for him. Whatever had happened, he'd caused it, and she was going to make him admit that.

"Perhaps we should give you two some time to discuss this alone." Mr. Hart rose, tugging on his wife's hand.

She resisted. "But—"

Mr. Hart ducked his head near her ear and murmured something that Amelia couldn't make out.

"Fine," Mrs. Hart huffed. "But don't think this is the end of the matter."

Her father shot her an apologetic look as he escorted her mother out of the drawing room.

Amelia stood. Sitting felt too vulnerable when Andrew was on his feet.

"Are you still seeing Miss Giles?" she asked, proud of herself when her voice didn't waver.

"No." He took a step forward. "I'm not. I swear it. I want only you."

She raised her chin. "Then how did she know that you were broke and married me for my dowry?"

A muscle in his jaw clenched. "Because I ended our relationship the night I discovered that I'd lost my fortune, and I told her I intended to search for a wife with a large dowry."

CHAPTER 25

Amelia's vision blurred, and she turned away from her husband. She couldn't think straight. Not with him standing right there.

Now that she thought about it, it made sense that he'd ended his relationship with Miss Giles when he'd lost his money. She'd just never considered the circumstances and how and when their relationship had ended with much specificity.

Honestly, it had been easier and more pleasant not to dwell on it. And why should she, when it hadn't seemed to matter?

Only now it turned out that perhaps it did matter.

She closed her eyes and did her best to regulate her breathing. "Would your arrangement with Miss Giles have ended if money had never become a problem?"

There was a quick intake of breath, as if he'd immediately begun to reply, followed by a hesitation. She grabbed fistfuls of her skirt and fought the urge to scream.

"I see."

She really did.

If Andrew hadn't lost his fortune, he would have continued his affair with Miss Giles.

Florence.

Money was all that had come between them.

Well, money and Amelia.

Florence was the woman he actually wanted. The one he'd chosen, when he'd been able to choose anyone. Amelia was just the woman he'd been forced to let into his life by circumstance. For now, she was a novelty, but how long would that last?

When the novelty faded, she'd have to accept the fact that even if it wasn't Florence Giles who came back into Andrew's life, there would be someone else like her.

Andrew reached for her hand, but she dodged him.

"I care for you," he said. "I promise, you are all I want."

"You don't—"

"That's why I didn't give in to Miss Giles's blackmail," he carried on, interrupting her.

Her lips parted. "What?"

Blackmail? What on earth was he talking about?

He moved closer. She stayed in place, relieved when he didn't try to touch her again.

"Listen to me properly before you decide what to think," he said quietly.

"All right." She supposed she owed him that much. He'd been good to her.

His fingers twitched, and he curled them into his palm. "As I said, I broke off my affair with Miss Giles when I found out about Mr. Smith. I explained the reasoning to her because we were close at the time, and I didn't want to hurt her without any explanation."

Amelia gritted her teeth. Of course he did. Even when he was failing, Andrew did his best to protect everyone's feelings.

"After we married, she made… advances toward me."

"She wanted you back," she said bluntly.

He nodded. "Yes. When I turned her down, she became quite persistent. At the Winston ball, she threatened me. She told me that if I didn't resume our affair, she would let everyone know how foolishly I'd lost my fortune. I'm sorry. I had hoped she wouldn't go through with it."

"So…." She dragged out the word, her thoughts whirring. "You didn't capitulate."

"Of course not," he said incredulously. "I would never."

She couldn't decide what to think of that. On one hand, she was pleased that he valued being faithful to her more than he valued his reputation. But on the other, he'd made a decision on something that potentially impacted them both —as well as Kate and Lady Drake—without consulting her.

She nibbled her lower lip, wondering where to go from here. "Thank you for being honest with me."

"Always." It was a vow.

"It means a lot to me that you care for me enough to do that." She rubbed at a tiny ink stain on her skirt. "But if you respected me properly, you'd have told me what was going on and discussed it with me before you acted."

"It was my problem to solve," he protested, moving toward her. "It was my fault we were in that situation."

"Perhaps," she allowed, circling around the chair, creating more space between them. It was difficult to think clearly when he was so close. "But a husband and wife are partners, are they not?"

He gave a short, jerky nod. "In some ways."

She narrowed her eyes. "We agreed to be partners in all the ways that matter. As such, you should treat me like an equal and not a fragile flower to be protected from the hardships of life."

He snorted. "'Fragile' isn't the word I'd use."

"Nor I." She edged toward the door. "It's sweet that you wished to protect me, but perhaps I could have helped.

Maybe together, we could have thought of a better way through this. Instead, you kept it from me until you were no longer able to."

He pressed his lips together, unable to deny the claim. "So, partner. What do we do now?"

She sighed, suddenly weary. "I am taking the carriage out. I need to think."

"Won't you stay and talk this through?"

"I'll be back later. Just allow me some time."

She left the drawing room and hurried up the stairs to change into a suitable outfit for venturing out of the house. Once her coat was on and her walking shoes ready to go, she tiptoed back past the drawing room and called for a carriage.

She wasn't quite sure where she wanted to go yet, so she asked the driver to go in the general direction of Hyde Park while she figured it out. A footman helped her inside and closed the door. She got comfortable and gazed out the window as they eased into motion.

They passed through the streets of Mayfair. It was still relatively early for a Saturday, so only a few people were out and about.

They drove past a street market, and she considered asking to stop but decided she'd better not without a maid. One could never trust how safe one would be in such a place. Better to go in pairs.

As they drew level with the entrance of the park, Amelia allowed her mind to drift. First, to the future she so badly desired. She and Andrew, happily married, perhaps with a little one. She'd spend her days writing and checking on the baby, her evenings reading, and her nights tangled up with her husband.

But that was all a fantasy, wasn't it?

It was more likely that she would end up pouring all her love into the baby, then writing, and reading before retiring to a cold, empty bed while her husband found solace elsewhere.

A couple of months ago, even that would have sounded like a dream, but now, she wanted more.

"Excuse me," she called forward through the open window. "I've decided where I'd like to go."

∽

When she left, Andrew considered chasing after Amelia but decided it would be best to give her time to calm down. Unfortunately, he had no idea where she would go.

Would she be safe?

He hated to think of her coming upon anyone who might be cruel. She wouldn't have gone to her parents—that, he was certain of. Not after the way her mother had spoken to her. But she didn't have any close friends to call on, nor any siblings.

Where would she go?

Damn, he should have asked before she left. Now he would worry until he set eyes on her again.

"What's happening?"

His gaze shot to the doorway where Kate hovered, wringing her hands.

"Did Amelia leave?" she asked.

"I'm afraid so."

She looked around. "What about her parents? Boden said they were here."

He sighed and ran his hand through his hair. "They're gone too."

She frowned. "What's wrong? Amelia and I were eating breakfast together when her parents arrived. I could tell she wasn't expecting them, and it was early for a social visit. Something must have happened."

He debated how much to tell her. He couldn't in good

conscience mention his mistress to his younger sister, but she did need to be warned of the situation.

"Word has spread that I lost our money and married Amelia to get her dowry," he admitted.

Kate's face fell. "Oh no. Does everyone know?"

He considered this. "The men at my club did, and so did Amelia's parents, so I assume most of the ton has heard."

Her shoulders slumped. "They will be gossiping about us, and not in a good way."

"I'm sorry." His gut squeezed. If he'd been a more responsible man, they'd never have ended up in this position. But then, he'd never have married Amelia either, so he wasn't sure he could bring himself to regret it.

She gasped, her eyes widening. "Poor Amelia." She bit her lip. "Surely people know you care for her and this isn't just a marriage of convenience?"

He was already shaking his head. "I've found that people tend to believe whatever story is the most compelling. No doubt they'll be saying that she bought and paid for an unwilling but impoverished husband."

It wasn't completely untrue, but it wasn't the whole story either.

"Is that why she left? She was upset?"

"Yes."

She clenched and unclenched her fists. "But where would she go?"

"I don't know." He hesitated, then asked, "Could you please get Mother? We need to decide how we're going to deal with this."

Lady Drake had more experience with the whims of society than he did. She'd be the one best placed to guide their next steps.

"Of course." Kate backed out of the doorway. "Is there anything else I can do?"

"Not right now. Well, perhaps we could use some more tea," he amended. Having something to do would make her feel better, even as menial a task as requesting another tea tray.

Kate nodded and glided away.

Andrew sat on the chaise. He crossed his legs and tapped one foot on the ground while he waited for his mother and sister to reappear.

When his mother entered, she took one look at him and grimaced. "Kate said you have bad news for me."

"Have a seat." He patted the cushion beside him. "You remember how I warned you that Mrs. Giles may cause some trouble?"

"Yes." She stacked her hands on her lap. "Has she started spreading rumors as she threatened to?"

"Yes, unfortunately. Mrs. Hart was here asking about it this morning, and the gentlemen at my club know too. There is no avoiding this."

Kate breezed into the room with Mrs. Smythe behind her. She waved her hand toward the table. "Please set the tea tray there, Mrs. Smythe."

A maid cleared the existing tray, and Mrs. Smythe set the new tea tray down. "Would you like me to pour?"

"No," Lady Drake said. "I'll take care of it."

Mrs. Smythe curtsied, and she and the maid left the room.

Kate sat on one of the chairs nearest to the chaise. "So, how shall we proceed?"

Andrew cleared his throat as Lady Drake got up and started fixing the tea. "You, my dear, will return to your chambers while Mother and I decide on that."

"But that's not fair," Kate protested. "This affects me as much as it does you. Why can't I help?"

"Because some of the things we need to talk about aren't meant for delicate ears," he said.

Kate looked between the two of them. "What aren't you telling me?"

Andrew sighed. "Just that there is a reason this rumor has spread now. You don't need to trouble yourself with the details, but Mother has experience that might be useful, and her ears are not as innocent as yours."

Kate pouted. "Mother, can't I stay? I'm old enough. I'll be out next season."

Lady Drake pinched the bridge of her nose. "I'm afraid your brother is right. He and I have things to discuss that are best said in private. We will let you know what we decide to do as soon as possible. You don't need to worry about being left out."

"Fine," Kate huffed. "You had better be telling the truth." She stood and, reluctantly, walked out of the room.

Lady Drake handed Andrew a cup of tea. "Here you go," she said. "I added plenty of sugar. I know you like it sweet."

"Thank you." He took the cup from her, blew across the surface of the tea, and raised it to his lips to sip. "Just how I like it."

"Tell me more about what happened with Miss Giles," Lady Drake said. "You gave me the general details, but I want to understand exactly why she feels like she needs to punish you."

So Andrew explained how he had ended his arrangement with Florence when he received news of the change in his financial situation. He told his mother how she'd hoped their relationship would resume after he married Amelia and how he'd disappointed her by turning her down.

When he was done, his mother studied him over the rim of her teacup, thoughts whirling behind her eyes.

"I can see Miss Giles's point of view," she said. "Her pride has been injured. But it was wrong of her to do something that hurts other people just because she has been hurt herself. After all, it isn't as if you meant to upset or offend her. You had a financial arrangement that you could no longer continue. She made it personal."

"It can be difficult not to take things personally, considering the kind of relationship we had," Andrew admitted. "But I won't tolerate her disrespecting Amelia. Amelia is innocent. She doesn't deserve this."

The corners of Lady Drake's eyes crinkled as she smiled. "You're rather fond of that woman, aren't you?"

"I am." He wasn't embarrassed by it. "So, back to the matter at hand. What do you suggest we do to combat the damage that's been done to our family's reputation?"

Lady Drake leaned back against the chaise and pursed her lips in thought. "We are already planning a ball, so I say we throw the biggest, most elaborate ball we possibly can in order to show the world that we aren't hiding. We aren't ashamed. And once we've done that, we retreat to the country house for Christmas."

He frowned. "But that would be cutting our time in London short."

"I know." She tapped her chin. "But if we throw our ball and then leave, we leave on our own terms. The ton will remember our ball and not whatever comes after. Because we can be certain that we will be a hot topic of discussion among the ton as soon as the ball is over. It's best to be gone for that."

He agreed, but he also wasn't sure that fleeing to the country would solve anything.

Apparently seeing his uncertainty, Lady Drake added, "I don't know about you, but I'd rather whisk Amelia away from here before she has to deal with a second round of gossip."

She had a good point. He didn't want Amelia to suffer more than she already had.

"Are you sure they won't say we are running?" he asked.

She shrugged. "I'm sure some will. But if we depart with

flair, then hopefully that's what they'll remember next season. There will be a new scandal before we return to London, which will dim their memories where we're concerned. Perhaps another duke will marry his former fiancée's twin."

Andrew laughed. "Wouldn't that be nice? But do we even have any more twins among the ton?"

"I doubt it, but I digress. All we need to do is make it through the season with our heads held high, and then we can recuperate in the country where no further gossip can upset your wife. Don't forget, there is a possibility she is with child, isn't there?"

Andrew startled. There was. Why had it not occurred to him that Amelia could be carrying his child at this very moment?

He'd thought about the possible birth of his heir in the abstract, but it had never quite struck him that his son or daughter could be developing even now. He and Amelia had certainly had enough sex for that to be true.

"Has Amelia said anything to you?" he asked, wondering if she'd given his mother any indication she might be pregnant.

Lady Drake shook her head. "I'm sure that when she knows, you'll be the first one she tells. But she's new to this, so she may not know what symptoms to watch out for."

And she was out there on her own, without his protection.

He hated the thought. Hated that his past was causing her distress. He should never have let her leave. He should have taken her into his arms and held her until she calmed.

"Where is Lady Longley?" Lady Drake asked.

Andrew buried his face in his hands. "I don't know. She left. She said she needed to think. But I don't know where she would have gone."

"Has she told you any places she likes to go in order to clear her head?" Lady Drake asked.

"No. I've already considered the options. She won't have gone to her parents' house, and she's never mentioned any particular friends."

"What about places she enjoys visiting?" Lady Drake straightened. "The park, perhaps. Or is there anywhere she likes to go to write or read?"

Andrew snapped his fingers. "The bookshop! That one I took her to after we married. Babbles, was it? No… Babbington Books. She loves it there. I should go."

He stood.

"No," she said sharply. "Let me go."

"What?" He didn't understand. "I'm the one who sent her running, so I'm the one who should go after her."

She pulled a face. "As far as she's concerned, you're the one who hurt her. Or at least, it's partially your fault that she is hurting. She's more likely to open up to me."

He bit back a sound of frustration. He understood, but he didn't like it. "Please bring my wife home."

CHAPTER 26

Amelia picked up the book and flipped through its pages, realizing too late that it was a romance. Sweet dialogue blurred in front of her eyes as tears filled them.

Even here, in a place that should be a sanctuary, she couldn't escape love.

"Excuse me, my lady," the proprietress, Mrs. Babbington, said, touching Amelia's shoulder. "Are you all right? You seem upset."

"Ugh, I am fine," Amelia said. "I think I got some dust in my eye."

"I am so sorry to hear that." Mrs. Babbington hesitated. "I find when I get dust in my eye, it sometimes feels better if I talk about it with someone. Do you think that might also be the case for you?"

Amelia sniffled. "There's nothing to talk about."

"Hmm. Maybe so. How is your book coming along?"

Amelia dabbed the corners of her eyes. "I finished another story."

"Very good. I look forward to reading it. Have you sent it to the publisher?"

Amelia nodded.

Mrs. Babbington's lips firmed. "Did they turn you down?"

"I haven't heard back yet." Although she did have to wonder whether publishers listened to rumors. Would this knock to her reputation damage her ability to publish her stories?

Surely not. Plenty of writers were controversial characters or not part of high society.

"So, perhaps it's man trouble that brings you here?" Mrs. Babbington suggested.

Amelia's instinctive response was to say no, but part of her thought it might be nice to have someone to listen.

"Yes," she whispered.

Mrs. Babbington tutted. "Why don't you come into the back room with me? We can have a glass of sherry, and you can tell me what's on your mind."

A laugh burst from Amelia, unbidden. "Sherry?" she asked. "At this time of day?"

Mrs. Babbington smiled warmly. "When affairs of the heart are involved, it's never too early for sherry."

"That's a philosophy I can agree with."

"Come with me, then."

Amelia followed her down the aisle of books, breathing in the smell of old and new paper. There was just something about the scent that reminded her of possibility. There were so many stories waiting to be read, tales waiting to be told, and she wanted to explore them all.

Mrs. Babbington guided her around the counter and through a door that led into the back of the shop. There was a desk against one wall, a small, enclosed fire for heating tea, and a pair of comfortable armchairs at the far end.

"Have a seat." Mrs. Babbington gestured toward the armchairs. "I'll just pour us a drink."

Amelia crossed the room and lowered herself onto one of the armchairs. The padding was soft and squishy, and although it had a faint musty odor, she could imagine being curled up there with a book for hours.

Mrs. Babbington retrieved a bottle of sherry from inside a drawer beneath the desk, along with two small glasses. She half filled each glass, pushed the cork back into the sherry bottle, and tucked it back into its place beneath the desk.

She carried the glasses to the armchairs and offered one to Amelia, who accepted the glass gratefully and inhaled the sweet aroma. Mrs. Babbington drank, and, cautiously, Amelia did the same.

"It's all right," she said, savoring the slight bite. "Better than the last time I tried it."

"I like it." Mrs. Babbington sat on the other armchair and crossed her legs. "Do you want to talk about what's happened, or would you prefer to rail about men in general?"

Amelia couldn't help smiling. "I've never had a friend to talk about men with before. I haven't spent much time with women my own age. Honestly, the closest thing I have to a friend is probably my husband's sister, and I can't really discuss my problems with her."

"No." Mrs. Babbington chuckled. "I don't suppose you can."

Amelia gulped down a mouthful of sherry and grimaced. "My husband married me for money. That's what it all boils down to."

"So, why has this upset you today? It doesn't seem as if it was a shock to you, and from what I saw of your interaction with the earl, you get along well enough."

"We do," Amelia agreed. "Honestly, that's half the problem. It's my fault. I've gone and fallen for him somewhere along the way, but he hasn't done the same."

Haltingly, she explained the beginning of her relationship with Andrew, their marriage, and, without going into too much detail, everything that had happened since. Mrs. Babbington listened without any judgment in her expression.

When Amelia finished, Mrs. Babbington sipped her sherry again and said, "Would you like my opinion?"

Amelia vacillated for a moment. It was nice to just be listened to, and she feared that if Mrs. Babbington gave her opinion, it may not be to Amelia's liking. But perhaps honesty was what she needed, so she nodded.

Mrs. Babbington straightened her shoulders. "What I've learned from my years of marriage is that men, no matter how well-intentioned, are fools when it comes to the women they care about. I believe that the earl cares for you. I could see it when you visited my bookshop together. I also have no doubt that he means well. He just… well, he made a bit of a mess of things, didn't he?"

A thud sounded inside the shop, stealing their attention, and then footsteps tapped on the wooden floor. They were light—possibly a woman's—and they were approaching the counter at a rapid clip.

Mrs. Babbington tossed back the rest of her sherry and rose. "I had best go see who that is."

Amelia started to get up, too, but the proprietress motioned for her to stay put.

"I'll return soon," she said. "You stay right here. If I take a while, you can find books in the cupboard beneath the desk to occupy yourself with."

Amelia looked around as Mrs. Babbington left. She had to admit to being a little bit jealous of the other woman. While Amelia may have had an incredibly privileged upbringing in terms of money, she had never been able to indulge her love of books quite as openly as she'd have liked to.

Mrs. Babbington, on the other hand, got to be surrounded by books every day.

She wondered whether the bookshop belonged to Mr. Babbington or if it was all Mrs. Babbington's. Plenty of women had jobs—she knew that just from looking within her own household—but no one ever talked about female shop owners or merchants. Women weren't "supposed" to own businesses. Their husbands were.

She heard voices through the open door and strained her ears to make out whatever was being said. She couldn't decipher individual words, but she could tell that Mrs. Babbington's customer was indeed a woman.

More conversation was exchanged, then footsteps approached. A woman in a dark blue day dress swept into the room behind the counter, her hazel eyes already seeking out Amelia.

She jolted upright. "Brigid?"

Lady Drake's sharp gaze took in the sherry glasses, and her lips quirked. "This looks like a good time. May I join you?"

Amelia knew she ought to stand, but her legs were shaking. She felt like a little girl who'd been caught doing something she shouldn't.

"I'm s-sorry," she stuttered. "I know this isn't entirely proper. I—"

"Balderdash," Lady Drake said bluntly. "Some days, sherry and friendly company are the most proper solutions to our problems. So, can I join you?"

"Of course you may," Mrs. Babbington answered for her. "Shall I pour you a glass?"

"Please do."

Lady Drake sank onto the armchair that Mrs. Babbington had vacated. The proprietress left the room and was back a moment later with a wooden chair. She positioned it in front of Amelia and Lady Drake, then hurried over to the desk to retrieve the bottle of sherry and pour another drink.

"It isn't often that I'm graced with the presence of two aristocratic ladies in my shop," Mrs. Babbington said, carrying the glass over and offering it to Lady Drake. "I hope you won't mind if I mention it to my husband tonight. I won't share your personal business, but I think he'll be quite tickled to hear what elevated company I entertained."

Amelia shook her head. "I have no issue with you telling him we were here. Lady Drake?"

Lady Drake was in the midst of swallowing sherry, so she nodded and gestured that her mouth was otherwise occupied. When she'd finished, she cradled the glass in her hands and gazed at Mrs. Babbington.

"Am I correct in assuming that my daughter-in-law has confided in you?" she asked.

Mrs. Babbington didn't answer, instead looking to Amelia for guidance.

"I have. She knows most of the details," Amelia said. "You can speak freely in front of her."

Lady Drake set her glass down and reached across to take Amelia's hand. "In that case, please allow me to apologize for any emotional pain you've experienced because of my family using you as a financial resource. You helped us, and we should have protected you better."

Amelia looked down at their joint hands and shrugged. "I was the one who proposed a marriage of convenience. I have no right to be upset because Andrew used to have a mistress. Even if he still did, I never asked for fidelity."

Lady Drake squeezed her hand. "You're such a strong woman. But even strong women can get emotionally involved when they don't expect to. Your expectations and desires don't have to remain static. They can change. An entire lifetime can't be anticipated or summed up in a single signed agreement."

"Ugh." Amelia buried her face in her hands. "I know. But I'm used to being practical. I don't know how to deal with this."

"With more sherry?" Mrs. Babbington suggested.

Lady Drake snorted. "An excellent idea. For what it's

worth, Amelia, I don't believe my son has been unfaithful to you—or that he ever intends to be."

Amelia raised her head and blinked, her bleary vision slowly clearing. "I don't know what to do," she whispered. "I'm falling in love with him, but I'm afraid he'll grow bored with me."

"Do you expect to grow bored with him?" Mrs. Babbington asked, picking up her sherry glass and studying the remnants of liquid inside.

Amelia frowned. "No."

Mrs. Babbington met her eyes. "Then why do you expect him to tire of you?"

Caught off guard, Amelia just stared at her. The proprietress made a good point. She was trying to predict the future, but her assumptions were flawed.

"I don't know," she admitted. "I'll think on it. Perhaps I ought to be more trusting of the connection between us."

"Good." Lady Drake rested her forearm on the arm of the chair. "In the meantime, let me tell you about our plan to minimize the damage done by Miss Giles."

Amelia and Mrs. Babbington listened as she explained her plan to throw an extravagant ball and then retreat to the countryside, where Amelia would have all the time and space needed to work things out with Andrew.

Apart from the ball, which she'd be quite happy not to attend, Amelia liked the sound of the plan. She could gladly spend lazy days with her new family at their country estate.

"Don't worry." Lady Drake released Amelia's hand and patted the back of it. "You are far from being one of the most scandalous couples of recent times. Has Andrew told you about the Duke of Ashford's marriage?"

"A little." She'd heard plenty at the time, since rumors had been flying.

"Oh, the Duchess of Ashford is a lovely woman," Mrs. Babbington said, leaning forward so she could participate more fully in the conversation. "She came here to buy books a couple of times, and the duke has collected orders on her behalf each time he came to Town this season."

"I'm eager to meet her." Amelia finished her sherry and placed the glass on the ground. "I've never met a woman who enjoys reading as much as I do—although, I must admit, that's possibly because I'm not terribly social and haven't spoken to many of my peers in depth."

"You'll like the duchess," Lady Drake assured her. "As Mrs. Babbington said, she's a sweet girl."

Sweet. Not a word Amelia would believe could ever be applied to her. But if the sweet Duchess of Ashford enjoyed reading, then she was sure they'd get along just fine.

The three women chatted for a while longer, but eventually, Amelia sighed and conceded that she and Lady Drake should probably return home before Andrew got too worried.

They bid farewell to Mrs. Babbington, making a promise to call again, and departed the shop. The carriage Amelia had taken was gone, but Lady Drake's was waiting, a footman standing out the front. He opened the door as they approached.

"I sent your driver home," she said. "I didn't see any reason for us to have two separate carriages."

"I see." Amelia suspected that her mother-in-law had also been trying to ensure that she didn't flee before they had a chance to speak.

Lady Drake gave her a knowing smile. "Climb in."

Amelia allowed the footman to assist her as she did so. Meanwhile, Lady Drake spoke to the driver. When Lady Drake joined her, she sat opposite Amelia rather than beside her, the better to hold her gaze while they talked.

"We're making a quick stop on the way home," Lady Drake said. "I hope you don't mind."

Amelia cocked her head. "Where?"

"Madam Baptiste's. We're going to commission dresses appropriate for the ball. Something tasteful but meant to stand out."

"What colors were you thinking of?" Amelia asked. They hadn't yet confirmed the color scheme. Their plans had gone off the rails when Lady Drake and Kate became ill.

"I like the idea of being bold." Lady Drake flashed her a grin. "No insipid pastels. Perhaps deep greens and blues."

Amelia nodded. "Blue suits me, and you look good in green."

"So I do."

Amelia considered Lady Drake. It had never occurred to her before, but she was rather young to be a widow with grown children.

"Do you ever intend to remarry?" she asked.

She was certain that if Lady Drake did, she would have plenty of suitors.

Lady Drake pursed her lips. "Perhaps one day, when my children are happily settled. Until then, I'm content as I am."

They arrived at the modiste, and Lady Drake waited for the door to be opened before stepping down.

She turned toward Amelia. "Let's make sure my son can't take his eyes off you."

CHAPTER 27

*London,
December 1820*

"Are you looking forward to the ball?" Kate asked from where she was sitting cross-legged on Amelia's bed.

Amelia grimaced. "About as much as I look forward to a visit from my mother," she muttered under her breath.

Kate frowned. "What was that?"

"I said I can't wait," Amelia declared, full of false cheer.

Kate's eyes narrowed. "Why do I not believe you?"

Amelia chuckled. "Because you're exceptionally bright."

Kate flushed. "Am not."

Amelia fought the urge to insist that she was. Her sister-in-law was very clever about particular things. She knew all about the latest fashions, and she was a talented artist, but she didn't consider herself to be intelligent because she wasn't academically inclined.

"My lady, this would be far easier if you'd stay still," Margaret said, attempting to gather Amelia's hair into an artful array of curls.

"Sorry, Margaret," she said, duly chastened.

"Well, I'm excited for you." The bed squeaked. Perhaps Kate was bouncing on the mattress. "The shade of blue that you and Mother chose is very flattering on you. I do wish you'd agreed to wear a ribbon of the same shade in your hair."

"I've agreed to the ball and the dress. That's enough."

"You're no fun. When I have my season, I shall wear the most exquisite gowns in shades of pink, blue, and green." Her voice became dreamy. "My shoes will match, and I'll dance all night."

"I don't doubt that. You'll have no shortage of suitors."

Kate wasn't destined to be a wallflower like Amelia. In the mirror, Margaret was smiling. Kate wasn't the only one excited for her season. The maid was eager to participate too. Amelia wouldn't be surprised if Kate and Margaret had already been practicing how they would dress her hair for her presentation at court.

Margaret bent over Amelia to slide a few hairpins into place. She winced as one scraped her scalp a little too sharply. Murmuring an apology, Margaret adjusted the pin.

"All done." She stood back. "Is it to your satisfaction, my lady?"

Amelia examined herself in the mirror. While her hair was dressed more elaborately than she would usually choose, she had to admit that it looked good. "It is."

"Now, for the dress." Kate sat upright and clapped excitedly. "I peeked at Mother's earlier. I like that it's in a similar style to yours, but yours is clearly more modern and intended for a younger woman."

Amelia shook her head. "It's amazing to me that you can tell so much just from looking at them. All I know is that they're similar without being the same."

Kate preened.

Margaret withdrew the dress from the wardrobe. Amelia undid her belt and allowed the dressing gown she was wearing to slide off her shoulders and drop to the floor. Her undergarments were already in place.

"If you'll just step into it like this." Margaret showed her where to put her feet. Once she was in the center, the maid lifted the dress and held it up. "One arm in here, and the other in there, then turn around."

Amelia slipped her arms through the holes and turned so Margaret could do up her buttons. She'd almost reached the top when there was a sharp knock at the door, followed by a deep voice.

"May I come in?" It was Andrew.

"Yes," she called back. "I'm almost ready."

She heard the door open and glanced over. Her husband looked spectacular in a black tailcoat over a gold-patterned shirt that brought out the flecks of gold in his eyes and a waistcoat that matched the color of her dress.

"Ladies, I'd like a moment of privacy with my wife, please," he said, bouncing on the balls of his feet.

"I'm nearly done," Margaret replied.

"I can finish." He strode over and took Margaret's place behind Amelia.

She closed her eyes as his fingertips brushed the sensitive skin between her shoulder blades. Based on the rustling of fabric, she assumed that Kate and Margaret were leaving.

"You chose well." His voice rumbled near her ear.

She tilted her head to give him better access, and he ran his lips up the length of her neck and nipped at the skin just beneath her ear.

"You can't seduce me before our very first ball," she reminded him as the door clicked shut.

His chuckle was sinful. "We're the hosts. It's not as if it's going to start without us. But you make a good point." He drew back, and she shivered, disappointed by the loss of his nearness.

"Is everything ready?" she asked, angling her body toward him.

"Mm-hmm." He brushed his lips over hers. "But I have a surprise for you."

A divot formed between her brows. "A surprise?"

He reached into his pocket and withdrew a black velvet bag. "These are for you."

Curious, she took the bag from him and loosened the drawstring. She reached inside and felt metal and polished stone brush against her fingertips. Jewelry of some variety.

She gripped a length of chain and pulled out a necklace, gasping as she revealed at least a dozen blue sapphires in gold settings. The stone intended to sit at the base of the throat was the largest, with the sapphires decreasing in size as they circled around the back of the neck.

"It's beautiful," she said, unable to take her eyes off it. She didn't wear jewelry often because she didn't like the way it was used to display wealth, but she could tell he'd bought this because he knew she would like it rather than for any other reason.

"There's more." His voice was husky.

She dipped her fingers back inside and pulled out a pair of earrings with matching sapphires and intricately spun gold. "These are for me?"

"Yes." He held out his hand, and she placed the earrings on his palm. "I bought them with the first payout from our new investments. It came through just the other day."

Gently, he slotted one earring into place and then turned her around to do the same on the other side. She passed him the necklace, and he looped it around her throat and latched it at the back, his touch whispering over the nape of her neck, leaving goose bumps in its wake.

"It's not a particularly practical purchase," she whispered.

His estate needed to be reestablished. Should he really have wasted money on an expensive gift for her?

"Maybe not," he agreed. "But it's beautiful, and you deserve it."

Her heart fluttered. She wrapped her arms around his neck and kissed him. "Thank you."

"You're very welcome." His forehead rested against hers, and for a moment, they just shared each other's air. But then a door slammed down the hall, and reality intruded. "We'd best go and greet our guests."

"Yes, we should." She linked her arm with his and allowed him to lead her from the bedchamber.

Lady Drake was already waiting at the top of the stairs. Her hair had been done similarly to Amelia's, and she was radiant in a rich green gown. Her eyes landed on Amelia's new jewelry and widened.

"Stunning," she said, the corners of her eyes creasing. "Perfect for you."

"Thank you, Brigid."

Together, the three descended the stairs to the foyer. The main entrance was wide open, and a dark-haired figure appeared in the entranceway, shaking rainwater from his hair.

"Ashford." Andrew beamed and crossed the space between them in several steps to clasp his friend's hand and drag him into an embrace. "So good of you to come."

Amelia blinked at him, surprised. "I didn't realize you would be here, Your Grace."

The duke gave her his customary half smile. "I wanted to show my support. I'll be returning home tomorrow."

She took his hand and held it for a few seconds. "Thank you. It means a lot that you made the effort when your family remains in the country."

His expression softened. "I'll be back to them before they even know I'm gone."

"Somehow, I doubt that." Surely a man so devoted to his

wife and daughter would receive the same devotion in return.

Lady Drake motioned behind them. "Guests are arriving. We should start a receiving line inside the ballroom." She patted the duke's cheek. "It's good to see you, Vaughan."

They made their way to the ballroom, where the duke quickly excused himself to the refreshments table. Amelia suspected he was the type of person who might need a couple of glasses of champagne to get through the evening.

She, Andrew, and Lady Drake lined up just inside the ballroom. As the guests began to arrive, they greeted each of them warmly. Amelia had studied the guest list ahead of time to make sure she knew who everyone was. With each person she correctly identified, she congratulated herself.

Everyone they spoke to was polite, but as the crowd grew, she became aware of whispers and stolen glances. One group of debutantes turned away from her as she looked over at them, and the loudest of the three giggled behind her hand.

Amelia's heart sank, and her shoulders climbed up nearer to her ears.

It wasn't working.

The ball was supposed to fix things, but all it had achieved was to emphasize the fact that the earl's family now had money and she was the reason why.

It was more obvious than ever that she'd bought herself a place among them.

Usually, that knowledge wouldn't bother her, but she hated to be the subject of all this public speculation. It was awful.

"The first song is about to start," Andrew said, taking her hand. "Dance with me."

They moved onto the dance floor, and as others clustered around, Andrew drew her closer.

"Ignore them." His voice wrapped around her like an

embrace, but it couldn't drown out the insidious whispering all around.

"It's not that easy," she said.

He twirled her as the first violin began to play, and her skirt flared around her, gleaming like a midnight sky in the light of the chandelier. "Nothing they say can stop us from leaving this week and enjoying Christmas in the country. It's all irrelevant."

Amelia didn't believe that the ton was irrelevant, but she appreciated him trying to calm her, and it did help to picture how they might spend the cool winter nights in front of a cozy fire in Suffolk.

"We can endure this," Andrew said. "And I promise that I'll give you the best Christmas ever to make up for it."

Amelia arched an eyebrow. "You can't make that promise. You don't know how good my past Christmases have been."

"Well, then I'll do my best." He held her tighter. "And I won't give you cause to doubt me again."

She wanted to believe him, but she wasn't sure that she could. He might mean it now, but no one could predict the future.

"Thank you," she whispered, regardless. The assurance was the best he could offer.

The dance ended, and he escorted her off the dance floor. A movement in the corner of her eye drew her gaze. Lady Drake was hurrying toward them. Unfortunately, before she reached them, Mrs. Hart appeared in front of Amelia.

She did not look happy.

Amelia's shoulders slumped. She'd always assumed that this ball would be her mother's moment of triumph, even more so than their wedding. However, it didn't look as though that was the case.

Mrs. Hart grabbed Amelia's arm and tugged her away from Andrew. "The gossip hasn't stopped." She looked around as if she expected everyone nearby to be listening to them. "You were supposed to fix this. Why should I be expected to deal with such disrespect? It was one thing when we weren't part of an aristocratic family, but we are now. This shouldn't be happening. Did you even try to make it stop?"

Amelia stared at her, astounded. "I'm doing the best I can."

"Well, do better," Mrs. Hart hissed. "This isn't how I expected to be treated when we joined the aristocracy."

Amelia glanced over her shoulder and saw her father approaching. She lowered her voice. "Tell me, how did you expect to be treated? You offered up a large dowry. The only reason we're part of the aristocracy now is because of that."

Mrs. Hart huffed. "If you were more socially adept, then we wouldn't be in this situation because you'd have already made powerful friends within the ton."

The barb struck true. Amelia's mouth fell open. She didn't know what to say. How could her mother be so cruel?

"Furthermore," Mrs. Hart continued, "if you had kept your husband satisfied—"

"That's quite enough," Mr. Hart interrupted, taking his wife by the arm. "This is not the place to have this conversation."

Amelia's eyes stung. She felt as if she'd been slapped. Her mother was blaming this on her. Blatantly telling her she wasn't good enough.

For years, she'd accepted this treatment. But she didn't have to now.

"I don't think this is a conversation that needs to be had at all," she said, looking around to see where Andrew had gotten to. Why wasn't he here with her?

She met her father's eyes, hating the knowledge that he could tell she was hurting but still allowed her mother to speak to her in such a way. After all, he hadn't said Mrs. Hart shouldn't say those things to Amelia, simply that the conversation ought to occur elsewhere.

Disappointed, she turned her back and stalked away.

She didn't know where she was going, only that she needed space. Deciding to get a drink and some fresh air, she made a beeline for the refreshments table. But before she reached it, she walked straight into Miss Wentham.

"Hello, Countess." Miss Wentham smirked. "It seems your first ball is a raging success. Although it's possible that has as much to do with the excellent gossip as it does your abilities as a hostess."

"What do you want?" Amelia asked. "I have no patience for games tonight."

Perhaps she shouldn't be so blunt with one of their guests, but Miss Wentham had never treated her with anything other than disdain, and she was tired of trying to be the better person.

Miss Wentham's smile grew. "I did warn you this would happen. I told you that the earl only wanted your money."

Amelia scowled. "Did it ever occur to you that I already knew that? I'm not quite as foolish as some people would like to believe."

Miss Wentham's brow furrowed. She opened her mouth, as if about to speak, but before she could, Amelia walked away.

All she wanted right now was to be alone. She had always known she didn't belong among the ton, but if she had ever deluded herself into thinking otherwise, this evening had provided all the proof she needed.

She wasn't one of them.

She didn't even think she wanted to be one of them.

As she hurried toward the balcony, her breath came in shallow gasps. Her throat was tight with emotion, and tears stung her eyes. She kept her head down and pushed past the guests.

Just as she reached the door, a murmur rippled through the crowd. Confused, she turned. The Duke of Ashford stood in front of her, blocking her view.

"Ignore them," he said. "They're all vultures. They mean nothing."

The murmur grew louder. Amelia tried to look around him.

"What the devil is she doing here?" The voice was Lady Drake's.

Amelia stretched onto her toes and peered toward the entrance, but immediately wished she hadn't. Heat rose up the back of her neck, and her blood rushed in her ears.

There, standing in the doorway, was Miss Giles.

CHAPTER 28

Andrew stared at Florence, unable to believe her audacity. She sashayed into the room, her head held high. If he didn't hate her so much in this moment, he might admire her gumption, but as it was, she could only be here for one reason.

To hurt him and humiliate Amelia.

Amelia.

He looked around for his wife, growing panicked when he didn't immediately find her. Her mother had snatched her away earlier, but he'd seen Mrs. Hart since then, so he knew they weren't still together.

She hadn't left, had she?

He gritted his teeth. He shouldn't have let Mrs. Hart speak to her in private. He should have known better. But at least if she wasn't here, she wouldn't have to witness this in person.

Unfortunately, it was at that moment he spotted her, standing near the balcony doors with Ashford and his mother.

Damn.

He hesitated, torn between whether to go to Amelia or

intercept Florence. He glanced from one woman to the other.

Amelia wasn't alone. She had support.

Would he like to go to her right now? Yes. But perhaps the best thing to do would be to get rid of the person causing her distress.

So thinking, he cut a line through the assembled guests toward Florence. Her eyes met his, and she smirked.

"All of this fuss for me?" she asked.

"You weren't invited," he told her coldly. "Why are you here?"

She laughed. "Why would I miss all the fun?"

"You think this is fun?" he demanded, heat simmering in his gut. "Distressing innocent women is fun for you?"

She rolled her eyes. "There is no need for your righteous indignation. I gave you a choice. You chose. Your wife should have known to expect this when she married you. If she didn't, that's her lookout."

Noticing that they were drawing attention, Andrew took her by the arm.

"Come with me. Let's talk in private."

"I am always happy to be in private with you," she cooed, pursing her lips suggestively.

"Keep your hands to yourself." He tugged her back out of the ballroom and down the corridor to his office.

She giggled. "So eager to get me all alone."

"What made you think you would be welcome here?" he asked, releasing her as though she'd burned him.

She shrugged one shoulder. "I've always been welcome around you before."

He crossed his arms. "That time has passed. You're making a spectacle of yourself—and of me."

"The attention doesn't bother me," she said, nothing but truth in her tone.

"I know." Attention never had bothered her. Whether

positive or negative, she thrived on it. "And if it were only us affected, that would be one thing. But it's not. You've carried through on your threat. It's over. I won't accept you doing anything else to upset my wife."

She sighed. "You're no fun these days. So serious all the time. So concerned about that mousey wife of yours. Why don't you just forget her for a little while and dance with me?"

"If you think I'm dancing with you, you're crazy."

Footsteps sounded outside, and they both turned toward the office doorway. Amelia appeared in the frame with Ashford at her back.

Andrew's chest squeezed. This was the first time Amelia had come face-to-face with Florence since finding out who she was to him. He instinctively reached for her, wanting to shield her from any pain or discomfort the situation might cause her, but she was too far away.

"I was sending her away," he said. "There's nothing happening here that you need to worry about."

But Amelia didn't seem insecure or cowed as he might have expected. Instead, she squared her shoulders and glared at Florence.

"You did not receive an invitation to this ball," she told his former mistress. "It's time for you to leave."

Florence raised her chin and stared Amelia down. "It's for Andrew to say whether I have to leave, not you."

He rolled his eyes. As they all knew, he'd been in the process of doing that exact thing when Amelia and Ashford had appeared.

Still, Amelia didn't shrink or waver. She looked down her nose at Florence. "Actually, it's not solely for Andrew to say. This is my home too. Considering the rumors you've spread, you're not welcome at any Longley property, including this one. Neither of us want to see your face again."

Florence sputtered and turned to Andrew. "Are you going to let her talk to me like that?"

Andrew moved over to stand beside Amelia. "Yes," he said simply. "I am."

Pride swelled in his chest. He took his wife's hand. She was strong, and he admired the hell out of her. Not only had she refused to let her insecurities get the better of her, but she was finally standing up for herself and fighting for what she wanted and deserved.

"But all I did was tell the truth," Florence protested, her hands on her hips.

"No," Amelia said. "You told the truth at the Benton ball, and while I think that was petty of you, I can understand why you did it. You lost Andrew. I know how upset I'd be if I lost him. But when you came here today, it wasn't about spreading the truth. It was to create a scene. There's no excuse for that. Now leave, or I'll have the duke escort you out."

One side of Florence's mouth hitched up, and cruel amusement filled her eyes. "The duke doesn't take orders from you."

"Perhaps not," Ashford agreed. "But I consider the countess to be a close friend, so I'm going to support my friend by escorting you to the door."

He brushed past Amelia and stopped beside Florence, gesturing for her to leave. When she didn't move, he began to reach for her, but she quickly darted out of the way.

"Don't touch me," she spat.

She shoved past them, jostling Andrew and stepping on Amelia's skirt, but she kept walking, so he didn't comment on it, simply relieved to see the back of her. Ashford followed close behind, no doubt to ensure she actually left the property.

Andrew guided Amelia fully inside the office and closed

the door. She was holding herself rigid, as if she wasn't sure how he was going to react to her treatment of Florence.

He raised her hand to his lips and kissed the back of it. "I'm so sorry you were subjected to that. I never expected that she would have the audacity to turn up at our ball."

"I know you didn't."

He couldn't quite decipher her tone. She didn't sound upset, necessarily, but her voice was loaded with emotion.

"Perhaps it was for the best," she continued, extracting her hand from his. "We had to face each other at some point, and now, she will no longer view me as someone she can walk all over."

He couldn't believe how calm she was. "I suppose that's certainly true."

"Besides." A small smile quirked her lips. "I got to look my demons in the eye and come out on top. But you'd better not put me through anything like this again. I deserve better."

"Better?" He shook his head. "No. You deserve everything."

And he would make sure she got it.

He drew her into his arms, moving slowly and giving her time to resist if she didn't want him. She melted against his chest, tilting her face toward his. He kissed her.

At first, it was the lightest brushing of lips, but then a delicious whimper escaped her, and she pressed closer, deepening the kiss.

He hummed his approval and cupped her bottom, wishing he could feel more of her through the fabric of her skirt. He flicked his tongue along the seam of her mouth, tasting the faintest hint of champagne, perhaps from her drink before the ball had begun. Her tongue met his, and they entwined, sliding sensuously against each other.

His hand curved around the side of her neck. The skin was smooth as satin beneath his fingers. He tilted her head back, and her lips left his. Her eyes fluttered open, the blue of them like pools he could swim in. They were slightly glazed, hazy with lust. The most beautiful things he'd ever seen.

"How did I get so lucky?" he asked, grazing the pad of his thumb along the ridge of her cheekbone.

She flushed. "I think I'm the lucky one."

She wasn't, but he knew it would take time and patience to prove that to her. He kissed her again, this time pouring his heart and soul into it, holding nothing back. She allowed him to drag her into a maelstrom of desire. Eventually, she pulled away.

"Our ball is still going just down the hall," she said. "We should get back to our guests."

Andrew stood firm. "I don't care about that. I don't care about most of the people here. Other than my family, and Ashford, they can go to hell for all I care."

She laughed but covered it quickly. "Even my parents?"

"Especially your parents." He kissed her forehead. "I appreciate that your father is helping me regrow my fortune, but he hasn't done right by you. He seems to view life as some kind of challenge for you to overcome, and perhaps that's made you stronger, but it's a father's job to be there when his daughter needs him, and he's let you down."

Her eyes were wide. "And my mother?"

He snorted. "Come, Amelia. You see the same thing I do when it comes to her. Her priorities are skewed. You should be more important than gossip, rumor, or social status. You're her daughter. A talented, intelligent, kind woman. You said earlier that you deserve better, and you really, really do."

She blinked rapidly, her eyes sparkling. "When we married, I never expected you to be like this. You've given me so much more than I ever imagined."

He gazed down at her, letting the full force of his affection shine through. "You are the one who has given me everything. I love you, Amelia. So much more than I ever knew was possible. My heart overflows with it. I feel that love with every breath I take. I don't give a damn what anyone else thinks, but I need you to believe me."

"Y-you love me?" she stammered. "Really?"

"I do." He held her hands in his. "More than anything."

She seemed stunned. "But… you never gave me any sign."

He grimaced. "It's come to my attention that despite our best efforts, you and I aren't always fantastic at communicating our feelings. I'm telling you now so there will be no misunderstandings. I love you, Amelia Drake. My heart beats for you. I won't say that I'm glad my family lost almost everything, but I'm ecstatic that that horrible situation brought me to you."

His heart raced frantically. Butterflies fluttered in his gut. He hadn't failed to notice that Amelia had yet to reciprocate his declaration. Honestly, she hadn't really said anything.

Did she feel the same?

He was sure she felt something. But maybe it was affection or friendship rather than the all-consuming love he felt for her.

"Sweetheart," he said, his tone pleading. "Say something."

"Oh." Her cheeks colored. The corners of her lips tipped up. "I'm sorry, I…."

"Yes?"

She nibbled on her lower lip. "It's so strange that we married for such unromantic reasons, and now you love me. You love me. I almost can't believe it. Certainly, no one else will."

"Then sod them all," Andrew said. "All that matters is that you believe me. Do you?"

CHAPTER 29

She did, she realized.

She believed him.

As far as she knew, Andrew had never lied to her. He may have omitted the truth at times, but he hadn't lied. So if he said he loved her now, she had no reason to doubt him. If she continued to hold herself back out of some misguided need to protect herself, she would be hurting not only herself but him too.

"I believe you," she whispered, holding his gaze. Flecks of gold twinkled in the depths of his irises. They were magical. Just like him. "And I love you too."

His face lit up. "You mean that?"

"Of course I do." She kissed him chastely. "How could I not? You believed in me all along. You encouraged me and supported me. You really see me in a way no one else ever has. I never stood a chance against you."

He cradled her face in his hands. "I will always be there for you, and I will do everything in my power to be worthy of you."

"You already are."

He brushed a kiss over her lips and then her forehead.

She closed her eyes, savoring the soft caress that filled her with a sense of warmth and comfort.

"So." She opened her eyes and tried to clear her thoughts. "Do you still want to leave for Suffolk? You know that it won't do as much to quell the gossip, considering that she turned up here."

Andrew laughed. "My practical countess. Always thinking ahead."

Her lips twisted wryly. "You love me. You just said so."

"I did," he agreed. "And I wouldn't have you any other way. Yes, sweetheart, I want to take you to Suffolk and show you where I grew up. I want to walk with you through the meadows I played in as a child and introduce you to the people who've known me my whole life."

Her heart beat a rapid rhythm. "I'd like that."

"I know."

She was about to open her mouth to protest being called predictable, but he stopped her with a finger to her lips.

"You're always so eager to discover new places," he continued. "Your fascination with the world around you is one of the things I love about you."

She softened. "Well, I love your kindness and generosity of spirit."

For a long moment, they gazed into each other's eyes. Then Andrew jerked his thumb toward the door.

"Do you really want to spend the evening at our ball?" he asked.

She narrowed her eyes. "No. I never particularly liked balls, and especially not after what just happened. They're bound to be gossiping already. But my parents are there, and so is your mother. Not to mention half the ton. We can't just leave."

"Can't we?" His eyes gleamed. "It's our ball. That means we get to make all the decisions. I say we hand off host duties to my mother—or to yours, who'd no doubt be thrilled with the responsibility—and then retreat to the bedchamber and celebrate properly."

She caught her lower lip between her teeth. His offer was so tempting, but surely it would be wrong to go along with it when this ball was supposed to be their social salvation.

"I want to," she admitted, leaning closer and breathing him in. "But it would be irresponsible."

"So be irresponsible," he whispered in her ear. "You and I have made too many decisions for the sake of others. This time, let's be selfish."

She drew back, looking up at him. Excitement simmered in her gut. "Really?"

He nodded, his expression serious despite the sparkle in his eyes. "Really."

She inhaled deeply. "Let's."

He kissed the top of her head and threaded his fingers through hers. "If we talk to my mother right now, we can escape again in only a few minutes. Don't make eye contact with anyone or stop if they call your name. We're on a mission. All right?"

She giggled, feeling lighter than she had in weeks. "I have tunnel vision. I will see and hear no one but your mother."

"Excellent."

Hand in hand, they strolled out of the office. Neither the duke nor Miss Giles were in the foyer, so Amelia assumed that she'd already left and he had returned to the ballroom.

As soon as they reached the doorway, a hush descended on the guests. The music kept playing, and the dancers continued dancing, but all the other guests' eyes were on them.

Amelia shivered. It wasn't the most pleasant sensation—especially not when she doubted they were thinking anything kind. But she held her chin high, kept her hand intertwined with Andrew's, and searched the gathering for Lady Drake.

"To the left of the dancers," she murmured. "Standing with the duke."

"I see her," he replied. "Don't forget what I said."

"I won't."

The crowd parted as they entered the room. Amelia heard someone say her name, but she didn't acknowledge them. A gentleman in a pink-and-gold waistcoat stepped in front of them, but Andrew whisked her around him. As they arrived at Lady Drake's side, the hush abated, and conversation rippled through the room.

"Mother." Andrew leaned close so no one could overhear them. "Would you consider acting as hostess in our stead while Amelia and I retire? It's been a particularly trying evening. You're welcome to pass on the duty to Mr. and Mrs. Hart, if you'd prefer."

Lady Drake glanced between them, her brows furrowed, her concern obvious. "Are you all right?"

His grip on her hand tightened. "We will be."

She nodded. "Good. I would be happy to stand in your stead, and I'm sure the Harts will be amenable to helping."

They'd better be, Amelia thought, *considering Mother was the one who wanted this ball to begin with.*

Yes, it had ended up being convenient in terms of attempting to combat the rumors, but she'd still never have planned a ball without encouragement from Mrs. Hart and Andrew.

Amelia turned to the duke. "Thank you for standing by me, Your Grace."

He bowed. "I will happily be your second whenever the role requires filling." His lips twitched. "Although I'd rather we avoid any duels. My wife would have my head if I were injured."

She laughed. "I don't intend on challenging Miss Giles to pistols at dawn, so I think you're safe on that front."

"We will bid you adieu," Andrew said. "Ashford, I know

how much you dislike these affairs. Please don't feel any need to linger on our account. We very much appreciate you making the effort to be here."

The duke inclined his head, and from his expression, she didn't think it would be long before he excused himself.

Andrew escorted Amelia back to the entrance. This time, fewer people paid them attention, although they did have to avoid a few wandering hands as guests tried to stop them for a quick word.

When they stood in the doorway, Andrew took Amelia by the hips and pulled her close. Her breath caught, and the back of her neck prickled with awareness. No one ever behaved so intimately in the public setting of a ball.

"May I?" he asked, curving his hand around between her shoulder blades and tipping her backward.

"Yes," she breathed, her eyes locked on his.

He kissed her.

Right there, in front of everyone.

Their lips parted, and he swallowed up her gasp and deepened the kiss. His tongue swept along hers.

How perfectly scandalous.

Someone whistled, and they broke apart. Her cheeks were burning, and she knew she must be bright red, but she couldn't bring herself to regret the kiss. Now all of these people knew he desired her. They would see that the Earl and Countess of Longley were married and very much in love.

It was heady.

Her mind was in a daze as Andrew led her out of the ballroom and into the corridor. He started to guide her toward the staircase, but a wicked idea occurred to her, and she stopped him.

"What is it, my love?" he asked.

With a mischievous grin, she glanced toward his office.

"This dress might be rather difficult to get out of, and I find myself too impatient to wait."

"I'm intrigued." He drew her knuckles to his lips. "What are you suggesting?"

She looked around and, certain they were alone, whispered, "You and me in your office."

His eyebrows shot up. "You won't be uncomfortable?"

She hesitated. "You'll lock the door?"

She loved the idea of being intimate with him while so many of their peers mingled nearby, none the wiser, but she didn't actually want anyone to walk in on them.

"Of course. If that's what you want?"

Her shoulders relaxed. "It is."

Decision made, they hurried to the office. She entered first, and he pushed her against the door. It clicked shut, and he turned the key, pinning her body against the wood.

Her breath came in short bursts. For some reason, the feeling of his powerful frame trapping her in place lit something up inside her. She angled her hips, seeking friction. He pushed his erection against her, sending a delicious zap of pleasure along her nerve endings.

He buried his face in the crook of her shoulder, his lips skimming along the sensitive skin. She shivered.

"So sweet," he murmured before biting lightly into the flesh.

She moaned. Part of her wanted him to bite harder and mark her. Such a bruise couldn't be dismissed as anything other than what it was: proof of his desire for her.

"You like that?" he asked, scraping his teeth over the delicate skin of her throat and nipping at the edge of her jaw.

"Mm-hmm." She ground against his hard cock, wishing the layers of her dress and his breeches were gone.

His lips tickled her as they curved into a smile. "My wanton wife."

"Only for you," she whispered. There was no one else

she'd ever trust enough to be like this with. No one else she'd want to be so intimate with.

"Yes." He sucked on her pulse point. "Mine."

She whimpered, then rolled them both so his back was against the door and she stood in front of him. She kissed the side of his neck, then sucked—hard—watching with delight as a red patch blossomed. A sign that he was hers as well.

Only hers.

"I am," he murmured, and she realized she'd said it aloud.

She blushed but didn't take it back.

"My countess." He cupped her face and kissed her. "I'm going to sit you on that desk, hike up your skirts, and completely and utterly own you. Any objections?"

She blinked at him, hardly able to think beyond the thick fog of need that had descended over her. "No."

"No?" He frowned.

"No objections."

"Thank God."

He bent and swept her into his arms, the movement made awkward because of the voluminousness of her skirts, but he didn't allow that to deter him. He carried her to the desk and set her down carefully. She shifted her bottom until she was sure she wouldn't fall and spread her thighs.

His eyes flashed, the gold flaring brighter than ever. "In case it isn't obvious, we're amending the agreement. If any other man ever lays a hand on you, it will be pistols at dawn."

She smirked. "As long as the same rule applies to you, then I see no issue with that."

"With this kiss, I bind you to me." He hesitated for just long enough for her to disagree.

When she didn't, he kissed her.

She dragged her fingers down his chest. "With this touch, I thee worship."

A shudder rolled through him, and he dropped to his knees. He lifted her skirt and ducked beneath it. A moment later, his breath whispered over her most intimate place. She felt him grab the waistband of her undergarments and ease them down; then he pressed a kiss to her.

She leaned back, her palms on the wood of the desk, supporting herself. Unable to see Andrew, she had no idea what he might do next. When his mouth fastened over her and his tongue gently probed her core, she jolted and gasped.

"Mm. Sweet." He teased her with his lips and tongue, circling around her bud, winding her tighter and tighter but never quite giving her enough.

She whimpered and thrust her hips forward, silently begging for more. Eventually, there was a slight pressure, and then one of his fingers slipped inside her. His tongue continued to circle her, driving her out of her mind. He crooked his finger, and she cried out.

"Shh," he teased. "We wouldn't want anyone to hear us."

He ducked out from beneath her skirts, and heat blasted through her at the sight of him. Lips damp, eyes bright, hair mussed. He looked delightfully rumpled.

"You still want this?" he asked, moving closer, his hands dropping to the desk as he caged her in.

"Yes. More than anything."

His pupils dilated, swallowing up the irises until only a thin band of color remained. "I love you so much."

Emotion tightened her throat. "I love you too."

With shaking hands, he undid his belt and lowered his breeches. His undergarment followed, and he stepped out of them, then grabbed the layers of her skirt and lifted them up around her waist. He shifted forward, the hair on his thighs scraping against the tender insides of her legs as he made his way to that hot, wanting part of her.

"Do it," she murmured, parting her thighs to reveal herself to him. "I need you."

"Fuck." A shudder rolled through him. "Easy, love. Too much of that and I won't last."

She grinned. "Then don't. We have all night."

She didn't know what was making her so brazen, but she never wanted it to end.

He fitted himself against her and pressed in. Her eyes widened as he filled her, and she exhaled slowly, allowing her muscles to relax. He held her gaze the entire time.

When he was deep within her, he began to rock. Just small movements at first, seating himself deeper and nudging her bud over and over again.

With one hand remaining in place behind her, she grabbed him with the other and yanked him toward her. "More."

His lips curved. "If you insist."

He drew out in one smooth motion and thrust back in so hard, her vision nearly whited out.

"Oh," she cried.

She needed more of that. Now.

Wrapping her legs around him, she urged him to do it again.

He did, and her head fell back, her mouth open, as starbursts of color exploded before her eyes.

She was so close. So close. Teetering on the brink. Just one more and...

He drove into her again, and she shattered, calling out his name. Pleasure like none she'd ever experienced turned her limbs languid even as she trembled from the overwhelming intensity, completely out of control of her own body.

"Fuck."

His hands slid beneath her bottom, and he lifted her against him. She clutched his shoulders as he thrust relentlessly into her, then groaned, rapture stealing across his face as he released within her.

Thankfully, he set her down before his legs gave out, and he collapsed onto the desk chair, his breeches still around his ankles.

"Wow." He patted his lap. "Come here."

Amelia lowered her feet to the floor, padded over to him, and sat. He wrapped his arm around her waist and held her close. She rested her head on his shoulder and closed her eyes as contentment washed over her.

They were quiet, but it was peaceful and perfect. Amelia smiled to herself. When she'd proposed her practical marriage to Andrew, she'd never have dreamed that she could be so happy with him—and have her writing too.

This was not at all how she'd foreseen the future playing out, but for once, she couldn't be more pleased that nothing had gone according to plan.

CHAPTER 30

*Suffolk,
December 1820*

As the carriage trundled along the tidy country road, Kate stuck her head out the window.

"We're almost there," she called. "Perhaps another mile or so."

Amelia's gut churned with both excitement and nerves. She was eager to see her new home. Andrew had told her such lovely stories about it. But she was also anxious to discover how the household staff would react to her presence.

Andrew had grown up among these people. The housekeeper, butler, and cook had all been there since he'd been a child, and she wanted them to like her.

Lady Drake smiled at her across the carriage. "They'll love you," she said, as if reading Amelia's mind.

Amelia supposed she would have a better idea of what was currently running through it than anyone else would. She had once been in Amelia's shoes, coming to this home for the first time. Although she'd at least been a member of the aristocracy prior to marriage.

"They will," Andrew confirmed, leaning over to kiss her cheek.

Warmth flooded her chest. She was so lucky to have him. In fact, she considered herself lucky to have all of them. She would always love her parents, but she hadn't spoken to them since the ball, and she wasn't sure how much time and energy she wanted to give them in future. Brigid and Kate had been far more accepting of her and caring toward her than her own family ever had been.

"There it is!" Kate was hanging out the window again, pointing to something in the distance.

"You know, Amelia can't see anything when you're in the way," Andrew pointed out.

Kate dropped back onto her seat and poked her tongue out at him—a more girlish gesture than any Amelia had seen from her. Perhaps returning to their home in the country reminded her of being little again.

Amelia shifted closer and looked through the window. She couldn't see much, but the silhouette of turrets against the skyline was unmistakable. The roof tiles were dark—perhaps gray or black—but slightly faded.

She kept an eye on the manor as they drew nearer and it came into view more clearly.

It was stunning.

Primarily built of orange and yellow stone and brick, it had over a dozen arched windows facing outward and a domed roof on the center section. A short flight of stairs led up to the main entrance, and the household staff were lined up along the paved area at the top and down the stairs.

A severe-looking older man and a short, thin woman with thick gray hair stood at the base of the stairs, awaiting the carriage. Amelia had already been briefed on the members of staff, so she knew these must be Alfred, the butler, and Harden, the housekeeper.

The carriage came to a stop in front of them, and they waited for a footman to open the door. Andrew stepped out first and then helped Amelia down. She straightened her back, remembering all her mother's lessons on good posture, and smiled politely at Alfred and Harden.

Andrew offered his hand to Lady Drake and then Kate. Once the whole party had disembarked, he linked arms with Amelia and escorted her over to greet the staff. Harden dropped into a curtsy, and Alfred bowed.

"Welcome home, my lord," Harden said, her hands clasped in front of her.

"Thank you, Harden. It's good to be back."

"My lord." Alfred dipped his head respectfully.

"Good afternoon, Alfred." Andrew raised his voice. "I'd like to introduce you all to the new countess. This is Lady Amelia Drake. My wife."

Amelia nodded to Alfred and Harden. "It's a pleasure to meet you."

Harden's thin lips lifted. "The pleasure is all ours, my lady. We feared the earl would never wed."

Andrew laughed. "Hey now, none of that. It's not as if I'm ancient."

"Of course not, my lord," Harden assured him, grinning slyly.

Lady Drake cleared her throat. "Shall we introduce the Countess of Longley to the household?"

"Oh, yes." Harden straightened and smoothed her dress. "Allow me."

The housekeeper escorted Amelia and Andrew along the line of staff, introducing each by name and position. Amelia did her best to commit the names and faces to memory, but she knew it would take a while before she remembered them all. There were simply too many.

She was glad that her dowry had ensured all of these people were able to remain employed. It was hardly enough money to do so indefinitely, but it bought them some time, and if Andrew and her father continued to manage it well, it could definitely support them into the future.

When they reached the top of the stairs and the end of the row of staff, Harden offered to show her around the inside of the manor.

"I would like that," Amelia told her.

"I'll accompany you," Andrew said. "I'm sure Mother and Kate would like to retire to their rooms for a while before dinner."

"Yes, please," Kate said at the same time as Lady Drake protested.

"I'll come with you," Lady Drake insisted. "I'll have plenty of time to rest later but only one chance to introduce my new daughter to our beloved home."

Amelia's heart warmed. "Thank you."

When she'd married Andrew, she'd never imagined that she'd receive a new mother figure as part of the arrangement, but she was so grateful she had.

Harden dismissed the staff, and as soon as they entered the manor, Kate vanished down a corridor and around a corner.

"All of the rooms for entertaining are on the ground floor," Harden said, gesturing down the corridors to the left and right. "The ballroom is directly behind us, and the drawing rooms, music room, and formal dining room are to the left. The kitchen and family room are farther along that corridor. To the right are the earl's office, the library, and the portrait gallery."

"There's a portrait gallery?" She'd heard of such things but had never seen one.

Harden nodded. "It displays portraits from over seven generations of the Drake lineage."

"That's incredible." Amelia didn't even know who her great-grandparents were, let alone anyone further back than that.

Harden smiled. "The family is proud of their heritage." She inclined her head. "Soon to be your heritage too."

Amelia started at that. It hadn't occurred to her that she or her children may one day be painted and displayed in the family's gallery.

"The family's chambers are upstairs on the left, and the guest rooms are to the right," Harden continued. "Come. Let's start in the ballroom."

They followed the housekeeper as she led them across the foyer to the ballroom. It was high-ceilinged and tastefully decorated, with a wooden floor, white walls, and gilt adornments above the mantle.

Harden showed them to the drawing room next, followed by the music room, where the sheer size of the grand piano stole her breath. The dining room was far more audaciously decorated than the ballroom, with massive crystal chandeliers hanging from the ceiling and gilt-framed paintings by some of the masters adorning the walls.

Amelia shook her head. When her mother saw that room, she'd be in heaven.

The morning room and the family's smaller dining area were, while also elegantly appointed, far warmer and more welcoming.

They reversed direction down the corridor. They didn't go inside the earl's office, but Amelia knew Andrew would let her look around whenever she wanted. They did, however, stop at the library.

And oh, how beautiful it was.

Amelia covered her mouth as they entered. Her eyes grew to the size of saucers. "It is… perfect."

Never in her life had she been inside such a beautiful library. It occupied two stories, with bookshelves lining every wall other than the one with windows out onto the courtyard. Stairs led to the second story, and comfortable brown leather chairs were tucked into the corners.

Andrew kissed her cheek. "I'm glad you like it. You can read anything you like, and you're welcome to add to it too. We have more than enough space."

She couldn't think of a better gift. "Thank you."

"Unfortunately, we must move on," he murmured. "You can return later and explore at your leisure."

Reluctantly, she allowed him to draw her away. The last place they were to visit on the ground floor was the portrait gallery. Once again, Amelia was awed. Portraits lined the walls. The oldest was on the nearest end of the room, and the most recent were farthest away.

As they strolled past the older paintings, many worn with age, she examined the faces. Some of the Drakes were austere, while others looked friendly. Many had the same auburn hair as Andrew. And many, she noted, had something of a mischievous twinkle in their eyes. She wondered if good humor was a family trait.

"There's so much history in here," she breathed.

"You will be a part of it." Lady Drake gestured to the part of the end wall that remained empty. "That space is for you, Andrew, and your children."

Andrew dipped his head beside Amelia's ear. "Did you notice the portrait of my parents?"

She studied the last painting before the empty space. In it, a woman who was obviously Lady Drake, albeit much younger, stood beside a handsome gentleman with dark reddish-brown hair a few years her senior.

"It's lovely." They looked happy together.

"His name was George," Andrew murmured.

"You have his smile." It sounded trite, but he really did.

Lady Drake snorted. "He inherited a lot more than that from his father. Drake men are born charmers. They're excellent at getting themselves into trouble but just as good at getting themselves out of it." Her tone was fond. She turned to Harden. "Shall we show the countess her bedchamber? I'm sure she would like a chance to rest before dinner."

"Yes, my lady."

They headed upstairs, bypassing the guest rooms in favor of going straight to the family wing. Harden indicated the door behind which each member of the family resided, but she and Lady Drake left once they'd unlocked the door to the countess's chambers.

Amelia's new bedchamber was undeniably feminine, with cream-colored walls, powder-pink carpet, and a white four-poster bed draped with gold hangings.

Andrew closed the door behind them, a wicked glint in his eyes. She went into his arms, leaning against his chest and kissing him.

"Let me welcome you home properly," he murmured, easing her sleeve down to expose her shoulder.

She closed her eyes and smiled. One thing was for certain, she'd never be locking the adjoining door between their bedchambers again.

∼

*Norfolk,
December 1820*

A COUPLE OF WEEKS LATER, ANDREW WOKE WITH HIS WIFE tucked against his body. He kissed the side of her neck and stroked her belly, wondering if his baby was growing inside her even now. The thought appealed to him.

"Wake up, my love," he whispered.

She mumbled sleepily and snuggled closer to him.

He grinned. "Sweetheart, it's Christmas."

At that, her eyes fluttered open. "It is?"

"Yes. We're at Ashford Hall, remember?" They'd traveled here to spend Christmas with Ashford, Emma, and their family.

Amelia rolled toward him, and he relaxed his hold on her. "Breakfast?"

He glanced at the clock, squinting through the dim light to make it out. "We have half an hour."

Unfortunately not long enough to make love to her, which was one of his new favorite ways to start the day.

She sighed. "I'd best call for a maid. It'll take me that long to make myself presentable."

He nuzzled the crook of her shoulder. "No need for that. I'll dress you."

She smiled at him. "You're very good at undressing me, but I'm not sure you're as skilled at the reverse."

He kissed the tip of her nose. "I'll prove it to you."

"All right, then."

He tossed back the covers and swung his legs off the edge of the bed, ignoring her squawk of protest. "Up we get, my love."

Grumbling something unintelligible, she crawled out of bed and rubbed her eyes. One of her cheeks was creased from the pillow.

Adorable.

His heart full of love, he wrapped his arms around her and peppered her with kisses. "What would you like to wear?"

She pursed her lips. "Perhaps the light green dress. If I put a red ribbon in my hair, it will be very festive."

"Indeed."

He retrieved the dress she'd mentioned and helped her into it. The buttons were, admittedly, more difficult to do up than to undo, but he managed.

That done, he got her to sit while he brushed her hair. She twisted it into a simple coil, and he looped a strip of red satin around the bundle and tied it in a bow. It was slightly lopsided but not too bad, all things considered.

They splashed cold water on their faces, dried them, and then he dressed himself quickly before they headed down for breakfast.

They shared a pleasant, hearty meal with Ashford and Emma, their daughter Lilian, Lady Drake, Kate, Emma's parents, and her younger sister, Sophie. Emma's twin, Violet, and her husband weren't in attendance, although considering the previous betrothal between Ashford and Violet, that was hardly surprising.

After breakfast, they retreated to the morning room, where a Christmas tree stood in the corner. The air was thick with the scent of pine, and the furniture had been rearranged around the tree, so they could gather there comfortably.

As Andrew sat and gestured for Amelia to join him, he listened in on her conversation with Emma. Amelia had allowed Emma to borrow a handwritten copy of her first Miss Joceline Davies novel, which was due to be printed next year, and the duchess had spent the evening prior reading.

Emma was enthusing over how much she'd enjoyed it, and Amelia's cheeks were flushed with joy.

"I'll be certain to send you a signed copy for your library once it's in print," Amelia said.

"I would like that very much." Emma smiled brightly, and Amelia smiled back.

Andrew exchanged a glance with Vaughan, pleased their wives were getting along well. Neither of them had any close friends, and it was obvious that they'd already bonded over their love of books. He suspected they would exchange letters regularly after the holiday ended.

"I don't get a season for another two years," Sophie complained, dragging his attention away from his wife.

"You're too young to have your first season next year," Lady Carlisle, Emma's mother, reminded her.

"It's all right." Kate sat beside Sophie and patted her knee. "I'll learn everything I can next season so I can tell you all about who to befriend and who to avoid when you join me."

Lady Drake frowned. "I thought you intended to marry in your first season, dear? Do you now plan to have more than one season?"

Kate shrugged. "It might be nice to share a season with a friend, and even if I do marry, I can still support her, can't I?"

"I suppose so." Their mother didn't seem to know what to make of that.

Frankly, Andrew didn't, either, except to hope that his investments continued to pay off so they could afford another season.

Emma clapped, cutting the conversation off. "Thank you all for coming," she said, her soft voice rising so they could all hear her. "We're so grateful to be surrounded by family for such a happy day. We're blessed to be here and to share it with you."

Ashford came to stand behind her, his hand resting on her waist.

"Now, the time for gift giving has finally arrived. Shall we begin with the youngest and work our way up?"

"Yes," Sophie urged, no doubt knowing that meant she would receive her gifts as soon as Lilian was done.

Andrew interlaced his fingers with Amelia's. She rested her head on his shoulder, and his heart swelled with joy. The sense of contentment and ease with those around him only grew as the youngest girls exclaimed excitedly over their gifts.

When it was Amelia's turn, he presented her with an elegant black box and watched as she took it from him curiously and tested the edges until she figured out how to open it. The lid flipped open, and she gasped, looking at him with sparkling eyes.

"It's beautiful." She kissed him, heedless of those around them. "The prettiest quill I've ever seen."

He felt a silly grin take over his face. "I hope you use it to write many more adventures for Miss Joceline."

Her expression was beatific. "I will."

When it was his turn, Amelia went first, offering him a cotton pouch. He felt it, frowning. Whatever was inside was soft. He had no idea what it could be. An item of clothing, perhaps? But it was awfully small.

"Open it," she urged.

He loosened the drawstring and looked inside the pouch, his confusion deepening. He reached inside, grabbed hold of something woolen and knitted, and pulled it out.

It was a baby bootie.

His heart racing, he withdrew a matching one, both made from sunshine-yellow wool.

He met her gaze, his throat thick with emotion. He coughed in an attempt to clear it. "Does this…." He drew in a deep breath. "Does this mean what I think it means?"

Amelia took his hand and placed it on her belly. "I'm pregnant. The doctor confirmed it before we left Suffolk, but I wanted to surprise you."

He tugged her into an embrace, being careful not to bump her stomach. He gave her a lingering kiss, breathing in her familiar minty scent.

"This is the best surprise you could have given me." He kissed her forehead, then the corners of her mouth, unable to bring himself to let go of her.

"I'm going to be a grandmother?"

With a happy sigh, Andrew released her, and they both turned to Lady Drake. Her eyes were shining, her fingertips pressed to her lips.

"You are," Amelia told her.

Lady Drake let out a small cry and rushed over to them, dragging them both into a hug. Kate piled on, and a laugh bubbled from Andrew.

This truly was the best Christmas he'd ever had.

Eventually, they returned to their seats and resumed the gift giving, but Andrew couldn't pay attention. He looped his arm around Amelia and caressed her belly, scarcely able to believe his luck. Only months ago, he'd been afraid that life as they knew it was over.

And it was.

But the life that had replaced it had brought him more happiness than he'd ever dreamed of.

When all the gifts had been distributed and the floor beneath the tree was bare, he took Amelia by the hand and led her back to their guest bedroom.

"How are you feeling?" he asked, sitting on the bed and pulling her down into his arms.

She relaxed against him, warm and trusting. "I'm well. A little tired, but I haven't felt sick at all. Mostly, my senses are just, well, especially sensitive. I'm told that's not unusual, but now that Emma and Lady Drake know, I can discuss it more with them to be sure."

He held her close. "Are you happy?"

Her bright eyes showed not an ounce of worry. "Very much so. Are you?"

"More than I ever have been." He wound his fingers through her hair, and his lips found hers in a kiss that lingered for too long to be entirely chaste. "Thank you, my love."

Her eyebrows drew together. "For what?"

He kissed her again. "For giving me everything that I never knew I needed."

EPILOGUE

*Suffolk,
About A Year Later*

"Pa-pa?" George chanted from where he was positioned on Amelia's hip.

"Papa is with Uncle Vaughan," Amelia told him, turning her face up into the sun. Although the sun was shining warmly on their backs, there was a faint coolness to the air as evening began to descend.

"Pa-pa," he insisted.

Amelia sighed. "Emma, do you have any idea where our husbands might be?"

Emma glanced over, her palm resting on her rounded belly. "Last I saw, they were in the gardens around the front."

Amelia laughed. "Of course."

The flowers were in bloom, and the garden at the entrance to Longley Manor was a vibrant blanket of purple, red, and yellow.

Together, the women walked around to the garden, pausing every now and then for Emma to get comfortable. The baby wasn't due for a while yet, but she'd confided in

Amelia that the pregnancy hadn't been particularly pleasant. Her back often ached, and she was nauseous on and off throughout the day, but she'd insisted on not being left inside on her own while the others enjoyed the sun.

Andrew came into view first. He was crouched in front of a flowerbed, encouraging Lilian to walk to him. The little girl lurched toward him, her gait uneven. When she was about halfway between him and Vaughan, she stumbled and fell to her knees.

Within seconds, Vaughan had scooped her into his arms. He kissed her belly, and Lilian shrieked and giggled. Emma picked up the pace and joined them, cooing and making a fuss over Lilian's efforts. Their little girl was growing more confident every day.

"Pa-pa!"

Andrew looked up, and a smile lit his handsome face. "Hello, little fellow."

He straightened, wiped his hands on his thighs, and headed over to Amelia. He greeted her with a kiss. "Want me to take him for a while?"

"That would be wonderful." She loved holding their son, but it seemed as if he was getting bigger and heavier every day.

She smiled. He was going to be a strong, healthy boy.

In a movement now practiced many dozens of times, they shifted George from her hip to his father's. Amelia felt a slight pang at the loss, but when Andrew kissed the top of George's downy head, her heart swelled with love.

"What's that smile about?" Andrew asked, squinting slightly into the sun.

She shrugged. "Just thinking about how lucky I am."

His mouth hitched in a lopsided grin. "I'm the lucky one. I have a wife I adore and a little boy to dote on who is still too young to get up to mischief."

She laughed. "Just wait. It will come."

She'd seen that firsthand with Lilian.

"And when it does, we'll be ready. Just think of the adventures we can have."

She cuddled closer to him and George. "I already have my perfect adventure."

In fact, she had it all.

A flourishing career, an adorable son, and a man who gave her a reason to smile every day.

Tears prickled in her eyes. She'd never dared to hope for a future as bright as this, but she would never, ever let it go.

THE END

EXCERPT FROM THE DUKE'S INCONVENIENT BRIDE

*London,
October, 1819*

Vaughan Stanhope, the Duke of Ashford, had never wanted a wife. Unfortunately, one could not get heirs without a wife, and without an heir, his title would pass to his bullying cousin, Reginald, and his brood of entitled brats.

Thus, here he was, in his best carriage, bedecked in his finest evening wear, and accompanied by his long-suffering friend, Andrew Drake, the Earl of Longley, on the way to a ball.

"I always knew you'd be the first of us to find a wife," Longley said, glancing out of the window as they arrived outside the Earl of Wembley's townhouse.

Vaughan scoffed and resisted the urge to look for himself. He was anxious enough without laying eyes on the crush of society that would no doubt be turning up tonight.

"Yes. After growing up with such a splendid example of matrimonial bliss, how could I possibly resist?"

Longley rolled his eyes. "Not because of your awful parents. Purely to spite that loathsome jackanapes, Reginald."

"Ah, yes. Him."

"Darling Reggie" as Vaughan's dearly departed mother had called him, had spent years tormenting him behind their parents' backs. Calling him names, mocking his shyness, and telling everyone who'd listen what a joke it was that he'd one day be a duke.

"He is the reason we're here, is he not?" Longley asked.

"In a roundabout way." At that moment, the carriage came to a stop. The door opened, and Vaughan climbed out, only too eager to be free of the conversation.

They made their way up the stone steps to the house's main entrance and stepped inside the foyer, where they were met by their hosts.

"Your Grace." The Earl of Wembley greeted Vaughan with a nod, then turned to Longley. "Lord Longley. Welcome to Wembley House."

"Felicitations. It seems as if you have a success on your hands," Longley said, and Vaughan shot him a look of gratitude for taking the lead. He was so much better in social situations than Vaughan was. Longley took the countess's hand and bowed over it. "My lady."

"Lord Longley," the countess demurred, then smiled slyly at Vaughan. "Your Grace, please allow me to introduce my eldest daughter, Lady Henrietta."

Vaughan acknowledged the girl with a tilt of his head. "Lady Henrietta. It's an honor to make your acquaintance."

Lady Henrietta's blond curls bounced as she angled her head back to look up at him, a friendly smile on her face. "The honor is all mine, Your Grace."

He glanced at Longley, who discreetly bumped him in the ribs with his elbow.

"I hope you will save me a dance," Vaughan said, the words difficult to get out past the lump in his throat. Still, this was what he was here for. To find a wife. Lady Henrietta was both pretty and suitable in terms of her connections. He could do worse.

"I would be delighted." She offered him her dance card and he filled a spot.

"We must move along," Longley urged as more guests arrived behind them. "Until later, Lady Henrietta."

They moved into the ballroom, which was massive, with high ceilings, white walls gilded with gold, and a polished wooden floor. It was also packed. Vaughan grew warmer, and not only from the mass of bodies pressing in around him. He and Longley seemed to have attracted a lot of attention with their arrival. Many young misses glanced their way, while their mothers studied the men more openly.

Heat prickled at the back of Vaughan's neck. He had the unmistakable feeling that he was being hunted. He drew in a shaky breath, his nostrils filling with the scent of the shrubbery somebody had felt the need to drag inside. He shrugged, trying to shake off the sensation of his skin being too tight for his body.

"Your Grace." A redheaded woman appeared in front of him with two younger ladies in tow. "Ah, and Lord Longley too." She looked like the cat that had eaten the canary.

"Lady Bowling," Vaughan replied, glancing over to make sure Longley hadn't beaten a rapid escape. His friend may be kind enough to have accompanied him tonight, but he had no desire for a wife of his own.

"May I present my daughter, Lady Esther, and her cousin, Miss Rose Hawthorne. They are new to society this season."

Vaughan blinked at the girls, one of whom wore a ridiculous feather construction in her hair, and the other of whom seemed to have been cinched so tightly into her ball gown that she might pass out at any moment.

"Charmed," Longley said, covering for Vaughan's hesitation. "I daren't hope that either of you lovely ladies have any space on your dance cards for His Grace or myself?"

The cards were proffered with much giggling and glee, and Vaughan dutifully added his name to each. They bid farewell to the group but had only made it another five paces before they were intercepted yet again.

By the time they reached the stairs leading to the upper balcony that overlooked the ballroom, Vaughan felt as if he hadn't drawn in a full breath for hours. A male voice called his name, but fearing yet another introduction to an eligible lady, he hurried up the stairs with Longley trailing behind him.

"Good lord, Ashford," Longley puffed as he drew even with Vaughan at the top of the stairs. "You're far less likely to find a wife up here than you were down there."

Vaughan surveyed the throng below, his pulse pounding madly in his temples. Even several feet above the revelry, he could hear the giggles, the inane chatter, and felt gazes following him.

"I did not realize it would be so…." He waved his hands, searching for a suitable descriptor. "Intense."

Longley chuckled. "'Tis the biggest ball of the season so far, which means every marriageable miss is seeking to make an impression. The fact that you are an unmarried duke, who has apparently decided to rectify your lack of a wife, makes you the plumpest catch here tonight."

Vaughan snorted. "You make me sound like a grouse."

"To the mamas of unwed young women, you might as well be."

Vaughan shook his head. "There must be a better way to find a wife."

Longley shrugged. "If you find one quickly, you won't have to subject yourself to many of these ghastly affairs. How many dances have you scheduled?"

"Almost half of them." His tone was morose. He enjoyed dancing, but not in cramped quarters such as this, and especially not with so many eyes on him.

Longley leaned on the balustrade. Vaughan followed his example, gazing out over the shining jewels of the ton.

"What do you want in a wife?" Longley asked. "Perhaps we can hasten the matter by being selective about the ladies to whom you offer your remaining dances."

Vaughan nodded. That made sense. "She must be well-mannered and respectable." His duchess would need to be able to smooth over his own occasional social missteps. "She does not have to be wealthy or from a titled family."

He pursed his lips, trying to quiet his thoughts, but it was difficult with the ruckus below. "She would ideally be popular and able to entertain herself, as I don't intend to spend much time together after we are wed."

There was a moment of silence, and then Longley asked, "Are you truly sure you wish to do this?"

~

Being Lady Violet Carlisle's twin sometimes made Emma feel invisible. Especially on nights such as these, when gentlemen were practically getting into fisticuffs to determine who would have the honor of dancing with Violet whilst seeming not to notice Emma at all. It made it difficult for Emma to find a man to fall in love with when they all wanted her sister.

With a sigh, Emma shrank back against the wall beside the refreshments table, watching as Violet spun across the dance floor on the arm of a viscount. She surveyed the gathering, searching for her mother, but her attention was halted by the sight of the square-jawed and remarkably well-built Earl of Longley, who seemed to be making his way directly to her.

Emma straightened, pushing her shoulders back and smiling in welcome. She had always liked the earl. Not only was he handsome, but he was also clever and kind. Perhaps he would spare her from another evening spent as a wallflower by asking her to dance.

"Lady Emma," he said, stopping in front of her. "You look well tonight."

She dropped into a curtsey. "As do you, my lord."

When she rose, he gestured toward the dance floor.

"Do you know when Lady Violet will next be free? I have someone to whom I'd like to introduce her."

Emma's heart sank. Of course the earl had not come over here to see her. As always, it was her sister whose company was desired.

"I believe she is free in two dances' time, my lord."

"Very good. My thanks, Lady Emma." He sketched a quick bow and left.

Emma turned to the table beside her and poured herself a drink. She sipped the lemonade and eyed the tiny pastries and cakes set out nearby. They had not eaten dinner prior to departing from Carlisle House because their mother had wanted them to look slim in their gowns.

Unfortunately, being hungry made Emma lethargic, which meant she lagged even further behind Violet in the beauty department than usual. She edged closer to the table and reached for a pastry, slipping it into her hand and quickly raising it to her lips. She glanced around, checking whether anyone had noticed, but of course, nobody was looking at her.

Nobody ever was.

She took another pastry and spied one of her acquaintances dancing with her new husband. Their heads were ducked close together, their gazes locked on each other. Emma sighed. They looked as though they were aware of no one else in the room.

How she wanted that.

Emma sipped her lemonade, wishing it were laced with something stronger. Something that would make the evening more tolerable. It wasn't that she didn't like balls. She rather thought she'd enjoy them if she weren't such a wallflower.

"Emma!"

Emma flinched and spun around. Her mother, Lady Carlisle, was making a beeline toward her around the edge of the ballroom, past the row of chairs where the spinsters and chaperones sat, drawing even with the refreshments table. Her eyebrows had climbed impressively high and her eyes were narrow as she appraised her erstwhile daughter.

"What on earth are you doing all the way over here?" her mother demanded. "Nobody will ask you to dance if you do not remain near the dancing."

Emma pursed her lips. She thought there were likely other, more pressing reasons she was not asked to dance, but far be it for her to say so.

"Sorry, Mother. I shall return with you momentarily."

She tried to finish her lemonade, but Lady Carlisle plucked the glass from her hand and put it on the table.

Emma sighed. "Very well."

Lady Carlisle took Emma by the arm and guided her back into the fray. Emma nodded at an acquaintance of hers who was, likewise, not particularly popular with the males of the aristocracy.

"Doesn't Violet look brilliant tonight?" Lady Carlisle asked, watching her other daughter with such pride stamped across her face that Emma had to look away. It was difficult to bear the knowledge that she never brought her mother the same level of joy.

"She does," Emma agreed because it was true. Violet sparkled tonight, as she did every night. The song ended, and there was a brief pause before the next one began. Violet was making her way toward them across the dance floor on the arm of a handsome gentleman Emma did not recognize.

The music started again, and Emma tapped her foot,

wishing somebody would ask her to dance. Even an elderly bachelor or a homely one would do. She did so love to dance.

"Mother," Violet said as they drew near. "This is Mr. Bently."

"Cousin to the Earl of Longley," Mr. Bently added—presumably to make himself look like a better catch to the Carlisle matriarch.

"He's quite a dashing dancer," Violet exclaimed.

Emma felt a pang of envy. She tried not to be jealous of Violet, but sometimes it was difficult.

"Lady Carlisle." The voice came from behind Emma and startled them all. Emma's hand flew to her chest as she turned toward it.

Lord Longley smiled broadly. He tipped his head. "Lady Emma. Lady Violet. Bently."

"Lord Longley." Violet's smile was beatific. Lord Longley was on her shortlist of prospective husbands. While Emma wanted to find a connection before she married, Violet was much more pragmatic. A title and a fortune would do nicely for her.

Lord Longley waited for the greetings to finish and then gestured to the man beside him, an austere-looking fellow with an immaculately tailored waistcoat, dark hair, and eyes the color of the sky on a cloudy morning.

"Please allow me to introduce you to my good friend, the Duke of Ashford."

Emma heard her mother's quick intake of breath. Violet was more subtle, but her eyes still widened. Emma didn't know why they were surprised. She wasn't. If the rumors were to be believed, the duke was looking for a bride, and Violet would make a remarkable duchess.

There was a chorus of "Your Graces" followed by curtseying, during which Emma surreptitiously watched the duke. His eyes were unusual and quite stunning, but he didn't have the same amiable air about him that Lord Longley did. In fact, while his mouth twitched slightly during the introduction, he didn't even smile.

When Emma found a husband, she'd want one who smiled regularly and laughed easily.

"A pleasure." The Duke of Ashford's voice was cool and cultured. He reminded Emma of what she imagined the character of Mr. Darcy from the novel she was reading would sound like. He turned to Violet. "Lady Violet, may I have this dance?"

Violet fluttered her eyelashes—dark, unlike Emma's overly pale ones—and smiled. "It would be an honor."

She took his hand and allowed him to lead her away. As soon as Violet left, Mr. Bently made his excuses, and the earl melted away into the crowd.

"Would you believe it?" Lady Carlisle asked, hushed but excited. "A duke."

"They look lovely together," Emma said. The duke had an intriguing dark handsomeness about him that did not appeal to her, but she knew many young ladies would go crazy for it. In conjunction with Violet's pale blond hair, strawberries-and-cream complexion, and dark eyebrows and eyelashes, they were a striking pair.

The song picked up, and Emma's foot tapped as she watched the dancers.

"Oh, Emma, please stop that," her mother snapped.

Emma scowled, but stilled her foot. All she wanted was to dance. And perhaps to eat a few more of those pastries.

When the dance finished, the duke returned Violet to them. His expression gave nothing away, but Violet appeared to be in raptures.

"His Grace is truly accomplished at the cotillion," she said.

The duke seemed to shrink an inch, and Emma frowned. She'd have expected him to either preen at the comment or not acknowledge it at all.

"It was a delightful dance," he said with all the enthusiasm Emma saved for when her governess had made her practice her sums as a girl.

He turned to Emma, and those pale gray eyes met hers. He hesitated, actually pausing to look at her, whereas many people simply swept straight over her. His lips parted, and anticipation fizzed in her stomach. Would he ask her to dance too?

ABOUT THE AUTHOR

Jayne Rivers adores regency romance books, especially those by Sarah MacLean and Julia Quinn. She writes feel-good stories with heroines she'd love to befriend and heroes she'd love to sweep her off her feet—if she wasn't married, of course.

Printed in Dunstable, United Kingdom